Family W
Na

Jules Gabriel Verne

Volume 33 of 54 in the

"Voyages Extraordinaires"

First published in 1889.

2013 Reprint by Kassock Bros. Publishing Co.

Printed in the United States Of America

Cover Illustration By Isaac M. Kassock

ISBN: 1484004957
ISBN-13: 978-1484004951

Jules Gabriel Verne (1828-1905)

The Extraordinary Voyages
of
Jules Verne
~

Table of Contents

FAMILY WITHOUT A NAME

Jules Verne

PART ONE

LEADER OF THE RESISTANCE

CHAPTER I - A FEW FACTS AND DATES

We pity the poor creatures who are flying at each other's throats for the sake of a few acres of ice." So said the philosophers at the end of the eighteenth century, referring to Canada, for whose possession the French and English were then at strife.

Two hundred years before that, when the Kings of Spain and Portugal claimed these American territories, Francis I had exclaimed, "I should like to see the clause in Adam's will, in which this vast heritage was left to them!"

And the king had the more reason for asking this, when, shortly afterwards, a part of these territories took the name of New France. The French, it is true, have not been able to keep possession of this magnificent American colony; but a large proportion of its population remains of French blood, and is connected with France by those ties of blood and natural instincts which international politics have some difficulty in breaking.

The few acres of ice now form a Dominion, with an area larger than that of Europe.

In the year 1534 a Frenchman landed, and took possession of this vast territory.

Jacques Cartier, of St. Malo, boldly advanced into its interior up the river, to which he gave the name of St. Lawrence. The following year the daring Malouin, continuing the exploration further westward, reached a group of cabins — Canada in the Indian tongue — from which has now sprung Quebec, and further westward still, he reached the village of Hochelaga, which is now Montreal. Two centuries later these cities in succession assumed the title of capital, concurrently with Kingston and Toronto, until, to put an end to their political rivalry, the town of Ottawa was declared to be the scat of government of the colony, which now bears the name of the Dominion of Canada.

A few facts, a few dates, will suffice us to trace the progress of this important state from its foundation to the period between 1830 and 1840, in which the events recorded in this history took place.

Under Henry IV. in 1595, Champlain, one of the best seamen of his time, returned to Europe, after a first voyage, in which he had chosen the site of

Quebec. He then took part in the expedition of De Mons, the bearer of letters patent for the exclusive trade in furs, which also gave him the right to dispose of land in Canada. Champlain, whose adventurous character kept him from much sympathy with commerce, withdrew from his bargain, and again sailing up the St. Lawrence, built Quebec in 1606. Two years before that the English had founded their colony in Virginia. The germs of national jealousy were thus called into being, and even in those times there were manifest the beginnings of the struggle which England and France were to wage in the New World.

At the commencement the Indians necessarily took sides in the quarrel. The Algonquins and the Hurons declared for Champlain against the Iroquois, who allied themselves with the English. In 1609 a battle was fought on the shore of the lake, which still bears the name of the French sailor, in which the Iroquois were beaten.

Two other voyages — in 1613 and 1615 — led Champlain to the almost unknown regions of the West on the shore of Lake Huron. Again he left America, and again he returned, and at length, after contending with intrigues of all sorts, he received in 1620 the title of Governor of New Franco.

A company was then formed, of which the constitution was approved by Louis XIII. in 1628. This company undertook to transfer to Canada in fifteen years 4000 French Catholics. Of several vessels sent on this errand, the first fell into the hands of the English, who sailed up the St. Lawrence, and summoned Champlain to surrender. He refused, but the want of resources, and any chance of help soon led to a capitulation, which in 1629 gave Quebec to the English. In 1632 Champlain departed from Dieppe with three vessels, and resumed the possession of Canada, which had been restored to France by the treaty of the 13th of July in that year. He laid the foundations of some new towns, established, under the direction of the Jesuits, the first Canadian college, and died on Christmas Day, 1635, in the land won by his enterprise and audacity.

For some time commercial relations existed between the French colonists and those of New England. But the French had to contend with the Iroquois, who had become formidable, owing to their numbers, for the European population did not exceed 2400; and so the company, whose affairs were becoming desperate, applied to Colbert, who sent them the Marquis de Tracy, at the head of a squadron. The Iroquois were repulsed, but at once returned to the attack, and a horrible massacre of the colonists took place near Montreal.

In 1665 the area of the colony had doubled, and there were 13,000 French in Canada. But the New Englanders now amounted to 200,000. War broke out in Nova Scotia, then called Acadia, and the New Englanders even reached Quebec, from which they had to retire in 1690.

At last, by the Treaty of Ryswick in 1697, France was assured in the possession of Canada, and the unsubdued nations, such as the Iroquois and Hurons, put themselves under French protection by the convention of Montreal.

In 1703, the Marquis de Vaudreuil, son of an earlier governor of that name, was appointed Governor-General of Canada, and, by reason of the neutrality of the Iroquois, found himself in a stronger position than his predecessors.

War began in Newfoundland, which had always been English, and in Acadia, which in 1711 escaped from Vaudreuil's hands. The Anglo-American forces were then concentrating for the conquest of Canada, when the Treaty of Utrecht confirmed the loss of Acadia, and assured a peace of thirty years with England.

During that period of repose the colony made real progress. The French built several new forts, to strengthen their hold on it. In 1721 the population was 25,000, in 1744 it was 50,000. It seemed as though the times of adversity were over. Nothing of the sort. With the war of the Austrian Succession England and France were enemies in Europe, and consequently in America. There was an alternation of reverse and success, and at length the Treaty of Aix-la-Chapelle, in 1747, left matters as they had been at the Treaty of Utrecht.

But although Acadia was henceforth a British possession, its people continued to be very French. And the United Kingdom encouraged Anglo-Saxon immigration, so as to obtain a preponderance of that race in the conquered provinces. France tried to do the same for Canada, but with poor success, and on the Ohio the rivals found themselves face to face.

Then it was that before Fort Duquesne, recently built by the compatriots of the Marquis de Vaudreuil, Washington appeared at the head of an Anglo-

American force. Had not Franklin just declared that Canada could not be suffered to belong to France?

Two fleets sailed from Europe — one from France, the other from England. After dreadful massacres in Acadia and the territories of the Ohio, war was officially declared by Great Britain on the 18th of May, 1756.

De Vaudreuil sent urgent demands for reinforcements and the Marquis de Montcalm arrived, and took command of the army. The first successes of the campaign fell to Montcalm. Fort William Henry, in the south of Lake George, a prolongation of Lake Champlain, was captured; and the Anglo-American troops were defeated at Carillon. But against these successes were to be set the surrender of Fort Duquesne by the French, the loss of Fort Niagara, and the capture of Quebec by General Wolfe in 1759. Montcalm was killed, Wolfe was killed.

Next year the French attempted to retake Quebec. They failed, and shortly afterwards had to surrender Montreal. At length, in 1763, a treaty was signed. Louis XV. renounced his pretensions on Acadia in favour of England, and gave up all Canada and its dependencies. New France existed no longer, except in the hearts of its children. But the English could not destroy a nationality when the majority of the people kept living the love of their old country; and in 1774 Great Britain restored the old French laws.

Although they had nothing further to fear from France the English soon found themselves at war with the Americans, who crossed Lake Champlain, took Carillon and Forts St. John and Frederick, and marched, under General Montgomery, to capture Montreal and be defeated before Quebec, where Montgomery was killed.

Next year — on the 4th of July, 1776 — there was proclaimed the Independence of the United States of America. The month before Montreal had been recaptured by the British.

And now came a period of great trouble for the French Canadians. The English feared that the colony would revolt and range itself under the Stars and Stripes the Americans had unfurled on the horizon.

In 1791 a new constitution divided the country into two provinces, Upper Canada in the West, Lower Canada in the East, with Quebec as its capital. Each province possessed a Legislative Council, nominated by the Crown, and an Assembly elected for four years by the freeholders of the towns. The population was then 135,000, of whom only 15,000 were of English origin.

In 1806 Le Catiadien was founded at Quebec; its motto was, "Nos institutions, notre langue et iios lois" and its object was to obtain this triple desideratum. In 1814 there was signed at Ghent the peace which ended the second American War, in which the successes and reverses were so equally shared.

Then the strife between the two races recommenced in Canada, but purely in the political field. The reforming deputies, led by the heroic Papineau, were unceasing in their attack on the government in all matters. The governor prorogued or dissolved the Assembly, but nothing was done. The opposition let nothing discourage them. The Loyalists, as they called themselves wished to abrogate the constitution of 1791, to reunite Canada in a single province, so as to obtain more influence for the English element, and to abolish the use of the French language, which had remained the parliamentary and judicial language. But Papineau and his friends protested with such energy that the project was abandoned.

The discussion grew more violent. The elections brought about serious collisions. In May, 1831, a riot occurred at Montreal, which cost the lives of three French Canadians. Meetings of the people took place in the towns and villages. An active propaganda was instituted throughout the province. A manifesto was drawn up, of ninety-two resolutions, enumerating the grievances of the French against the English, and demanding the prosecution of the Governor-General, Lord Aylmer. The manifesto was adopted by the Chamber, in spite of the opposition of a few reformers, who considered it insufficient. In 1834 new elections took place. Papineau and his partisans were again elected. Faithful to the protest of the preceding Chamber, they insisted on the prosecution of the Governor-General. But the Assembly was prorogued in March, 1835, and Lord Aylmer was replaced by Lord Gosford as Commissioner, with whom were associated two other Commissioners, for the purpose of inquiring into the causes of the agitation. Lord Gosford explained the conciliatory intentions of the Crown, but the deputies refused to recognize the powers of the commission of inquiry.

But by immigration the English party were gradually reinforced — even in Lower Canada. At Montreal, at Quebec, constitutional associations were formed to put down the reformers. The governor had to dissolve these associations, which were against the law, but they remained ready for action all the same. It was obvious that the attack would be vigorous on both sides. The Anglo- American element became more audacious than ever. It was proposed to Anglicize Lower Canada by every means; and the patriots resolved on resistance, whether legal or not.

Such was the situation in Canada in the year 1837, at the commencement of this story. It is important for us to keep well in view the antagonism between the French and English elements, the vitality of the one, the tenacity of the other.

It was to concert measures rendered necessary by a probable insurrection, that the Governor, Lord Gosford, the Commander-in-Chief, Sir John Colborne, Colonel Gore, and the Chief of the Police, Gilbert Argall, met together on the evening of the 23rd of August.

The Indians designate by the word "Kebec "any narrowing of a river produced by a sudden approach of its banks. Hence the name of Quebec. The city is built on a promontory, a sort of Gibraltar, just above where the St. Lawrence opens out, like an arm of the sea. The upper town is on the steep hill which commands the river, the lower town extends along the banks, where the warehouses and docks are built, where the streets are narrow, and the footpaths paved with wood. The houses were mostly built of wood, a few unimposing buildings there were: — the Governor's house, the English and French cathedrals, an esplanade crowded with loungers, a citadel occupied by a sufficient garrison — such was Champlain's old city, a much more picturesque place than the modern towns of North America.

From the governor's garden the view extended afar over the superb river, with its waters divided by Orleans Island down stream. The evening was splendid. The cool atmosphere was untroubled by the keen north-west breeze which is at all seasons so hurtful in the St. Lawrence valley. In the shade of a square, one of its faces lit by the light of the moon, rose the quadrangular pyramid raised to the memory of Wolfe and Montcalm.

For an hour the governor-general and other high personages had been conversing on the gravity of a state of affairs which kept them continually on the alert. The symptoms of an approaching revolt were only too evident. They must be prepared for every eventuality.

"How many men have you?" asked Lord Gosford of Sir John Colborne.

"Very few unfortunately," said the general. "And yet I ought to draw off some of the troops from the country."

"What are the numbers?"

"I cannot muster more than four battalions, and seven companies of infantry, for it is impossible to withdraw any from the garrisons of the citadels of Quebec and Montreal."

"What artillery have you?"

"Three or four field-guns."

"And cavalry?"

"A picquet only."

"If you have to scatter those troops over the neighbouring counties," said Colonel Gore, "there are not enough. It is very unfortunate that you had to dissolve the constitutional associations formed by the Loyalists We should then have had hundreds of volunteers, whose help we should not despise."

"I could not allow those associations," said Lord Gosford. "Their contact with the population would have led to disturbances every day. We must avoid everything that may provoke an outbreak. We are on a powder-magazine, and we must walk in list shoes."

The governor did not exaggerate. He was a man of great ability, and conciliatory disposition. Since his arrival in the colony he had shown much kindness to the French colonists, having — as the historian Garncau remarks — " a dash of Irish gaiety, which was not out of sympathy with Canadian gaiety." If the rebellion had not yet broken out it was owing to the circumspection, the kindness, the spirit of justice which Lord Gosford had shown. By nature and -conviction he was opposed to violent measures.

"Force," he said, "may compress, but it does not suppress. In England they forget that Canada is neighbour to the United States, and that the United States ended by gaining their independence. I see that in London the ministry wants a policy of aggression. By the advice of the Commissioners the House of Lords and House of Commons have adopted a resolution to prosecute the opposition deputies, to make use of the public funds, to alter the constitution, so as to double the number of English electors. But that does not show much wisdom. There will be bloodshed on one side or the other."

There was good reason for expecting this. The measures adopted by the British Parliament had produced an agitation which only wanted an opportunity to declare itself. Secret councils, public meetings, kept opinion in a state of excitement. Revocations were being exchanged at Montreal as at Quebec between the reformers and the partisans of English domination, and the police knew that a call to arms had been distributed throughout the country. The governor-general had been hanged in effigy. All that could be done was to be prepared for the outbreak.

"Has Monsieur de Vaudreuil been seen at Montreal?" asked Lord Gosford.

"He does not seem to have left his house," said Gilbert Argall. "But his friends Farran, Clerc, Vincent Hodge, are constantly visiting him, and are in daily communication with the liberal deputies, and particularly with Gramont of Quebec."

"If an outbreak occurs, it will doubtless have been prepared by them," said Sir John Colborne.

"Then why not arrest them?" asked Colonel Gore. "Why does not your lordship destroy the plot before it is hatched?"

"If it is not hatched already!" said the governor- general, who turned to the chief of the police and continued, "Did not M. de Vaudreuil and his friends figure in the insurrections of 1832 and 1835?"

"They did," said Sir Gilbert Argall, "or rather there was good reason for supposing so; but positive proof was wanting, and it was impossible to prosecute them, just as it had been in 1825."

"That proof should be obtained at any price," said Sir John Colborne, "so that we might put a stop to the intrigues of these reformers once for all. There is nothing more hateful than civil war! But if it comes to that, we must make the work short and sharp."

To speak in this way was characteristic of the commander-in-chief of the British forces in Canada. Sir John Colborne was the man to put down a revolution with all due vigour, but to take part in secret surveillance such as falls to the lot of the police was most unpalatable to him. Owing to this it was that for many months Gilbert Argall's emissaries had had the whole task of watching the proceedings of the French Canadian party. The towns, the parishes of the St. Lawrence valley, and more especially those in the counties of Vercherts, Chambly, Laprairie, Acadie, Terrebonne, and Deux Montaignes, had swarmed with detectives. At Montreal, in place of those constitutional associations of which Colonel Gore regretted the dissolution, the Doric Club — with its members the most violent of loyalists — had taken upon itself to suppress the insurgents by the most rigorous of means. And Lord Gosford feared that at any moment, day or night, the outbreak might occur.

It can be understood, therefore, how the governor's friends urged him to support the bureaucrats — as the Crown's partisans were called — against the partisans of the national cause. Besides, Sir John Colborne was not the man for half-measures, as appeared later on, when he succeeded Lord Gosford in the government of the colony. Colonel Gore, an old soldier and Waterloo hero, was, of course, for acting vigorously, and without delay.

On the 7th of May in this year a meeting had been held at Saint Ours, a small village in Richelieu county, in which the principal reformers took part. The resolutions then agreed to became the political programme of the French opposition.

One of the resolutions was "Canada, like Ireland, should rally round a man endowed with a hatred of oppression, and a love of his country, which nothing, neither promises nor menaces, can shake."

This man was Papineau, whom popular sentiment declared to be an O'Connell.

At the same time the assembly decided to abstain as much as possible from consuming imported articles, and only to use the products of the country, so as to deprive the government of the revenue obtained from the duties on foreign merchandise.

Lord Gosford replied to these declarations on the 15th of June, by a proclamation forbidding seditious meetings, and ordering the magistrates and officers of the militia to disperse them.

But although Papineau was the ostensible leader, there was another who worked in the dark, and so mysteriously that the principal reformers had seldom seen him. Around this personage quite a legend had grown, which had given him extraordinary influence over the minds of the masses. Jean-Sans-Nom was the name under which alone he was known.

"And this Jean-Sans-Nom," asked Sir John Colborne; "have you got on his track yet?"

"Not yet," said the chief of police. "But I have reason to think that he has reappeared in Lower Canada, and that he has even been in Quebec."

"And your men have not been able to put their hands on him!" exclaimed Colonel Gore.

"That is not an easy thing to do."

"Has this man really the influence they ascribe to him?" asked Lord Gosford.

"Certainly," said Argall, "I can assure your lordship that his influence is very great."

"Who is he?"

"That is what they want to know," said Sir John Golborne. "Is it not so, Argall?"

"That is so. It is not known who he is, whence he comes, or whither he goes. He has appeared in this way, almost invisibly, in all the late insurrections. There can be no doubt that Papineau, Viger, Lacoste, Vaudreuil, Farran, Gramont, all the leaders, in fact, look for him to strike in when the time comes. Jean-Sans-Nom has become a sort of supernatural being among the people in the districts of the St. Lawrence above Montreal and below Quebec. If the legend is to be believed, he has all the qualifications of a leader, extraordinary boldness, and courage above suspicion. And, above all, there is the mystery of his incognito."

"You think he has been in Quebec?" asked Lord Gosford.

"The information I have received leads me to suppose so," said Argall. "And I have put on his track all the smartest men I know, among them that Rip, who showed so much intelligence over the Morgaz affair."

"Simon Morgaz," said Sir John Colborne, "who in 1825 so conveniently handed over for a consideration his accomplices in the Chambly plot?"

"The same."

"Do you know what has become of him?"

"Only one thing," said Argall, "that .he was cut by all the French Canadians he betrayed, and that he disappeared. He may have left America. He may be dead."

"But could not what succeeded with Simon Morgaz.

succeed again with these reformers?" asked Sir John Colborne.

"Don't think that, general!" answered Lord Gosford. "They are above that sort of thing. That they are enemies of English influence, and dream of obtaining for Canada the same independence as the United States is true. But to hope to buy them, to turn them into traitors by promises of money or honours, will never do! I don't think you will find a single traitor amongst them."

"They said the same of Simon Morgaz," said Sir John Colborne ironically, "and yet he gave up his friends. And who knows if this Jean-Sans-Nom is not to be bold?"

"I don't think so," said the chief of the police.

"Anyhow," said Colonel Gore, "whether he is to be sold or hanged, the first thing is to catch him, and if he has been seen at Quebec — "

As he spoke a man appeared on one of the paths of the garden, and stopped about ten yards off.

Argall recognized the man, who, however, did not belong to the regular brigade of Comeau, who was at the head of the Canadian police.

"That is Rip, of Rip and Co." said he, addressing Lord Gosford. "Your lordship will allow me to hear what he has to say?"

Lord Gosford nodded, and Rip approached respectfully, and waited for Argall to speak to him, which he did in these terms.

"Have you made sure that Jean-Sans-Nom has been seen in Quebec?"

"I have, your honour!"

"And why was he not arrested?" asked Lord Gosford.

"Your lordship must excuse my associates and myself," said Rip; "but we did not receive warning in time. The day before yesterday we heard of Jean-Sans-Nom as having visited one of the houses in the Rue de Petit-Champlain,

14

next door to the tailor's shop. I surrounded the house, which is occupied by Sebastien Gramont, Advocate and Deputy, who is very prominent in the reformist party. But Jean-Sans-Nom was not there, although Gramont had certainly had dealings with him. And our search was useless."

"Do you think the man is still in Quebec?" asked Sir John Colborne.

"I cannot answer in the affirmative, your excellency," said Rip.

"You do not know him?"

"I have never seen him. And in fact there are very few that have."

"Do you know which way he went when he left Quebec?"

"I do not."

"And what do you think?" asked the Minister of Police.

"My idea is that he has gone towards Montreal, where the agitators seem to be concentrating. If an insurrection is being planned it is in that part of Lower Canada that it will break out. I suspect that Jean-Sans-Nom is lying close in some village on the bank of the St. Lawrence."

"And that," said Argall, "is where we ought to look."

"Well, give the necessary orders," said the governor.

"Your lordship will be satisfied. Rip, to-morrow you will leave Quebec with the best men you have. I will watch Monsieur de Vaudreuil and his friends, who are certainly in communication with Jean-Sans-Nom. Try and get on his track by any means. It is the governor- general's special order."

"And it will be faithfully obeyed," said Rip. "I will go to-morrow."

"We approve in advance," said Gilbert Argall, "of all you think necessary to effect the capture of this dangerous partisan. We want him dead or alive, before he can raise the French by his presence. You are intelligent and zealous, Rip; you showed that a dozen years ago in the Morgaz affair. We again reckon on your zeal and intelligence. Go."

Rip was preparing to leave, and had already taken a few steps backward when he stopped.

"May I ask your honour a question?" he asked.

"A question?" said Argall.

"Yes, your honour, for it is necessary it should be answered, in order that the books of Rip and Co. may be kept in proper form."

"What is it?"

"Is there a price on Jean-Sans-Nom's head?"

"Not yet!"

"There ought to be!" said Sir John Colborne.

"There is," said Lord Gosford.

"What is the amount?" asked Rip.

"Four thousand dollars."

"It is worth six thousand," said Rip. "I shall have to pay travelling and other special expenses."

"Very well," said Lord Gosford.

"It will be money your lordship will never regret."

"If it is gained — " added the minister.

"It will be, your honour!"

And with this promise — a rather hazardous one, it seemed — the chief partner in Rip and Co. retired.

"This Rip seems to know what he is about," said Colonel Gore.

"And gives us confidence in him," said Argall. "This reward of six thousand dollars will improve his finesse and his zeal. That Chambly affair brought him something considerable, and though he is fond of his business, he is fonder still of the cash it brings him. You must take him as he is, and I know no one more likely to catch Jean-Sans-Nom, if Jean-Sans-Nom will let himself be caught!"

The general, the minister, and the colonel took leave of Lord Gosford. Then Sir John Colborne gave Colonel Gore his orders to set out immediately for Montreal, where his colleague, Colonel Wetherall, was waiting, with orders to prevent, as much as possible, the spread of the insurrectional movement in the neighbouring districts.

CHAPTER II - TWELVE YEARS BEFORE

Simon Morgaz! A name execrated in the humblest huts of Canada! A name devoted for long years to public execration! Simon Morgaz! The traitor who betrayed his brothers, and sold his country.

In 1825 — twelve years before the insurrection of 1837 — a few French Canadians had organized a conspiracy, with the object of withdrawing Canada from the English domination, which weighed on it so heavily. They were bold men, active, energetic, of good position, sprung, for the most part, from the early immigrants, who had founded New France. No wonder that they -could not believe that their colony had been abandoned to England for ever. And even admitting that the country could not return to the defendants of Cartier and Champlain, had they not the right to be independent? And it was to gain its independence that they risked their heads.

Amongst them was Monsieur de Vaudreuil, a descendant of the old governors of Canada under Louis XIV. — one of those families whose French names have become geographical names in Canadian cartography.

At this time M. de Vaudreuil was thirty-five years of age, having been born in 1790, in the county of Vaudreuil, situated between the St. Lawrence on the south and the River Ottawa on the north, on the confines of the province of Ontario.

M. de Vaudreuil's friends were, like him, of French origin, although successive alliances with Anglo Americans had changed their French names. Such were Professor Robert Farran of Montreal, Franfois Clerc, a rich landowner of Chateauguay, and a few others, to whom either birth or fortune assured extensive influence over the population of the villages and country.

The real chief of the conspiracy was Walter Hodge, who was of American nationality. Although he was then sixty, age had not cooled the heat of his blood. During the War of Independence he had been one of those daring volunteers known as "skinners," whose wild violence Washington had to tolerate, on account of the vigour with which they harassed the Royal Army. At the end of the eighteenth century, as we know, Canada had been tempted by the United States to enter the American federation; and this explains why an American like Walter Hodge should have joined this conspiracy, and even become its chief. He was one of those who had adopted as his motto the four words which comprise the Monroe doctrine, "America for the Americans."

Walter Hodge and his companions had never ceased from protesting against the exactions of English administration, which became more and more intolerable. In 1822 their names figured in the protest against the union of Upper and Lower Canada, with those of the two brothers Sanguinct, who, eighteen years later, with so many other victims, were to pay with their lives for their attachment to the national party. They fought with pen and speech against the lands being so partitioned among the bureaucrats as to strengthen the English element. They had attacked all the governors, Sherbrooke, Richmond, Monk, and Maitland, and associated themselves in every way with the deputies of the opposition.

In 1825, however, the conspiracy had a definite object, and was organized without the participation of the Liberals of the Canadian Assembly. If Papineau and his colleagues, Cuvillier, Bedard, Viger, Quernel and others, were not admitted to its secrets, Hodge could count on them to assure its consequences if they succeeded.

At the outset it was proposed to seize on the person of Lord Dalhousie, who in 1820 had been nominated to the post of Governor-General of the English colonies in North America. On his arrival, Lord Dalhousie seemed to have resolved on a policy of concession. Thanks to him, the Roman Catholic Archbishop of Quebec was officially recognized, and Montreal, Rose, and Regiopolis became the sees of three new bishops. But the British Cabinet had refused Canada the right of self-government. The members of the Legislative Council, nominated for life by the Crown, were all English by birth, and rendered quite helpless the House of Assembly elected by the people. Out of a population of 600,000 inhabitants, including 525,000 French Canadians, three-quarters of the government functionaries were of English descent. And the question had again arisen of proscribing the legal use of the French language throughout the colony.

To seize on Lord Dalhousie and the principal members of the Legislative Council, provoke a popular movement in the counties of the St. Lawrence, install a provisional government until an election had constituted a National Government, and raise the Canadian Militia against the Regular Army, such were the plans of Walter Hodge, Robert Farran, Francois Clerc, and Vaudreuil.

With Walter Hodge and his partisans there was connected a certain Simon Morgaz, whose position and origin it is needful for us to know.

In 1825 Simon Morgaz was forty-six years old. An advocate in a country where there are more advocates than clients, just as there are more doctors than patients, he lived in a struggling way at Chambly, a village on the left bank of the Richelieu, a dozen leagues from Montreal, on the other side of the St. Lawrence.

He was a resolute man, whose energy had been remarked when the reformers protested against the proceedings of the British Cabinet. His pleasant manner and prepossessing face, made him generally liked. No one imagined that the personality of a traitor would one day stand manifest from such a winning exterior.

Simon Morgaz was married. His wife was eight years younger, being then thirty-eight. She was of American origin, and was the daughter of Major Allen, whose bravery during the War of Independence may be appreciated from the fact that he was one of Washington's aide de-camps. A true type of loyalty, he would have surrendered his life to save his word with the tranquillity of a Regulus.

It was at Albany, in the State of New York, that Simon Morgjz and Bridget met and became acquainted. The young lawyer was a French Canadian, as Major Allen well knew — for he would never have given his daughter to the descendant of an English family. Although Morgaz possessed no personal fortune, yet with what came to Bridget on the death of her mother a certain comfort, if not wealth, was assured to the young couple. The marriage took place at Albany, in 1806.

Morgaz and his wife might have been happy, but they were not. Not that Morgaz ever failed in his treatment of his wife, for he always entertained for her a sincere affection, but a passion devoured him — a passion for gambling. Bridget's patrimony was dissipated in a few years, and although her husband was recognized as a talented advocate, his work did not suffice to fill up the gaps in his fortune. It was not misery but penury that his wife had to bear with. Bridget never reproached her husband; her advice had been useless; she accepted the trial with resignation and with courage, although the future was most unpromising.

It was not only for herself that Bridget had to fear. During the first years of her married life she had had two children, to whom she had given the same baptismal name, with a slight difference. The elder, Joann, was born in 1807; the younger, Jean, in 1808. Bridget devoted herself entirely to the education of her sons. Joann was of a gentle disposition; Jean of a more lively temperament, though both were energetic enough in their gentleness and vivacity. They took evidently after their mother, being serious in thought, and having a taste for work, and a straightforward way of looking at things, which was certainly wanting in Simon Morgaz. To their father they were always respectful, but there was none of that natural ease and confidence without reserve which is the very essence of blood relationship. For their mother their devotion was unbounded, their affection overflowing. Bridget and her sons were united by a double chain of filial and maternal love which nothing could ever break.

After their childhood, Joann and Jean had been sent to the school at Chambly, where they gained the reputation of being among the best pupils in the junior division. When they were twelve and thirteen they had gone to the college at Montreal, where they soon came to the front. Two years elapsed, and they had just finished their education when there occurred the events of 1825.

As a rule, Simon Morgaz and his wife resided at Montreal, where the advocate's office was in daily danger of having to shut up, but they had managed to retain possession of a small house at Chambly. It was there that Walter Hodge and his friends met, when Morgaz had joined the plot of which the first act would be the arrest of the Governor-General, and the next the installation of a provisional government at Quebec.

Under this modest roof in the village of Chambly the conspirators fancied they were in greater safety than they would have been at Montreal, where the police surveillance was very keen. Nevertheless they acted with great prudence, so as to throw all attempts at espionage off the scent. Arms and ammunition had been stored in the house without their transport evoking the least suspicion.

But the Governor got wind of the plot, and set a special watch over the proceedings of those deputies who formed the permanent opposition. As we said before, however, Papineau and his colleagues did not know of the plans of Hodge and his associates. That the 26th of August had been fixed for the call to arms would have been a surprise to both friends and enemies.

On the evening of the 25th of August the house of Simon Morgaz was entered by the police, under the guidance of Rip, just as the conspirators had met. There was no time to destroy their secret correspondence, or burn the lists of their supporters. The police seized the arms hidden in the cellars. The plot was discovered, and there were taken to Montreal under a strong escort, Walter Hodge, Robert Farran, Francois Clerc, Simon Morgaz, Vaudreuil, and a dozen others.

What had happened was as follows: there was then at Quebec a certain Rip, who kept a private inquiry and detective office, and who was frequently employed on government business, not without a consideration. A matter of police was to him merely a matter of cash, and he passed it through his books just as he would have done a matter of commerce, charging so much for the job — so much for a search, so much for an arrest, so much for surveillance, &c. &c. He was a very shrewd man, very keen, very daring, quite a man of the world, in fact, with his hand, or rather his nose, in everybody's business; and what is more, he was quite devoid of scruples, and had not the shadow of a moral sense.

In 1825, Rip, who had just started his agency, was thirty- three years of age. Already his mobile physiognomy and cleverness in disguises, had enabled him to have a hand in several matters under different names. For some years he had known Simon Morgaz, with whom he had had business in law matters. Certain circumstances which would have appeared insignificant to every one else made him think that the advocate of Montreal was concerned in some way with the conspiracy of Chambly. He pressed him close; he pried into the secrets of his private life; he frequented the house, although Bridget took no pains to hide the antipathy she felt for him.

A letter seized at the post-office went far to prove the advocate's complicity. The minister of police, informed by Rip of the result of his inquiries, recommended him to act judiciously with Morgaz, whom he knew to be in pecuniary difficulties; and one day Rip suddenly gave the unhappy man the choice between two alternatives — to be prosecuted for treason, or to receive the enormous sum of a hundred thousand piastres, or dollars, the value being the same, and reveal the names of his accomplices and the details of the conspiracy at Chambly.

The advocate was astounded. Betray his companions! Sell them for gold! Hand them over to the scaffold! But nevertheless he succumbed; he accepted the price of his treason, he revealed the secrets of the conspirators, after receiving a promise that his infamy would never be divulged. It was even agreed that the police should arrest him at the same time as Walter Hodge and his friends, that he should be tried by the same judges, and that he should be sentenced — and it could only be a sentence of death — and then he could escape.

This abominable scheme was concocted between the minister of police, the head partner of Rip & Co. and Simon Morgaz.

Things happened as had been arranged. On the day named by the traitor, the conspirators were surprised in the house at Chambly, and on the 25th September, 1825, they were all tried together.

The only reply the prisoners made to the charge was to attack the British ministry. To the legal arguments they answered with arguments of the purest patriotism. Did they not know that they were condemned in advance, that nothing could save them?

The trial lasted for several hours, and all would have gone as arranged, when a circumstance occurred that revealed the conduct of Simon Morgaz.

One of the witnesses, Mr. Turner, of Chambly, declared that he had frequently seen the advocate in conference with Rip. It was a flash of revelation. Walter Hodge and Vaudreuil, who for some time had been suspicious of Morgaz, owing to his strange behaviour, saw their suspicions confirmed by the evidence. The conspiracy had been conducted so secretly, and had been so easily discovered, that it was obvious some traitor had been at work. Rip was examined and plied with questions, to which he could only reply with embarrassment. Simon Morgaz tried to defend himself; but he launched forth into such improbabilities and curious explanations, that his companions and also his judges soon made up their minds. A scoundrel had betrayed his accomplices, and that traitor was Simon Morgaz.

An irresistible feeling of repulsion arose among the prisoners and the public who crowded the court.

"President of the Court," said Walter Hodge, "we demand that Simon Morgaz be removed from this dock, which is honoured by our presence, and dishonoured by his. We do not wish to be contaminated any longer by contact with this man."

Vaudreuil, Clerc, and Farran joined Hodge, and, unable to restrain themselves, attacked Morgaz, to whose assistance the warders had to come. The President of the Court ordered Morgaz to be taken back to prison. Howls accompanied him; the threats of which he was the object told him he was looked upon as a traitor, whose treason would cost him his life at the hands of the more ardent apostles of Canadian independence. Walter Hodge, Francis Clerc, and Robert Farran were found to be the chief of the Chambly conspiracy, and sentenced to death. On the 27th of September, after another appeal to the patriotism of their brothers, they died on the scaffold.

The other accused, among whom was M. de Vaudreuil, whether it was that they seemed to be less compromised, or that the Government wished to inflict the capital punishment only on the leaders, were allowed to escape with their lives. Sentenced to imprisonment for life, they did not receive their liberty till 1829, when a general amnesty was granted to political offenders.

What became of Simon Morgaz, after the execution? An order of release allowed him to leave the prison at Montreal, and he hastened to disappear.

But universal reprobation weighed on his name and that of those who were in no way responsible for his treason. Bridget Morjraz was brutally hunted from the house she occupied at Montreal, and from the house at Chambly, where she had gone while the proceedings were in progress. She took with her her two sons, who had been hunted from college, as their father had been hunted from the dock in the court of justice.

Where had Simon Morgaz decided to hide his unworthy existence, when his wife and children joined him a few days afterwards? In a distant village a long way from Montreal.

But Bridget did not believe that her husband was guilty, nor did Joann nor Jean. The four retired to the village of Vercheres, in the county of that name, on the bank of the St. Lawrence. They hoped that no suspicion would denounce them to public animadversion. They lived miserably on the resources which remained to them, for Simon, although he had received the reward for his treason, took care not to have recourse to it before his wife and sons. In their presence he always protested his innocence, and cursed the injustice which had fallen on his family and on him. If he had been a traitor, would he not have the price of his treason to support him? Would he be reduced to penury in this way?

And Bridget judged from this that her husband was guiltless. She rejoiced at this result, which gave the lie to his enemies. Appearances were against him. He could not explain them. He was the victim of a horrible combination of circumstances. He would justify himself some day. He was innocent!

With his two sons a difference was observable in their attitude regarding their father. The eldest, Joann, kept himself aloof, and did not dare to think of the opprobrium thus fallen on the name of Morgaz. The arguments for and against presented themselves to his mind, and he rejected them as being unable to fathom them. He would not be his father's judge, so much did he fear that the judgment would be against him. He shut his eyes, he was silent, he kept himself apart when his mother and his brother would have reasoned with him. Evidently the unhappy boy feared to find guilty the man whose son he was.

Jean, on the contrary, behaved differently. He believed in the innocence of the accomplice of Hodge, Farran, and Clerc, although the presumptions were overwhelming. More impetuous than Joann, less master of his judgment, he allowed himself to be carried away by his instincts of filial affection. He would have defended his father publicly. When he heard people talk of Simon Morgaz, his heart leapt, and his mother had to interfere to prevent an outburst. Thus did the unfortunate family live at Vercheres under an assumed name, and the fury with which the people of the village would have risen against them, had their real name been known, can be imagined.

But the people at Vercheres soon began to be troubled about this family, whose origin they knew not, whose life was so mysterious, whose incognito was never betrayed, suspicion arose concerning them.

One night Morgaz and his family went away. They crossed the St. Lawrence, and lived for a few days in one of the villages on the left bank of the river. There attention was directed to them, and they left that village. They were now wanderers, hated by all. Vengeance, it might be said, blazing torch in hand, pursued them, as, in biblical legends, Abel's murderer was pursued. Morgaz could settle nowhere. He crossed the counties of Assumption, Terrebonne, Deux-Montagnes, Vaudreuil, towards the east, towards the less-inhabited parishes.

25

Two months after the trial, father, mother, and sons had fled beyond the territories of Ontario. At Kingston they were recognized at an inn, and had to leave it immediately. Simon had but just time to escape during the night. In vain Bridget and Jean would have defended him. They could scarcely get away from being ill-treated, and Joann might have been killed, as he protected their retreat.

They met again on the borders of a lake, a few miles beyond Kingston. They went along the southern shore, so as to enter the United States, for refuge could no longer be found in Upper Canada. Better to gain some lost country, among some Indian tribe. It was in vain. The unhappy man was repulsed everywhere. Everywhere he was recognized, as if he bore a mark of infamy on his forehead.

It was the end of November. It was weary travelling in this fearful weather, in the glacial breeze and rigorous cold of the winter season in the lake country. As they journeyed through the villages, the sons bought provisions, while the father kept in hiding. They slept, when they could, in abandoned huts, when they could not, in the clefts of the rocks, or under the trees of the interminable forests that covered the land.

Simon Morgaz became more and more gloomy and savage. He never ceased exculpating himself, as if some invisible accuser followed his steps, and shouted "Traitor! traitor!" And now he seemed unable to look his wife and children in the face. Bridget tried to comfort him with affectionate words, and though Joann kept silence, Jean never ceased to protest.

"Father, father!" he would say, "do not give in! Time will do justice on your calumniators. They will see that they have been deceived, that appearances were against you! You to have sold your country indeed!"

"No, no!" Simon would answer; but in so feeble a voice that it was almost inaudible.

The family, wandering from village to village, at last reached the western end of the lake, a few miles from Fort Toronto. They had got to the river Niagara, to where it enters the lake, to cross over to the American bank.

Did Morgaz wish to stop? Would it not be better to go further west, and reach a country so distant that the rumour of his infamy had not spread therein? But where was he going? His wife and sons did not know, for he always led the way, and all they had to do was to follow.

On the 3rd of December, in the evening, exhausted with fatigue and want, they had halted in a cave half hidden by brushwood and briars — doubtless some haunt of the wild beasts now abandoned. The little food that remained to them was spread on the sand. Bridget had succumbed to physical and mental lassitude. At any cost, Montcalm must find in the neighbouring village an Indian tribe who, for a few days, would grant the hospitality which Canadians never refuse.

Joann and Jean, tortured with hunger, were eating some cold venison. But neither Simon nor Bridget could eat anything.

"Father," said Jean, "you must recruit your strength."

Simon Montcalm made no reply.

"Father," said Joann. and this was the first time he had spoken to him since their departure from Chambly, "we can go no further! Mother cannot stand any more fatigue. Here we are on the American frontier; are you going to cross it?"

Simon looked at his eldest son, and his eyes fell almost immediately. Joann continued, —

"Look at the state mother is in. She cannot move! This torpor will deprive her of all the energy she has left! To-morrow it will be impossible to rouse her. My brother and I can go on, doubtless! But we must know where you are going. What is it you intend to do?"

Simon Morgaz did not reply. He bowed his head, and went to the back of the cave.

Night fell. No sound troubled the solitude. Thick clouds covered the sky as though to cover all in a dense mist. Not a breath pierced the atmosphere. Heavy flakes of snow began to fall. The cold was intense. Jean gathered some dead wood and lit a fire in a corner, so that the smoke would float outwards.

Bridget, stretched on a bed of grass that Joann had gathered, lay without a movement. The little life that remained to her only betrayed itself by the painful breathing, broken by long and sorrowful sighs. While Joann held her hand, Jean fed the fire.

Simon Morgaz lay, half-crouching in the darkness, in an attitude of despair, as if he were horror-stricken at himself, when the reflection of the fire occasionally lighted up his face.

Then the firelight gradually sank, and Jean felt his eyes close in spite of all lie could do.

How long did he remain asleep? He did not know. But when he awoke, the fire was nearly out.

He rose, threw an armful of wood on the fire, which he revived by blowing, and the cave was again lighted up.

Bridget and Joann, close together, continued motionless. But Simon Morgaz was not there!

When had he left the place? When his wife and sons were sleeping?

With a fearful presentiment, Jean rushed out of the cave. As he did so, he heard the report of firearms.

Bridget and Joann leapt up suddenly. They also had heard the report, which seemed to be close by.

With a shriek of terror, Bridget staggered to her feet, and fled from the cave.

The three had not gone twenty yards when they saw a corpse on the snow.

It was the body of Simon Morgaz. He had shot himself in the heart with his pistol. He was dead.

Joann and Jean recoiled, overwhelmed. The past rose before them. Was it true that their father was guilty? Had he in a crisis of despair put an end to an existence he had found too hard to be borne?

Bridget threw herself on her husband's body. She clasped it in her arms. She could not believe in the infamy of the man whose name she bore.

Joann raised his mother and took her back to the cave, where his brother and he brought their father's body to the place it had occupied a few hours before. A pocket-book slipped on to the ground. Joann picked it up, and when he opened it, a roll of bank-notes fell. It was the reward for which Simon Morgaz had betrayed the leaders of the Chambly Conspiracy. The mother and the two sons could no longer doubt.

Joann and Jean knelt by Bridget's side.

And before the corpse of the traitor who had done justice on himself, there knelt a dishonoured family, whose name must die with him who had dishonoured it.

CHAPTER III - A HURON NOTARY

IT was not without good reason that the Governor and Sir John Colborne, and the minister of police and Colonel Gore, had consulted together on the measures to be taken for the repression of the reformists. In fact, a formidable insurrection of the French Canadians was about to take place.

But if Lord Gosford and his staff had good reason to be busy, nothing seemed to trouble a certain young fellow, who, on the morning of the 3rd of September, was supposed to be "engrossing" in the office of Mr. Nick, in Bon Secours market-place, Montreal. "Engrossing" is not quite the word, perhaps, to apply to the absorbing occupation in which the second clerk, Lionel Restigouche, was employed at the time — nine o'clock in the morning. A column of irregular lines neatly written was stretching out at much length down a nice page of bluish paper, which in no way resembled the parchment of a deed. At times, when Lionel's hand stopped while an idea took shape, his eyes looked listlessly out of the half-opened window towards the column in Jacques Cartier Place in honour of Lord Nelson. Then his look would become animated, and his pen would resume its course, as he gently swayed his head as if beating time to some regular rhythm.

Lionel was barely seventeen. His face, almost feminine still, was French in type, and very pleasant in expression; his hair was light and rather long, perhaps, and his eyes were as blue as the water in the great lakes. Though he had neither father nor mother, Mr. Nick might be said to be both to him, for the estimable notary was as fond of him as of his own son.

Lionel was alone in the office. There was no one with him, not even one of the other clerks, who were out on business, not even a client, although Mr. Nick's office was one of the busiest in the town. And Lionel, feeling sure he would not be interrupted, was taking his ease, and had just signed his name with a wonderful flourish below the last line on his page, when he heard some one remark, — "What are you doing there, my boy? "It was Mr. Nick, who had entered without Lionel's noticing him, so absorbed had he been in his work.

Lionel's first movement was to slip the paper in question under the blotting-pad, but the notary stepped up and snatched away the suspicious document before the clerk could stop him.

"What is this, Lionel?" he asked. "An agreement? An engrossment? An office copy of — "

"Mr. Nick, believe me — "

The notary had put on his spectacles, and with knitted brows ran his eyes over the page in astonishment. "What is this?" he exclaimed. "Lines all unequal! Margin all down one side! Margin on the other! So much good ink wasted, so much good paper wasted by these useless margins!"

"Mr. Nick," answered Lionel, blushing to the ears, "that came to me — by chance — "

"What came to you — by chance?"

"The verses."

"The verses! You write your drafts in verse, do you? Is not prose enough for you to draught a deed in?"

"That is not a deed, if you please."

"What is it, then?"

"A piece of poetry I have composed for the meeting of the Lyre-Amicale."

"The Lyre-Amicale!" exclaimed the notary. "Do you imagine, Lionel, that it was for you to figure at the meeting of the Lyre-Amicale, or any other Parnassian association, that I took you into my office? Was it for you to abandon yourself to these versifying gymnastics that I made you my second clerk? Would it not have been better for you to be passing your time canoeing on the St. Lawrence, or showing off your dandyism in the paths of Mont Royal or the park of Sainte Helene! Indeed! A poet in a notary's office! A clerk's head with a halo round it! Why, it is enough to frighten clients away!"

"Do not be angry, Mr. Nick," said Lionel in a piteous tone. "If you only knew how our melodious language lends itself to verse! It lends itself so nobly to rhythm, cadence, and harmony. Our poets Lemay, Elzear, Labelle, Franfois Mons, Chapemann, Octave Cremazie — "

"Messieurs Cremazie, Chapemann, Mons, Labelle and Lemay do not fulfil the important functions of second clerk that I know of. They are not paid — to say nothing of board and lodging — six dollars a month, nor are they paid by

31

me. They have not to draw up contracts of sales, nor draught bills, and they can Pindarize as they please!"

"Mr. Nick — this time — "

"Yes, this time you wished to be the laureate of the Lyre-Amicale?"

"I did so foolishly presume — "

"And may I ask what is the subject of this effusion? Probably some dithyrambic evocation to Tabellionope, the muse of the Perfect Notary."

"No," said Lionel.

"Then what do you call your rhyming machine?"

"Will-o'-the-wisp."

"Will-o'-the-wisp!" exclaimed Mr. Nick. "Do you address verses to Will-o'-the-wisps?"

And probably the notary would have held forth on jinns elves, brownies, goblins, water-sprites, ases, cucufas, farfadets, and all the poetic figures of Scandinavian mythology, when the postman knocked at the door and appeared on the threshold.

"Ah! is that you, my friend?" said Mr. Nick. "I took you for a will-o'-the-wisp."

"A will-o'-the-wisp, Mr. Nick?" said the postman. "Do I look like one?"

"No; you look more like a postman who has brought me a letter."

"Here it is, Mr. Nick."

"Thank you!"

The postman retired as the notary caught sight of the handwriting, and immediately opened the letter.

Lionel picked up his sheet of paper and put it in his pocket.

Mr. Nick read the letter very carefully; then he returned it to the envelope and looked at the postmark. The postmark was that of St. Charles, a small village in the county of Vercheres, the date was that of the 2nd of September, the day before. After thinking for a minute or so, the notary returned to his philippic against the poets.

"Ah, you worship the muses, Lionel? Well, as a punishment, you will accompany me to Laval, and you will have time on the road to improve your verses. We must be off in an hour, and if we meet any will-o'-the-wisps, you can do the polite to them."

With that the notary passed into his private office, while Lionel prepared for the journey, which was not unpleasing to him. An excellent man was Mr. Nick, and much appreciated for the correctness of his judgment and the value of his advice. He was then aged fifty; his engaging physiognomy, his large, beaming face expanding amid a cluster of curly hair which had once been very black, but was now growing grey; his quick, cheery eyes, his splendid teeth, his laughing lips, his pleasant manners, all went to form a very pleasant companion. One thing should be noted: under Mr. Nick's well tanned skin it could be seen that Indian blood flowed in his veins.

It was so, and the notary did not seek to hide it. He was descended from the old natives of the country, those who possessed the soil before Europeans crossed the ocean to conquer it. At this time there were many marriages between the French and Indians. Saint Castin, Enaud, Nepisigny, Entremont, and others married squaws, and even became chiefs of Indian tribes.

Nick by descent was a Huron; that is to say, he came from one of the four chief families of the Indian branch. Although he bore the sounding name of Nicholas Sagamore, he was always known as Mr. Nick, and he was quite content to be so called.

His race was not extinct. One of his innumerable cousins was chief of the Peaux-Rouges, and reigned ever a Huron tribe in the north of Laprairie county, west of Montreal.

There is nothing strange in such a state of things in Canada. Quebec possesses an honourable tabellion, who, by birth, has a right to brandish the tomahawk, and shout the war-cry of a tribe of the Iroquois. Happily, Mr. Nick did not belong to that tribe of perfidious Indians. No! Descended from the Hurons, who were nearly always friends of the French, he had nothing to blush for. And so Lionel was proud of his master, the undoubted descendant of the great chiefs of North America, and he only waited for an opportunity to celebrate his deeds in verse.

33

At Montreal Mr Nick had always preserved a prudent neutrality between the two political parties. And, as both respected him, both had recourse to his services. It seemed as though hereditary tendencies had in him undergone a complete change. Never had the warlike fancies of his race awoke in him. He was only a notary — a perfect notary — placid and conciliating. And he seemed to have no desire to perpetuate the name of the Sagamores, for he had never taken a wife, and never thought of taking one.

As we said above, Mr. Nick was preparing to leave the office in company with his second clerk. He would only be away a few hours, and his old servant Dolly would keep dinner waiting for him.

The town of Montreal is built on the southern shore of one of the islands of the St. Lawrence. The island is from ten to eleven leagues long, and five or six wide, and lies in a huge estuary formed by an enlargement of the river a little below the junction of the River Ottawa. It was here that Jacques Cartier discovered the Indian village of Hochelaga, which in 1640 was granted by the King of France to the congregation of Saint Sulpice. The town took its name from Mont Royal, by which it is commanded, and was in a very favourable position for the development of trade. In 1760 it had 6000 inhabitants. It extends at the foot of a picturesque hill, which has been made into a magnificent park, and which shares with another park on the island of St. Helene, in providing attractive walks for a large number of the people of Montreal. A superb tubular bridge, nearly three miles long, which did not exist in 1837, now joins the city to the right bank of the river.

Montreal has become a great city, more modern in aspect than Quebec, and consequently less picturesque. There can be visited, not without some interest, the two cathedrals, Protestant and Catholic, the Bank, the Exchange, the General Hospital, the Theatre, the Convent of Notre Dame, the McGill University, and the Seminary of Saint Sulpice. To the west is the English or Scotch quarter; to the east is the French quarter. The two races are the less inclined to mingle from the fact that nearly all the trade is in the hands of merchants of British origin, and this was more particularly the case in 1837. The magnificent waterway of the St. Lawrence assured the prosperity of the town, which it put in communication, not only with the counties of Canada, but also with Europe.

Like the rich merchants of London, those of Montreal have their offices in a different place to their dwelling- houses. When business is over they return to the northern suburbs, to the slopes of Mont Royal, and the circular avenue surrounding its base. There rise the private houses, some of which are like palaces, and the villas draped in verdure. Beyond the opulent quarter the Irish are crowded in their Ghetto of St. Anne, at the mouth of the Lachine Channel, on the left bank of the St. Lawrence.

Mr. Nick was very well off. Like the commercial notables, he could every evening have retired to one of the aristocratic habitations of the upper town under the leafy shades of St. Antoine. But he was one of the old school of notaries, whose horizon is bounded by the four walls of their office, and who justify their name of note-watchers by watching night and day the contracts, minutes, and family papers confided to their care. The descendant of the Sagamores thus lived in the .old house in the Bon Secours market-place; and it was thence, that on the morning of the 3rd of September, he set out with his second clerk to find a vehicle to take him from the island of Montreal to the island of Jesus, which is separated from it by one of the minor branches of the St. Lawrence.

The first thing Mr. Nick did was to go to the Bank, along the wide streets bordered with rich shops and kept up with much care by the municipality. At the bank he told Lionel to wait in the vestibule while he went into the central hall to return in a quarter of an hour and go on to the coach office.

The vehicle he hailed was one of those two-horse affairs known as "buggies" by the Canadians. They are a kind of char-a banc, hung on springs, as easy as possible, but very strong, and made so as to be suitable to the hardness of the roads. They can hold half-a-dozen travellers.

"Eh! Mr. Nick!" said the driver of the buggy, as he caught sight of the notary, who was always greeted with this cordial exclamation.

"I myself, and my clerk!" said Mr. Nick, with his habitual good-humour.

"Are you all right, Mr. Nick?"

"Yes, Tom, and you ought to try and be as well as I am. You wouldn't ruin yourself with physic — "

"Nor with physicians," said Tom.

"When are we off?" asked Mr. Nick.

"Now."

"Any one going with us?"

"No one yet," said Tom; "but some one may turn up at the last moment."

"I hope so! I hope so, Tom! I like to talk as I travel, and when you want to talk I have noticed that it is as well not to be alone."

Mr. Nick's wishes were apparently not to be satisfied this time. The horses were harnessed. Tom cracked his whip, but no traveller appeared.

The notary took the end scat, and Lionel sat down beside him; Tom gave a last look round, up and down the road, and then mounted the box, gathered up the reins, whistled to his horses, and the noisy affair began to move, just as some passers-by, who knew Nick — and who did not know him, the excellent man? — wished him a pleasant journey, to which he replied by a little salute with his hand.

The buggy went away uphill, towards Mont Royal. The notary looked to the right and left with as much attention as the driver, but for a different reason. It seemed as though no one that morning was going to the north of the island, to have a chat with Mr. Nick.

The vehicle had reached the circular promenade, and the horses were breaking into a trot, when a man came forward, and beckoned the driver to stop. He sat down on the seat, in front of Lionel, having first saluted Mr. Nick and his clerk. The buggy went off at a gentle trot, and a few minutes later, at a turning on Mont Royal, was out of sight of the galvanized iron roofs of the houses of the town, which were shining in the sun like so many silvered mirrors.

The notary had seen the newcomer enter the vehicle with the most lively satisfaction. Now he could talk for the twelve miles that separated Montreal from the upper branch of the St. Lawrence. But it did not seem as though the traveller was in a humour to indulge in conventional conversation. He had given a glance at Mr. Nick and Lionel, and then settled himself in a corner, and, with his eyes half closed, seemed to be absorbed in his reflections.

He was a young man, about twenty-nine years of age. With his slight figure, energetic face, resolute look, manly features, high forehead, and dark hair, he was a typical French Canadian. What was he? Where did he come from? Mr. Nick, who knew everybody, did not know him, and had never seen him before. Looked at closely, the young man seemed to have passed through much trouble, and to have been educated in the school of misfortune.

That the unknown belonged to the party agitating for national independence was apparent from his dress, which was almost that of a backwoodsman. For a cap he wore a blue tuque, crossed on his chest was a sort of cape, and his trousers were of some coarse grey stuff, tied up with a red Sash. All was home-made; and, as will not have been forgotten, the use of home-made fabrics alone was a political protest, owing to its excluding such manufactured products as were imported from England. It was one of the thousand ways of defying the home authorities, and the way was not without precedent. A hundred and fifty years before, the Bostonians had proscribed the usage of tea out of hatred to Great Britain. And, in imitation of them, the Canadians had proscribed the use of stuffs manufactured in the United Kingdom. As to Mr. Nick, he, as a neutral, wore trousers of Canadian make, and coat of cloth imported from England. But, in the patriotic garments of Lionel there was not a single thread that had been woven beyond the Atlantic.

The buggy rolled along over the rough ground of Montreal Island, across to the minor branch of the St. Lawrence; and long did the journey seem to Mr. Nick, who was naturally so loquacious. But, as the young man did not seem disposed to begin, Mr. Nick fell back on Lionel, in the hope that their travelling companion would end by joining in the conversation.

"Well, Lionel," said he, "and how about this will-o'- the-wisp?"

"The will-o'-the-wisp?" asked the clerk.

"Yes! I have quite tired myself with looking, and yet I haven't seen it on the plains."

"There is too much daylight, perhaps," said Lionel, keeping up the pleasantry.

"Perhaps if we sang the old song. —

'Come along cheerily, goblin queer!

Come along cheerily, neighbour dear!'

But no — the goblin will not answer. By-the-bye, Lionel, you know how to get away from the blandishments of will-o'-the-wisps?"

37

"Certainly, Mr. Nick. All we have to do is to ask them what day of the month Christmas is; and, as they do not know, you have time to escape while they are looking about for an answer."

"I see you are acquainted with the tradition. Well, until one of that sort stops the road, suppose we have something to say about the one you have got in your pocket."

Lionel blushed slightly.

"You really wish it?"

"Yes, my boy! It will pas℈ a quarter of an hour or so."

* And the notary continued, addressing the young passenger, —

"You do not object to listen to a little versification, do you, sir?"

"Not at all," answered the passenger.

"It is a piece of poetry that my clerk has composed for the meeting of the Lyre-Amicale. These fellows fight shy of nothing! Come on, my young poet, present your piece — as they say to the gunners!"

Lionel was only too pleased to have a listener who would, perhaps, be more indulgent than Mr. Nick. And he drew forth his bluish paper, and read as follows: —

"The Will-o'-the-Wisp.

"A wayward flame that none can reach.

That doth its nightly guard deceive.

And in the darkening hours of eve.

Nor on the wave, nor on the beach.

A trace behind doth leave.

"A flame so quick to fade and flee.

In purple oft, and oft in white!

To solve this mystery of light.

The will-o'-the-wisp pursued must be.

And captured in its flight."

"Yes," said Mr. Nick; "captured, and put in a cage!"

Lionel continued, —

"Is it a phantom from afar?

Is it the hydrogen of the mire?

Would that its origin were higher!

Comes it not from a distant star?

Algol, or Vega of the Lyre?"

"That is for you to say, my boy!" said Mr. Nick, with a nod. "That is your business!"

Lionel continued, —

"To me, the soft and furtive breath Of sylph, or elf, or sprite, it seems.

As lightly float its fitful gleams.

When slowly wakes the plain beneath The morning's golden beams.

Is it the glimmer of the lamp Borne by the spectre, who would rest On the roof-ridge where the wine is press'd.

When through the night-air chill and damp The moon floats manifest?

'Is it the spirit of a fay.

That seeking, half concealed.

What peace a wicked world can yield.

Doth, like a gleaner, limp away.

Finding but nothing in the field?"

"Perfect!" said Mr. Nick. "Are you at the end of your descriptive comparisons?"

"Oh! No! Mr. Nick," said the clerk.

And he continued: —

"Is it the image of a form That all acknowledge fair Distorted by the troubled air?

Or the last flash of the dying storm Traced by its lingering glare?

"Did it from the path escape.

Traced by a falling meteorite That in its swift Icarian flight Was luminous, had weight, and shape.

And vanish'd in the night?

"Still on its path shoots radiance forth; And pale reflections cling.

And rays of mystery fling.

Like the auroras of the north Light as a night-moth's wing!"

"What do you think of all this troubadourish jingle?" asked Nick of his fellow-passenger.

"I think," said the stranger, "that your clerk has imagination, and I am curious to know to what else he will compare his will-o-the-wisp."

"Go on, Lionel, then."

Lionel had blushed at the young man's compliment, and with a clear voice he continued, —

"Doth it glow in that hour of sighs When the living are a-bed.

And the flutteing flag is spread.

That the Angel of the Darkness flies In memory of the dead?"

"Brrr!" said Mr. Nick.

"When night is clothed in her gloomiest robe.

And the given time is nigh.

And hush'd is every cry.

Is it the signal that the globe Sends upwards to the sky?

"And such a light as on ocean floats And, as the wandering spirits race Along their weary voyage through space.

The harbours of the universe denotes And their lone resting-place?"

"Well done, young poet!" said the stranger.

"Yes not bad! Not at all bad!" said Mr. Nick. "Where did you find all that, Lionel? That is all, I suppose?

No, Mr. Nick," said Lionel, and in a still more marked voice he read, —

"But beware, dear maid, if in your eyes The light of love it seems!

Chase it from your dreams!

That light to flame will never rise Brightly as it gleams!"

"A trap for the girls, indeed!" said Mr. Nick. "I should have been much surprised if there had not been a little love in view in these anacreontics! After all, it is the usual thing at your age! What do you think, sir?"

"Quite so," said the stranger; "and I fancy that — "

The stranger stopped in the middle of the sentence at the sight of a group of men at the side of the road, one of whom hailed the driver to stop.

The horses were pulled up and the men approached the vehicle.

"Mr. Nick, I believe!" said one of the men, lifting his hat.

"And Mr. Rip!" said the notary, adding in an undertone, "We must mind what we are up to!"

Luckily neither Mr. Nick, nor his clerk, nor the detective remarked the change in the stranger's face when Rips name was mentioned. He grew pale, not with the paleness of fear, but with that which is inspired by insurmountable horror. Evidently he would have sprung at the man. But, turning away his head, he controlled himself.

"Are you off to Laval, Mr. Notary?" asked Rip.

"As you see, Mr. Rip. Business will keep me there only an hour or two, and I hope to be back at Montreal this evening."

"That is your affair!"

"And what are you doing with your men?" asked Mr. Nick. "Always in ambush at the government cost. Are you going to capture a scoundrel or so?

41

There are plenty to take, for they multiply like weeds. It would be much better for them to turn honest men — "

"That's so, but they want the taste."

"The taste! You are always pleasant, Mr. Rip! Are you on the track of some criminal?"

"Criminal to some; hero to others. It all depends on the point of view."

"What do you mean?"

"The presence in the island has been reported of the famous Jean-Sans-Nom — "

"Ah! The famous Jean-Sans-Nom! Yes! The patriots have made him a hero, and not without good motives! But her Gracious Majesty does not seem to be of the same opinion, or Gilbert Argall would not have put you on his track."

"That's so."

"And you say they have seen this mysterious agitator in Montreal Island?"

"They claim to have done so," said Rip. "But I begin to doubt it."

"Well, if he did come here, he is almost sure to have got away by this time," said Mr. Nick. "He's not very long in one place. Jean-Sans-Nom is not easy to get hold of."

"Quite a will-o'-the-wisp," said the stranger to the young clerk.

"Good! Very good!" exclaimed Mr. Nick. "Lionel, you ought to bow! And, by-the-bye, Mr. Rip. if you meet a will-o'-the-wisp on the road, will you please catch him by the collar, and bring him to my clerk? It will please the wandering flame to hear how he has been treated by a disciple of Apollo!"

"Certainly!" said Rip. "If we are not obliged to go back to Montreal, where I expect fresh instructions."

Turning to the stranger, Rip continued, —

"And you are accompanying Mr. Nick?"

"To Laval," said the unknown.

"Where I'm in a hurry to go. Good-bye, Mr. Rip! If I cannot wish you good luck, for the capture of Jean- Sans-Nom would be a sad blow for the patriots, I can at least wish you good morning!"

"And I can wish you good day, Mr. Nick."

The horses resumed their trot. Rip and his men disappeared at a turning in the road.

A few minutes afterwards, the notary said to the stranger, who had leant back in the corner.

"I hope Jean-Sans-Nom will not let them catch him. They have been looking for him so long — "

"And they will have to look!" exclaimed Lionel. "And that confounded Rip will — "

"Hush, hush, Lionel! That is not our business."

' This Jean-Sans-Nom seems accustomed to outwit the police!" said the stranger.

"Just so, sir. If he is taken, it will be a great loss to the French-Canadians."

"He'll not be wanting in friends, Mr. Nick, and he is not a man to be taken."

"It doesn't matter," said the notary. "I have heard that it would be a great pity. After all, I don't take such interest in politics as Lionel, and it is better not to say much."

"But," continued the young man, "we were interrupted when your clerk's poetical inspiration — "

"He has finished inspiring, I suppose?"

"No, Mr. Nick!" said Lionel, thanking the stranger with a smile.

"What, not out of breath yet?" exclaimed the notary. "Here's a will-o'-the-wisp that was a sylph, an elf, a sprite, a spectre, a spirit, a phantom, a flash of lightning, an aerolite, a ray, a flag, a harbour-light a spark of love, and is not that enough? What else can it be?"

"I should like to know!" said the stranger.

"Then continue, Lionel, continue, and get to the end of it, if it has an end!"

Lionel, accustomed to Mr. Nick's pleasantries, began to read, —

"Whatever thou art, whatever thy name.

I would thy hidden projects know.

And share thy very thoughts: and so.

Absorb'd in thee, mysterious flame.

With thee would ever go,

"When settling on the silent trees Your wide wings in the twilight loom; Or, in the graveyard's darker gloom.

Softly called by the whispering breeze To guard the marble tomb."

"That is very pathetic!" said the notary.

"Or, where the seething billon s race —

The good ship driven on her side.

And by the tempest fiercely plied —

With all a spectre seagull's grace.

About the labouring hull to glide.

"A closer union could we claim If fate would heed the prayer I lisp.

To make us one, my will-o'-the-wisp.

To be born with you, my frolicsome flame!

To die with you, my will-o'-the-wisp!''

"Ah! that's very good!" said Mr. Nick. That's the sort of ending that suits me. You might sing it, —

'To be born with you, my frolicsome flame!

To die with you, my will-o'-the-wisp."

What do you say, sir?"

"Sir," said the stranger. "I hope the poet will accept all my compliments; and maybe win the prize at the meeting of the Lyre-Amicale. His verses have

44

enabled us to pass a very pleasant time, and never did a journey seem so short to me!"

Lionel was extremely flattered, and drank to the full of the praise the stranger gave him. And Mr. Nick was not at all displeased at the eulogiums addressed to his clerk.

Meanwhile the buggy had made good progress, and eleven o'clock had but just struck when they reached the northern branch of the river.

At this time the first steam-boats had already appeared on the St. Lawrence. They were not very powerful or very swift, and resembled the present day "tugs" more than any other craft afloat.

In a few minutes the boat had taken Mr. Nick, his clerk and their fellow-passenger across the middle branch of the river, whose greenish waters were still mingling with the blackish waters of the Ottawa.

There they parted company, after many compliments and much hand-shaking.

Then, while the stranger walked straight for the streets of Laval, Mr. Nick and Lionel turned off away from the town, towards the cast of Jesus Island.

CHAPTER IV - THE VILLA MONTCALM

The Island of Jesus, lying between the two upper arms of the St. Lawrence, is smaller than the Island of Montreal. It comprises the county of Laval, the name of which belongs to the Catholic University of Quebec in memory of the first bishop instituted in Canada.

Laval is also the name of the chief town of the island, which is situated on its northern bank. M. de Vaudreuil's house was three miles further down the St. Lawrence.

It was a house of agreeable aspect, surrounded by a park of about fifty acres, with stretches of grass and high thickets, and having the river bank for a boundary. It was built somewhat in the French taste, and had it not been for the swift, tumultuous course of the St. Lawrence, one might have supposed that the Villa Montcalm, as it was called, was on the banks of the Loire, a few leagues from Chenonceaux or Amboix.

M. de Vaudreuil had taken part in all the later insurrections of the French Canadians. He had figured in the plot to which the treason of Simon Morgaz had given so tragic an ending. A few years later an amnesty had restored him to liberty.

His house was built on the river bank. In its ebb and flow, the tide washed the lower step of the terrace, which was sheltered by an elegant verandah running along the front of the house. Behind, under the tranquil shadows of the park, the river breeze bore an aerial freshness, which tempered the heats of the Canadian summer. People who cared for shooting or fishing, could shoot or fish from morning till night. There was game in abundance on the plains of the island; the fish were in the creeks of the St. Lawrence, which the distant undulations of the hills shut in as with a frame of verdure.

The manners were those of the seventeenth century. An English author, Russell, has very justly said, "Lower Canada is a France of the olden time, under the white flag and fleur-de-lis." A French author, Reveillaud, has written, "It is the field of refuge of the old regime. It is a Brittany or a Vendee of sixty years ago. On the American continent the colonist has kept with jealous care the modes of thought, the childish beliefs and the superstitions of his fathers." This was true in those days; the French race had remained very pure in Canada, and without mixture of foreign blood.

46

On returning to the Villa Montcalm, in 1829, M. de Vaudreuil found himself in easy circumstances. Although his fortune was not a large one, yet he could have remained in retirement had not his ever-ardent patriotism forced him into aggressive politics.

At the time our story begins, M. de Vaudreuil was forty-seven years of age; his greyish hair made him appear somewhat older; but his quick glance, keen blue eyes, tall stature, robust constitution, assuring him of health under all trials, and his sympathetic and prepossessing face, made him the perfect type of a French gentleman. He was a true descendant of the bold men who crossed the Atlantic in the eighteenth century to found the most beautiful of colonies.

He had been a widower for ten years. The death of the wife he had loved with the deepest affection had left an irreparable void in his existence. His life was now centred in his only daughter, in whom her mother lived again.

At this time, Clary de Vaudreuil was in her twentieth year. Her graceful figure, abundant dark brown hair, large gloomy eyes, rich colour, and somewhat serious expression, made her like some of Fennimore Cooper's heroines, handsome rather than pretty, and more commanding than attractive. As a rule, she maintained a frigid reserve, or rather her whole life was concentrated in the only love she had yet felt — the love of her country.

Clary de Vaudreuil was a patriot. During the events of 1832 and 1834, she had closely studied the various phases of the insurrection. The leaders of the opposition regarded her as the bravest of the many women whose devotion they had secured. And when M. de Vaudreuil's political friends met at the Villa, Clary took part in their conferences, saying little, but listening, observing, and taking part in the correspondence with the committees. The French had absolute confidence in her, for she deserved it, and they had the most respectful friendship for her, and she was worthy of it.

However, in her impassioned heart another love had come of late to mingle with her love for her country — a love ideal and vague, which did not even know him who inspired it.

In 1831 and 1834, a mysterious personage had played an important part in the many attempts at rebellion. He had risked his head with an audacity, a courage, a disinterestedness, that were well calculated to impress the imagination of the sensitive. Throughout Lower Canada his name was repeated with enthusiasm — or rather the formula that served him for a name,

47

which was none other thin Jean-Sans-Nom. In the day of battle he came to the very forefront; when the strife was over, he disappeared. But it was felt that he was working in the dark, that his hand never ceased to prepare the future. In vain the authorities had sought to discover his retreat. Even Kip and Co. had failed. Nothing was known of the man's origin, of his past life, or his present life. One thing only was certain, that his influence was all-powerful among the French Canadians. And a legend had risen around him, and the reformists waited to see him appear, waving the flag of independence.

Such was the anonymous hero whose deeds had made so deep an impression on Clary dc Vaudreuil. Her most secret thoughts invariably turned to him. She regarded him as a supernatural being. She lived in mystic communion with him. In loving Jean-Sans-Nom with the most ideal of loves, it seemed to her she loved her country all the more. But this sentiment she kept close in her heart. And when her father saw her wandering away in the park, and walking so pensively, he little thought she was dreaming of the young patriot who in her eyes symbolized the revolution.

Among the political friends who often met at the Villa Montcalm, there were many whose relatives had taken part with M. de Vaudreuil in the unhappy conspiracy of 1825. Among these friends we may mention Andrew Farran and William Clerc, whose brothers Robert and Francis, had been executed on the 2Sth of September, 1825; there was also Vincent Hodge, the son of Walter Hodge, who had been betrayed with his companions by Simon Morgaz. With them a Quebec advocate, the Deputy Sebastian Gramont — in whose house it had been falsely reported to Rip that Jean-Sans-Nom was a visitor — frequently shared in the hospitality of M. de Vaudreuil.

The most ardent of these was certainly Vincent Hodge, who was then a young man of thirty-two. Of American descent by his father, he was of French descent by his mother, who had died of grief a short time after her husband's execution. Vincent Hodge had found it impossible to live near Clary, without admiring her, without loving her, and this was in no way displeasing to M. de Vaudreuil. Vincent Hodge was a distinguished-looking man, genial and pleasant in manner, though a little too much of the typical frontier Yankee. Clary could not have chosen a husband more worthy of her — brave beyond reproach, earnest in character, and true in sentiment; but she had not even noticed that she was the object of his attention. Between her and Vincent Hodge there could be only one bond — that of patriotism. She appreciated his good qualities, but she could not love him. Her life, her thoughts, her aspirations, belonged to another, to an unknown she waited for, who would one day appear.

M. de Vaudreuil and her friends observed with attention the progress of events in the Canadian provinces. Opinion was in a very excited state, but it no longer concerned itself, as in 1825, with a mere personal plot against the governor. It was rather a general conspiracy in a state of latent heat. For the rebellion to break out it only needed a chief to appeal to the people, and raise every parish in the adjoining county. And then, without a doubt, M. de Vaudreuil and his friends would take a leading part in the insurrection.

Never had circumstances been more favourable. The reformers were loud in their protests, denouncing the exactions of the Government which claimed to seize on the public revenue without the consent of the legislature. The newspapers — among them the Canadian founded in 1806, and the Vindicator of more recent origin — fulminated against the crown and its agents. They reported the speeches made in Parliament or in public meetings by Papineau, Viger, Quesnel, Saint Real, Bourdages, and many others who rivalled each other in the talent and audacity of their attacks. A spark would be enough to provoke a popular explosion. This was well known to Lord Gosford. And the partisans of the French were as well acquainted with the fact as his lordship.

Matters had reached this stage, when, in the morning of the 3rd of September, a letter arrived at the Villa Montcalm. The letter, posted the night before at Montreal, informed M. de Vaudreuil that his friends, Vincent Hodge, Andre Farran and William Clerc had been invited to visit him that evening. M. de Vaudreuil did not recognize the hand which had written the letter and signed it in these words: — A Son of Liberty.

M. de Vaudreuil was much surprised at the communication, and also at the way in which it had been made. The night before he had seen his friends at Montreal, at the house of one of them, and had left them without anything being said of a meeting on the morrow. Had Vincent Hodge, Farran, and Clerc received a similar letter? That might be so; but might it not be some plot on the part of The police? This suspicion was natural enough after the Simon Morgaz experience.

But all that could be done was to wait. When Vincent Hodge, Farran and Clerc arrived, if they came, they could perhaps explain what at present seemed inexplicable. Such was Clary's opinion when she read the letter. Her eyes were riveted on the mysterious writing as she examined it attentively. A strange spirit was here. Where her father saw only a snare spread for himself and his political friends, she seemed, on the contrary, to believe in some powerful intervention in aid of the French cause. Was there at last to be revealed the hand that would seize the threads of a new uprising, and guide it to success. "Father," she said, "I have confidence! "However, as the rendezvous was appointed for the evening, M. de Vaudreuil thought he would first go over to Laval. Perhaps he might learn what had happened to bring on the projected conference. He could be there to receive Vincent Hodge and his two friends when they landed on the island. But just as he was going to give the order to get ready, his servant appeared to inform him that a visitor had arrived.

"Who is he?" asked M. de Vaudreuil quickly. "Here is his card," said the servant. M. de Vaudreuil took the card, read the name it bore, and immediately exclaimed, —

"The excellent Mr. Nick? He is always welcome, bid him come in!"

An instant later, the notary found himself in the presence of M. de Vaudreuil and his daughter. "You, Mr. Nick!" said M. de Vaudreuil. "In person, and ready to pay my respects to yourself and to Mademoiselle Clary!"

And he shook hands with M. de Vaudreuil, after having favoured his daughter with the official salute which the ancient notaries have kept to themselves from time immemorial.

"Mr. Nick," said M. de Vaudreuil, "this is an unexpected visit, but it is a pleasant one nevertheless."

"Very pleasant for me," said Mr. Nick. "And how are you, M. de Vaudreuil? You both look flourishing enough. You certainly seem to live well at the Villa Montcalm! I ought to take back with me to Bon Secours a little of the air you breathe here."

You need not do that, Mr. Nick! Come and see us oftener.:'

"And stay a few days," said Clary.

"And my office, and my deeds!" exclaimed the loquacious notary. "They won't leave me much time for holiday-making! To say nothing of the wills, for people live to be so old in Canada, that they will end by never dying. What with our octogenarians and centenarians, we are a long way out of the bounds of ordinary statistics. But as for the marriage settlements, they completely tire me out! By-the-bye, six weeks ago I was at Laprairie with one of my clients — one of my good clients, you understand — when I had to draw up the settlements for his nineteenth youngster!"

"That must have been Thomas Harcher, I am sure!" said M. dc Vaudreuil.

"Exactly, and it was at your farm at Chipogan that I attended."

"It is a large family, Mr. Nick."

' It is that, M. de Vaudreuil, and note that I am in no hurry to have done with the documents that concern it."

"Well, Mr. Nick," said Clary, "it is likely that we shall meet you at Chipogan. Thomas Harcher has so insisted on our being present at his daughter's wedding, that if nothing keeps us here, my father and I are going to give him the pleasure!"

"And give me the pleasure too," said Mr. Nick. "Is it not a pleasure for me to see you! I have only one complaint to make, Mademoiselle Clary."

"And what is that Mr. Nick?"

"That you always receive mc here as a friend and never as a notary."

Clary smiled at the insinuation, and almost immediately resumed her habitual gravity.

"But," said M. de Vaudreuil, "it is not as a friend, my dear Nick, that you are here to-day, you have come as a notary!"

"So I have! So I have! But not on account of Mademoiselle Clary! But all in good time! The time will come right enough! But, M. de Vaudreuil, I beg to inform you that I have not come alone."

"What! You have a companion? And you let him wait in the antechamber? I'll order him in."

"No! No! It is not worth while! It is only my second clerk — a boy who makes verses — did you ever hear of such a thing? — and who runs after will-o'-the-wisps. Figure to yourself a clerk-poet, or a poet-clerk,

51

Mademoiselle Clary! As I wish to speak with you in private, M. de Vaudreuil, I told him to take a walk in the park."

"You did well, M-. Nick! But we must refresh this young poet."

"Useless! He drinks nothing but nectar, and not even that unless it is of the latest vintage."

M. de Vaudreuil could not help laughing at the pleasantries of this excellent man, whom he had known for so many years, and whose advice had always proved so valuable in the management of his personal affairs.

"I will leave you with my father, Mr. Nick," said Clary.

"I beg you will remain, mademoiselle! "Said the notary. "I know I can speak in your presence, even of things that may have reference to politics — at least I suppose so, for as you know, I never meddle — "

"Well, well, Mr. Nick," said M. de Vaudreuil, "Clary can assist at our interview. Sit down, and then you can talk at your ease."

The notary look one of the cane chairs that furnished the room, while M. de Vaudreuil and his daughter installed themselves on a sofa in front of him.

"And now, my dear Nick," said M. de Vaudreuil, "what has brought you here?"

"To give you that," said the notary.

And he drew from his pocket a bundle of bank-notes.

"Money!" said M. de Vaudreuil, who could not hide his extreme surprise.

"Yes, money, and good money, and whether it pleases you or not, a good round sum!"

"A good round sum!"

"Judge for yourself! Fifty thousand dollars in beautiful notes of legal tender!"

"And this money is intended — "

"For you — for you alone!"

"And who sent it me?"

"Impossible for me to tell you, for the very excellent reason that I do not know!"

"What use is to be made of this money?"

"Neither do I know that."

"And how have you been instructed to remit me such a sum?"

"Read!"

The notary handed him a letter which contained only a few lines: —

"Mr. Nick, notary at Montreal, will at once remit to the president of the committee of reformists of Laval at the Villa Montcalm, the balance standing to our account in his office books.

"J. B.J.

"September 2nd, 1837."

M. de Vaudreuil looked at the notary, understanding as little as before of the reason of the errand.

"Mr. Nick," said he, "where was this letter posted?"

"At Saint Charles, in the county of Vercheres."

Clary took the letter. She examined the writing. Perhaps it was in the same hand as the letter which warned M. de Vaudreuil of the visit of his friends Hodge, Clerc. and Farran? No! Nothing of the sort. There was no resemblance in the handwriting of the two letters, as she showed her father.

"You have no suspicion, Mr. Nick," she asked, "who can be the writer of this letter, who signs himself J. B. J.?"

"None, Mademoiselle Clary."

"But it is not the first time you have been in communication with this person?"

"Evidently."

"Or rather with these persons, for the letter docs not say my account, but our account, which would lead us to think that the three initials belong to three different names."

53

"Quite so," said Mr. Nick.

"I observe also," said M. de Vaudreuil, "that as it is a question of account, you must have made certain payments before this."

"M. de Vaudreuil," said the notary, "I will tell you all I know, and which it seems to me you ought to know!"

And, taking time to collect his thoughts, he continued as follows: —

"In 1825, a month after the sentence which cost the lives of some of your dearest friends, and deprived you of your liberty, I received a packet containing bank notes amounting to the enormous sum of one hundred thousand dollars. The packet had been posted at Quebec, and contained a letter couched in these terms: — ' This sum of one hundred thousand dollars is placed in the hands of Mr. Nick, notary of Montreal, for him to dispose of, according to instructions he will subsequently receive. His discretion is counted on to say nothing of the deposit entrusted to his care, nor of the use to which it may eventually be put.'"

"And it was signed?" asked Clary.

"It was signed J. B. J." answered Mr. Nick.

"The same initials?" said M. de Vaudreuil.

"The same?" repeated Clary.

"Yes, mademoiselle. As you may think, I could not be more surprised than I was at this mysterious deposit. But after all, as I could not send back the money to my unknown client, and as I did not care to inform the authorities, I paid in the hundred thousand dollars to the bank at Montreal, and I waited."

Clary de Vaudreuil and her father listened to Mr. Nick with the greatest attention. Had not the notary said in his heart that the money was destined for political purposes? And, as they were soon to see, he was not deceived.

"Six years later," he continued, "a sum of twenty- two thousand dollars was demanded by a letter signed with these enigmatic initials, to be sent to the village of Bourgade, in the county of that name."

"To whom?" asked M. de Vaudreuil.

"To the chairman of the Reformist Committee, and a little time afterwards there broke out the revolt you remember. Four years elapsed, and in a letter signed with the same initials, I was requested to send twenty-eight thousand dollars to Sainte Martine, this time to the president of the county of Chateauguay. A month later there came that violent reaction which marked the election of 1834, and brought about the prorogation of the Chamber, and was followed by the demand to impeach the Governor Lord Aylmer!"

M. de Vaudreuil reflected a few moments on what he had heard, and then said. —

"And so, my dear Nick, you see a connection between these different demonstrations, and the sending of the money to the reformist committees."

"I, M. de Vaudreuil!" said Mr. Nick, "I see nothing! I am not a politician! I am a simple administrator! I have only to return the sums I have received on deposit, and in the way I am instructed. I tell you things as they are, and I leave you to draw your conclusions."

"Good! My prudent friend!" said M. de Vaudreuil, with a Smile. "We will not compromise you. But if you have come to-day to the Villa Montcalm — "

"It is to do for the third time what I have already done twice. This morning, the 3rd of September, I have been instructed, first, to dispose of the balance of the sum that had been remitted to me, being fifty-thousand dollars; and, secondly, to place it in the hands of the president of the committee at Laval. That is why, M. de Vaudreuil, you being the president of the said committee, I have brought you the said sum. Now, to what use is it to be put? I do not know, and I do not wish to know. It is in the hands of the president mentioned in the letter, and if I did not send it through the post, but preferred to bring it myself, it was because it gave me an opportunity of seeing my friend, M. de Vaudreuil and Mademoiselle Clary, his daughter!"

Mr. Nick had finished his story without interruption. And then, having said what he wanted to say, he arose, went out on to the terrace, and looked at the boats, which were ascending and descending the river.

M. de Vaudreuil, deep in his reflections, kept silence. A similar train of thought was exercising the mind of his daughter. He had no doubt that this money, mysteriously deposited with Mr. Nick, was to be employed for the needs of the cause, and for an approaching insurrection. Was it not a singular coincidence that the money had come the very day that "A Son of Liberty" had called together the most intimate friends of M. de Vaudreuil?

The conversation was resumed, and continued for some time. And with the loquacious Mr. Nick how could it be otherwise? He informed M. de Vaudreuil of what M. de Vaudreuil knew far better, the political situation in Lower Canada. And these things, as he did not cease to repeat, he only spoke of with extreme reserve, having no desire to be mixed up in them. His object was to put M. de Vaudreuil on his guard, for there had certainly been an increase in the activity of the police in the county of Montreal.

And with regard to this Mr. Nick was led to say, —

"What the authorities particularly dread is that a chief should put himself at the head of a popular movement, and that this chief should be the famous Jean-Sans- Nom."

At these words Clary rose, and went to lean on the window opening into the park.

"Do you then know this audacious agitator?" asked M. de Vaudreuil.

"I do not know him," said the notary. "I have never seen him, and I never met anybody who knew him. But he exists, there is no doubt of that! And I imagine him to be a true hero of romance — a young man of tall stature, of noble features, and thrilling voice — unless he is some good old patriarch, bent and broken by age. With such personages you do not know what to think!"

"Whatever he may be," answered M. de Vaudreuil, "Heaven grant that the thought may come to him to put himself at our head, and we will follow him as far as he likes to lead."

"Well, M. de Vaudreuil, that will not be long first."

"You say so?" said Clary, returning quickly to the middle of the room.

"I say so, Mademoiselle Clary — or rather, I say nothing! That is wiser!"

"Speak! speak!" said the girl. "What do you know?"

"What others know doubtless," answered Mr. Nick. "That Jean-Sans-Nom has reappeared in the county of Montreal. At least, so runs the report — unfortunately — "

"Unfortunately?" said Clary.

"Yes, for if so, I fear our hero will not escape the police. This very day, as I was crossing the island of Montreal, I met the bloodhounds that Gilbert Argall had put on his track, and among them was the head of the house of Rip and Co."

"What? Rip?" said M. de Vaudreuil.

"Himself," said the notary. "He is a clever man, and should be led on by a good reward. If he catches Jean- Sans-Nom, the condemnation of the young patriot — yes, decidedly, he ought to be young — the condemnation is certain, and the national party will provide another victim."

In spite of her self-control. Clary turned pale, her eyes closed, and it was with difficulty she could restrain the beatings of her heart. M. de Vaudreuil walked hurriedly backwards and forwards in the room.

Mr. Nick, wishing to remove the painful effect produced by his last words, added, —

"After all, he is a man of uncommon audacity, this Jean-Sans-Nom. He has, up to the present, managed to escape. And if he is closely pressed, every house in the county will give him a refuge, and all doors will be open to him — even the door of Mr. Nick's office, although Mr. Nick does not meddle with politics."

Thereupon the notary took his leave of M. and Mademoiselle de Vaudreuil. He had no time to spare if he wished to return to Montreal before dinner-time — that regular and ever-welcome hour at which he completed one of the most important deeds of his existence.

M. de Vaudreuil would have had the horses out to give him a lift to Laval; but, like a prudent man, Mr. Nick declined. The less that was known of his visit to the Villa Montcalm the better. He had good legs, thank Heaven, and a mile more or less would not trouble one of the best walkers among Canadian notaries. And was he not of the blood of the Sagamores, the descendant of those hardy Indian people whose warriors for months used to follow the war-path, &c. &c.

In short, Mr. Nick called Lionel, who doubtless had been following the muses along the park piths, and up along the river bank the two soon struck the road to Laval.

In three-quarters of an hour they reached the quay just as Vincent Hodge, Clerc and Farran were landing from the tug on their way to the Villa Montcalm.

As they passed the notary was saluted with the inevitable "Good morning, Mr. Nick!" Crossing the river, they mounted the buggy, and returned to the house in Bon Secours market-place just as the old servant, Dolly, was placing the soup on the table.

Mr. Nick immediately sat down in his large arm-chair, and Lionel placed himself in front of him while he hummed, —

To be born with you, my frolicsome flame.

To die with you, my will-o'-the-wisp.'

And above all," he added, "if you swallow a few verses as you eat, please take care of the bones."

CHAPTER V - THE UNKNOWN

WHEN Vincent Hodge, William Clerc and Andrew Farran reached the villa, they were received by M. de Vaudreuil.

Clary had just gone to her room. By the window opening on to the park she let her looks wander over the country which the Laurentides bounded on the horizon The thought of this mysterious being, so vividly recalled to her memory, occupied her whole thoughts. He had been reported as being in the district. He was being sought for in the island of Montreal. For the island of Jesus to offer him a refuge he would only have to cross the arm of the river! Would he demand shelter at the Villa Montcalm? That he had friends there ready to welcome him he could not doubt. But to take shelter under the roof of M. de Vaudreuil, the president of one of the reformist committees, would expose him to the greatest danger. The villa would be watched, and Clary had a presentiment that Jean-Sans-Nom would come, if it were only for a day, an hour. And in her excited state, desirous to be alone, she had left the drawing-room before the friends of M. de Vaudreuil were introduced.

William Clerc and Andrew Farran — both about the same age as M. de Vaudreuil — were two old officers of the Canadian militia. Deprived of their rank after the sentence of the 25th of September which sent their brothers to the scaffold, sentenced themselves to imprisonment for life, they had only recovered their liberty on account of the amnesty to which M. de Vaudreuil owed his. The party saw in them two men of action who only asked for a second opportunity of risking their lives in an appeal to arms. They were energetic, and inured to fatigue by their hunting expeditions in the woods and plains of Three Rivers, where they owned large estates.

As soon as Vincent Hodge had clasped M. de Vaudreuil's hand, he asked him if he knew that Farran, Clerc and himself had been each invited by letter?

"Yes," said M. de Vaudreuil; and doubtless the letter you received, like that I had, was signed A Son of Liberty:'

"That's it!" said Farran.

"You don't suspect an ambush?" asked Clerc. "In arranging this rendezvous, may they not intend to catch us when we are in consultation?"

"The Legislative Council," said M. de Vaudreuil, "has not yet deprived Canadians of the right of meeting at each other's houses that I am aware of!"

"Perhaps not," said Farran; "but who sent the letter, and why did he not sign his name?"

"That is certainly strange," said M. de Vaudreuil, "and particularly as this personage, whoever he may be, does not state his intention of being present at the rendezvous. The letter I had merely informed me that you three were to meet me here this evening — "

"And ours contained no other information," said Clerc.

"It is difficult to understand," said Vincent Hodge, "why the unknown should have arranged matters in this way if he did not propose to be present; and I believe he will come."

"Well!" said Farran; "let him come. We shall see what sort of a man he is, and we will listen to what he has to say. And we can show him out, if it does not suit us to have anything to do with him."

"Vaudreuil?" asked Clerc. "Your daughter knows of this letter, what does she think?"

"Nothing suspicious," said M. de Vaudreuil.

"We must wait," said Vincent Hodge.

But if he intended to be at the rendezvous, the man who signed the letter would have to take certain precautions. It would be night before he reached the villa — at least that would only be prudent under the circumstances.

Conversation ranged over the political situation, which had become so critical. Such a state of things could not last. And as bearing on this matter, M. de Vaudreuil mentioned that as president of the county of Laval, he had received from Mr. Nick, the notary, a considerable sum which was certainly destined for the use of the cause.

While they walked in the park till dinner was ready, Vincent Hodge, Clerc and Farran confirmed what Mr. Nick had said. The police were on the alert. Not only were Rip and his men engaged, but detachments of regular police were scouring the country, doing their utmost to strike the trad of Jean-Sans-Nom. Evidently the appearance of this personage would be sufficient to provoke a rising. It was, therefore, not impossible that the unknown was to inform M. dc Vaudreuil concerning this.

About six o'clock, M. de Vaudreuil and his friends returned to the drawing-room, where they found Clary. William Clerc and Farran greeted her in the only way authorized by their age and intimacy. Vincent Hodge was more reserved. Respectfully he shook hands, and then he offered her his arm, and with her led the way to the dining-room.

The dinner was abundant, as was the case in Canada in those days in the poorest as well as the richest houses. It consisted of fish from the river, of venison from the neighbouring forests, and of vegetables and fruits gathered in the kitchen-garden of the villa.

During dinner, no mention was made of the meeting so impatiently awaited. Before the servants it was best to say nothing, although they had been in the house for years.

After dinner, the evening was so fine, the temperature was so mild, that Clary went and sat under the verandah. The St. Lawrence caressed the lower steps of the terrace, bathing them with its waters which the slack of the tide held level in the twilight. M. de Vaudreuil and his guests smoked as they leant over the balustrades, exchanging but few words, and always in a low voice.

It was just after seven o'clock. Night began to close in and hide the lower depths of the valleys, while the 16ng twilight retired across the plains to the west; the stars began to appear in the opposite zone of the sky.

Clary looked up and down the St. Lawrence. Would the unknown come by the river? It seemed so, if he wished to leave no trace of his passage. It was easy for a small boat to slip along the river among the grass and reeds of its bank. If he landed at the terrace, the mysterious personage could enter the villa without being seen, and could leave it again without any of the people in the house having the least suspicion of his presence.

As, however, it was possible that the visitor might not come by the St. Lawrence, M. de Vaudreuil had given orders to admit at once any one presenting himself at the villa. A lamp in the drawing-room showed but a little light through the curtains of the windows sheltered by the thick glass of the verandah. Outside nothing could be seen of what was passing within.

61

But if all was quiet on the side of the park, it was not so on the river. From time to time boats came into view, sometimes on the left bank, sometimes on the right; sometimes they met, and a few words were interchanged, and then they rowed away in different directions.

M. de Vaudreuil and his friends attentively watched these comings and goings, the object of which they fully understood.

"Those are police boats," said Clerc, "Yes," said Vincent Hodge, "and they are watching the river — and — "

"Perhaps the Villa Montcalm!"

The words were spoken in a low voice, and it was neither M. de Vaudreuil nor his daughter, nor either of his guests, that uttered them.

A man, hidden among the thick grass below the balustrade, rose on the right of the steps, and at a quick step crossed the terrace. He raised his toque, and, with a slight bow, said, —

"The Son of Liberty, who wrote to you, gentlemen!"

M. dc Vaudreuil, Clary, Vincent Hodge, Clerc, and Farran, surprised by the sudden apparition, endeavoured to recognize the man who had entered the villa in so strange a fashion. His voice was as unknown as his face.

"M. de Vaudreuil," said the man, "you must excuse my coming here in this strange way, but it was important that no one should sec me come, as it is important that no one should see me go."

"Come in," said M. de Vaudreuil.

Then they all entered the drawing-room, and the door was immediately closed.

The man was the young stranger in whose company Mr. Nick had travelled from Montreal. M. de Vaudreuil and his friends remarked, as the notary had done, that he was a French Canadian.

After bidding adieu to Mr. Nick at Laval he had gone to a humble tavern in the lower quarters of the town. There, in a dark corner of the room, he had waited till dinner time, glancing through the newspapers. His impassive countenance gave no sign of the sentiments aroused by what he read, although the journals were most violent in their partisanship for or against the Crown.

Queen Victoria had just succeeded her uncle, William the Fourth, and in impassioned articles a discussion was carried on as to the changes which the new reign would bring about in Canada. But although it was a woman's hand that held the sceptre of the United Kingdom, it was feared it would rest heavily on the colony.

Till six o'clock the young man had remained in the tavern where he dined, and at eight o'clock he had started.

If a spy had followed him, he would have seen him make for the river bank, and glide through the thick grass, and reach the villa, where he arrived three-quarters of an hour afterwards. The unknown had waited a little before appearing on the terrace, and we know how he had intervened in the conversation between M. de Vaudreuil and his friends.

And now, with the doors and windows shut, they could speak without fear of being overheard.

"Sir," said M. de Vaudreuil, "you will not be surprised if I first ask you who you are?"

"I told you when I arrived, M. de Vaudreuil. I am like all of you, a Son of Liberty."

Clary made an involuntary gesture of disappointment. Perhaps she expected another name. Would this man persist in his incognito even in the Villa Montcalm?

"Sir," said Farran, if you arranged a meeting here between us and M. de Vaudreuil, it was doubtless in order to confer with us on matters of some importance. Before talking freely to you, it is only natural that we should like to know with whom we have to deal."

"You would have been imprudent, gentlemen, not to have asked me that question," said the young man. "And it would be unpardonable of me if I had refused to answer it."

And he handed them a letter.

The letter informed M. de Vaudreuil of the visit of the unknown, in whom he might place entire confidence, even if he did not give his name. It was signed by one of the principal leaders of the Opposition in Parliament, the advocate Gramont, deputy for Quebec, and one of the political associates of

M. de Vaudreuil. Gramont added that if the visitor asked M. de Vaudreuil's hospitality for a few days, he could accord it him with every confidence that it was for the interest of the cause.

M. de Vaudreuil read this letter to his daughter and friends, and then added, —

"Sir, you can consider yourself at home here, and you can remain as long as it suits you at the Villa Montcalm."

"Two days at the outside, M. de Vaudreuil," replied the young man. "In four days I must have rejoined my companions at the mouth of the St. Lawrence. I thank you for your welcome. And now, gentlemen, I beg you will listen to what I have to say."

He then spoke with precision of the state of public opinion at the moment. He showed that the country was ready to rise against the loyalists and the agents of the Crown. This he had seen himself in a reformist campaign during the last few weeks in the counties of the Upper St. Lawrence and the Ottawa. In a few days he was to pay a last visit to the parishes in the eastern counties, so as to knit together the elements of an approaching insurrection, which would extend from the mouth of the river to the territories of Ontario. To this levy in mass neither Lord Gosford, with the representatives of authority, nor General Colborne, with a few thousand redcoats, had adequate forces to oppose, and Canada — he did not doubt — would at last throw off the yoke."

The unknown spoke with a coolness that showed that at all times and in every place he could retain his self- control; that a fire burned within him; and that his thoughts were inspired by the most ardent patriotism. As he gave certain details as to what he had done and what he intended to do, Clary never took her eyes off him. All that he said told her that she had before her the hero in whom, in her imagination, was incarnated the Canadian revolution.

When he had ended the account of his proceedings, he added, —

"A chief is needed by the partisans of our autonomy, and when the time comes a chief will arise to take the lead. Meanwhile a committee of action should be formed to concentrate individual efforts. Will you and your friends join this committee? All of you have already suffered in your families, in your persons, for the national cause.

This cause has cost the lives of our best patriots, of your father, Vincent Hodge, of your brothers, William Clerc and Andrew Farren — "

"By the treason of a scoundrel!" said Vincent Hodge.

"Yes, of a scoundrel!" repeated the young man. And Clary detected a slight change in his voice, which had been so clear till then. "But," added he, "the man is dead."

"Are you sure of that?" asked Clerc.

"He is dead," replied the unknown.

"Dead! This Simon Morgaz! And it was not I that did justice on him!" exclaimed Vincent Hodge.

My friends," said M. de Vaudreuil, let us say no more about the traitor, and allow me to reply to the proposition that has been communicated to us. Sir," said he, turning to his guest, "what our people have already done we are prepared to do again. We will risk our lives, as they risked theirs. You can depend upon us in all things, and we will undertake to centralize at this Villa Montcalm the efforts in which you have taken the initiative. We are in daily communication with the different counties in the district, and at the first signal we will risk our lives. Your intention is, you say, to leave us in two days to visit the eastern parishes? Be it so. At your return you will find us ready to follow the chief, whoever he may be, who will unfurl the flag of independence."

"Vaudreuil has spoken for us all," said Vincent Hodge. "We have but one thought — to withdraw our country from oppression and assure it the right to be free."

"And which, this time, it will conquer!" said Clary, advancing towards the young man. But at the same moment he stepped towards the door opening on to the terrace.

"Listen, gentlemen!" he said.

A strange noise was heard in the direction of Laval; a distant clamour, of which it was difficult to recognize the nature or the cause.

"What is it?" asked William Clerc.

"Has a rising taken place already?" asked Farran.

"Heaven grant it may be nothing!" said Clary. "It would be to begin too soon."

"Yes. too soon," said the stranger.

"What can it be?" asked M. de Vaudreuil. "Listen! The noise approaches us."

"It sounds like a trumpet-call," said Farran.

Brazen notes traversing space at regular intervals became heard at the villa. Was it an armed detachment on the march for M. de Vaudreuil's house?

M. de Vaudreuil opened the door of the room, and his friends followed him on to the terrace.

They looked towards the west, but there was no suspicious light in that direction. Evidently the noise did not come across the plains of Jesus Island. But suddenly a confused noise was heard nearer, and at the same time came a sound of trumpets.

"There it is," said Vincent Hodge.

And he pointed with his finger to the St. Lawrence up towards Laval. In this direction a few torches were giving a light but little stronger than that reflected by the misty waters of the river.

Two or three minutes passed. A boat dropping down with the tide came near the bank a quarter of a mile up stream. The boat contained a dozen persons, whose uniform it was easy to recognize in the torchlight. It was a constable, accompanied by a detachment of police.

From time to time the boat stopped. Immediately a voice, preceded by a blast from the trumpet rose on the air, but it was impossible to hear what it said at the Villa Montcalm.

"That is a proclamation," said William Clerc.

"And it ought to be of importance," said Farran, "for the authorities to issue it at this hour."

"Wait," said M. de Vaudreuil, "and we shall soon hear — "

"Would it not be better for us to return to the drawing- room?" said Clary, addressing the stranger.

"Why should we?" said he. "What the authorities think good to proclaim ought to be good for us to hear."

Meanwhile, the boat, followed by a few canoes, had come opposite the terrace.

A blast was given from the trumpet. And this is what M. de Vaudreuil and his friends distinctly heard: —

"By the Governor-General of the Canadian Provinces.

"A Proclamation.

"This 3rd of September, 1837.

"A reward is hereby offered for Jean-Sans-Nom, who has reappeared in the counties of the Upper St. Lawrence. Six thousand dollars will be paid to whoever will arrest him, or cause him to be arrested.

"For Lord Gosford.

"Gilbert Argall, "Minister of Police?'

Then the boat resumed its course down stream.

M. de Vaudreuil and his friends remained motionless on the terrace, which was then enveloped in the darkness of the night. Not a movement had escaped the unknown, as the constable's voice repeated the terms of the proclamation. The girl alone, almost unconsciously, made a step towards him.

M. de Vaudreuil was the first to speak.

"Again a reward offered to traitors!" he said. "It will be useless this time, I hope, for the fair renown of Canada!"

"It is too much to hope that they will find another Simon Morgaz!" exclaimed Vincent Hodge.

"May heaven protect Jean-Sans-Nom!" said Clary, in a voice thrilling with emotion.

There were a few moments of silence.

"Let us come in and go to our rooms," said M. de Vaudreuil. "I will see that one is got ready for you," said he, addressing the unknown.

"I thank you," was the reply; "but it is impossible for me to stay longer in this house — "

"And why?"

"When, an hour ago, I accepted the hospitality you offered me, I was not in the position that this proclamation has put me?"

"What do you mean? "That my presence can now only compromise you, for the Governor-General has put a price on my head. I am Jean-Sans-Nom!"

And Jean-Sans-Nom bowed, and was walking towards the river bank, when Clary stopped him with her hand.

"Remain here," she said.

CHAPTER VI - THE ST. LAWRENCE

The valley of the St. Lawrence is probably one of the largest that geologic agencies have sculptured on the face of the globe. Humboldt gives it an area of 270,000 square leagues — an area almost equal to that of Europe. The river, in its capricious course, dotted with islands, barred with rapids, broken with falls, traverses the rich valley of Lower Canada. At the mouth of the river, in the large bay beyond the estuary, lie the Magdalen Islands, the islands of Cape Breton and Prince Edward, and the large island of Anticosti, which the very different- looking coasts of Labrador and Newfoundland shelter from the violent winds of the Northern Atlantic.

It is not till the middle of April that the breaking-up commences of the ice accumulated by the long rigorous period of winter in Canada. The St. Lawrence then becomes navigable. Ships of large tonnage can then reach the region of the great lakes, those fresh-water seas which stretch, like a string of beads, across what has been so poetically called "the land of Fennimore Cooper." At that time the river, served by the ebb and flow of tide, it as animated as a roadstead when a treaty of peace has just raised the blockade. Sailing-vessels, steamers, timber- rafts, pilot-boats, coasters, fishing-boats, pleasure-boats, and canoes glide on the surface of its waters, now clear of their thick covering. It is life for half a year, after half a year of death.

On the 13th of September, about six o'clock in the morning, a cutter left the little port of St. Anne, which is situated in the mouth of the St. Lawrence, on the southern bank. She was manned with five of those fishermen who ply their profitable trade from the rapids of Montreal to the island of Anticosti; and, after casting their nets and lines where the instinct of their trade directs them, sell their salt-water and fresh-water fish from village to village, or rather from house to house — for there is almost an unbroken chain of houses along both banks to the western boundary of the province. The fisherman's trade is, perhaps, the most honoured of all in Canada, especially along the river-side, where there are from ten to fifteen thousand fishing-boats, and more than 30,000 fishermen working on the river or its branches.

The cutter had a passenger, making six men in all on board, who was a fisherman only in his dress. But it would have been difficult to recognize in him the young man who for two days had been a guest at the Villa Montcalm.

Jt was Jean-Sans-Nom.

While he stayed at the villa he had given no explanation of the incognito under which he concealed himself and his family. Jean was the only name he had given to M. and Mademoiselle de Vaudreuil.

In the evening of the 3rd of September, when their conference was over, Vincent Hodge, William Clerc, and Farran had returned to Montreal. It was not till two days after he arrived at the villa that Jean took his leave.

During this short stay, what hours were passed in talking of the new attempt which was to free Canada from the English yoke! With what passion Clary heard the young patriot glorify the cause which was so dear to both of them! He seemed to have shaken off some of the coldness he had shown at first, and which he seemed to have put on. Perhaps he was submitting to the influence of the thrilling spirit of the girl whose patriotism agreed so well with his own.

It was on the evening of the 5th of September that Jean had left the villa to resume his wandering life, and finish the campaign of reformist propaganda in the counties of Lower Canada. No one in the house suspected that he was Jean-Sans-Nom. Rip and Co. started on a false trail, had not discovered his retreat. He had left the villa secretly as he had arrived, had crossed the St. Lawrence in the ferry-boat at the end of the island, and struck into the interior, towards the American frontier, so as to cross it if necessary. As it was in the districts on the upper river that the search was being prosecuted, and naturally so, on account of his having just been through them, he reached, without recognition or pursuit, the river St. John, which forms in part the boundary of New Brunswick. At the little port of St. Anne, his bold companions were waiting for him, and on their devotion he could reckon without misgiving.

They were five brothers — the eldest, Pierre and Remy, were twins, in their thirtieth year, the three others — Michel, Tony, and Jacques, aged twenty-nine, twenty- eight, and twenty-seven — of the numerous family of Thomas Harcher and his wife Catherine, of the farm of Chipogan, in Laprairie county.

A few years before, at the outbreak of the rising of 1831, Jean-Sans-Nom, closely pressed by the police, had found refuge in this farm, which he did not know belonged to M. de Vaudreuil. Thomas Harcher received the fugitive into his family as if he had been one of his sons. If he was not ignorant that lie had given shelter to a patriot, he certainly did not know that this patriot was Jean-Sans-Nom.

While he lived at the farm, Jean — he was known by no other name — had made close friends with Pierre and Remy. Their sentiments were the same as his. They were keen supporters of the French party, with a bitter hatred of everything that "smelt English," as the saying then went in Lower Canada.

When Jean left Chipogan, it was on board the boat in which the five brothers cruised on the river from April to September. Ostensibly they carried on the trade of fishermen, which gave them access to all the houses on the river-side. In this way they baffled pursuit, and prepared a new insurrectional movement. Before his arrival at the Villa Montcalm, he had visited the counties of Ottawa, in the province of Ontario. Now, as he sailed up the river, he could give the last orders to the people of Lower Canada.

The cutter had just left the port of St. Anne. Although the tide had begun to run out, a fresh breeze from the eastward filled her sails, and the Champlain — such was her name — made good progress.

The climate of Canada is not so temperate as that of the United States, and is very warm in summer and very cold in winter, although the country is in the same latitude as France. This is probably because the warm current of the Gulf Stream is deflected from its coast, and does not moderate the excess of temperature.

During this first fortnight of September, the temperature was very high, and the sails of the Champlain were filled with an almost scorching wind.

"We shall have a hot passage to-day," said Pierre, "particularly if the wind drops at noon."

"Yes," said Michel, "And may the sun frizzle up the gnats and the black mosquitoes! They are in thousands on this beach of St. Anne!"

"Brothers, this heat will end, and we shall soon rejoice in the mildness of the Indian summer."

It was Jean who had given his companions the fraternal name of which they were so worthy. And he was right in boasting the beauties of the Indian summer of Canada, which occurs in the months of September and October.

"Are we to fish this morning?" asked Pierre Harcher, "or are we to go up the river?"

"Fish till ten o'clock," said Jean; "and then we can sell our fish at Matane."

71

"Then we must make a board towards Mons," replied Pierre, who was captain of the Champlain. "The water is better there, and we can return to Matane when the tide slackens."

The sheets were shortened in, the boat luffed, and, heeling to the breeze with the stream in her favour, she headed across for the point of Mons, on the north side of the river, which is here between nine and ten leagues wide.

After an hour's sail the Champlain lay to, and with her jib-sheet hauled aft, and speed reduced, her crew began to fish. They were in the middle of this magnificent estuary, bordered by a zone of cultivable land extending to the north, to the foot of the first slopes of the chain of the Laurentides, and to the south to the Notre Dame mountains, whose highest peaks rise 1300 feet above the sea.

Pierre Harcher and his brothers were skilful at their trade. They had plied it in every part of the river. Amid the rapids of Montreal they had taken quantities of shad by means of fascines. About Québec they had fished for salmon or gasperaux, come up at the spawning season into the higher reaches of the river. It was seldom that their "tides" were not extremely profitable.

This morning the gasperaux were abundant. Frequently the nets were almost full enough to break. And about ten o'clock the Champlain, filling her sails, headed off" for Matanc.

It was better to make for the southern bank of the river. On the northern bank the villages are scattered, and the people few. The land is barren, being little but an accumulation of chaotic rocks. With the exception of the valley of the Saguenay, by which the overflow of Lake St. John escapes, and which is alluvial, the yield of the soil is poor, except with regard to the rich forests with which the land is widely covered.

On the south of the river, on the contrary, the land is fertile, the villages numerous, and, as we have said, it is as though a panorama of houses extended from the mouth of the river, all the way to Quebec. If tourist; are attracted by the picturesque scenery of the Saguenay valley, or that of Malbay, the Canadian and American bathers — principally those whom the burning heats of New England drive to the more bracing climate of the great river — chiefly frequent the southern bank.

It was to that side, to the market of Matane, that the Champlain brought her first load of fish. Jean, and two of the Harchers — Michel and Tony — went from door to door with the product of their toil. It might have been remarked that Jean remained in some of these houses much longer than is usually taken in traffic of this kind, and that he entered the houses and exchanged a few words, not only with the servants, but with the masters. And it might also have been remarked that at certain humble dwellings he gave back to the buyers more money than his comrades had received.

The same proceedings went on during the following days in the villages along the river, at Rimouski, at Bic, at Trois Pistoles, at Caconna beach, one of the fashionable bathing resorts on the banks of the St. Lawrence.

At Riviere-du-Loup, a little town reached on the morning of the 17th of September, the Champlain was boarded by the men charged with watching the river. But all was well. For some years Jean had been borne on the cutter's list as if he had been one of Thomas Marcher's sons. Never would the police have supposed that under the guise of a fisherman there was hidden the man they wanted, whose head was worth six thousand dollars to whoever would betray it.

When the police had gone, Pierre Harcher remarked, —

"It might be better for us to get to the other bank."

"So we think," said Michael.

"And why?" asked Jean. "Is it because our boat appeared suspicious to these men? Is it because things have not gone on in the customary way? Is it that they doubt that I am one of your family?"

"As I really think you are!" said Jacques, the youngest of the five, who was of a sprightly disposition. "Our father has so many children that one more cannot embarrass him, and he might mistake you for one!"

"And," said Tony, "he loves you like a son, and we all love you as if you were of the same blood!"

"And are we not?" said Remy, "Are we not all French?"

"Certainly!" said Jean. "But I do not see why you should be afraid of the police."

"You can never be too prudent," said Tony.

"Of course not," said Jean, "and if it is only for the sake of prudence that Pierre is going to cross the river — "

"Which it is," said Pierre, "for the weather will soon change."

"That is another thing," said Jean.

"Look here," said Pierre, "the north-east breeze will soon spring up, and I have an idea it will be rather fresh. I feel it! We must think of our boat, and I do not care to lose it on the rocks of Riviere-du-Loup or Kamouraska!"

"Be it so!" said Jean. "Let us get across to Tadoussac, if possible. We can then go up the Saguenay to Chicoutimi, and then we shall neither lose our time nor our trouble."

"Quick, then," said Michael, "Pierre is right This north-easter is not far off. If it catches the Champlain before we are across, we shall go a hundred times further towards Quebec than towards Tadoussac."

And away went the Champlain to the northward, eating into the wind, which at once began to freshen.

It was eight o'clock in the evening. Pierre Harcher was not mistaken when he caught sight of the long, narrow clouds that announced the coming of the storm. There was barely time to get under the shelter of the northern coast.

Five or six leagues separate Riviere-du-Loup from the mouth of the Saguenay. It was rather rough work on the passage. The wind swooped down on the Champlain when she was but a third of the way across. Sail had to be reduced, and every reef taken in, and yet the mast bent as if it would break. The surface of the river rose in huge waves as if it had been the sea. and the waves dashed against the cutter's bow and covered it with foam. It was rather dangerous for a boat of only a dozen tons. But the crew were steady and skilful. More than once they had braved the storm in the open sea between Cape Breton and Newfoundland. And the seamanship of the crew is as worth taking into account as the seaworthiness of the ship.

But Pierre Harcher would have enough to do to reach the mouth of the Saguenay, and it would take him three more hours. When the tide ebbed it would make the sea worse, although it would keep the cutter on her course. Those who have not been caught in one of these north-east gales in the valley of the St. Lawrence, can have little idea of their violence. They are quite a scourge in the counties below Quebec.

Fortunately the Champlain found shelter under the northern bank, and as night fell, entered the mouth of the Saguenay.

The storm, lasted but a few hours. On the 19th of September, at dawn, Jean could resume his campaign up the Saguenay, which flows past the high cliffs of Capes Trinity and Eternity, which measure some eighteen hundred feet in height. In this picturesque county is some of the finest scenery in Canada, and amongst other gems is the marvellous bay of Haha. The Champlain reached Chicoutimi when Jean put himself in communication with the members of the Reformist Committee, and in the morning, taking advantage of the tide, he resumed his voyage to Quebec.

Meanwhile, Pierre and his brothers did not forget that they were fishermen by trade. Each evening they cast their net and their lines. And in the morning they landed at the villages on each bank. On the northern side, along the county of Charlevoix from Tadoussac to the Bay of St. Paul, they visited Malbay, Sainte Irenee, and Notre- Dame-des-Eboulements, whose significant name is only too well justified by its situation amid a chaos of rocks. Then there were the shores of Beaufort and Beaupre, where Jean did useful work by landing at Chateau-Richer, and then there was Orleans Island just below Quebec.

On the southern bank the Champlain put in successively at Saint Michel, at Point Levi. Certain precautions had to be taken, for the surveillance of this part of the river was very strict. It would have been better, perhaps, not to have stopped at Quebec where the cutter arrived in the evening of the 22nd of September. But Jean had an appointment with the advocate, Sebastian Gramont, one of the most ardent deputies of the Opposition.

When darkness had quite set in, Jean made his way towards the higher quarters of the town, and by the Rue du Petit-Champlain reached Gramont's house.

For some years Jean and Gramont had been in communication with each other.

Gramont, then thirty-six years of age, had taken an active part in all the political manifestations of the later years — in that of 1835 especially — for which he had been imprisoned.

It was then that there began his connection with Jean- Sans-Nom, who had, however, told him nothing of his birth or relations. Gramont knew but one thing, that when the time came his friend would put himself at the head of the insurrection. Not having seen him since the abortive attempt of 1835, we waited for him to-night with lively impatience.

When Jean arrived he was cordially welcomed.

"I have only a few hours to give you," he said.

"Well," said the advocate, "let us employ them in talking of the past and of the present."

"Of the past! No!" said Jean. "Of the present — of the future — of the future above all!"

Ever since he had known him Gramont had felt that in Jean's life there had been some great misfortune, some great grief, and he could not discover the cause. Even as he stood there, he affected so much reserve that he even avoided shaking hands with him. But Gramont had not insisted on knowing his friend's secrets. When it suited him to confide in him, he would be ready to listen.

During the few hours they passed together, they talked about the political situation. On his part, the advocate informed Jean of the state of opinion in Parliament. In return, Jean informed the advocate of the measures already taken with a view to the rising, of the formation of a Central Committee at the Villa Montcalm, and of the results of his journey through Upper and Lower Canada. He had only to traverse the Montreal district to finish his campaign.

Gramont listened with extreme attention, and saw grounds for great hope in the progress made by the cause during the last few weeks. There was not a village where money had not been distributed for the purchase of arms and ammunition.

Jean then learnt the last movements of the authorities at Quebec.

"In the first place, my dear Jean, there was a rumour that you were here a month ago. There were search warrants out for you, and even this house was searched, it having been falsely reported that you were here. I had a visit from the detectives, and among others a certain Rip — "

"Rip!" exclaimed Jean in a voice as though the name burnt his lips.

"Yes-the head of the firm of Rip & Co." replied Gramont. "Remember he is a very dangerous man."

"Dangerous!" muttered Jean.

"And it would be well for you to beware of him," added Gramont.

"To beware of him!" said Jean. "Yes, to beware of him, as if he were a scoundrel."

"Do you know him?"

"I know him," said Jean, who had recovered his equanimity, but he does not know me yet!"

"That is the important point!" added Gramont, somewhat surprised at his guest's behaviour.

Then Jean, turning the conversation to another subject, asked a question as to the proceedings in Parliament during the last few weeks.

"The opposition," said Gramont, "is very strong. Papineau, Cuvillier, Viger, Quesnel, and Bourdage are constant in their attacks on the Government measures. Lord Gosford would prorogue the House, but he fears that it would be the signal for an uprising."

"Would that it may not take place till we are ready!" said Jean. Do not let the Parliamentary leaders imprudently precipitate matters."

"They shall be warned, and they will do nothing to interfere with your plans. At the same time, in view of a possible insurrection, the Governor-General has taken certain measures. Sir John Colborne has concentrated all the troops he can dispose of, so as to move them quickly to the villages on the St. Lawrence, where the outbreak is most probable."

"There — and at twenty other places at the same time — at least I hope so. The people must all rise on the same day, at the same hour, that the bureaucrats may be overwhelmed by numbers. If the movement is only local, there is a chance of its being choked off at the beginning. It was to make it general that I have been journeying east and west, and am going through the centre. I am off this very night"

"Go, then, Jean, but do not forget that the soldiers and volunteers of Sir John Colborne are cantoned round Montreal under Colonels Gore and Withcrall. It is there we shall have the resistance."

"We will arrange everything so as to get all the advantage of the first shot," said Jean. "The committee at the Villa Montcalm is well placed in view of a combined rising, and I know the energy of M. de Vaudreuil, who is the leader of it. In the counties of Vercheres, St. Hyacinthe, and Laprairie, which adjoin that of Montreal, the most ardent Sons of Liberty have communicated to the towns and villages the fire of their patriotism."

"And it has even reached the clergy!" said Gramont.

In public as in private, in sermons and interviews our priests preach against English tyranny. A few days ago, in the very Cathedral of Quebec, a young preacher dared to appeal to the national sentiment, and his words had such an effect that the minister of police would have arrested him. But Lord Gosford opposed the rigorous measure, as he thinks he can remain good friends with the Canadian clergy. All he did was to have the bishop send the preacher away from the town, and now he is continuing his mission through the counties of Montreal. He is a real tribune of the pulpit, his eloquence is most persuasive, and he is held back by no personal consideration, and he will assuredly devote to our cause the sacrifice of his liberty and his life."

"Did you say this priest was a young man?" asked Jean.

"He is hardly thirty."

"To what order does he belong?"

"To the Sulpiciens order."

"And his name?"

"The Abbe Joann."

Did the name evoke any remembrance in Jean's mind? Gramont might well think so, for Jean remained silent for a few seconds. Then he took leave of the advocate, although he had been offered hospitality till the morning.

"I thank you, my dear Gramont," he said. "But I must rejoin my companions before midnight. We must start with the tide."

"Good-bye, then," said the advocate. "Whether your enterprise succeeds or not, you will, none the less, be one of those who have done much for our country!"

The friends separated. And then Jean returned to the Champlain, and, her anchor being weighed, she started at once on her voyage up the river to Montreal.

CHAPTER VII - FROM QUEBEC TO MONTREAL

At midnight the cutter was several miles up the stream. During the clear moonlight night Pierre Harcher could navigate in safety, although he had to tack from one bank to the other, owing to the wind blowing freshly from the westward.

The Champlain did not stop, except for a little just before the dawn. A mist lay on the wide prairies, extending from either shore. Soon the tops of the trees in the background appeared above the mist, which the rising sun began to dissipate, and the course of the river again became visible.

A number of fishermen were already at work, towing their nets and lines behind the little boats that rarely leave the upper course of the St. Lawrence or its affluents to the right and left. The Champlain soon made one of the fleet engaged in its morning labours between the shores of the counties of Portneuf and Lotbiniere. And the brothers Harcher dropped anchor on the northern shore, and set to work with them. They wanted a few baskets of fish to sell in the villages, as soon as the tide allowed them to go up the river, in spite of the head wind.

While they were fishing, several bark canoes came alongside the Champlain, such light canoes as a man can put on his shoulder when he has to take to the portages — those parts of the river which are unnavigable, owing to the rocks that obstruct it, or the falls, or rapids, or eddies which are so frequent in Canadian rivers.

The men in the canoes were mostly of Indian race.

They came to buy the fish, and take it to the towns and villages in the interior, up the numerous streams with which the land abounds. Occasionally they were French Canadians who came alongside the Champlain, and, after a few minutes' conversation, returned to the shore to accomplish the errand on which they were sent.

Had the brothers been in search of gain or pleasure as they fished, their wish would have been amply satisfied. With net and line they did marvels. Pike, perch, maskinongis and touradis, and a quantity of white-fish, which gourmets appreciate for its excellent flesh. The crew of the Champlain would be heartily welcomed in the houses by the river-side. They were favoured by splendid weather, such as is almost peculiar to the happy and incomparable valley of the St. Lawrence. Delightful was the aspect of the neighbouring country from the banks of the river away to the Laurentides. As Fennimore Cooper poetically says, they were all the more beautiful for having assumed their autumn livery — the green and yellow livery of the last five days.

The Champlain first ran in shore on the left bank, in the county of Portneuf. In the town of this name, and in the villages of St. Anne and St. Stanislas, there was some business to transact. At certain places it is possible that the Champlain left more money than she received for her fish; but the Harchcrs made no complaint.

During the next two days Jean sailed in this way from shore to shore. In the county of Lotbiniere, on the right bank, at Lotbiniere and at St. Pierre-les-Bosquets — in the county of Champlain, on the opposite side at Batisean — then on the other side, at Gentilli, at Doucette, the principal reformists received their visits. At Nicolet, in the county of that name, M. Aubineau, a justice of the peace, and one of the most influential inhabitants, communicated with Jean. There he learnt, as he had at Quebec, that the Abbe Joann was travelling through the parishes, exciting the people by his preaching. M. Aubineau then spoke of the ammunition and weapons of which they were in need "You will soon receive," said Jean, "a raft of timber, which ought to have left Montreal last night, and which will bring you guns, and powder and lead. You will then be armed in time. But do not rise till the signal is given. If necessary, you can enter into communication with the committee, at the Villa Montcalm, in the Island of Jesus, and correspond with its president — "

"M. de Vaudreuil?"

"Yes."

"Agreed."

"Did you not tell me that the Abbe Joann had passed through Nicolet?"

"He was here six days ago."

"Do you know where he went, when he left you?"

"Into the county of Vercheres, and, unless I am mistaken, he was going into Laprairie county."

Thereupon Jean took leave of the justice of the peace, and returned on board the Champlain, just as the Harchers returned, after selling their fish. The river was then crossed obliquely, towards the county of St. Maurice.

At the mouth of the river of that name stands one of the most ancient towns in the country, that of Three Rivers, at the opening of a fertile valley. At this time there had just been established here a cannon foundry, managed by a French-Canadian Company, employing only French- Canadian workmen. Here was an anti-loyalist centre, which Jean could not neglect. The Champlain went a few miles up the St. Maurice river, and Jean entered into communication with the committees formed in the parishes.

The foundry, having been recently established, was not as yet in working order. A few months later it might have been able to furnish the reformists with the cannon of which they were so much in need. It was possible, however — if they worked night and day — that they could turn out the first guns in time to use them against the artillery of the royal troops. Jean had a very important interview on the subject with the heads of the committees.

If a few of the pieces could be made in time, there would be no difficulty in finding hands to use them.

After leaving Three Rivers, the Champlain coasted along the county of- Maskinongi, put in at the little town of the same name, and on the night of the 24th of September entered the widening of the St. Lawrence known as Lake St. Peter. This is a lake about five leagues long, bounded upstream by a series of islets, which extend from Berthier, a town of the county of that name, up to Sorel, in the county of Richelieu.

Here the Harchers cast their nets, or rather towed them behind, and slowly drifted upwards with the stream. Thick clouds covered the sky, and the darkness became so thick that it was impossible to see cither bank of the river.

A little after midnight, Pierre, on the look out forward, caught sight of a light farther up stream.

"That is a ship's light, I think," said Remy.

"Look after the nets," said Jacques. "We have thirty fathoms out, and they will be lost if that ship comes across them."

"Well, starboard the helm," said Michel. "There's room enough."

"The wind is failing," said Pierre. "We are drifting."

"We had better haul in the nets," said Jean. "That will be safer."

"Yes, and lose no time," said Remy.

The brothers were preparing to haul in the nets, when Jean observed, —

"Are you certain that it is a ship coming down the river?"

"I am not so sure," said Pierre. "Anyhow, it is coming very slowly, and the light is almost on the water-line."

"It may be a cage," said Jacques.

"If it is a cage," replied Remy, "the more reason for avoiding it. We must keep clear! Haul away!"

The Champlain might have lost her nets, if the brothers had not made haste without even stopping to clear away the fish in the meshes. There was not a moment to lose, for the light was only a couple of cable-lengths away.

A cage in Canada is a raft of timber, composed of from sixty to seventy "cribs "or sections, and amounting to at least a thousand cubic feet. As soon as the liver is clear for navigation, a number of these cages daily descend the river to Montreal or Quebec. They come from the immense forests of the West, which form one of the inexhaustible resources of Canada. Imagine a floating mass, five or six feet out of the water, like an enormous pontoon without a mast. Its trunks have been squared by the woodmen's axes, or cut into bundles and planks by the saw-mills near the waterfalls on the Ottawa. Thousands of these rafts come down the river from the month of April to that of October, avoiding the falls and rapids by means of slides built in narrow canals by the side of the river. Some of the cages are stopped at Montreal, and there loaded for Europe, but most of them go on to Québec.

These rafts are, as may be supposed, a great hindrance to navigation, particularly in the narrow subsidiary branches of the stream. They float down with the tide, and it is almost impossible to steer them. Ships and fishing boats have to avoid them, as they may damage them seriously. And it will be understood how eagerly the Harchers worked to get in their nets, which were in the way of the cage the calm prevented them avoiding.

Jacques was right. It was a cage. A light in front indicated the direction it was following. It was hardly twenty fathoms away when the Champlain had all her nets in. In the silence of the night a voice was heard singing the well-known song, the air of which is almost a national one. It was easy to recognize that the singer was a French-Canadian.

"As I came from the wedding I felt very weary.

And at the clear fountain I lay down to rest."

Doubtless Jean recognized the singer's voice, for he came up to Pierre, who was rowing his hardest to keep the Champlain clear, and said, —

"Board him!"

"Board him?" asked Pierre.

"Yes! It is Louis Lacasse."

"We'll drop back with him!"

"Five minutes at the most," said Jean. "I have only a few words to say to him."

In a moment the helm was put down, and the Champlain ran alongside, and was moored forward.

The man on the raft stopped his song, and shouted, —

"Look out with that cutter!"

"There's no danger, Louis Lacasse," said Pierre Harcher. "It is the Champlain."

Jean had jumped on the raft, and ran up to Lacasse, who as soon as he recognized him by the light of the lantern, said, —

"My respects to you, Monsieur Jean!"

"Thank you, Lacasse."

"I thought I should meet you, but I reckoned you would come when I was moored for the flood tide. But since you are here — "

"Is all aboard?" asked Robert.

"All is aboard, hidden under the planks and between the beams. It is well stowed, I can tell you!" added Lacasse, lighting his pipe.

"Did the custom-house officers board you?"

"Yes, at Vercheres. They stayed prying about for half an hour, but they saw nothing. It is shut up, as if it was in a box."

"How many?" asked Jean.

"Two hundred muskets."

"And swords?"

"Two hundred and fifty."

"Where do they come from?"

"Vermont. Our American friends have been busy, and they have not cost us much. But we had a lot of trouble in getting them to Fort Ontario. Now there are no more difficulties."

"And ammunition?"

"Three casks of powder, and several thousand bullets. If each one kills its man, there will soon be not a redcoat left in Canada."

"You know where these things are to go?" asked Jean.

"All right," said Lacasse. "Never fear! There is no danger of surprise! During the night, at low tide, I can moor my cage, and the canoes can come alongside and take their share. But I don't go lower than Quebec, where I hand over to the Moravian, outward bound to Ham- burg."

"It is understood," said Jean, "that before you reach Quebec you have disposed of the last gun and last cask of powder."

"All right."

"You are sure of the men who are with you?"

"As yourself! And when the guns begin to talk, they will not be behind."

Jean gave him a number of dollars which he put into his large pouch without counting them. Then there was a general hand-shaking with the cutter's crew, and Jean returned on board the Champlain, which paid off towards the left bank. And as the cage continued to float down stream there was heard the sonorous voice of Lacasse, beginning again, —

"And at the clear fountain I lay down to rest."

An hour afterwards the breeze returned with the flowing tide. The Champlain reached the numerous islets which bound the lake of St. Pierre, and coasted the counties of Joliette and Richelieu which lay opposite each other. Then she put in at the river-side villages of Montreal county and the county of Vercheres, where the women had fought so bravely against the Indians in the seventeenth century.

While the cutter stopped for a time, Jean visited the reformist chiefs and acquainted himself with the state of public opinion. Often they spoke to him of Jean-Sans- Nom for whom a reward had been offered. Where was he at the moment? Would he appear when the fight was over? The patriots were reckoning upon him. In spite of the Governor-General's proclamation, he could come without fear into the county, and there for an hour, for twenty-four hours, all houses would be open to him.

Jean was much affected at these proofs of unshrinking devotion. Yes! He was waited for like a Messiah by the French-Canadians! And then he would restrain himself to answer, —

"I do not know where Jean-Sans-Nom is; but the day will come when he will be where he ought to be."

About the middle of the night of the 26th of September, the Champlain had reached the southern branch of the St. Lawrence which separates the island of Montreal from the south bank.

The Champlain was near the end of her voyage. In a few days the brothers would lay her up for the winter when the navigation of the river was impracticable. Then Jean and his friends would go to Laprairie county, to the farm of Chipogan, where the family would all meet for the wedding.

Between the island of Montreal and the right bank, the arm of the St. Lawrence is barred by the rapids which are one of the curiosities of the country. There is also a lake like that of St. Pierre, where the Champlain had met the raft of Louis Lacasse. It is called the Saut de Saint Louis, and it is situated opposite Lachine, a small town built above Montreal, and a popular watering-place. It is like a tumultuous sea into which pour the waters of one of the branches of the Ottawa. Thick forests still clothe the right bank around a village of Christianized Iroquois, the Caughnawaga, whose little church raises its modest steeple above the mass of verdure.

In this part of the St. Lawrence, the ascent is very difficult. The descent may be much easier than is desirable, for a wrong movement of the helm might send the boat across the rapids. But the sailors, accustomed to these dangerous passes — particularly the fishermen — are very skilful in manoeuvring on the tumultuous waters. By keeping close to the southern bank and hauling on to a rope, it is not impossible to reach Laprairie, the chief town of the county of that name, where the Champlain was generally laid up for the winter.

About midday the cutter was a little below Lachine. Whence came this name, which is that of a vast Asiatic empire? Simply from the first navigators of the St. Lawrence. When they reached the neighbourhood of the country of the great lakes, they believed they were on the shore of the Pacific Ocean, and consequently not far from the Celestial Kingdom.

The captain of the Champlain steered for the right bank, and he reached it about five o'clock in the evening close to the boundary between Montreal county and Laprairie county.

Then it was Jean said to him, —

"I must go ashore now."

"Will you not come with us to Laprairie?" asked Pierre.

"No. I must visit Chambly, and by landing at Caughnawaga I shall not have so far to go."

"There is a great deal of risk in that," said Pierre. "And I shall not part with you without anxiety. Why do you leave us, Jean? Stay a couple of days with us, and we can go away together as soon as the Champlain is dismantled."

"I cannot," said Jean; "I must be at Chambly this very night."

," Shall two of us go with you?" asked Pierre.

"No; I must go alone."

"And you will remain at Chambly?"

"Only a few hours. I expect to be off again before daylight."

As Jean did not appear desirous of explaining why he must go, Pierre did not insist, and contented himself with adding, —

"Shall we wait for you at Laprairie?

"That is useless. Do what you have to do, and do not be anxious about me."

"Then we shall meet — "

"At the farm of Chipogan."

"You know we ought to be all there during the first week in October?"

"I know."

"Don't fail, Jean. Your absence would give much pain to my father, my mother, and all of us. We shall have a family gathering at Chipogan, and as you are a brother, you must be there to make the family complete."

"I will be there, Pierre."

Jean shook hands with all the brothers. Then he went into the cabin, and dressed himself as he had been on his visit to the Villa Montcalm. A minute afterwards he had jumped on to the bank, and with an "au revoir" had disappeared under the trees the thick masses of which surrounded the Indian village.

The brothers set to work, and with a great effort hauled their boat up against the stream, taking advantage of the eddies in the shelter of the promontories. At eight o'clock the Champlain was moored in a small creek at the foot of the first houses of Laprairie.

The brothers Harcher had finished their fishing season, and during the six months had sailed 200 leagues down and up the great river.

CHAPTER VIII - AN ANNIVERSARY

IT was five o'clock in the afternoon when Jean left the Champlain. He was about three leagues from the village of Chambly, to which he was going.

What was he to do at Chambly? Had he not already finished his propagandist work through the south-western counties before his arrival at the Villa Montcalm? Yes, certainly. But he had not yet visited this parish. Why? No one could have said; he had told no one, and he could scarcely have told himself. He went to Chambly as if he were being attracted there and repelled at the same time, and he was fully cognizant of the battle that was raging within him.

Twelve years had passed since Jean had left the village where he had been born. He had never returned to it. There was no fear of his being recognized. After so long an absence, would he himself have forgotten the street in which stood the house in which he had passed his childhood?

No! These souvenirs of early life could not be effaced from so vivacious a memory. As he came out of the riverside forest he saw himself again among the prairies which he had formerly crossed to the ferry over the St. Lawrence. It was no longer a stranger wandering in the land, but a child of the country. He showed no hesitation in crossing certain fords, in taking certain cross roads, and cutting off certain corners, to shorten his road. And when he reached Chambly he would have no hesitation in recognizing the little square in which stood the paternal house, the narrow read by which he oftenest entered it, the church to which his mother took him, the school where he had begun his studies before he had gone to finish them at Montreal.

Once again Jean wished to see the places he had kept away from for so long. When he was about to risk his head in a desperate struggle an irresistible desire had brought him back to the spot where his miserable existence had commenced. It was not Jean-Sans-Nom visiting the reformists of the county, but the boy returning, perhaps for the last time, to the village where he had been born.

Jean walked quickly, so as to reach Clambly before night and leave it before morning. Absorbed in his painful remembrances, his eyes saw nothing of what would formerly have attracted his attention, neither the elk passing in the woods, nor the birds of a thousand kinds that flitted among the branches, nor the game which ran along the furrows.

A few labourers were still at work in the fields. He turned off, so as not to have to reply to their cordial greeting, desiring to cross the country unobserved and enter Chambly without being seen.

It was seven o'clock when he saw the church-steeple rising among the trees. In little more than a mile he would be there. The sound of the bell was borne to him on the wind. And instead of exclaiming, "Yes, it is I! I, who have returned to what I once loved so well — to my nest — to my cradle!" he was silent, and asked himself in terror, "What have I come to do here?"

However, the interrupted ringing of the bell told him it could not be the Angelus that was ringing. To what service, then, were the faithful of Chambly being summoned at so late an hour?

"So much the better," said Jean, "they will be at church. I shall not have to pass the open doors; they will not see me; they will not speak to me; and if I do not ask shelter of any one, no one will know that I have been."

And he continued his journey. But for an instant the idea of returning came to him. No. It was an invincible force which drew him forwards.

As he approached Chambly, Jean looked about him with more attention. Notwithstanding the changes that had taken place in the twelve years, he recognized the houses, the enclosures, and the farms on the skirts of the village.

When he reached the main street he glided along by the houses, whose aspect was so French that it might have been the capital of a bailiwick in the seventeenth century. Here lived a friend of the family, with whom Jean had passed his holidays. There lived the cure of the parish, who had given him his first lessons. Were these worthy men alive? Then a higher building rose on the right. It was the school he had gone to each morning.

The road led him up to the church. The paternal house occupied a corner of the square on the left, with its back overlooking a garden, in which the trees grouped with the belt of trees that surrounded the village. The night was dark. The half-open door of the church allowed a glimpse to be seen within, where a crowd was just visible in the light of the lustre hanging from the roof.

Jean, having lost his fear of being recognized, would have mingled with this crowd. He would have entered the church and taken part in the service, and knelt on the benches where he had used to pray. But at first he felt himself drawn towards the other side of the square, and he turned to the left, and reached the corner where his father's house used to stand.

He remembered it. All the details returned to him — the gate which shut off the little front garden, the dovecot on the gable to the right, the four windows on the ground floor, the door in the middle, the window to the left on the first floor where he had so often seen his mother among the flowers that framed it. He was fifteen when he had left Chambly for the last time. At that age things are already deeply graven on the memory. Here it was that the house ought to be which had been built by his ancestors at the beginning of the colony — but house there was none!

In its place there was nothing but ruins. Gloomy ruins, not such as time had made, but such as had been made by violence. There could be no mistake. Burnt stones, blackened walls, charred beams, heaps of ashes, white now, and telling of the time when the house had been the prey of the flames!

A horrible thought crossed Jean's mind. Who had lighted the flame? Was it the work of chance or carelessness? Was it the hand of justice?

Irresistibly he was attracted, and he glided among the ruins. He stumbled against some ashes heaped on the ground. A few owls flew off; doubtless no one came there. Why, then, in this most frequented part of the village, had these ruins been allowed to remain? Why, after the fire, had the ground not been cleared?

During the twelve years he had been away Jean had never heard that the house had been destroyed, that it was now but a pile of stones blackened by the fire.

He stood still, full at heart, and thinking of the sorrowful past and the more sorrowful present.

"Eh! What are you doing there, sir?" asked an old man, stopping on his way to church.

Jean did not hear him, and did not reply.

91

"Hallo!" the old man shouted. "Are you deaf? You must not stop there. If they see you there, you may hear something you won't like."

Jean came out of the ruins on to the road, and said to the man, —

"Were you speaking to me?"

"Yes, to you. You must not go in there."

"And why not?"

"Because the place is accursed."

"Accursed!" murmured Jean, but in so low a tone that the old man did not hear him.

"You are a stranger here, sir?"

"Yes," said Jean.

"And you have not been to Chambly for many years?"

"Yes, many years."

"Then it is not surprising that you do not know. Believe me, it is good advice I am giving you — do not go back into those ruins."

"And why?"

"Because you can only soil yourself with the cinders. It is the house of a traitor!"

"Of a traitor?"

"Yes, of Simon Morgaz."

Which the unhappy man knew only too well!

And so, of the house from which his father had been driven twelve years before, of the dwelling which he had wished to see for the last time, and which he thought was still standing, there remained only a few bare walls. And tradition had made the place so infamous that no one dare approach it, and none of the people of Chambly could pass it without a malediction! Twelve years had gene, and in this village, as throughout Lower Canada, there had been no diminution in the horror inspired by the name of Simon Morgaz!

Jean had lowered his eyes, his hands trembled, he felt as though he would faint. Had it not been for the darkness, the old man would have seen the blush of shame overspread his face.

"You are a French-Canadian?"

"Yes," answered Jean.

"Then you cannot be ignorant of the crime that Simon Margaz committed?"

"Who docs not know it?"

"No one, in truth. You come from the eastern counties, doubtless?"

"Yes — from the east — from New Brunswick."

"That is a long way off. Perhaps you did not know that the house had been destroyed?"

"No! An accident, probably?"

"Not at all, sir; not at all. It would have been better, perhaps, if it had been destroyed by the fire of Heaven 1

And that will happen some day, for God is just! But we have anticipated His justice! The day after Simon Morgaz had been hunted from Chambly, we burnt down his house. And that his memory might never perish we left the ruins in the state you see. And it is forbidden to go near them; and no one would soil himself with the dust of this house."

Jean stood motionless, and listened. The animation with which the old man spoke showed that the feeling against all belonging to Simon Morgaz was as violent as ever. Where Jean had come for souvenirs of his family there were only souvenirs of shame.

But as the old man spoke, he drew further and further away from the ruins towards the church. The bell had just ceased its last call. The service was about to begin. The chanting could already be heard, interrupted by long pauses, and the old man said, —

"I must now leave you, sir, unless it is your intention to accompany me into the church. You will hear a sermon that will have much influence hereabouts — "

"I cannot," said Jean. "I must be at Laprairie before daylight."

93

"Then you have no time to lose, sir. The roads are safe enough. For some time the police have been out day and night, in pursuit of Jean-Sans-Nom, whom, thanks be to Heaven, they have not caught. We think a good deal of that young hero, sir, and if I can believe what rumour says, he will here find all the gallant fellows ready to follow him."

"As in all the county," said Jean.

"Much more, sir. Have we not to atone for the shame of having been the neighbours of Simon Morgaz?"

The old man was fond of talking, that was evident. But at last he was really going, had turned to go, when Jean asked him, —

"My friend, perhaps you knew the family of this Simon Morgaz?"

"I did, and well. I am seventy now, and I was fifty-eight at the time of this abominable affair. What has become of him? I don't know! Perhaps he is dead. Perhaps he has gone to a foreign land, under another name, so that they cannot throw his own in his face! But his wife, his children! Ah! how I pity the poor things! Madame Bridget I used to see so often, always good and kind, though she was not very rich! All the village loved her! What she has had to suffer, poor woman — what she must have suffered!"

How can we describe what was passing in Jean's mind. Before the ruins of the house, where the last act of the treason had been accomplished, where the companions of Simon Morgaz had been betrayed, to hear the name of his mother, to be reminded of the misery of her life, it was almost more than human nature could bear. Jean must have been a man of extraordinary strength of will to restrain the cry of anguish which rose to his lips.

And the old man continued, —

"And I knew the two sons, sir! They took after her! Ah! the poor boys! Where are they at this moment? Every one here liked them for their frankness and good- heartedness. The elder was more serious and studious, and the younger more playful and determined, taking up the defence of the weak against the strong. His name was Jean. His brother's was Joann, just the same as that of the young preacher who is to address us tonight."

"The Abbe Joann?" exclaimed Jean.

"Do you know him?"

94

"No. But I have heard of his sermons."

"Well, sir, if you do not know him, you ought to make his acquaintance. He has come through the western counties, and every one has been rushing to hear him. You will see what enthusiasm he will arouse. If you can delay your departure an hour — "

"I am with you," said Jean.

With the old man he entered the church, where they found some trouble in finding scats.

The first prayers had been said, and the preacher had just entered the pulpit. — _

The Abbe Joann was thirty years of age. In his impassioned face, his penetrating look, his full, persuasive, voice, he resembled his brother, being beardless, like him. In both could be traced the characteristic features of their mother. To see him, or to listen to him, it was easy to understand the influence he had over the crowd attracted by his reputation. As the mouthpiece of the Roman Catholic faith and the national faith, he was an apostle in the true sense of the word, a child of the brave race of the missionaries capable of yielding their lives for their belief.

The Abbe Joann began his sermon. All that he said for his God could, it was evident, be said for his country. His allusions to the state of affairs in Lower Canada were designed to incite his hearers, with whom patriotism only waited an opportunity for declaring itself openly. His gestures, his words, so worked on his hearers, that a murmur ran through the church when he appealed to Heaven for help against the spoilers. His thrilling voice sounded like A trumpet as his arm seemed to lift on high the flag of independence.

Jean, in the shadow, sat and listened. It seemed as though he himself were speaking through his brother's lips. The ideas were the same, the aspirations were the same. Both were working for their country, each in his own way, one with words, the other with deeds, and both ready to sacrifice their lives for the cause.

In these days the Catholic clergy possessed a real influence in Lower Canada, from both a social and intellectual point of view. The priests were looked upon as sacred persons. There was a struggle in progress between the old Catholic beliefs, implanted by the French element in the colony, and the

Protestant beliefs which the English sought to introduce among all classes. The Catholics rallied round their cures, and the political movement that sought to wrest the Canadian provinces from English hands received no slight encouragement from this alliance between the clergy and their flock.

The Abbé Joann belonged to the order of Sulpicians. And this order, as the reader may not be aware, had possessed large tracts of land since the early conquest, and drew from them important revenues. Thus it followed that the Sulpicians were one of the most honoured and powerful corporations in Canada, and their priests, as the richest landowners, were the most influential of the inhabitants.

The sermon, or rather the patriotic harangue of the Abbé Joann, lasted three quarters of an hour. It aroused such enthusiasm among the congregation, that had it not been for the sanctity of the place, it would have been greeted with repeated applause. The heart-strings of the people had been stirred by the patriotic appeal. It may be thought strange that the authorities allowed a reformist propaganda to be conducted under the cloak of religion. But it would have been difficult to seize on any sentence clearly appealing for insurrection, and the pulpit enjoyed a liberty which the Government could not lightly interfere with.

The sermon over, Jean remained in a corner of the church while the crowd passed out Would he then recognize the Abbé, clasp him by the hand, exchange a few words with him, before rejoining his companions at the farm of Chipogan? Probably the two brothers had not seen each other for several months, when they had parted each to take up his own side in the work of revolution.

Jean was waiting behind the farthest pillars of the nave, when a violent tumult was heard without. It seemed as though the people were manifesting their angry feelings with extraordinary violence. At the same time there were flashes of light, which even penetrated the church.

The congregation went out, and Jean, carried with them in spite of himself, reached the middle of the square.

What was the matter?

Before the ruins of the traitor's house a great fire had just been lighted. A few men, who were soon joined by children and some women, were feeding the fire with armfuls of dry wood.

Cries of horror and shouts of hatred rent the air.

"To the fire with the traitor! To the fire with Simon Morgaz!"

And then a figure of a man, clothed in rags, was dragged towards the flames.

Jean understood. The population of Chambly were proceeding to burn Simon in effigy, just as in London they used to burn the effigy of Guy Fawkes.

It was the 27th of September, the anniversary of the day on which Walter Hodge and his companions, Clerc and Farran, had died on the scaffold.

Seized with horror, Jean would have fled. He could not move from the ground, where his feet seemed to be fastened. He looked at his father, overwhelmed with blows and insults, dragged in the mud, a prey to a delirium of hate. And it seemed that all this opprobrium recoiled on him, Jean Morgaz.

At this moment the Abbé Joann appeared. The crowd divided to let him pass.

He also understood the meaning of the popular manifestation. And at the same instant he recognized his brother, whose livid face was lighted by the flames, as a hundred voices shouted the odious date and the infamous name.

The Abbé could not restrain himself. He stretched out his arm, and rushed towards the fire as they were going to hurl the effigy into it.

"In the name of the God of mercy," said he, "have pity for this unhappy man's memory! Has not God a pardon for all crimes?"

"Not for the crime of treason against your country, of treason against those who have fought for her!" replied one of the men. And in a moment the fire had devoured the effigy of Simon Morgaz, as it did at each anniversary.

The shouts redoubled, and ceased not till the fire was extinct.

In the gloom no one noticed that Jean and Joann stood hand in hand together, and bowed their heads. And then, without uttering a word, they left the horrible scene, and fled from the village to which they were never to return.

CHAPTER IX - THE MAISON-CLOSE

Six leagues from Saint Denis lies the town of Saint Charles, on the north bank of the Richelieu in the county of Saint Hyacinthe which adjoins that of Montreal. It is in descending the Richelieu, one of the largest affluents of the St. Lawrence, that we reach the little town of Sorel, where the Champlain had put in during her last fishing cruise.

At this time an isolated house stood a few hundred yards this side of the sudden bend made by the main street of Saint Charles.

It was a humble and cheerless-looking dwelling, consisting of only one floor, with a door and two windows facing the small front yard where weeds abounded. As a rule the door was shut; the windows were never open, not even behind open-panelled shutters which were closed over them. If daylight reached the interior, it was only through the two other windows which opened on the garden at the back.

This garden was but a small square patch, surrounded by high walls, festooned with much long pellitory, and having a bordered well in one of the corners. In the small space were a few vegetables, a few fruit trees, pears, nuts and apples, left to the care of nature. A small yard taken from the garden close to the house, contained five or six fowls to furnish the quantity of eggs needed by the daily consumption.

Inside, the house had but three rooms, with only such furniture as was strictly necessary. One of the rooms to the left as you entered, served as a kitchen; the others to the right were bedrooms. The narrow passage which separated them formed the communication between the front door and the garden.

The house was humble and miserable, but it was evident that it was designedly so, and that it was of their own choice that those who lived there, lived in misery and humility. If a mendicant knocked at the door of Maison-Close — as it was called in the town — never was he allowed to depart without a small gift. Maison-Close might well have been called Maison-Charitable, for charity was there to be had at all hours.

Who lived there? A woman, alone, dressed in black, and never without a long widow's veil. She rarely left the house — once or twice a week, only

99

when some in- indispensable errand obliged her to go, or on Sundays to attend the service. But when she went on her errand, she waited till night, or rather till evening had come, and glided through the dark streets, quickly entered the shop, spoke in a low voice but few words, paid what was asked without attempting to bargain, and returned with her head bowed, her eyes on the ground, like a poor creature who was ashamed of being seen. When she went to church it was at dawn to the first service, and she kept herself apart, in an obscure corner, kneeling as if absorbed in herself. Beneath her veil her immobility was terrible; she would have seemed to be dead if it had not been for the sighs which escaped her. Once or twice some good people would have assisted her, would have offered their services, would have interested themselves in her, would have spoken words of sympathy; but she wrapped herself more closely in her widow's veil, and recoiled from them as if she were an object of horror.

The inhabitants of Saint Charles knew nothing of this stranger — or rather this recluse. Twelve years before she had arrived in the town to take possession of this house, which had been bought on her account at a very low price, for the people to whom it belonged had been trying to sell it for some time, and had found no applicant.

One day the inhabitants learnt that the new owner had arrived in the night, though none had seen her enter. Who had helped her to remove her scanty furniture, they knew not. Never did anybody enter her house. As she lived then so had she lived ever since her appearance at Saint Charles, in a sort of coenobitic isolation. The walls of Maison-Close were those of a cloister, and no one had been inside them.

But did not the people of the town endeavour to pry into this woman's life, to learn her secret? At first they were rather astonished, and there was some gossip about the owner of Maison-Close. It was supposed this, and it was supposed that. Then they began not to trouble about her. Within her means she seemed charitable to the poor, and that went for much in the esteem of all.

Tall, bent more by grief than age, the stranger seemed to be about fifty. Under the veil which fell almost to her waist was hidden a face which had once been beautiful, a high forehead, and large black eyes. Her hair was quite white, and her look as though it were impregnated with the ineffaceable tears which had filled her eyes for so long. The character of the face, formerly so gentle and smiling, was now one of gloomy energy and implacable will.

But had public curiosity kept careful watch on Maison- Close it would have discovered that it was not absolutely closed to visitors. Three or four times a year, invariably at night, the door was opened to one stranger, sometimes to two, who neglected no precaution in arriving and leaving unseen. Did they remain a few days in the house, or only a few hours? No one could say. Whenever they left, it was before daylight. There could be no doubt the woman was in communication with some one outside.

It was the 30th of September, 1837, and eleven o'clock at night. The high road after crossing the county of South Hyacinthe from west to east, passes Saint Charles and runs on.

It was then" deserted. Profound obscurity enwrapped the sleeping town. There was no one to see the two men who came along the road, glided up to the wall of Maison-Close, opened the gate, which was only fastened with a latch, and knocked at the door in a way that was evidently a preconcerted signal.

The door was opened, and shut almost instantly. The two visitors entered the first room to the right, lighted by a night-lamp giving too feeble a light to be seen outside.

The woman seemed in no way surprised at the arrival of these two men. They clasped her in their arms and kissed her forehead with quite filial affection.

They were Jean and Joann. The woman was their mother, Bridget Morgaz.

Twelve years before, after the expulsion of Simon Morgaz, driven away by the people of Chambly, no one had doubted but that the unhappy family had left Canada to expatriate themselves in some part of North or South America or in some distant corner of Europe. The money obtained by the traitor would enable him to live comfortably wherever he might go; and, taking another name, he would escape the contempt which would have pursued him round the world.

As we know, things did not happen in this way. One night Simon Morgaz shot himself, and no one knew that his body lay in some undiscoverable spot on the northern bank of Lake Ontario.

Bridget Morgaz, Jean and Joann saw all the horror of their position. Mother and sons might be innocent of the crime of her husband and their father, but prejudices were such that they would have neither pity nor pardon. In Canada their name would be an object of universal reprobation. They resolved to renounce the name without thinking of taking another. What did they want with a name, poor creatures! when the world had only disgrace for them?

The mother and her sons did not leave the country.

Before leaving Canada, they had a task to fulfil, and this task, even if they gave their lives for it, they all three resolved to accomplish.

It was to repair the wrong Simon Morgaz had done his country. Had it not been for the treason suggested by that hateful tempter, Rip, the plot of 1825 had a good chance of success. Had the Governor-General and the leaders of the British army been carried off, the troops could not have been able to resist the French- Canadians, who would have risen to a man. But an act of infamy had betrayed the secret of the conspiracy, and Canada had remained under the English yoke.

Jean and Joann would resume the work interrupted by their father's treachery. Bridget, who boldly faced the terrible position, showed them that it ought to be the object of their existence. The brothers, who were then seventeen and eighteen, understood their duty, and devoted themselves entirely to the work of reparation.

Bridget Morgaz resolved to live only on her own private income, and would keep none of the money found in the suicide's pocket-book. All of it ought to be used for the Reformist cause. It was secretly deposited in the hands of Mr. Nick, at Montreal, under the conditions we know. A part was kept by Jean to be distributed by him to the Reformists. It was thus that in 1831 and 1835 the committees had received the money needful for the purchase of arms and ammunition. In 1837 the balance, which was still considerable, had been sent to the committee at the Villa Montcalm and confided to M. de Vaudreuil.

Bridget had retired to the house at Saint Charles, and there her sons came secretly to see her. For the last few years each had followed a different road to arrive at the same end.

Joann, the eldest, had, under the influence of religious ideas, developed by the bitterness of his position, resolved to be a priest — but a priest militant. He had entered the congregation of the Sulpicians, with the intention of upholding the imprescriptible rights of his country. His natural eloquence, fortified by the most ardent patriotism, attracted the people to him. And in these later days his renown had increased, and he was then at the height of his power.

Jean had taken part in the revolutionary movement not so much by his words as by his deeds. Although rebellion had failed in 1831 and 1835, his reputation had not diminished. Among the masses he was looked upon as the mysterious chief of the Sons of Liberty. We know to what a high place he had risen in the Opposition councils. It seemed as though the cause of independence was in the hands of one man, and that Jean-Sans-Nom, as he called himself, was the only man from whom the patriots were waiting for the signal of a new insurrection.

The hour was at hand. Before making the attempt, Jean and Joann had met by chance at Chambly, and come to Maison-Close to see their mother, perhaps for the last time.

And now they were here with her, seated by her side. They held her hands; they spoke to her in a low voice. Jean and Joann told her how things stood. The struggle would be terrible, like every supreme struggle.

Bridget, imbued with the sentiments with which their hearts were full, gave herself over to the hope that at last their father's crime would be atoned for by her sons.

"My Jean, my Joann," she said, "I want to share your hopes, to believe in your success."

Yes, mother," said Jean, "you must believe in it. In a few days the movement will have begun — "

"And may God give us the triumph a sacred cause deserves!" added Joann.

"May God help us!" said Bridget. "And perhaps I shall at last have the right to pray for — "

Up to then never had a prayer escaped the lips of this unhappy woman for the soul of him who had been her husband.

"Mother," said Joann, "mother — "

"And you, my son," said Bridget, "have you prayed for your father, you, a priest of the God who pardons?"

Joann bowed his head, and did not reply.

Bridget resumed, —

"My sons, up to now you have both done your duty; but do not forget that you have only done your duty. And if our country owes to you the day of its independence, the name you formerly bore, the name of Morgaz — "

"Exists no longer!" said Jean. There is no rehabilitation possible for it. You can no more restore it to honour than you can restore to life the men whom our father's treason sent to the scaffold. What Joann and I are doing is not that the infamy attached to our name may disappear. That is impossible! It is not a bargain of that sort we would conclude. Our efforts are to repair the wrong done to our country, not the wrong done to ourselves. Is that not so, Joann?"

"Yes," said the young priest. "If God can pardon, I know man cannot. Our name will always be a hateful one."

"But cannot it be forgotten?" asked Bridget, kissing her sons on their foreheads, as if she would efface the indelible stigma."

"Forgotten!" exclaimed Jean. "Go to Chambly, and you'll see if it is forgotten."

"Jean," said Joann. "Be silent!"

"No, Joann. Our mother ought to know. She has strength enough to hear all, and I would not leave her the hope that rehabilitation is possible."

And Jean, in a low voice and in broken speech, told her what had happened at Chambly.

Bridget listened without even a tear rising to her eyes. She could not even weep.

But was it, then, true that hope there was none? Was it possible that the remembrance of the treason was unforgettable, and that the responsibility of the crime would descend to the innocent? Was it written in the human conscience that the stain on the family name could never be effaced?

For some minutes not a word was exchanged between the mother and her sons. They did not even look at one another. Their hands parted; they suffered terribly. Everywhere, as at Chambly, they were pariahs, outlaws, repulsed by society, under the ban of humanity.

About three o'clock Jean and Joann began to think of leaving their mother. They must go without the risk of being seen. They intended to separate as they left the town. They must not be seen together on the road by which they crossed the country. No one must know that that night the door of Maison-Close had opened to the only visitors who ever crossed it.

The brothers rose. At the moment of a separation which might be eternal they felt how strong was the tie which bound them together. Fortunately, Bridget was unaware that a reward had been offered for Jean's apprehension. Although Joann was not ignorant of this, the terrible news had not yet reached his mother's solitude. Jean said nothing of it to his mother. What was the good of adding to her sorrows? And had not Bridget cause enough to fear that she would never see her son again?

The moment of separation had come.

"Where are you going, Joann?" asked Bridget.

"Into the southern parishes," said the young priest. "There I will wait to rejoin my brother when he is at the head of the patriots."

"And you, Jean?"

"I am going to the farm of Chipogan, in the county of Laprairie. There I will rejoin my companions, and concert the final measures — amid those family joys which are denied to us, mother. Those gallant fellows have received me like a son. They will give their lives for mine. But if they knew who I was, if they knew the name I bear! Ah! wretches that we are, whose contact is defilement! But they shall not know it, neither they nor any one else."

Jean had fallen back into the chair, with his head in his hands, overwhelmed beneath the weight which every day lay more heavily on him.

"Arise!" said Joan. "That is the expiation! Be strong enough to suffer! Arise, and let us go!"

"Where shall I see you again?" asked Bridget. "Not here any more," said Jean. "If we win, we win all three leave the country. We will go far away where no one will recognize us. If we give our country her independence, it must never be known that she owes it to the sons of Simon Morgaz."

"And if all is lost?" asked Bridget. "Then, mother, you will not see us again, in this country or in any other. We shall be dead!"

The brothers threw themselves for the last time into Bridget's arms. The door opened and shut again.

Jean and Joann walked for about a hundred yards together, and then they separated after a last look at Maison-Close, where the mother was praying for her sons.

CHAPTER X - THE FARM OF CHIPOGAN

The farm of Chipogan was about seven leagues from THE town of Laprairie, in the county of that name. It occupied a gentle rise in the ground on the right bank of a small tributary of the St. Lawrence. By repute it was a fine property, extending over some four hundred acres, belonging to M. de Vaudreuil, and rented by Thomas Harcher.

In front of the house, and along the stream, lay a vast chessboard of prairie, in quite a triumph of geometrical design, squares upon squares all duly fenced, and in flourishing cultivation. The soil was a rich black mould, three or four feet thick, resting on a bed of clay, as is usually the case in the district all the way up to the slopes of the Laurentides.

In the square fields, which were in the highest state of cultivation, grew different kinds of such cereals as are common in Central Europe. Behind the house, and extending to the hilly woodland which closed the view, lay a wide stretch of rich pasture, which served as the grazing-ground of the usual domestic animals and several horses of the vigorous Canadian breed so esteemed by the Americans.

The forest once covered all the country bordering on the St. Lawrence from its estuary to the great lakes. But what vast clearings have been made in them by the hand of man! What superb trees, rising a hundred and fifty feet in the air, are still falling under the thousands of axes which trouble the silence of the mighty woods where the birds swarm in myriads! The lumbermen find profitable but regrettable work in felling the oaks, maples, ashes, chestnuts, aspens, birches, elms, walnuts, hornbeams, pines and firs, which, sawn and trimmed, go to form the strings of rafts that descend the river. If, at the end of the eighteenth century, Cooper's hero — Natty Bumppo, Hawk- eye, the Deerslayer, or the Leatherstocking — could regret the massacre of the trees, what would he have said to the pitiless destroyers who exhaust the fecundity of the soil by their reckless waste?

But this reproach could not apply to the lessee of Chipogan. Thomas Harcher knew what he was about, and his men served him well. His farm worthily bore the reputation of being a model of scientific cultivation at a time when Canadian agriculture was two centuries behind the age.

The farm of Chipogan then was one of the best in the district of Montreal. The rotation of crops saved the land from impoverishment. The fruit trees in the large kitchen garden were of the different kinds that flourish in Europe, and they were cut and pruned, and trained with care. All of them fruited well except, perhaps, the apricot and the peach, which succeed better in the south of Ontario than in the province of Quebec. But the others did honour to the grower, particularly the apples which were of the "famous "sort with red translucent flesh. With regard to the vegetables, the red cabbages, pumpkins, melons, sweet potatoes, bluets — the name given to the blackish bilberries eaten at dessert — there were gathered enough, twice a week, to supply the market at Laprairie. In short, with the hundreds of bushels of cereals, the crop of fruit and vegetables, and the thinning of the few acres of forest, the farm was a profitable investment for M. de Vaudreuil, and there was no likelihood that in Thomas Harcher's hands it would become exhausted, and sink into a mere waste of weeds and briars.

The Canadian climate is well suited for agriculture. In place of rain it has the snow which falls from the end of November to the end of March, and protects the green carpet of the fields. The keen dry cold is preferable to continual rain storms. In no part of the temperate zone is vegetation so rapid; the corn sown in March is ripe in August, and the hay is made in June and July.

The farm buildings were grouped within a fence of palisades, twelve feet high. A gate with stone pillars gave the sole means of access — an arrangement due to the time when precautions had to be taken against Indian attacks. At the time of my story the Indians were living on good terms with the colonists. And two leagues to the eastward, at the village of Walhatta, there was prospering the Huron tribe of Mahogannis, who often visited Thomas Harcher to exchange the spoils of the chase for the products of the farm.

The principal building consisted of a two-storey house, quite square, containing the number of rooms required by Harcher's family. A large room occupied the greater part of the ground floor between the kitchen and the larder on one side, and the apartment specially reserved for the farmer, his wife and younger children on the other.

In the yard in front of the house, and behind abutting on the kitchen garden, stood the outhouses extending up to the palisades. There were the stables, cattle-sheds and stores; the houses and runs of the American rabbits whose skins woven in strips yield an extremely warm fabric, and the poultry yard with the prairie hens, who multiply more abundantly in the domesticated than in the wild state.

The large room on the ground floor was simply but comfortably furnished with articles of American manufacture. It was there that the family had their meals and passed their evenings, the gathering place for the Harchers of all ages, who liked to be together when the day's work was over. We need not be astonished at finding that a library of books held the first place, and that the second was occupied by a piano, to the music of which every Sunday the boys and girls danced French waltzes and quadrilles with much enthusiasm.

The work of the farm required a large staff. But Thomas Harcher found enough hands in those of his own family, and not a single hired servant was employed.

The farmer was then in his fiftieth year. A French- Canadian by birth, he was a descendant of those hardy fishermen who had settled in Nova Scotia the century before. He was the perfect type of the Canadian settlers, who are not called peasants but "habitants" in North America. Tall, broad-shouldered, powerful in body and limbs, a strong head, greyish hair, keen-sighted, with we'll set teeth and a large mouth, which looked as though it could deal with an ample supply of food, and a good- tempered, frank physiognomy, he had made many firm friends in the neighbouring parishes. And he was an implacable enemy of the English.

He would have sought in vain throughout the valley of the St. Lawrence for a better companion than his wife, Catherine. She was then about forty-five, as strong as her husband, and as young as he was in body and mind, a little rough, perhaps, in features and bearing, but good-natured and brave, and in fact quite the "mother "as he was the "father," in every acceptation of the word. They were an excellent couple, and so healthy that they promised to live to a hundred, for the Canadian climate is very favourable to longevity.

One reproach, perhaps, might be levelled at Catherine Harcher, a reproach, however, that she shared with all the women of the district, who are excellent housekeepers on condition that their husbands clean the house, make the beds, lay the table, pluck the fowls, milk the rows, churn the butter, peel the potatoes, light the fire, wash the crockery, dress the children, scrub the furniture, and do the washing. However, Catherine did not push to the extreme that spirit of domination which makes the husband the slave of the wife in most of the French-Canadian houses. To be just, it should be said that she did her share of the daily work. Nevertheless Thomas Harcher willingly submitted to her wishes and whims, and a fine family she had given him, ranging from Pierre, the first-born, down to the last baby, aged only a few weeks, who was soon to be christened. In Canada the fruitfulness of marriage is really extraordinary. Families of twelve and fifteen are quite common. Those of twenty are not rare, and even those of twenty-five are occasionally heard of. It is not so much the family as the tribe which is developed under the influence of the patriarchal customs.

If Ishmael Bush, Fennimore Cooper's old pioneer in The Prairie, could point with pride to his seven sons, without counting his daughters, the issue of his marriage with the robust Esther, with what a feeling of superiority he would have been overwhelmed by Thomas Marcher, who was the father of twenty-six children, all very much alive at the farm of Chipogin!

fifteen sons and eleven daughters, of all ages within a few weeks of thirty. Of the fifteen sons four were married; and of the eleven girls two were married, and with the seventeen grandchildren of their marriages and their mothers and fathers, the Harcher family numbered just fifty-two in the direct line!

The five eldest we know. They formed the crew of the Cham plain, the devoted companions of Jean. We need not give the names of the other children, or say anything about their peculiarities of character. Sons, daughters, grandsons and granddaughters never left the farm. They worked at it under the direction of their chief. Some were in the fields, where work never failed them. Some were in the woods, employed as lumbermen, and they had plenty to do. Two or three went hunting in the forests near Chipogan, and furnished the game for the large family table. In these woods there still abounded elk, cariboo — a kind of large reindeer — bison, deer, roebuck, without mentioning the diversity of smaller game, furred and feathered, divers, wild geese, ducks, woodcock, snipe, partridges, quail and plover.

Pierre Harcher and his brothers, Remy, Michael, Tony and Jacques, when the cold obliged them to abandon the waters of the St. Lawrence, came to winter at the farm, and took to hunting for furs. They were among the most intrepid and indefatigable of backwoodsmen, and sent their more or less valuable furs to the markets at Montreal and Quebec. At that time, black bears, lynxes, wild cats, martens, badgers, minks, foxes, beavers, ermine", otters, and musk rats had not gone off towards the north, and there was a good trade in furs, for it was not necessary to travel in search of them to the distant shores of Hudson's Bay.

To lodge all this family of children and grandchildren quite a barracks was required, and the huge square building contained in addition a few spare rooms for the guests that Thomas Harcher occasionally received, county friends, farmers of the vicinity, and voyageurs who worked the rafts down the tributaries to the main river. And there were rooms reserved for M. de Vaudreuil and his daughter when he came to visit the farmer's family.

It was on the 5th of October that M. de Vaudreuil and his daughter arrived. It was not only a business relationship which united M. de Vaudreuil and Thomas Harcher, it was a reciprocal affection of friendship on one side and devotion on the other, which had not failed for many years. And much were they bound together by their politics, for the farmer and his master were devoted body and soul to the reformist cause.

The family was now complete. Three days before Pierre and his brothers had left the cutter dismantled at the quay of Laprairie, and taken up their winter quarters at the farm. There was absent only the adopted son, who was not the least loved of the dwellers at Chipogan.

But Jean was expected during the day. If Jean did not arrive, he must have fallen into the hands of the emissaries of Rip, and the news of his arrest would soon have spread throughout the country.

The time was not far distant when the lord of the manor was the godfather of all the children of his copyholders, which might be counted by hundreds. M. de Vaudreuil had up to the present only stood for two of the farmer's family. This time it was Clary who was to be godmother to the twenty-sixth child, and Jean was to be godfather. And the girl was pleased at this bond which united them for a few short moments.

It was not only for a christening, however, that the farm of Chipogan was to make holiday.

When Thomas Harcher received his five sons, "My boys," he said, "you are welcome. You have come at a good time."

"As we always do, father," said Jacques.

"No better than always. To-day we are united for the christening of the last baby. To-morrow there is the first communion of Clement and Cecile, and the day after there is the wedding of your sister Rose with Bernard Miquelon."

"Things are flourishing in our family!" said Tony.

"Yes, not bad, my boys," said the farmer, "and it is not unlikely that next year I shall call you together on an exactly similar occasion."

And Thomas Harcher laughed a sonorous laugh, while Catherine embraced the five manly boys.

The christening was to take place at three o'clock in the afternoon. As soon as Jean came they would go in procession to the parish church, rather more than half a mile away.

Thomas, his wife, his sons, his daughters, his sons-in-law, and his daughters-in-law, and his grandchildren, had all put on their best clothes for the occasion, and seemingly would not put them off again for the next three days. The daughters had white bodices and glaringly coloured skirts, with their hair floating over their shoulders. The sons had put off their working waistcoats and Norman caps, and wore their Sunday costume of black hooded cloak, parti-coloured belt, and shoes of plaited cowskin.

The evening before M. and Mdlle. de Vaudreuil had taken the boat to cross the St. Lawrence opposite Laprairie, and had been met by Thomas Harcher, who had brought them on in the buggy.

On the way M. de Vaudreuil had warned the farmer that he must be on his guard. The police were sure to know he had left the Villa Montcalm, and it was possible that he was the object of special surveillance.

"We will keep our eyes open, master," said Harcher, in whose use of the word there was nothing servile.

"Up to the present you have seen nothing suspicious in the neighbourhood?"

"Not even a Canouache!" such being the term of contempt by which he spoke of certain Indians in the west.

"And your adopted son," said Clary, "has he arrived at the farm?"

"Net yet; and that makes me anxious."

"Since he left his companions at Laprairie you have had no news?"

"None."

And since the visitors had been installed in the two best rooms of the farm, Jean had not come. However, everything had been prepared for the ceremony of baptism, and if the godfather did not arrive during the afternoon they would not know what to do.

Pierre and two or three of the others had gone a good league on the road to meet him. But Jean had not been there, and twelve o'clock was just about to strike.

Thomas and Catherine were talking together on the subject.

"What shall we do, if he docs not come before three o'clock?" asked the farmer.

"We will wait!" said Catherine.

"What will we wait for?"

"Well, not for the arrival of our twenty-seventh!" said the lady.

. "And how many more?"

"You are merry, Monsieur Harcher."

"I am not merry! But if Jean is too late, we may have to do without him."

"Do without him!" exclaimed Catherine. "Not at all. I told him he should be godfather to one of our children, and we will wait till he comes."

"But if he does not come?" asked Thomas, who did not understand the christening being put off indefinitely. "If something has happened to make it impossible for him to come — "

"No evil prophesying, Thomas," said Catherine. "If we do not christen to-day, we can christen to-morrow, I suppose?"

"Well, to morrow is the first communion of Clement and Cecile, our sixteenth and seventeenth!"

"Well, the day after?"

"That is the wedding of Rose with Bernard Miquelon!"

"That is enough, Thomas! We can do them all at once if necessary. But when a baby has the chance of having a godfather like Jean, and a godmother like Mademoiselle Clary, we need not be in a hurry to get others in their place!"

"And the curé has been told!" said Thomas to his intractable better half.

"That is my business," said Catherine. "Our curé is an excellent man, and he shall not lose his fee; and he would not like to disoblige clients like us!"

And in truth there were few of his parishioners who gave him so much to do as Thomas and Catherine.

As time went by the anxiety grew greater. If the Harchers did not know that their adopted son was Jean-Sans-Nom, the Vaudreuils did, and were in great fear about him.

And they asked Pierre Harcher under what circumstances Jean had left the Champlain.

"It was at the village of Caughnawaga that we landed him," said Pierre.

"On what day?"

"On the 26th of September, about five in the afternoon."

"Then he has been away for nine days?" said M. de Vaudreuil.

"Yes, nine days!"

"And he did not say what he was going to do?"

"His intention," said Pierre, "was to visit the county of Chambly, where we had not been during the whole of our fishing cruise."

"Yes, that is a reason," said M. de Vaudreuil. "But I am sorry he ventured alone in a place where the police are sure to be on the watch."

"I offered to let Jacques and Tony go with him," said Pierre; "but he refused."

"And what is your idea about it all?" asked Clary.

"My idea is that Jean had long intended to go to Chambly, but said nothing about it to us. As we had agreed to land at Laprairie and return together to the farm, he did not tell us until we were off Caughnawaga."

114

"And when he went away, did he promise to come here for the christening?"

"Yes," said Pierre; "he knew he was to hold the baby with you, and that without him the family would not be complete."

After this formal promise the only thing to do was to wait.

But if the day went by and Jean did not appear, alarm would be justifiable. For a resolute man such as he was not to appear on the appointed day meant that the police had got hold of him. And then, as M. and Mdlle de Vaudreuil knew only too well, he was lost.

At this moment the gate in the fence opened, and a savage appeared.

A savage — for in Lower Canada all Indians are so called, even in official documents.

The savage was a Huron, and of pure race — as was obvious from his beardless face, his prominent cheekbones, his small sparkling eyes. His tall stature, his quick, penetrating glance, the colour of his skin, the fashion of his hair, made him an unmistakable type of the indigenous American.

The Huron was clothed almost in the Canadian manner. He belonged to the tribe of the Mahogannis, who occupied a village of fourteen or fifteen fires in the north of the county. The tribe, as we have said, had frequent dealings with the farmer of Chipogan.

"What is the matter, Huron?" asked Thomas Harcher as the Indian advanced and solemnly shook hands.

"Will Thomas Harcher reply to the question I will ask him?" replied the Huron, in the guttural tone peculiar to his race.

"And why not," asked the farmer, "if my reply will be of interest to you?"

"Then my brother will listen, and judge what he ought to say."

By this one form of speech, in which the savage asks in the third person, with the most dignified air, for probably some very simple reply, there can be recognized the descendant of the four great nations who formerly possessed the territory of North America. They were divided into Algonquins, Hurons, Montagnais, and Iroquois, who comprised the tribes of Mohawks, Oncidas, Onondagas, Tuscaroras, Delawares, Mohicans, which one chiefly meets with in the works of Fenimore Cooper. Really there remain but the scattered fragments of the ancient races.

After a short silence, the Indian, with an imposing gesture, resumed: —

"My brother knows the notary, Nicholas Sagamore, of Montreal?"

"I have that honour."

"Is he not coming to the farm of Chipogan?"

"That is true."

"Can my brother inform me if Nicholas Sagamore has arrived?"

"Not yet," said Thomas Harcher. "We do not expect him till to-morrow to draw up the marriage settlements between my daughter Rose and Bernard Miquelon."

"I thank my brother for the information."

"Have you an important communication for Mr. Nick?"

"Very important," replied the Huron. "To-morrow the warriors of my tribe will leave our village of Walhatta and come to visit him."

"You will be welcome at Chipogan," said Thomas Harcher.

And thereupon the Indian stretched out his hand to the farmer and solemnly retired.

A quarter of an hour afterwards the gate was again opened. This time it was Jean, whose arrival was welcomed with shouts of joy.

Thomas and Catherine Harcher, their children and grandchildren, rushed on to him, and it took him some time to reply to the greetings of all those who were so pleased to see him again.

Time was pressing, and M. de Vaudreuil, Clary and Jean could only exchange a few words. But as they were to pass three days at the farm together, they would have leisure enough to talk over affairs later on. Thomas Harcher and his wife were in a hurry to get to the church. They did not want to keep the curé waiting. The godfather and godmother were ready, and it was time to start.

"Let us get away," said Catherine, who had been going from one to the other, scolding and ordering them about. "Come along, my son," she said to Jean; "give your arm to Mademoiselle Clary. And Thomas? where is Thomas? There will be no end to this! Where is Thomas?"

"Here I am, wife."

"You have got to carry the baby."

"All right."

"And don't let it fall."

"All right. I have carried twenty-five to the curé, and now I've got in the way of it."

That'll do!" said Catherine, interrupting him. "Be The procession left the farm in the following order: — At the head was Thomas, with the baby in his arms, and Catherine close by. M. de Vaudreuil, his daughter, and Jean came next; then followed the family of three generations, in which the ages had become so intermixed that the baby just born had many nephews and nieces older than himself among the children of his brothers and sisters.

It was a bright, sunshiny day, but at this time of the year the temperature would have been rather low if the sun had been hidden by the clouds. The procession passed under the trees, along the winding footpath at the end of which rose the spire of the church. A carpet of dry leaves covered the ground. The autumnal tints were thick on the chestnuts, birches, oaks, beeches, aspens, which here and there had their branches bare, while the firs and pines still retained their foliage of green.

As the procession passed on, several friends of Thomas Harcher, farmers in the neighbourhood, joined in. And it was quite a hundred strong when it reached the church, including a few strangers who had been attracted by curiosity.

Among the strangers, Pierre Harcher noticed a man whose manner seemed suspicious. Evidently he had come from a distance. Pierre had never seen him before, and it seemed to him that the intruder was taking stock of the farmer's family.

Pierre had good reason to mistrust the man. He was one of the police-officers who had received orders to keep an eye on M. de Vaudreuil since his departure from the Villa Montcalm. Rip, engaged in searching for Jean-Sans-Nom, whom he believed to be hidden in the suburbs of Montreal, had sent off the man with orders to watch not only M. de Vaudreuil, but also the Harcher family, whose reformist opinions were known to him.

As they walked side by side, M. de Vaudreuil and his daughter and Jean talked over the reasons of Jean's delay in reaching the farm.

"I heard from Pierre," said Clary, "that you had left him to go to Chambly and the parishes in the vicinity."

"Quite so," said Jean.

"Did you come here straight from Chambly?"

"No; I had to go into the county of St. Hyacinthe, and I could not get back at once, as I had hoped. I had to go a long way round — "

"Were the police on your track?" asked M. de Vaudreuil.

"Yes," said Jean; "but I was able with a little difficulty to again escape them."

"Every hour of your life you are in danger," said Mdlle de Vaudreuil. "There is not a moment but your friends tremble for you. Since you left the Villa Montcalm our anxiety has been unceasing."

"That," said Jean, "is why I am so eager to end this life which I have to fight for so unceasingly, so eager to act in broad daylight face to face with the foe! Yes! the time has come when the battle should begin! But at this moment let us forget the future for the present. This is a truce, a halt before the battle! Here, Monsieur de Vaudreuil, I am only the adopted son of this brave and honest family."

The procession had arrived, and the little church could hardly hold the crowd.

The curé was on the threshold, near the modest stone vase which served for the baptismal ceremonies of the many new-comers of the parish.

Thomas Harcher presented, not without some pride, the twenty-sixth offspring of his marriage with the no less proud Catherine. Clary de Vaudreuil and Jean stood side by side while the curé went through the usual ceremony.

"And you name this child?" asked the curé.

"Jean, like his godfather!" said Thomas Harcher, holding out his hand to the young man.

One of the ancient customs of France still exists in the towns and villages of Lower Canada. In the rural parishes the Catholic clergy are supported by the so-called tithes, but the tithe there is the twenty-sixth of the fruit and crops of the land, and by a strange tradition this twenty- sixth is not confined to the crops alone.

And so Thomas Harcher was not astonished, when the baptism was over, to hear the curé say, in a loud voice, —

"This child belongs to the Church, Thomas Harcher. He may be the godson of the godfather and godmother you have chosen, but he is my pupil! Are not children the fruit of the family? As you have given me the twenty- sixth of your corn harvest, so is the twenty-sixth of your children given to the Church this day!"

"We recognize your right," replied Thomas Harcher, "and my wife and I submit to it with good grace."

The child was then taken to the vicarage, where it was received in triumph.

Henceforth, by the tradition of the tithe, little Jean belonged to the Church, and as such he would be brought up at the expense of the parish.

And when the procession was formed to return to the farm of Chipogan there was cheering again and again in honour of Thomas and Catherine Harcher.

CHAPTER XI - THE LAST OF THE SAGAMORES

Next day the ceremonies were resumed. There was another procession to the church, with a similar reception in going, and a similar gathering on the return.

Young Clement and Cecil Harcher, the one in his black coat, looking like a little man, the other in her white dress looking like a little bride, figured among the first communicants from the neighbouring farms. If the other "habitants "were not as rich in offspring as Thomas Harcher of Chipogan, yet they had a very respectable number of olive branches. The county of Laprairie was quite crowded with the blessings of the Lord, and could vie with the most prolific villages of Nova Scotia.

This day Pierre saw no more of the stranger whose presence had given him some anxiety the day before. The detective had disappeared. Had he suspected anything with regard to Jean-Sans-Nom? Had he gone to report to his chief at Montreal?

When the family returned to the farm, their chief business was to do justice to the luncheon. Everything was ready, thanks to the multiple directions Thomas Harcher had received from Catherine. He had to see after the table, the kitchen, the cellar, with the help of his sons be it understood, who had their share of the maternal scoldings.

"It is well for them to get used to it," said Catherine. "It will come more natural to them when they have a house of their own."

And it really was an excellent apprenticeship.

But if the luncheon of the day took a deal of seeing after, what about that of the morrow? A table to be laid for a hundred? Yes! that was the number, reckoning the friends of the bridegroom. And we must not forget Mr. Nick and his second clerk, who would attend for the signing of the settlements. An incomparable wedding in which Farmer Harcher came into rivalry with Farmer Gamache, of Cervantesque memory!

But that was to take place to-morrow. To-day all that could be done was to welcome the notary. One of the Harchers had gone off to Laprairie to bring him at three o'clock with the buggy.

Catherine remembered that Mr. Nick was a hearty eater as well as a man of taste, and she did not expect that his food would be quite to his liking.

"It will be all right," said the farmer. "You can take things quietly, Catherine."

"I shall not take things quietly," said Catherine. "There is sure to be something wanting at the last moment, and I won't hear of that if I can help it."

Thomas Harcher went his way saying to himself, —

"Excellent woman! A little fussy undoubtedly. She won't hear of this! And she won't hear of that! And yet she isn't at all deaf nevertheless!"

M. de Vaudreuil and Clary had had a long conversation with Jean regarding his journey through the counties of Lower Canada. They told Jean the state of affairs in Montcalm county since his departure. Farran, Clerc, and Hodge had frequently been to the Villa as also had the advocate Gramont, who had then gone to Quebec to interview the chief deputies of the opposition.

After luncheon M. de Vaudreuil had gone in the buggy to confer with the president of Laprairie County and return with the notary.

His daughter and Jean accompanied him along the lovely road from Chipogan, shaded with huge elms, which bordered a little stream running into the St. Lawrence. He had started before the buggy, and was not overtaken till he was half a league from the farm. He took his seat by Pierre Harcher and soon disappeared at a rapid trot.

Jean and Clary returned through the shady tranquil woods that lay beside the stream. They had a clear road among the underwood and beneath the branches, which in Canadian forests grow upwards. From time to time the axe of the lumberman resounded as it struck the tree trunks. The reports of a gun were heard in the distance, and occasionally a couple of deer would appear amid the bushes, which they would clear at a bound. But hunters and woodcutters remained hidden in the thickets, and it was through a profound solitude that Clary and Jean walked slowly towards the farm.

They were soon to separate. Where and when would they see each other again? Sore were their hearts at the thought of the coming parting.

121

"Do you think you will soon come back to the Villa Montcalm?" asked Clary.

"M. de Vaudreuil's house will be carefully watched," said Jean. "And for his sake it would be better. I should keep our friendship secret."

"But you are not going to take refuge in Montreal?"

"No, although it would be easy to avoid pursuit in so large a town. I should be safer with Vincent Hodge, or Farran or Clerc than in the Villa Montcalm."

"But not more welcome!"

"I know that, and I never shall never forget that during the few days I spent with you, your father and you treated me like a son, like a brother!"

"And so we ought to do," said Clary. "To be united by the same sentiments is to be united by the same blood. It sometimes seems to me as though you were always one of our family. And now if you are alone in the world — "

"Alone in the world," repeated Jean, hanging his head. "Yes — alone - alone."

"Well, after the triumph of our cause our house will be yours! But meanwhile, I understand you require a safer retreat than the Villa Montcalm. You will find it, for where is the habitant who would shut the door against a fugitive?"

"Nowhere that I know of," said Jean, "and there is not one who would betray me."

"Betray you!" exclaimed Mademoiselle de Vaudreuil. "No! the time for treason has passed! In all Canada we shall never again see a Simon Morgaz!"

The name uttered with such horror made the blush rise to the young man's forehead, and he had to turn away to hide his emotion. Clary had not noticed it; but when he returned his face betrayed such suffering that she asked anxiously, —

"What is the matter with you?"

"Nothing," he said, "nothing. Palpitation to which I am occasionally subject! It seemed as though my heart would burst. It is now over!"

Clary looked at him as if to read his innermost thoughts.

To change the conversation, he continued, —

"The best thing for me would be to take refuge in one of the neighbouring countries where I can remain in communication with M. de Vaudreuil and his friends."

"But without going far from Montreal?"

"No. For probably it will be in the neighbouring parishes that the insurrection will break out. Besides it does not matter much where I go."

"Perhaps," said Clary, "the farm of Chipogan might still be the safest place."

"Perhaps."

"It would be difficult to discover your retreat among the farmer's numerous family.

"Probably, but if it were discovered, it might have serious consequences for Thomas Harcher I He docs not know that I am Jean-Sans-Nom, on whose head a price has been set."

"Do you think, then," said Clary, "if you were to tell him that he would hesitate."

"No, certainly not," said Jean. "He and his sons are patriots. I have seen that clearly enough while we were engaged on our propagandist campaign together. But I would not have Thomas Harcher a victim to his affection for me. And if the police were to find me with him, they would arrest him. I would rather give myself up."

"Give yourself up!" murmured Clary, in a voice that sorrowfully declared her anguish of mind.

Jean bowed his head. He understood only too well the nature of the feelings to which he had given way almost in spite of himself. He felt the chain that was binding him more and more closely to Clary de Vaudreul. But could he love the girl? The love of a son of Simon Morgaz! What opprobrium! And what treason, too, for he could never tell the name of the family from which he came! No! He must flee away and never see her again!

When he was himself again, he said, —

"To-morrow night I shall leave the farm of Chipogan, and I shall not appear again until the hour of the struggle. Then I shall have no need of concealment!"

His features grew animated for a moment, and then resumed their usual calm.

Clary looked at him with an indefinable expression of sorrow. She would have known something of his former life. But how could she ask him without paining him by some indiscreet question?

However, after giving him her hand, which he only just touched, she said,
—

"Jean, pardon me if my sympathy for you makes me put aside a reserve I ought perhaps to retain. There is a mystery in your life — a past of misfortune! You have suffered much?"

"Much!" said Jean.

And as if the avowal had escaped him unawares, he immediately added, —

"Yes, much, because I have not been able to give my country that which she has the right to expect from me."

"The right to expect," said Clary, "the right to expect from you?"

"Yes, from me," said Jean, "as from all Canadians, whose duty it is to sacrifice themselves to give their country her independence."

Clary saw well enough that there was a load of misery hidden under this burst of patriotism. She would have known what it was to share it, to lighten it, perhaps! But how could she if Jean persisted in these evasive replies?

"Jean," she said, "I hope the national cause will triumph! The triumph will be chiefly due to your devotion, your courage, the ardour with which you have inspired its partisans. You will have a right to their recognition."

"Their recognition, Clary de Vaudreuil?" said Jean, starting suddenly. "No! never!"

"Never? If the French Canadians to whom you have given liberty demand that you remain at their head."

"I should refuse!"

"You could not!"

"I should refuse, I tell you!" in a tone so positive that Clary remained silent. But more gently lie added, —

"Clary de Vaudreuil, we cannot read the future. I hope that events will turn to. the advantage of our cause. But it would be better for me to die in defending it."

"To die! you!" exclaimed Clary, her eyes filling with tears, "to die, Jean! And your friends?"

"Friends? My friends? ".

And his expression was that of some miserable wretch, who throughout an opprobrious life had been put under the ban of humanity.

"Jean," said Clary, "you have had much trouble in the past, and you are in trouble now! And what makes your position all the more sad is that you cannot, or rather will not, confide in any one, not even in me, who would so willingly share in your trouble. Well, I can wait, and I ask you only to believe in my friendship."

"Your friendship!" murmured Jean; and he took a step backwards as if even his friendship might disgrace her.

But were not the only consolations that could help him support his horrible existence those he would find in the friendship of Clary de Vaudreuil? While he was at the Villa Montcalm he had felt his heart full of the ardent sympathy with which he had inspired her, and which he felt for her. But, no! it was impossible! Unhappy man! If ever Clary learnt whose son he was, she would repulse him with horror! A Morgaz! And as he had told his mother, if he and Joann survived this last attempt, they would disappear! Yes, once their duty was accomplished, the dishonoured family would go far away, so far away that people would never hear of them again.

Silently and sadly Clary and Jean returned together to the farm.

About four o'clock there was a great uproar at the gate. The buggy was returning, signalled from afar by the shouts of joy with which the guests welcomed the arrival of M. de Vaudreuil, Mr. Nick, and his young clerk.

What a welcome they gave to the notary!

"Mr. Nick! How do you do, Mr. Nick?" exclaimed the elders, while the younger members of the family hugged him in their arms, and the little ones jumped on his knees.

"Yes, my friends, here I am!" he said, all smiles. "It is really I, and no one else! But be calm I It is not necessary to tear my coat, I assure you."

"Now, children, clear off," said Catherine.

"Truly," said the notary, "I am enchanted to see you, and to be here with my dear client, Thomas Harcher."

"Mr. Nick," said the farmer, "it is very kind of you to come!"

"And I would have come from much farther, if necessary from the end of the world, from the sun, from the stars, yes, Thomas, from the stars!"

That is an honour for us, Mr. Nick," said Catherine, Signalling to her eleven daughters to drop a curtsey.

"And for me," said Mr- Nick, "a pleasure I Ah.

Madame Catherine, you are always charming! When will you cease to grow young!"

"Never! never!" said the fifteen sons of the family. "I must have a kiss, Madame Catherine!" said Mr. Nick. "You will allow me?" he asked the farmer, after he had bestowed a loud smack on the lady's cheek. "As often as you like," said Thomas Harcher. "Now it is your turn, Lionel," said the notary ''Kiss Madame Catherine!"

"Willingly," said Lionel, who received a double kiss in exchange for his own.

"And now," said Mr. Nick, "I hope the charming Rose will have a happy wedding. I used to dance her on my knee. Where is she?"

"Here I am, Mr. Nick," said Rose, blooming with health and good-humour.

"Yes, you are charming," said the notary, "and so charming that I must really plant a kiss on each of those cheeks, which are worthy of the name they bear!"

And he kissed them well and truly. But this time Lionel was not invited to share in the tribute — very much to his regret.

126

"Where is the intended?" asked Mr. Nick. "Has he forgotten the day? where is he?"

"Here," said Bernard Miquelon.

"Ah! He's a fine lad, a good-natured lad!" exclaimed Mr. Nick. "I would kiss him too, to complete — "

"Come on, Mr. Nick," said the young man, opening his arms.

"Good! "said Mr. Nick, shaking his head. "I fancy Bernard Miquelon would rather have one kiss from Rose than two from me! And so, Rose, kiss your future husband in my place!"

Which Rose in some confusion did, amid the applause of the whole family.

"Eh!" said Catherine, "I think you must be thirsty, Mr. Nick, and your clerk also?"

"Very thirsty," said Mr. Nick.

"Extremely thirsty," said Lionel.

"Now, Thomas, what are you looking at? Go and get a good drink for Mr. Nick, and as good a one for his clerk? Shall I have to ask you again?"

No! once was enough, and the farmer hurried off, followed by two or three of his daughters, while Mr. Nick, who had just caught sight of Clary de Vaudreuil, went up to speak to her.

"Well, my dear young lady," he said, "at the last visit I paid to the Villa Montcalm we made an appointment to meet at the farm of Chipogan, and I am happy — "

He was interrupted by an exclamation from Lionel, whose surprise was very natural. Was he not face to face with the young unknown who had so sympathetically received his poetical effort a few weeks before?

"But, it is Monsieur — Monsieur — " he repeated. M. de Vaudreuil and Clary looked at each other anxiously. How did Lionel know Jean? and if he knew him, did he know that the Harchers did not knew they had given shelter to Jean-Sans-Nom?

"Quite so," said the notary, turning to the young man. "I recognize you, monsieur! You were our travelling companion, when my clerk and I went in the buggy to the Villa Montcalm at the beginning of September.

"That is right, Mr. Nick," answered Jean, "and it is with much pleasure, believe me, that I find you here, accompanied by the young poet."

"Whose poem received honourable mention at the Lyre Amicale!" said the notary. "It is evidently a nursling of the Muses that I keep in my office to draught my deeds!"

"Accept my compliments, my young friend," said Jean, "I have not forgotten your charming

"To be born with you, my frolicsome flame.

To die with you, my will-o'-the-wisp."

"Ah! monsieur!" said Lionel, very proud of the praise of the two lines that had lingered in the memory of so good a judge.

In listening to this exchange of compliments Clary and her father were much relieved. Mr. Nick then told them how they had met Jean on the way from Montreal to Jesus Island, and Jean was introduced to Mr. Nick and his clerk as the adopted son of the H archers. The explanations ended by a hearty shake of the hands all round.

Then Catherine's imperious voice was heard, —

"Now then, Thomas! Come along! Will you never have done? Are you going to let Mr. Nick and Mr. Lionel die of thirst?"

"It is ready, Catherine, it is ready!" said the farmer. "Don't be impatient!"

And he invited the notary to follow him into the dining- room.

Neither Mr. Nick nor Lionel wanted much pressing. Taking their places at a table on which were some coloured cups, and napkins of startling whiteness, they refreshed themselves with toddy, an agreeable beverage composed of gin, sugar and cinnamon, and flanked with crisp toast-a little something to enable them to wait till dinner-time without fainting.

Then all set to work on the last preparations for the grand fête of the morrow, which would doubtless be long remembered at the farm of Chipogan.

128

Mr. Nick strolled about from one to the other. He had a kind word for every one, while M. de Vaudreuil, Clary and Jean talked of more serious matters as they walked under the trees in the garden.

About five o'clock all the relatives and guests assembled in the larger room for the signature of the marriage contract. Mr. Nick, of course, presided at this important ceremony, and that he comported himself with all due dignity and notarial grace can be imagined.

The various wedding presents were then handed to the young couple. Not one of the brothers or brothers- in-law, not one of the sisters or sisters-in-law, but had made some purchase for Rose Harcher and Bernard Miquelon. And so numerous were the articles of ornament and use that the young couple could well have set up housekeeping on them. But when Rose had become Madame Miquelon she would still remain at Chipogan. Bernard and the children would merely be a welcome increase to the family of Thomas Harcher.

The most valuable presents were given by M. de Vaudreuil and his daughter. For Bernard Miquelon there was an excellent gun that rivalled the favourite weapon of Leatherstocking. Rose had a necklace which made her look more charming than ever. Jean gave the sister of his companions a box fitted with such a set of the needful implements for cutting, sewing and embroidery, as could but give the greatest of pleasure to a good housewife.

And at each gift there were clapping of hands and shouts of applause, which were redoubled when Mr. Nick solemnly placed on the young couple's fingers their wedding ring which he had bought from the best jeweller of Montreal, and which already bore their names.

Then the marriage contract was read, in a loud, intelligible voice in proper notarial style. There was some sign of emotion when Mr. Nick announced that M. de Vaudreuil, out of friendship to his tenant, Thomas Harcher, added a sum of five hundred dollars to the bride's dowry.

Five hundred dollars! when, half a century before, a bride with a dowry of fifty francs was considered a rich match in the Canadian provinces.

"And now, my friends," said Mr. Nick, "we will proceed to the signature of the contract. The young couple first, then the father and mother, then Monsieur and Mademoiselle de Vaudreuil, then — "

"We will all sign!" exclaimed all present, with a shout that deafened the notary.

And then old and young, friends and relatives, came one after the other to add their signatures to the contract which was to assure the future of the two young people.

That took some time! In fact, the passers-by now entered the farm, attracted by the joyous tumult within, and put their signatures to the deed, so that pages and pages would have to be added if the state of things were to continue. And why should not all the village and all the country crowd in when Thomas Harcher offered his visitors the choice of the most varied drinks, in addition to the whisky that flows as naturally towards Canadian throats as the St. Lawrence towards the Atlantic.

Mr. Nick inquired if the ceremony were ever to end. The worthy man beamed with joy; he was inexhaustible; he had a cheery word for all, while Lionel, passing the pen from one to another, found he would soon require a new one, as it was being used up by the interminable column of signatures that grew longer and longer.

"Is that all?" asked Mr. Nick, after an hour.

"Not yet!" said Pierre Harcher, who had gone to the door to sec if any one were on the road.

"Who is coming now?" asked Mr. Nick.

"A troop of Hurons!"

"Let them come in! let them come in!" said the notary. "Their signatures will do no dishonour to the contracting parties. What a contract it is, my friends! I have drawn up hundreds in the course of my life, but never have I seen the names of so many good people at the bottom of the last page!"

The Indians now appeared on the scene and were welcomed with loud shouts of welcome. They did not wait for an invitation, but swarmed in, fifty in number — men and women. And amongst them Thomas Harcher recognized the Huron who had presented himself the day before to ask if Mr. Nick were coming to the farm of Chipogan.

Why had the tribe of Mahogannis come from their village of Walhatta? Why had they arrived in gala costume to visit the notary of Montreal?

It was for a reason of great importance, as we shall see immediately.

The Hurons were all in their war-paint. Their heads were surmounted by feathers, their long thick hair fell on to their shoulders from which hung a multi-coloured cloak; their bodies were clothed in deerskin, their feet were shod with moccasins of elk leather; they were armed with the long rifles which for many years had replaced among the Indian tribes the bows and arrows of their ancestors. But the traditional axe, the war-tomahawk, hung from their belts.

A coat of fresh paint bedecked their faces. Azure blue, lampblack and vermilion, accentuated the astonishing relief of their aquiline noses, their large nostrils, and huge mouths furnished with a double row of curved and regular teeth, their high, square check-bones and their small, keen eyes, whose black orbits glowed like embers.

The deputation was accompanied by a few of the Walhatta women — doubtless the youngest and best- looking of the tribe. These squaws wore a bodice of embroidered stuff with the sleeves leaving the forearm bare, a petticoat of glaring colours, "mitasses "of cariboo leather, ornamented with hedgehog quills and laced on their limbs, and soft moccasins braided with glass beads imprisoned their feet whose smallness a Frenchwoman might envy.

The Indians had, if possible, doubled the gravity which was habitual to them. With much ceremony they advanced to the threshold of the large room where stood Monsieur and Mademoiselle de Vaudreuil, the notary, and Thomas and Catherine Harcher, while the rest of the party occupied the courtyard.

Then the one who seemed to be the chief, a Huron of tall stature and about fifty years of age, holding in his hand a cloak of native work, addressed the farmer solemnly as follows, —

"Is Nicholas Sagamore at the farm of Chipogan?"

"He is!" said Thomas Harcher.

"And I add that I am he," said the notary, much surprised that he could be the object of the visit.

The Huron turned towards him, raised his head proudly, and in a more imposing tone, continued, —

"The chief of our tribe," said he, "has been called by the great Wacondah, the Mitsimanitou of our fathers. Five moons have passed since he went to the happy hunting-grounds. His heir is now Nicholas, the last of the Sagamores. To him henceforth belongs the right of burying the tomahawk of peace, or unearthing the tomahawk of war."

A profound silence greeted this unexpected declaration. It was well known in the country that Mr. Nick was of Huron origin, and that he was descended from the great chief of the tribe of Mahogannis; but no one had imagined, and he least of all, that the order of heredity would call him to the head of an Indian people.

And then, amid a silence that none dare disturb, the Indian resumed, —

"At what time will my brother take his seat at the fire of the Great Council of his tribe, clothed in the traditional mantle of his ancestors?"

The spokesman of the deputation never supposed that the notary would refuse, and presented him with the mantle.

And as Mr. Nick, absolutely dumbfounded, hesitated to answer, there was a shout — in which fifty others joined — of "Honour! Honour to Nicholas Sagamore!"

It was Lionel who had raised the enthusiastic shout. That he was proud of the good fortune that had come to his master, and considered that the distinction was reflected on the clerks in his office, and more especially on himself, and rejoiced at the idea of henceforth marching by the side of the great chief of the Mahogannis, we need not waste time in insisting.

De Vaudreuil and his daughter could not help smiling at the astounded look of Mr. Nick. Poor man! While the farmer and his children and friends offered him their sincere felicitations, he did not know what to reply.

Then the Indian again asked him the question from which there was no escape.

"Will Nicholas Sagamore follow his brothers to the wigwams of Walhatta?"

Mr. Nick remained silent. Be it well understood he would never consent to resign his profession to reign over a Huron tribe. But, on the other hand, he did not like to hurt by a refusal the Indians of his race who called him by the right of succession to such an honour.

"Mahogannis," said he at last, "I did not expect this. I am indeed unworthy of it. You understand — my friends — I am only here as a notary! — "

He stammered; he was at a loss for words; he was unable to reply.

Thomas Harcher came to his assistance. "Hurons!" said he, "Mr. Nick is Mr. Nick at least till this ceremony of marriage is completed. After that, if it pleases him, he will leave the farm of Chipogan free to return with his brothers to Walhatta!"

"Yes! After the wedding!" shouted the throng who wished to keep the notary.

The Huron shook his head, and took counsel with the deputation.

"My brother cannot hesitate," he said. "The blood of the Mahogannis runs in his veins and imposes on him rights and duties which he will not refuse — "

"Rights! rights! Be it so!" murmured Mr. Nick, "But duties-"

"Does he accept?" asked the Indians. "He accepts!" said Lionel, "I am sure of it! And in witness of his sentiments he should at once be clothed with the royal mantle of the Sagamores!"

"The imbecile!" said Mr. Nick between his teeth. "Why will he not be quiet!"

And with a thump the pacific notary strove to calm the stormy enthusiasm of his clerk.

Monsieur de Vaudreuil saw that Mr. Nick only wished to gain time. Addressing the Indian, he said that assuredly the descendant of the Sagamores did not think of withdrawing from the duties his descent imposed upon him. But a few days, a few weeks perhaps, were necessary for him to put matters in order at Montreal. It was necessary, therefore, to give him time to set his affairs in order.

"That is wise," said the Indian. "And as my brother accepts, let him receive as the pledge of his acceptance the tomahawk of the great chief called by the Wacondah to the happy hunting-grounds, and let him wear it in his belt!"

Mr. Nick took the favourite weapon of the Indian tribes, and, much puzzled by not having a belt, he rested it piteously on his shoulder.

The deputation then uttered the traditional "liugh" of their race, a sort of exclamation of approval in use in the Indian languages.

Lionel could hardly restrain himself for joy, although his master appeared particularly embarrassed at a position which might make him a laughing-stock in the brotherhood of Canadian notaries. With his poetic gifts he saw that he was already called upon to celebrate the mighty deeds of the Mahogannis, and shout in lyric verse the watery of the Sagamores — though how he was to find a rhyme for tomahawk he did not quite see.

The Hurons were about to retire, regretting that Mr. Nick's duties prevented him from accompanying them, when Catherine had an idea.

"Mahogannis," she said, "it is a marriage feast that brings us together to day at the farm of Chipogan. Will you remain in the company of your new chief? We offer you hospitality, and to-morrow you take your places at the feast, in which Nicolas Sagamore will occupy the seat of honour."

There were thunders of applause when Catherine Harcher had formulated her thoughtful proposition, and they rose even louder and longer when the Mahogannis accepted an invitation made with such goodwill.

Thomas Harcher had only to lay the wedding-table for fifty more — and this did not embarrass him in the least, for the room was large enough for even this increase of the party.

Mr. Nick had to resign himself to his fate — for he could not do otherwise — and he received the accolade of the warriors of his tribe, whom he would willingly have sent to perdition.

And with the merry dancing of the young folk in rounds and reels, the second day of the festivities at Chipogan came to an end.

CHAPTER XII - TIIE DINNER

THE great day had arrived — the last of the successive ceremonies of baptism, communion, and marriage, in which the good folks of Chipogan had taken such delight. The marriage of Rose Harcher and Bernard Miquelon had been celebrated in the morning before the State official, and would now take place at the church. Then, in the afternoon, the wedding feast would bring together the guests, whose numbers had received such a large addition. In truth it was time to finish, or the county of Laprairie and even the district of Montreal would have gathered at Thomas Harcher's hospitable table.

On the morrow the party would break up. The De Vaudreuils would return to the Villa Montcalm. Jean would leave the farm, and would not reappear until the day he put himself at the head of the reformist party. His companions on the Champlain would continue their occupation as hunters and trappers, and wait till the time came to rejoin their adopted brother, while the family generally would return to the customary work of the farm. The Hurons would go back to the village of Walhatta, where they expected to give Nicholas Sagamore a triumphant reception when he came for the first time to smoke the calumet by the hearth of his ancestors.

But Mr. Nick had been as little pleased as possible with the homage he had received. He had no intention of giving up his office for the chieftainship of any tribe, and he had been talking the matter over with Monsieur de Vaudreuil and Thomas Harcher, and his perplexity was such that they had some difficulty in keeping from laughing at him.

"You are amusing yourselves," he said. "It is easy to see that you have no throne ready to open at your feet."

"My dear Nick," said M. de Vaudreuil, "there is no need to take it seriously."

"And how can I take it otherwise?"

"The men will not insist on it when they see you are in no hurry to betake yourself to the wigwam of the Mahogannis."

"You do not understand them," said Mr. Nick. "They will never leave me alone. They will follow me to Montreal! They will make demonstrations I cannot escape! They will besiege my door! And what will old Dolly say? You will see it will end by my marching forth with moccasins on my feet and feathers on my head!"

And Nick, who was always ready for a laugh, ended by sharing in the hilarity of his friends.

But it was with his clerk that he had the chief crow to pick. Lionel — out of malice — treated him already as if he had accepted the succession of the defunct Huron. He no longer called him Mr. Nick! He spoke to him only in the third person, and employed only the emphatic language of the Indians. And as it was the appropriate thing for every warrior of the prairies, he had given him a choice of surnames, such as Elkhorn or the Subtle Lizard, corresponding to those of Hawkeye or the Longue Carabine.

About eleven o'clock the procession was formed in the courtyard. It was admirably arranged, and such as would have inspired a young poet, if Lionel's muse had not been occupied with higher themes.

At the head marched Bernard Miquelon and Rose Harcher, one holding the little finger of the other, and both of them beaming with happiness. Then came the De Vaudreuils, with Jean by their side; then the fathers and mothers and sisters and brothers of the happy pair; then Mr. Nick and his clerk, escorted by the members of the Huron deputation. The notary would have dispensed with this honour had he been able to. To Lionel's extreme regret, his master required only the native costume, the tattooing of the body and the colouring of his face, to worthily represent the line of the Sagamores.

The ceremony was performed with all the pomp suitable to the position occupied by the Harcher family in the district. There was a great ringing of bells, a grand accompaniment of hymns and prayers, and much firing of gun?. And in this noisy concert of gun-firing the Hurons took part with a skill and precision that would have won the approval of Natty Bumppo, the celebrated friend of the Mohicans.

Then the procession returned to the farm. Rose Miquelon on her husband's arm this time, nothing having occurred to mar the proceedings in any way.

Then the party separated for a time. Mr. Nick being in no way loath to leave his Mahogannis, and breathe more at his ease in the society of his Canadian friends. And more piteously than ever he continued to say to M. de Vaudreuil, "In truth, I do not know how I shall get rid of these savages!"

Meanwhile if any man was busy, driven about, and stormed at from noon to three o'clock — the hour at which the wedding feast was to begin in accordance with ancient custom — that man was Thomas Harcher. True, Catherine and her sons and daughters did all they could to help him; but the preparation of a feast of this importance left him not a minute's respite.

It was not only the number of diners he had to satisfy, as the diversity of tastes. And the bill of fare comprised all the ordinary and extraordinary dishes known in Canadian cookery.

On the immense table — at which one hundred and fifty guests were to sit — were disposed as many spoons and forks wrapped in a white napkin and flanked by a metal cup. There were no knives, for each guest had to use his or her own. There was no bread, only the maple-sugared cake being admissible at a wedding feast. The cold meats were on the table, the hot were served in due order.

There were earthen pots of hot soup, from which perfumed vapours escaped; there were fried fish and boiled fish from the sweet waters of the St. Lawrence and the lakes, trout, salmon, eels, pike, white fish, shad, touradis and maskinongis; there were ducks, pigeons, quails, woodcock, snipe, and fricasseed squirrels; there were turkeys, geese, bustards, fattened on the farm, some of them roasted a sparkling golden brown, some of them drowned in a sea of spices; then there were hot oyster patties, forcemeat pies, huge onions, legs of mutton, chines of roast boar, maize puddings, fawn cutlets, and deer steaks; then those wonderful haunches of venison, which make Canada the envy of the epicures of the two worlds, the bison hump so much esteemed by the hunters of the prairies, cooked in its natural fur and garnished with fragrant leaves! Add to all these, the sauce-boats in which floated relishes of a score of kinds; mountains of vegetables, brought to perfection in the last days of the Indian summer; pastry of all kinds, particularly those cracknels or fritters, for the making of which Catherine Harcher's daughters enjoyed an unequalled reputation; varieties of fruit from the orchard; and a hundred flagons of different forms of cider, beer, wine, and spirits for dessert.

The large room had been very artistically decorated in honour of Bernard and Rose Miquelon. Garlands of leaves ornamented the walls, appropriate shrubs stood in the angles, hundreds of nosegays of fragrant flowers ornamented the window bay. At the same time, guns, pistols, carbines — all the weapons of a family of many sportsmen — were arranged in glittering trophies.

The newly-married couple occupied the middle of the table, which was of horseshoe shape, like the Falls of Niagara, which, a hundred and fifty leagues to the southwest, precipitate their deafening cataracts. And they were indeed cataracts which were to be engulfed in the abysses of these French-Canadian stomachs!

On each side of the newly-married pair were the DeVaudreuils. Jean and his companions of the Champlain were opposite to them, between Thomas and Catherine Harcher. Mr. Nick was enthroned with the principal warriors of his tribe, anxious to witness, no doubt, how their new chief comported himself. And in this respect Nicholas Sagamore promised to display an appetite worthy of his lineage. Contrary to tradition, and for this special occasion, the children were admitted to the large table among their relatives and friends, and around them circulated a squad of negroes, engaged for this particular service.

By five o'clock the first assault had been delivered. At Six there was a truce, not to carry away the dead, but to give the living time to recover their breath. Then it was that the toasts and speeches began.

Then followed happy wedding songs, according to ancient custom, for at every meeting at dinner, as at supper, the women and the men sang alternately the old songs of France.

Then Lionel recited a flattering epithalamium composed expressly for the occasion.

"Bravo, Lionel, bravo!" shouted Mr. Nick, who had drowned in the bowl the cares of his future sovereignty.

The good old fellow was very proud of his young poet's success, and he proposed the health of the gallant laureate of the Lyre Amicale!

At this proposal the glasses were filled to the brim, and held towards Lionel, who was so happy and confused that he could think of no better reply than the toast, —

"To Nicholas Sagamore! To the last branch of the noble tree on which the Great Spirit has hung the destinies of the Huron nation!"

There were thunders of applause. The Mahogannis stood up round the table and brandished their tomahawks as if they were about to hurl themselves against the Iroquois, or Mungos, or any other tribe of their enemies.

Mr. Nick, with his placid figure, seemed much too pacific for such bellicose warriors! In truth this blockhead of a Lionel had much better have kept silence.

When the effervescence had calmed down, the second course was attacked with renewed vigour.

Amid the noisy manifestations, Jean, Clary, and Lerfillier had every facility for conversation in a low tone. In the evening they were to separate. If the De Vaudreuils did not leave till the morning, Jean had resolved to go that night so as to seek a safer retreat away from the farm of Chipogan.

"But," said M. de Vaudreuil, "would the police think of looking for Jean-Sans-Nom among Thomas Harcher's family?"

"Who knows if the detectives are not on my traces?" answered Jean, as if he had a presentiment of evil, "and if that should happen, when the farmer and his sons learn who I am — "

"They will defend you," said Clary. "They would die for you"

"I know it," said Jean, "and then in return for the hospitality they have given me I should leave behind me ruin and misfortune! Thomas Marcher and his children would by obliged to quit their home for having defended me! And so I am anxious to get away from the firm."

"Why do you not return secretly to the Villa Montcalm?" said M. de Vaudreuil. "The risks which you would spare Thomas Harcher are those to which it is my duty to expose myself, and I am ready to do so! In my house the secret of your retreat would be well kept."

"That proposition Mademoiselle de Vaudreuil has already made to me in your name, but I have had to decline it."

"But," said M. de Vaudreuil, "it would be convenient for the final measures you have to devise. You could communicate with the members of the committee every day. When the rising takes place Farran, Clerc, Hodge and are ready to follow you. Is it not probable that the first outbreak will occur in Montreal county?"

"That is so," said Jean, "or rather in one of the adjoining counties, according to the positions occupied by the royal troops."

"Well, then," said Clary, "why do you not accept my father's offer? Is it your intention to again traverse the neighbouring parishes? Have you not ended your propagandist campaign?"

"It is ended," said Jean, "and I have now only to give the signal."

"Then what are you waiting for?" asked M. de Vaudreuil.

"I am waiting for something to complete the exasperation of the reformists," said Jean, "and which will soon happen. In a few days the deputies of the opposition will refuse the Governor the right he assumes to dispose of the public revenues without the authority of the Chamber. Besides, I know from a sure source that the English Parliament intends to pass a law permitting Lord Gosford to suspend the constitution of 1791. The result of that will be that the French-Canadians will be without any guarantee of a share in the representative system attributed to the colony, and which as it is leaves them so little freedom of action! Our friends, and with them the liberal deputies, will resist this excess of power. Probably Lord Gosford, to put a check on the reformist demands, will dissolve or prorogue the Chamber. The day he does so the country will rise, and we shall only have to guide the revolution."

"There is no doubt," said M. de Vaudreuil, "that such a provocation on the part of the loyalists will bring about a general revolt. But the English Parliament will hardly dare to go so far. If this attempt against the rights of the Franco-Canadians does take place, are you sure it will be soon?"

"In a few days," said Jean. "Sebastien Gramont told me so."

"And till then," asked Clary, "how are you to escape?"

"I must throw the detectives off the track."

"Have you a hiding-place in view?"

"I have."

"Where you will be safe?"

"Safer than elsewhere."

"Far from here?"

140

"At St. Charles, in the country of Verchères."

"Be it so," said M. de Vaudreuil. "No one can be a better judge of the matter than yourself. If you think you can keep the place of your retreat secret, we do not insist on our offer. But do not forget that at any hour of the day or night the Villa Montcalm is open to you."

"I know it, Monsieur de Vaudreuil, and I thank you."

Amid the incessant exclamations of the feasters, in the increasing tumult of the room, it can easily be believed that no one had heard this conversation, which was carried on in a low tone. Occasionally it was interrupted by some noisy toast or striking repartee, or rousing chorus. And it seemed about to finish when Clary asked a question that produced a very surprising reply.

What was it urged the girl to put this question? Was it a suspicion or a regret that Jean thought it his duty to still retain a certain reserve towards her?

"There is, then, somewhere a house in which you can hide that is more hospitable than ours?"

"More hospitable? No! But as hospitable," said Jean, not without emotion.

"And which is it?"

"My mother's."

Jean uttered the words in such a tone of filial affection that Clary was deeply moved. It was the first time that Jean, whose past had been so mysterious, had alluded to his family. He was not then alone in the world as his friends believed. He had a mother who was living in secret in the village of Saint Charles. Doubtless Jean went to see her sometimes. The house was open to him when he required quiet and repose. And it was there he was going to wait for the strife to begin.

Clary made no answer. Her thoughts were drawn towards this distant house. How happy she would be to know this mother! She must be a heroic woman, a patriot she would love, a patriot she loved already! Assuredly she would see her some day. Was not her life indissolubly bound up with that of Jean-Sans-Nom, and who was it could break the bond? Yes, at the moment of separating from him, perhaps for ever, she felt the power of the attraction that drew them towards each other.

141

The feast was near its close, and the gaiety of the guests, excited by the frequent libations, was showing itself in many ways. Compliments to the happy couple flew in from all sides. It was an extremely good-humoured uproar, amid which could be heard ever, now and then —

"Honour and happiness to the young people."

"Long live Bernard and Rose Miquelon."

And there was health-drinking to Monsieur de Vaudreuil and his daughter, and to Catherine and Thomas Harcher.

Mr. Nick had given the feast a grand reception. If he had not been able to retain the austere dignity of a Mahoganni it was because that was quite contrary to his open and communicative nature. But it is well to add that the representatives of his tribe had somewhat departed from their ancestral gravity under the influence of the good cheer and good wine.

They had filled their glasses in the French style to salute the Harcher family, whose guests they were, when Lionel, who could not keep still, went round the table with a compliment addressed to all he passed. It occurred to him to say to Mr. Nick in a very loud voice, —

"Nicholas Sagamore, will you not say a few words in the name of the tribe of Mahogannis?"

In the happy temper in which Mr. Nick found himself, lie did not receive the suggestion unkindly.

"Do you think so, Lionel?" he asked.

"I think, great chief, that the time is come for you to wish happiness to the bride and bridegroom."

"If you think this is the time I will do so! "And the excellent man arose and claimed silence by a gesture full of Huron dignity.

There was a lull immediately.

"Young people," he said, "an old friend of your family cannot leave you without expressing his acknowledgments for — "

Suddenly Mr. Nick stopped. The sentence remained incomplete on his lips. His look was directed towards the door.

142

A man stood on the threshold, whose arrival no one- had noticed.

Mr. Nick had recognized him, and he exclaimed in a tone in which surprise mingled with uneasiness, —

"Mr. Rip!"

CHAPTER XIII - MUSKETRY AT DESSERT

The head of the house of Rip and Co. was not accompanied by his own men.

Behind him were a dozen of Gilbert Argall's force, in addition to forty of the volunteers, who occupied the main entrance into the courtyard. It seemed as though the house was surrounded.

Was it a simple domiciliary visit or was it an arrest with which the head of the Harcher family was threatened. In either case it must be a matter of importance to induce the minister of police to send so strong a detachment to the farm of Chipogan.

Monsieur De Vaudreuil and his daughter were terror- stricken when the notary uttered Rip's name. They knew that Jean-Sans-Nom was in the room. They knew that to Rip in particular had been entrusted the duty of tracing him. And what could they think but that he had discovered his retreat and was about to arrest him? If Jean fell into Gilbert Argall's hands he was lost.

By a supreme effort of the will, Jean had not even started when he heard the name. There was hardly a change in his colour. No movement, not even an involuntary one, betrayed him; and yet he had just recognized Rip, whom he had met the day the buggy took Nick and Lionel from Montreal to Jesus Island! Rip, who had been in pursuit of him for two months! Rip, the tempter, who had caused the infamy of his family in urging his father, Simon Morgaz, on to treachery.

And yet he remained cool and collected and showed no sign of the hatred which raged within him, while M. de Vaudreuil and his daughter trembled at his side.

But if Jean knew Rip, Rip did not know him. He did not know that the traveller he had met for a moment on the road from Montreal was the man on whose head a price had been put. What he knew was that Jean-Sans- Nom ought to be at the farm of Chipogan. And this is how he had again got on his track.

A few days before Jean had been met five or six leagues from Saint-Charles, after leaving Maison Close, and had been reported as a suspicious stranger as he left the country of Verchères. Noticing that the alarm had been given, he had fled into the interior of the county, and, not without many narrow escapes of falling into the hands of the police, he had reached Thomas Harcher's farm.

But Rip's men had not lost sight of him, as he thought, and they were soon almost certain that he had taken refuge at Chipogan. Rip was at once communicated with. Knowing not only that the farm belonged to M. de Vaudreuil, but that M. de Vaudreuil was there at that very time, Rip had no doubt but that the stranger was Jean-Sans-Nom; and giving orders to some of his men to mix with the guests at Harcher's, he reported to Gilbert Argall, who put at his disposal a squad of police and a detachment of Montreal volunteers. And under such circumstances, Rip had just reached the doorway, assured that Jean-Sans-Nom was among the guests of the farmer of Chipogan.

It was five o'clock in the afternoon. The lamps were not alight, and it was still daylight in the room. In an instant Rip had looked round the company, but Jean- Sans-Nom received no more of his attention than the rest.

Thomas Harcher, seeing his courtyard invaded by a body of men, rose and said to Rip, —

"Who are you?"

"I have my orders from the minister of police."

"What to do?"

"You will hear. Are you not Thomas Harcher of Chipogan?"

"Yes, and I demand by what right you enter my house."

"In accordance with the duty that has been entrusted to me. I am about to make an arrest."

"An arrest!" exclaimed the farmer — " an arrest in my house! — and who is it to be?"

"A man for whose apprehension a reward has been offered by the Governor, and who is here!"

"His name."

"He calls himself," said Rip, in a loud voice, "or rather he is called, Jean-Sans-Nom!"

145

The reply was followed by a long murmur. What! It was Jean-Sans-Nom whom Rip had come to arrest, and whom he affirmed was at the farm of Chipogan.

The attitude of the farmer, of his wife and his children, and all present, was so obviously that of profound astonishment, that Rip thought his men must have been on a false scent Nevertheless he reiterated his demand, and this time still more decidedly.

"Thomas Harcher," he said, "the man I seek is here, and I summon you to deliver him up."

At these words Thomas Harcher looked at his wife, and Catherine, seizing his arm, said, —

"Answer him."

"Yes, Thomas," said Mr. Nick, "answer him. It seems to me that the reply is easy enough."

"Very easy in fact," said the farmer, who, turning towards Rip, continued, "Jean-Sans-Nom is not at the farm of Chipogan."

"And I say he is, Thomas Harcher!" said Rip quietly.

"No, I tell you, he is not! He has never been here! I do not even know him! But I say that if he had come to ask me for shelter I would have given it him, and if he was in this house; I would not surrender him."

There could be no mistake about the significant demonstrations with which the farmer's announcement was received. Thomas Harcher had expressed the sentiment of all who were with him. If Jean-Sans-Nom had taken refuge at the farm there was not one who could be base enough to betray him.

Jean, impassable all the time, heard all that passed. M. de Vaudreuil and Clary dared not even look at him for fear of drawing Rip's attention towards him.

"Thomas Harcher," continued Rip, "you are doubtless aware that by a proclamation, dated the 3rd of September, 1837, a reward of six thousand dollars is offered to whoever will arrest or cause to be arrested this Jean-Sans-Nom!"

"I know it," said the farmer, "and all in Canada know it. But there has not yet been found a Canadian scoundrel enough to commit so odious a betrayal, and he never will be found."

"Well said, Thomas!" exclaimed Catherine, and her children and friends supported her.

Rip continued unmoved, —

"Thomas Harcher," he said, "if you know of the proclamation of the 3rd September, 1837, perhaps you do not know of the new announcement which the Governor- General made yesterday, under date of the 6th October!"

"I do not know of it," said the farmer, "and if it is like the other, and offers an encouragement to traitors, you need not inform me of it."

"You shall hear it all the same," replied Rip, and unfolding a paper, he read as follows: —

"'It is required of all inhabitants of the Canadian towns and territories that they should refuse help and protection to Jean-Sans-Nom, on pain of death to all who give him shelter.

"' For the Governor-General.

"' Gilbert Argall.

Minister of Police.'"

And so the Government had gone to this length! After TART I. — M

offering a reward for Jean-Sans-Nom, they had now threatened the death penalty against whoever gave him shelter!

The act provoked the most violent protests on the part of all present. Thomas Harcher, his sons, his guests had risen from their seats to rush at Rip, and chase him from the farm with all his police and volunteers, when Mr. Nick interposed.

His look was serious. Like the rest of those in the room, he felt a very natural horror at the new announcement of Lord Gosford which Rip had just read.

"Monsieur Rip," he said, "he whom you seek is not at the farm of Chipogan. Thomas Harcher has told you so, and I reiterate it. You have therefore nothing

147

to do here, and you would have done better to have kept that regrettable document in your pocket. Believe me, Monsieur Rip, you would be well advised not to force your presence on us any longer."

"Well said, Nicholas Sagamore!" said Lionel.

"Yes! Go away — at once!" said the farmer, whose voice trembled with anger. "Jean-Sans-Nom is not here! But if he comes — in spite of the governor's menaces — I will receive him! Now, leave the house! Leave it, I say!"

"Yes! Yes! leave it!" said Lionel, whose exasperation Mr. Nick tried in vain to calm.

"Take care, Thomas Harcher!" replied Rip, "you will do no good against the law, nor against the force I have to support me. Police and volunteers, I have fifty men with me. Your house is surrounded."

"Get out! clear out!"

And shouts arose, and threats were directed against Rip.

"I will not go until I have made sure of the identity of all those who are here! "said Rip.

At a sign from him the police from the courtyard approached the door ready to enter the room.

Through the windows Monsieur de Vaudreuil and his daughter could see the volunteers posted round the house.

In view of an imminent collision, the children and women, with the exception of Clary and Catherine, hurried into the neighbouring rooms. Pierre Marcher and his brothers and friends had taken down the weapons hung on the walls. But inferior as they were in numbers, how could they prevent Rip from doing his duty?

Monsieur de Vaudreuil went from window to window to see if Jean could escape in the rear of the farm by crossing the garden. But in this direction, as in the other=, flight was impracticable.

Amid the tumult Jean remained motionless by the side of Clary, who would not leave him.

148

Mr. Nick then tried a last effort at conciliation, as the police were about to enter the room.

"Mr. Rip! Mr. Rip!" he said, "you are going to cause bloodshed, and quite uselessly, I assure you! I repeat, and I give you my word, Jean-Sans-Nom is not at the farm."

"And if he were," said Thomas Marcher, "I repeat, I would fight for him till death!"

"Good! Good!" said Catherine, rendered enthusiastic by her husband's attitude.

"Do not you interfere in this matter, Mr. Nick!" said Rip. "It does not concern you, and you may have to repent too late! I will do my duty whatever happens! And now, make room there! Make room there!"

A dozen police entered the room, and Thomas Harcher and his friends rushed at them to turn them out and shut the door.

And Mr. Nick shouted as a last effort, — "Jean-Sans-Nom is not here. Mr. Rip, I assure you he is not here!"

"He is here!" said a loud voice that made itself heard above the uproar.

There was silence for a moment.

Jean, motionless, with his arms crossed, looked straight at Rip and said, —

"I am Jean-Sans-Nom!"

Monsieur de Vaudreuil had seized the young man's arm, while Thomas Harcher and the others exclaimed, —

"He! Is he Jean-Sans-Nom?"

Jean showed with a gesture that he wished to speak. There was silence again.

"I am the man you seek," he said to Rip; "I am Jean- Sans-Nom."

And then, turning to the farmer and his sons, he continued —

"Forgive me, Thomas Harcher, forgive me, my brave companions, if I have hidden from you who I was, and thank you for the hospitality which for five years I have received at the farm of Chipogan. But the hospitality, which I

149

accepted so long as it caused you no danger, I can accept no longer now it means death to all who give me shelter! Yes, thanks on the part of him who was here but your adopted son, and who is Jean Sans-Nom for his country!"

An indescribable movement of enthusiasm received this declaration.

"Vive Jean-Sans-Nom! Vive Jean-Sans-Nom!" resounded on all sides.

And when the shouts had ceased, Thomas Harcher said. —

"And now, as I said we would fight for Jean-Sans-Nom, let us fight for him till death."

In vain Jean would have interposed to stop so unequal a strife. No one would listen to him. Pierre and the elder ones threw themselves on the police who obstructed the doorway and thrust them out. The door was immediately shut and barricaded with the heavy furniture. To get into the room or even into the house, the only way was by the windows, which were a dozen feet from the ground.

An attack would have to be made, and that in the dark.

for the night had begun to fall. Rip, who was not a man to give way, took his measures for executing his warrant and launching the volunteers against the house.

Pierre Harcher, with his friends and companions, posted himself at the windows ready to fire.

"We will defend you, in spite of yourself, if necessary!" said they to Jean, who was now powerless to stop them.

The farmer had prevailed on Clary de Vaudreuil and Catherine to rejoin the other women in one of the side rooms, where they would be safe out of gunshot. Only the men were left in the room, thirty all told.

For the Mahogannis could not be reckoned among the defenders of the farm. The Indians were indifferent to all that had passed, and had maintained their habitual reserve. The matter did not concern them no more than it did Mr. Nick and his clerk, who had no side to take either for or against authority: and the notary intended to remain absolutely neutral. Resolved to receive no blow and to give none, he did not cease to appeal to Lionel, who was breathing forth fire and flame. Bah! the young clerk would hardly listen to him, so excited was he at the chance of fighting for Jean-Sans-Nom, who was not only the popular hero, but also the sympathetic listener who had so favourably received his attempts at poetry.

"For the last time," said Mr. Nick, "I forbid you from mixing yourself up in this matter!"

"And for the last time," said Lionel, "I am astonished that a descendant of the Sagamores refuses to follow me on the war-path!"

"I will follow no other path but that of peace, you stupid boy, and you will do me the favour of leaving the room, where you can only get some injury done you."

"Never!" exclaimed the bellicose poet.

And from one of the Mahogannis he seized the tomahawk that hung from his belt.

Jean began to organize the resistance as soon as he saw that his companions had decided to meet force with force. During the struggle he might manage to escape, and now, whatever might happen, the farmer and his people were in open rebellion against authority, and could not be more compromised than they were already. Rip and his men must first be driven off. Then he could see what was best to be done. If the assailants tried to break in the doors of the house, it would take time. And before reinforcements arrived from Laprairie and Montreal, the police and volunteers might be driven out of the courtyard. And so Jean resolved to make a sortie and clear the approaches.

Arrangements were made accordingly. To begin with, a score of gunshots rattled from the front windows, and Rip and his men were obliged to retreat to the palisades. Then the door was quickly opened, and Jean, followed by Monsieur de Vaudreuil, Thomas Harcher, Pierre, and his brothers and friends, rushed into the courtyard.

A few volunteers lay on the ground. Some of the defenders were also wounded, as in the semi-darkness they hurled themselves on the besiegers. A hand-to-hand struggle followed, in which Rip bravely took his share. But his men began to lose ground; if they were to be driven out of the gate and have it shut against them, they would find it very difficult to get over the high palisading.

To drive them out, Jean and his brave companions tried every effort. If he could do so, he might get away across country, and even beyond the Canadian frontier, to wait till the time came for him to reappear at the head of the insurgents.

It need not be said, that although Lionel had gallantly joined the combatants, Mr. Nick had not left the house. Resolved to maintain strict neutrality, he did no more than wish well to Jean-Sans-Nom and all the defenders, among whom he had so many personal friends.

But notwithstanding their bravery, the inhabitants of the farm could not make head against the police and volunteers, who began to get the better of them. They had to retreat little by little towards the house for shelter. The room would then be invaded. All issue would be cut off, and Jean-Sans-Nom would have to surrender.

And the forces of the besieged were sensibly diminish- in"-. Already two of the elder Harchers, Michael and Jacques, and three or four of their companions had been carried into one of the adjoining rooms, where Clary de Vaudreuil, Catherine, and the other women took care of them. And the battle would be lost if some reinforcement did not come to Jean's rescue.

Suddenly a change occurred in the state of affairs.

Lionel had just run into the room covered with blood from a flesh wound in his shoulder.

Mr. Nick caught sight of him.

"Lionel! Lionel!" he exclaimed, "you would not listen to me, you insupportable boy!"

And seizing the young clerk in his arms lie would have dragged him into the room with the wounded.

Lionel refused.

"It is nothing! It is nothing!" said he. "But, Nicholas Sagamore will you let your friends be beaten, when your warriors are only waiting for a word from you to help them?"

"No! No!" exclaimed Mr. Nick, "I have no right to give it! To take part against the constituted authorities!"

And as one very last effort he threw himself among the combatants, to stop them by his objurgations.

And he met with no success, but was immediately surrounded by the police and dragged out into the courtyard.

This was too much for the Mahoganni warriors, whose bellicose instincts could not stand this sort of thing. What! Their great chief arrested and ill-treated! A Sagamore in the hands of his enemies, the Pale Faces!

It was too much! And the war-cry was heard above the din of battle.

"Forward! Forward, Hurons!" shouted Lionel, who was quite beside himself.

The intervention of the Indians suddenly changed the fortunes of the strife. Tomahawk in hand, they hurled themselves at their assailants, who, exhausted by the hour's battle, began to retreat.

Jean-Sans-Nom, Thomas Harcher, and their friends felt that a well-sustained effort would drive Rip and his men out of the enclosure. They re-took the offensive. The Hurons vigorously helped them, after rescuing Mr. Nick, who was astonished to find himself encouraging them with his voice if not with his hand, which was still incapable of flourishing the tomahawk of his ancestors.

And that was how a notary of Montreal, the most pacific of men, got into trouble for defending a cause which concerned neither the Mahogannis nor their chief.

The police and volunteers were soon forced through the gate, and as the Indians pursued them for a mile beyond the neighbourhood, Chipogan was completely cleared.

It was a bad business, evidently, and would figure on the wrong side in the next profit and loss account of Messrs Rip and Co.

PART TWO

INTO THE ABYSS

CHAPTER I - THE OPENING SKIRMISH

The affair at Chipogan Farm had far-reaching repercussions. From Laprairie County the news quickly spread through the neighbouring provinces. Public opinion could hardly have found a more favourable opportunity for expressing itself. This was not merely a brush between the police and the French-Canadians — a brush in which the agents of the law and the loyal volunteers had come off second best. What was much more serious was the motive with which the detachment had been sent to Chipogan. Jean-Sans-Nom had reappeared. The chief of police, Gilbert Argall, had learned of his presence at the farm, and had tried to arrest him. The attempt had failed, and the man in whom the French cause was personified was free and would no doubt soon make use of his freedom.

Where had Jean-Sans-Nom taken refuge, after he left Chipogan? The most active, the most careful, the most persistent search had not disclosed his hiding-place. But, although much disappointed at his failure, Rip did not despair of success. Besides his own personal interest the reputation of his firm was at stake, and he would play out the game until he won. The government knew whom they had to deal with, and neither withdrew their confidence from him nor spared their encouragement. And now Rip, having been face to face with the young Reformist, knew him personally. He was no longer pursuing him in the dark.

Since the fiasco at Chipogan a fortnight had elapsed. The last week of October had begun, and whatever he did Rip could learn nothing.

The day after the attack, Thomas Harcher found he had to leave Chipogan. He put in order all his most pressing business and set off with his older sons across the forests of Laprairie County, to take refuge in the United States territory, impatient to see how events would turn out. St. Albans, on Lake Champlain, offered him every security. There the police agents could not reach him.

If the movement stimulated by Jean-Sans-Nom were successful, if Lower Canada recovered its autonomy and were freed from Anglo-Saxon oppression, Thomas Harcher would quietly return to Chipogan; if not, he could stay and hope that oblivion would come with time, or that an amnesty would cover the past offences and things would gradually resume their former course.

The farm was not left without a mistress. During the winter, when agricultural work was suspended, nothing would suffer under Catherine's superintendence. And Pierre and his brother could still go on with their hunting across the regions adjoining the Canadian colony. In six months there would in all probability be nothing to stop their recommencing their fishing along the St. Lawrence.

Thomas Harcher had only too good reason for getting into safety. Next day Chipogan was occupied by a detachment of regular troops from Montreal. Catherine, having nothing to fear for her husband and her older sons, those more directly compromised in the affair, made the troops welcome. The police, by the governor's orders, did nothing in the way of reprisals, and the energetic woman knew how to keep herself respected by her garrison.

As at Chipogan Farm, so at the Villa Montcalm. The authorities watched it, but did not occupy it. M. de Vaudreuil, realising that he had openly espoused the Reformist cause, took care not to return to his home. A warrant for his arrest had been issued, and had he not taken to flight he would have been imprisoned in Montreal, so that he could no longer have taken his place in the insurrection. Where did he hide? With one of his political friends, no doubt, but so secretly that it was impossible to find exactly where he had taken refuge.

Clary de Vaudreuil returned alone to the Villa Montcalm, where she kept in touch with the leading Reformists. Jean-Sans-Nom she knew to be with his mother at Saint Charles: more than once, by different hands, she had received letters from him. And if Jean spoke only of the political situation she knew full well what else was disturbing his heart.

The part that the Hurons had played in the Chipogan affair will not have been forgotten: but for their intervention the volunteers would not have been repulsed, and Jean-Sans-Nom would have fallen into the hands of Rip's myrmidons.

But what had brought about their intervention? Was it the pacific lawyer of Montreal? Certainly not. On the contrary, all his efforts had been directed towards preventing bloodshed. He had thrown himself into the struggle only to separate the combatants. If the Walhatta warriors had taken part in the fight it was simply because Nicholas Sagamore had been seized by the attackers, and was in danger of being treated like a rebel. What was more natural than that the Indian warriors should defend their chief? None the less, their intervention had brought about the repulse and dispersal of the detachment just as it was about to capture the house. So Mr. Nick was responsible for their defeat; and not without reason Mr. Nick felt that his freedom was in danger.

Seeing himself so seriously compromised in a matter that did not really concern him, and not caring, under the circumstances, to return to Montreal until the excitement had calmed down, he had allowed himself to be carried off to Walhatta village, to his ancestral wigwam. His office had to be shut up indefinitely, his practice would suffer, and old Dolly would be in despair. But what was to be done? Better be Nicholas Sagamore among the Mahogannis than Mr. Nick in jail.

Lionel, it need hardly be said, had followed his master to the Indian village, amid the thick woods of Laprairie county. He, too, had fought against the volunteers, and he could not well escape punishment. But if Mr. Nick mourned in petto, Lionel rejoiced continually at the turn events had taken. He had no regret at having fought for Jean-Sans-Nom, the recognised hero of the French-Canadians. He even hoped that matters would not stop there, and that the Indians would declare in favour of the insurgents. Mr. Nick was no longer Mr. Nick; he was a Huron chief. Lionel was no longer his clerk; he was the right hand of the last of the Sagamores.

So there was some reason to fear that the Governor-General would punish the Mahogannis for their intervention at Chipogan. But prudence imposed on Lord Gosford a well-justified restraint. Reprisals would have given the Indian tribes an opportunity of coming to the aid of their brothers, and of rising in mass — a dangerous complication as matters then stood. And so Lord Gosford judged it best not to pursue either the Walhatta warriors or their new chief by right of inheritance, and Mr. Nick and Lionel went unmolested in their retreat.

Lord Gosford was carefully following the proceedings of the Reformists, who were still carrying on their agitation. The district around Montreal was especially placed under police supervision, for an insurrectional movement was expected in the adjoining parishes of Richelieu. Steps were taken to check it at the outset, if it could not be prevented, and the soldiers under Sir

John Colborne went into quarters in Montreal county and the surrounding regions. The Reformists could not conceal from themselves that the attack would be difficult to withstand, but this did not stop them. Their cause, they felt, would be supported by the whole of the French-Canadians, who only awaited the signal to rush to arms since the affair at Chipogan had revealed the presence of Jean-Sans-Nom. If the popular agitator had not yet given the signal, it was because the anti-Liberal pronouncements he expected from the English Cabinet had not yet been made.

But, concealed in the mysterious Maison-Close, where he had rejoined his mother, Jean had not ceased to watch the course of events. During the six weeks that had elapsed since his arrival at Saint Charles, the Abbé Joann had several times visited his brother at night, to give him the political news. They hoped that the suspension of the 1791 Constitution, and the dissolution or prorogation of the Canadian Assembly, in which this would result, would soon take place.

Twenty times Jean, in his ardour, was on the point of leaving Maison-Close, to traverse the country and sound the call to arms, in the hope that the people of the towns and villages would rise at his voice and make good use of the arms given out from the reformist centres during his last season's fishing on the St. Lawrence. At the very outset, perhaps, the loyalists would be overwhelmed by numbers — and then what could the authorities do but submit? But the Abbé Joann had dissuaded him by pointing out that a first repulse would be dangerous, and would spoil all the chances that might come later. And, indeed, the troops were mustered round Montreal, and ready to advance on any points where rebellion might break out.

The Reformists had, therefore, to act with extreme circumspection, and they felt it advisable to wait until public exasperation had been raised to its height by the measures of Parliament and the exactions of the servants of the Crown.

Hence the delay which, to the extreme impatience of the Sons of Freedom, dragged on interminably.

When Jean had fled from Chipogan he had expected that October would not end before a general insurrection broke out in Lower Canada. But on the 23rd, when there had been nothing so far to indicate that the uprising was near at hand, the measures that Jean had foreseen provoked an outburst.

On the report of the three commissioners they had appointed, the British Parliament had decided that the public revenue should be expended without waiting for approval by the Canadian Assembly, that the leading Reformist Deputies should be prosecuted, that the constitution should be amended by demanding from a French elector double the qualification of an English elector, and that the Ministers should not be responsible to the Chambers.

These violent measures set the whole of Lower Canada in a ferment. They had aroused the patriotic emotions of the French-Canadians; it was more than the people could bear, and on both banks of the St. Lawrence they flocked to the public meetings.

On 15th September, at Laprairie, a meeting took place at which those present included a delegate from France under the orders of the French Government, and the Chargé-d'Affaires of the United States at Quebec.

In several of the most important towns, an immediate break was demanded with Great Britain, the Reformists were urged to pass from words to deeds, and it was decided to apply for help to the United States. A fund was started for the receipt of subscriptions, however small or large, in support of the popular cause.

Processions carried banners with slogans which evoked outbursts of cheers: ' Tyrants begone! The people are awake!'

' Union of the people; terror of the rulers.'

' Rather a bloody battle than the oppression of a corrupt power.'

A black flag, displaying a death's head and cross- bones, bore the names of the most unpopular governors, and in honour of old France a white flag bore on one side an American eagle encircled with stars and on the other a Canadian eagle holding in its beak a sprig of maple with these words: — ' Our future! Free as the air!'

These showed how excited the people had become. Great Britain had some reason to fear that the colony would at one blow sever the bond that bound it to herself. The representatives of the authority took serious steps to cope with a supreme struggle, but all they were willing to see were the threats of a faction while they were really faced with a national awakening.

On 23rd October there was a meeting at St. Charles, the village where Jean-Sans-Nom was in hiding at his mother's. Six counties had sent their representatives, thirteen deputies spoke, and among them was Papineau, then at the height of his popularity. More than six thousand persons, men, women and children, assembled from ten leagues round, were encamped in a large field around a column surmounted by a Cap of Liberty. And to show that the military element made common cause with the civilians, a company of the militia were brandishing their weapons at the foot of the column.

Papineau, in a speech preceded by even more fiery orators, seemed, if anything, too moderate in advising the crowd to keep within the bounds of constitutional agitation.

In reply, the chairman, amid frantic interruptions, retorted: ' The time has come to melt our spoons into bullets! ' And the representative of Acadie improved upon this by his energetic words: ' The time for talk is over! Now it's lead that we must hurl against our enemies!'

Thirteen resolutions were then adopted, while the cheering was reinforced by salvoes of musketry from the militia.

The resolutions began by affirming the rights of man and the right and the need to resist a tyrannical government; they then incited the British soldiers to desert their colours, encouraged the people to refuse to submit to the magistrates and to those officers of the militia who were nominated by the government, and finally to organise themselves as the Sons of Freedom.

Then Papineau and his colleagues filed before the symbolic column, while a choir of the young people chanted a hymn at the tops of their voices.

It seemed that enthusiasm could reach no greater height than this. Yet it did, for after a few moment's silence somebody else appeared upon the scene. This was a young man whose face showed a passionate enthusiasm: climbing on to the pedestal of the column, he raised above the heads of the thousands around him the flag of Canadian independence. Several of the people recognised him, but even before they did so, the lawyer Gramont shouted his name, and the crowd repeated it amid frantic cheers: 'Jean-Sans-Nom! Jean-Sans-Nom! ' Jean had just left Maison-Close. For the first time since the last insurrection in 1836, he showed himself publicly; then, having added his name to those of the other agitators, he disappeared. But he had been seen once more and the effect was immense.

161

What had taken place at St. Charles was soon known all over Lower Canada, and the resulting enthusiasm may well be imagined. Further meetings were held in most of the other parishes. In vain the Bishop of Montreal, Monsignor Lartique, tried to calm the excitement by counselling evangelical moderation. The explosion was close at hand. M. de Vaudreuil, in his hiding-place, Clary at the Villa Montcalm, received two letters whose handwriting they well knew. The same information reached Thomas Harcher and his sons at St. Albans, the American village in which they were waiting to cross the frontier.

At this season of the year, the winter sets in with that suddenness peculiar to the climate of North America.

The broad plains offer no obstacle to the storms from the Polar Regions, and the Gulf Stream, swerving towards Europe, fails to heat them by its generous waters. There is no transition, so to speak, between the warmth of summer and the cold of winter. The rain falls almost incessantly, traversed occasionally by a fugitive ray of sunshine robbed of its heat. In a few days the trees, stripped bare to the tips of their branches, have strewn the ground with a shower of leaves which the snow will soon bury all over the Canadian territory. But neither the attacks of the storm nor the exacting temperature of the climate would keep the patriots from rising at the first signal.

It was under these conditions that, on 6th November, the two parties came into collision at Montreal.

On the first Monday of each month the Sons of Freedom assembled in the large towns to make a public demonstration. On this occasion the Montreal Reformists wanted to make the demonstration as large as possible, and the meeting was called in the very heart of the city, between the walls of a court leading out of the Rue Saint Jacques.

At the news of the meeting the members of the Doric Club posted up a proclamation that the time had come to crush the rebellion at its birth, and inviting the loyalists, the constitutionalists, and the bureaucrats, to meet on the Place d'Armes.

The Reformist meeting was held at the time and place indicated, and Papineau was warmly applauded, while other orators also won enthusiastic acclamations.

Suddenly a shower of stones fell into the court. The loyalists were attacking the Reformists. Armed with sticks, the latter formed themselves up in five columns, rushed out, threw themselves on the members of the Doric Club, and drove them back to the Place d'Armes. Then pistol-shots rang out here and there. One of the orators received a violent blow which stretched him on the ground, and one of the most determined Reformists had his thigh pierced by a bullet.

The members of the Doric Club, though repulsed, did not regard themselves as beaten. Knowing that the redcoats would come to their aid, they dispersed along the streets of Montreal, broke Panineau's windows, and sacked the office of the Vindicator, a Liberal newspaper, which had long supported the French-Canadian cause.

Because of this outbreak the Reformists were investigated, and warrants were issued for the arrest of the leaders, who had to take flight. Monsieur de Vaudreuil, who had come out of hiding, was again forced to seek refuge in his hiding-place, where the police had sought for him in vain since the affair at Chipogan.

And it was then that Jean-Sans-Nom again appeared.

After the bloodshed which had occurred on 6th November, a few of the leading citizens had been arrested not far from Montreal, and on the 22nd a detachment of cavalry was escorting them to the city.

One of the boldest advocates of the national cause, ' the handsome Viger ' — as the insurgents called him — was notified of the arrest of two of his friends, though the man who brought the message was unknown to him.

'Who are you?' asked Viger.

'That doesn't matter,' the man replied. ' The prisoners are in a carriage which is now approaching Longueil, and they've got to be rescued.

'Are you alone?'

'My friends are waiting for me.'

'Where shall we join them?'

'On the road.'

'Come along, then!'

And off they went. Neither Viger nor his companion lacked for supporters, and they reached Longueil at the head of a number of patriots, whom they posted in front of the village. But the alarm had been given, and a detachment of loyalists ran up to reinforce the escort. The officer in command then warned the people of the village that if they joined Viger their homes would be given to the flames.

'Nothing to be done here,' the unknown decided when these threats were reported to him. ' Come on.'

'Where to?' asked Viger.

'Two miles from here. Don't let's give the bureaucrats an excuse for any reprisals. They may come only too soon!'

'Let's get on! ' Viger agreed.

Followed by their men, they crossed the fields. Reaching Trudeau Farm, they took up their position in a nearby field. It was time. A cloud of dust, rising a quarter of a mile away, announced the approach of the prisoners and their escort.

The carriage arrived, and at once Viger went up to the officer in command.

'Halt!' he snapped. ' And hand over your prisoners in the name of the people!'

'Look out there!' the officer shouted to his men. ' Ready!'

'Halt!' repeated the stranger.

Suddenly someone rushed to seize him. This was one of Rip and Co.'s men — one of those who had been at Chipogan Farm.

'Jean-Sans-Nom!' he shouted as soon as he had confronted him.

'Jean-Sans-Nom!' exclaimed Viger, dashing up to his companion.

And suddenly, with irresistible enthusiasm, the cheers broke out.

As the officer was ordering his men to capture Jean- Sans-Nom, he was overthrown by a sturdy Canadian, who had jumped into the road. Meanwhile the others posted behind the hedge were awaiting orders from Viger. He gave them as loudly and confidently as if he had a hundred followers.

Meanwhile Jean had made for the carriage; he was accompanied by several comrades, as determined to defend him as they were to free the captives. But as soon as the officer had regained his feet he gave the word to fire. Six or seven shots rang out. Viger was struck by two bullets, though not mortally; one grazed his leg, the other carried away the tip of his little finger. He replied with a shot from his pistol, and wounded the leader of the escort in the knee.

Then a panic broke out among the detachment's horses, several of which had been wounded. Thinking they had to do with a thousand men, the loyalists dispersed across the country and the carriage was left unguarded. Jean-Sans-Nom and Viger threw open its doors, and the prisoners were released, and escorted in triumph into a village nearby.

But when the affair was over, and Viger and his companions looked around for Jean, he was nowhere to be found. No doubt he had hoped to keep his incognito until the fight was over, for he had had no reason to suppose that he would meet with one of Rip's men, and that his identity would be revealed. Now the fight was over, he had hastened to disappear without anyone's noticing which way he had gone. And yet none of the reformists doubted but that they would see him again when the blow was to be struck which was to give Canada her independence.

CHAPTER II - ST. DENIS AND ST. CHARLES

The day could not be far distant when the people would rush to arms. Already both factions were ready. But where would be the field of battle? Evidently in the regions near Montreal, where the popular effervescence was rapidly assuming proportions disquieting to the Government; especially demanding attention were the two rich parishes traversed by the Richelieu stream and situated a few leagues apart. They were St. Denis, where the Reformists were centralised, and St. Charles, where Jean, who had returned to Maison-Close, was preparing to give the signal for the insurrection.

The Governor-General had taken all the measures that circumstances demanded. To surprise him in his Residence, to imprison him, to substitute the popular for the royal authority, was no longer to be dreamed of even by the most enthusiastic of the reformists. The attack might well come from the bureaucrats; and the Reformists had had to take up positions where resistance could be organised most favourably. To transform the defensive into the offensive, that was their aim. A victory here would mean that the people would rise on each side of the St. Lawrence, and so lead to the annihilation of Anglo-Saxon tyranny from the mouth of the river to Lake Ontario.

Lord Gosford was fully aware of this. His troops were but few, and if the revolt became general, they would be overwhelmed by numbers. Hence it was advisable to strike at the disaffection by a double blow, at St. Denis and at St. Charles. And this was what he attempted after the affair at Longueil.

Sir John Colborne, the commander-in-chief, divided his army into two columns. At the head of one was Lieutenant-Colonel Wetherall; at that of the other was Colonel Gore.

Colonel Gore's preparations were soon made, and he left Montreal on the 22nd of November. His column consisted of five companies of fusiliers and a detachment of cavalry, but his artillery was limited to one field gun. He reached Sorel on the evening of the same day. Although the weather was abominable and the road almost impracticable, he did not hesitate to get on the march in the middle of a very dark night.

His plan was to attack the insurgents at St. Charles after he had dispersed those at St. Denis, but first he meant to make certain arrests, to be carried out by the deputy-sheriff who was accompanying him. He had already left Sorel a few hours previously when Lieutenant Weir of the 32nd regiment arrived with a despatch from Sir John Colborne. The despatch being urgent, the lieutenant at once set out after him, but as he travelled across country, he reached St. Denis before the troops, and there he fell into the hands of the patriots.

Doctor Nelson, who was in charge of the defence, interrogated the young officer, and extracted the information that the troops were already on the march, and would arrive in the morning. And he then handed over the lieutenant to a few of his men to be treated with the respect due to a prisoner of war.

The preparations were hurriedly completed. Among other companies of the patriots were those who called themselves the ' Beavers ' and the ' Snow-shoes,' who were skilled in the use of arms, and whose conduct was to be very brilliant in the affair that followed. Under Nelson's orders were Papineau and a few other deputies, as well as De Vaudreuil, and his comrades. At a hint from Jean they had come to rally the Reformists, although they had not found it easy to elude the Montreal police.

Clary de Vaudreuil, too, had just arrived with her father, whom she had not seen since they left Chipogan. Because of the warrant issued against him, De Vaudreuil had been forced to cease all communication with the Villa Montcalm, and he had been very uneasy at leaving his daughter alone and exposed to so many dangers. When he decided to go to St. Denis he had sent word to ask her to join him there, and this Clary did without hesitation, never doubting a definite success, for, as she knew, Jean was about to put himself at the head of the Reformists. M. de Vaudreuil and his daughter were thus re-united in a friend's house in the village.

A decision was then reached by the leaders, and to this Papineau had to consent, very much against his will. Dr. Nelson and a few others reminded this courageous deputy that his place was not on the battle-field, and that his life was too valuable for him to risk needlessly. So he felt it his duty to leave St. Denis for some place of safety where he could be out of reach of the police agents.

The whole night was spent in casting bullets and making cartridges. The doctor's son, with his comrades and De Vaudreuil and his friends, had got to work without losing an instant. Unfortunately their armament left much to be desired. Their muskets were few, and were only flint-locks, which often missed fire, and whose range did not exceed a hundred yards. During his expedition on the St. Lawrence, Jean, it will be remembered, had distributed arms and ammunition. But as each county had to have its share with a view to a general rising, these weapons could not be concentrated at any one centre — this would have been desirable at St. Charles and St. Denis, where the first shock was to take place.

During that cold, dark night Colonel Gore advanced on St. Denis. Just before he reached it two French- Canadians fell into his hands, and they informed him that the insurgents would not let him enter the village and that they would fight on till death.

Colonel Gore, without giving his men any rest, harangued them, and warned them they were to expect no quarter. Then, dividing them into three detachments, he stationed one in a small wood covering the village on the east, another along the river, while the third, with its one gun, advanced along the road.

At six in the morning Dr. Nelson, Vincent Hodge and De Vaudreuil mounted their horses to reconnoitre the road from St. Ours. The darkness was still so deep that they nearly fell into the hands of the advance guard of the regulars. Retreating at once, they returned to St. Denis, and gave orders to break down the bridges, and ring an alarm from the church bell. In a few minutes the Reformists had mustered.

How many were there? From seven to eight hundred, a few armed with muskets, the others only with scythes, forks, or pikes, but all determined to die in repulsing Colonel Gore's forces.

Dr. Nelson posted sixty of those men who had muskets in the upper floor of a stone house by the roadside; among these were M. de Vaudreuil and Vincent Hodge. Twenty-five yards away, behind the walls of a distillery, were thirty of the others, including William Clerc and Farran. In a store nearby were a dozen men under the orders of the Deputy Gramont. Those who had to trust to cold steel were in ambush behind the walls of the churchyard.

After half-past nine that morning, just as the final arrangements were made, there came a tragic event which was never thoroughly cleared up, not even at the criminal investigation which took place later.

Lieutenant Weir, who was being escorted along the road, caught sight of Colonel Gore's advance guard, and tried to escape so as to rejoin it; but he slipped, and before he could regain his feet he was killed by a sword-thrust.

The battle then began. A cannon-ball aimed at the stone house struck two men just as a third was shot at one of the windows. For a few minutes there was a brisk exchange of fire. The soldiers in the open paid dearly for the contemptuous indifference with which they exposed themselves to the fire of these ' peasants,' as their leader had called them. They were decimated by the defenders in the stone house, and three of the gunners fell, fuses in hand, at the piece which they were serving.

The projectiles, however, broke down the wall, and soon the upper floor of the house no longer afforded any shelter.

'To the ground floor!' shouted Dr. Nelson.

'Yes,' added Vincent Hodge, ' and then we'll be nearer the red-coats.'

They went down, and the musketry once more began with renewed violence. The reformists displayed extraordinary courage, even advancing up the road right into the open. The doctor sent his aide-de-camp to order them to retire, but the man fell dead, shot in two places.

For an hour the musketry duel continued, on the whole to the disadvantage of the assailants, who had now taken cover behind the walls and the piles of wood. Then Colonel Gore, seeing that his ammunition was running out, ordered Captain Markman to turn the position.

This Markman attempted to do, not without losing the greater part of his men. He himself was hit and thrown off his horse, so that he had to be carried to the rear by his soldiers. Things were already going badly for the royalists, when there came a loud shouting in the road, and they realised that an attempt was being made to surround them.

A man had suddenly appeared on the scene — that very man around whom the French-Canadians were used to rallying as they would round a flag.

'Jean-Sans-Nom! Jean-Sans-Nom!' they shouted, as they brandished their weapons.

169

It was Jean, at the head of a hundred insurgents from the other villages. They had crossed the Richelieu under fire, and one of the missiles had broken the oar of the boat in which Jean had been standing.

'Forward, Snow-shoes and Beavers!' he shouted, as he led his comrades on.

At his voice, the patriots rushed upon the royalists, while those besieged in the house, encouraged by this unexpected reinforcement, made a sortie. Colonel Gore had to beat a retreat towards Sorel, leaving a number of prisoners and his one gun in the hands of the victors. He had lost thirty killed and as many wounded, as against twelve killed and four wounded on the side of the reformists.

Such was the affair at St. Denis. In a few hours the news of the victory spread through the whole region, and even to the riverside counties of the St. Lawrence.

This was encouraging for the reformists; but it was only a beginning. And as they were waiting for orders, Jean shouted these words, as though making a rendezvous for another victory: 'Patriots — on to St. Charles!'

He had not forgotten that the village was threatened by Colonel Wetherall.

An hour later, M. de Vaudreuil and Jean, after bidding farewell to Clary, whom they had told of their victory, had rejoined their companions on the road to St. Charles. Thence he would lead his comrades on.

There, two days later, was to be decided the fate of the 1837 insurrection.

The village, where the Reformists had concentrated their forces, had become the main centre of the rebellion, and it was on this that Colonel Wetherall was marching in considerable strength.

Here Brown and the other leaders had organised the defence. They could trust the fiery population, who had already shown their feelings by expelling one of the gentry, accused of favouring the English-Canadians; and it was round this person's house that Brown, the insurgent leader, had formed a camp where he could concentrate all the forces he had at his disposal.

St. Denis is not more than six miles from St. Charles, where the sound of the guns had been heard during the 23rd. Before night its people had heard that the royal troops had been forced to beat a retreat towards Sorel. The impression produced by this first victory was profound: the doors of all the houses were thrown wide open, and the people swarmed out into the street, a prey to a kind of patriotic delirium.

One house alone remained shut — the Maison-Close by the turning in the main road, some distance away from the camp. Bridget's dwelling was thus in less danger than those further in if the camp should be attacked and stormed by the royal troops.

Bridget, still as ever alone, was waiting ready to receive her sons, if circumstances should force them to seek shelter. But just then the Abbé Joann was visiting the parishes of Upper Canada and preaching insurrection; and Jean, no longer hiding himself, had reappeared at the head of the patriots. His name was now passing from mouth to mouth all along the St. Lawrence. Cut off from the world as Maison-Close was, the name had reached it, and with it the news of the victory at St. Denis, with which he was so intimately associated.

And Bridget was wondering whether Jean would not come to the camp at St. Charles, to visit his mother, to cross her threshold to tell her what he had done and what he meant to do, and to embrace her perhaps for the last time. But that depended on the course the insurrection took, and so she kept herself ready at any time of the night or day to receive her son at Maison-Close.

Hearing of the defeat at St. Denis, Lord Gosford, fearing that the victors would reinforce the patriots at St. Charles, had sent orders to Colonel Wetherall to retreat. "It was too late. The messengers despatched from Montreal by Sir John Colborne were stopped on the road, and instead of retiring the column continued its movement on St. Charles. It was now impossible for anyone to prevent the encounter between the insurgents stationed at the village and the soldiers of the regular army.

On the 24th Jean-Sans-Nom had reached the defenders of the camp at St. Charles, and with him had come De Vaudreuil, Farran, Clerc, Hodge and Gramont. Two days previously farmer Harcher and his five sons, after leaving St. Albans, had crossed the American frontier and come to St. Charles, resolved to do their duty to the end.

It must be realised that no one doubted of a final success, neither the political leaders of the opposition party, nor De Vaudreuil and his friends, nor Thomas Harcher, nor his valiant sons, nor any of the village people, who were over-excited at the thought that it had fallen to them to strike the last blow at Anglo- Saxon tyranny.

Before attacking St. Charles, Lieutenant-Colonel Wetherall had told Brown and his followers that if they would surrender they would come to no harm. This proposal was unanimously rejected: that it had been made at all showed that the royalists felt themselves unable to capture the camp. No! they must never be allowed to march on St. Denis and take sanguinary reprisals. As soon as Wetherall's column appeared, it would be repulsed, it would be dispersed. A new defeat awaited the royalists, a complete defeat, assuring a final victory. Such was the belief of the patriots.

But it would be wrong to suppose that the defenders of the camp were in great strength. They were only a handful of men, but they were the élite of the party. Leaders and rank and file numbered only a couple of hundred, armed with scythes, pikes, clubs, and fire-lock muskets, and in reply to the royal artillery they had but two guns, and these were almost unserviceable.

While they were making ready to receive him, Colonel Wetherall marched rapidly towards them, unhindered by the obstacles which winter can produce in these regions. The weather was cold, and the earth dry, so that the men could make good progress, and the guns rolled easily over the hardened ground, without having to be dragged through the snow or the swamps.

The reformists were ready for them. Enthusiastic at their previous victory, electrified by the presence of their leaders, and above all by that of Jean-Sans-Nom, the reception they gave to Colonel Wetherall's proposals had already been described. To his demand for them to lay down their arms, they were ready to reply with musket-shots, and scythe-swings, and pike-thrusts.

However, the camp, being at the end of the town, had certain disadvantages which there was no time to remedy. It was covered on one side by a river, and defended on the other by a thick abattis of trees which surrounded the house, and it had been protected by entrenchments, but it was commanded by a hill to its rear which the insurgents were not strong enough to occupy.

If the royalists were to capture this hill, there would be no shelter, except the house, which they had pierced with loop-holes. Could it in such circumstances withstand an assault, and if they were besieged, would Brown and his comrades be in sufficient force to repulse their assailants?

About two in the afternoon, a distant noise was heard, and much disorder followed. A number of women and children, and old men, were seen hastening across the fields towards St. Charles. They were the country-people in full flight. In the distance thick clouds of smoke were rising in the air. As far as the eye could reach all the farm-houses were in flames. Wetherall's columns were advancing through the desolation and slaughter which marked his path.

Brown succeeded in stopping such of the fugitives as were in a condition to fight; leaving the command to Marchessault, he went out to rally them. Marchessault made the final arrangements, and stationed his forces under cover of the abattis which protected the camp.

'It is here,' he announced, 'that the fate of our country will be decided! It is here we must defend our country .

'To the death!' exclaimed Jean-Sans-Nom.

And then the sound of gun-fire was heard, and the patriots realised that right from the outset the royal troops were being handled to the best advantage.

For Wetherall to expose himself to the fire of the insurgents drawn up along the abattis would have been most injudicious. With his three or four hundred infantry and cavalry and his two guns, he could easily command the camp and wipe out the defenders. So he gave orders to skirt the entrenchments and to occupy the hill in the rear.

This movement was executed without difficulty. The two guns were dragged up into position, and the fight broke out with equal energy on both sides. And all this had taken place so quickly that Brown, still occupied in rallying the fugitives scattered over the countryside, could not get back to the camp, and had to make off to St. Denis.

Though insufficiently sheltered, the patriots defended their position with admirable courage. De Vaudreuil and the other leaders, with Harcher and his sons, all who had firearms, returned shot for shot to the besiegers' fire. Jean-Sans-Nom encouraged them by his very presence. But what he longed for was the battle-field, the hand-to-hand struggle in which he could lead the bravest. His energy was paralysed by this long-range combat.

This nevertheless lasted as long as the entrenchments held good. If the defenders of the camp had brought down more than one red-coat, they

173

themselves were not without serious losses, for twelve of them had fallen, some wounded, some killed. Amongst these was Remy Harcher, stretched in a pool of blood, his chest torn open by grape-shot. When his brothers lifted him to carry him into the house, life was already extinct. Farran, with his shoulder broken, had been taken there already. De Vaudreuil and Hodge, after putting him in shelter, had returned to their places in the defence.

But soon the house, their last refuge, had to be evacuated. Destroyed by the guns, the abattis no longer protected the camp, and Colonel Wetherall gave orders to carry the position at the point of the bayonet.

Many valiant patriots perished; their ammunition exhausted, they fought on with clubbed muskets. Though some, after a heroic resistance, succeeded in cutting their way through their assailants, there fell so many other Reformists that their number was never known, for the river swept away many of the bodies.

Among those persons more intimately connected with this narrative were several victims. If Jean-Sans-Nom had fought like a lion, always at the head of his men, always in the thick of the fight, openly and known to all who were for or against him, if it were only by a miracle that he escaped unhurt, it was not so with others. Some had been dangerously wounded, and had been carried to the rear by Thomas and Pierre Harcher, who thus saved them from the atrocious massacre that followed. William Clerc and Vincent Hodge as recklessly exposed themselves: a score of times they had been seen in the thick of the fight, musket and pistol in hand. At one critical moment they had followed Jean-Sans- Nom towards the battery on the hill, where he would have been killed had not Vincent Hodge turned aside the blow that one of the gunners had aimed at him.

'Thanks!' said Jean, ' but maybe you were wrong. It will soon be all over now.'

And to his mind it would have been well if the son of Simon Morgaz had fallen there where the cause of freedom was about to perish on the St. Charles battlefield.

He threw himself back into the fight, just in time to see De Vaudreuil lying on the ground, covered with blood. He had received a sabre stroke from one of Wetherall's horsemen who were scouring the neighbourhood to scatter the insurgents.

And then a voice seemed to speak in Jean's mind, a voice which implored: 'Save my father!'

Concealed amid the smoke of the musketry, Jean crawled towards De Vaudreuil, who was by now unconscious and perhaps dead. He took him in his arms, and carried him along the entrenchments; and then, as the horsemen were off pursuing the rebels with unheard-of ferocity, he succeeded in reaching the upper part of St. Charles, among the burning houses. Here he took refuge in the church porch.

It was then five in the evening, and the sky would already have been dark if the flames had not been rising above the ruins of the village. The insurrection, victorious at St. Denis, had been vanquished at St. Charles, nor could it be said that the victory had compensated for the defeat. No! the defeat would have worse results for the national cause than the victory had advanced it; and it had shattered every hope of the insurgents.

Those of the combatants who had not succumbed were forced to disperse without getting any orders for rallying. William Clerc, accompanied by Andrew Farran, who had only been slightly wounded, went off across country and, after many dangers, managed to reach the frontier, not realising what had happened to De Vaudreuil and Hodge.

And now, what would become of Clary de Vaudreuil, in the house at St. Denis, where she was waiting for tidings? Would she not have everything to fear from the reprisals of the loyalists if she could not get away?

So meditated Jean, as he sat hidden in the church. De Vaudreuil had not returned to consciousness, though his heart was beating feebly. If he were seen to at once, could he possibly be saved? Where and how could this be done? There was no room for hesitation. That very night he must take him to Maison-Close.

Maison-Close was not far off — only a few hundred yards, down the main street of the village. In the darkness, as soon as Wetherall's men had left St. Charles, or when they had settled down for the night, Jean could carry the wounded man to his mother's home.

His mother! M. de Vaudreuil with Bridget — with the wife of Simon Morgaz! And if ever he learnt under whose roof Jean had brought him!

175

But had not he, the son of Simon Morgaz, been a guest at the Villa Montcalm? Had he not been De Vaudreuil's companion-in-arms? Would it not be snatching him from death? Would it do any harm to M. de Vaudreuil to owe his life to Bridget Morgaz?

But he need never know! Nothing need betray the incognito which hid the miserable family.

Jean had his plan ready; it now only remained to put it into execution — in a few hours at the outside.

And then his thoughts returned to that house at St. Denis, where Clary de Vaudreuil would learn of the patriots' defeat. If her father did not return to her, would she not think he was dead? Would it be possible to let her know that M. de Vaudreuil had been taken to Maison-Close, and to get her away from the village, now handed over to the vengeance of its conquerors?

The anxiety told on Jean, and worse even than this was his torture at the thought of this terrible disaster for the national cause. All his hopes after the victory of St. Denis, what might have been its effects — the rising of the counties, the success of the insurrection in the valleys of the Richelieu and the St. Lawrence, the royal army rendered powerless, the gaining of independence, his reparation to his country for his father's treachery — all was lost — all!

All? Perhaps there would still be a chance of continuing the struggle? Was the cause dead in the hearts of the French-Canadians because a few hundred had fallen at St. Charles? No! Jean would set to work again. He would fight on to death.

Although night had fallen, the village was still noisy with the shouts of the soldiers and the cries of the wounded, and the streets were still alight with the flames. After destroying the camp, the fire had seized on the neighbouring houses. Where would it stop? If it were to reach the end of the village? If Maison-Close were to be destroyed? If Jean were to find neither his home nor his mother?

The thought terrified him. For himself he could always get away into the woods, and escape during the night. Before daylight he would be out of reach. But what would become of De Vaudreuil? If he fell into the hands of the royalists, he was lost, for not even the wounded had been spared in the bloody conflict.

But towards night calm seemed to return to St. Charles. Its people had either been driven out, or, after Colonel Wetherall's forces had gone, they had sought refuge in the few houses spared by the fire. The streets were now deserted, and he must take advantage of this.

Jean went to the church door, opened it, threw a quick glance around and descended the steps. No one was there, and the place was half lighted by the reflection of the distant flames.

Jean returned to M. de Vaudreuil, who was lying at full length near a pillar. He raised him in his arms. This was a heavy burden even for a man like Jean, and he would have to carry it as far as the turning in the main road, as far as Maison-Close. He crossed the square, and made his way quickly along the neighbouring street. It was time. Scarcely had he gone twenty yards, when there came a loud noise, and the tramping of horses.

It was a detachment of cavalry returning to St. Charles. Before pursuing the fugitives, Wetherall had ordered the troops to pass the night in the village, and it was the church itself which he had decided to use as a bivouac.

Immediately afterwards, the horsemen swarmed into the nave, not forgetting to take precautions against a counter-attack. And not merely the men; they had brought their horses with them. No need to stress the profanations indulged in by the soldiery, drunk with bloodshed and alcohol, in a building consecrated to Catholic worship.

Jean made his way along the deserted street, stopping every now and then to take breath. And always that fear that when he reached Maison-Close, he would find it in ruins.

At last he reached the road, and stopped before his mother's house. It was lost in the shadows; the fires had not yet reached it. But through the windows there came not a gleam of light.

Jean, carrying De Vaudreuil, pushed the gate open, and dragging himself to the door, he gave the agreed signal.

A moment later the two were safe in the house of Bridget Morgaz.

CHAPTER III - DE VAUDREUIL AT MAISON-CLOSE

'Mother,' Jean laid the wounded man on the bed used by himself or his brother whenever either of them passed the night at Maison-Close, ' Mother, if this man isn't looked after he'll lose his life.'

'I'll look after him, Jean!'

'It will cost you your own life, mother, if Weatherall's soldiers find him here.'

'My life! Does my life count for anything, my son?'

Jean did not care to tell her that her guest was De Vaudreuil, one of Simon Morgaz's victims. It would only have recalled painful memories. Better for Bridget not to know it. The man whom she was sheltering was a patriot. That gave him a right to her devotion.

Bridget and Jean had gone back to the door. They listened. There was a distant noise near the church, but all was quiet on the main road. The last of the reflections of the fires kindled in the upper part of the village had gradually begun to die away, as had the shouts of the loyalists. The arson and pillage had stopped. Though a score of so of houses had been reduced to ashes, Maison- Close was one of those which had escaped destruction. But Bridget and Jean had everything to fear from the victors when the morning sun should light up the ruins of St. Charles.

During the night they had had more than one alarm.

From hour to hour the soldiers and volunteers making their rounds had passed in front of Maison-Close; they were keeping an eye on the outskirts of the village as far as the turning in the main road. Now and then they had halted. Had orders to search the house been given? Were the police about to knock at the door and summon the inmates to open it? And it was not for himself that Jean trembled, but for De Vaudreuil, who would meet his fate in his mother's house!

These fears were not to be realised, for that night at any rate. Bridget and her son sat down beside the wounded man. All they could do for him they had done. But they must get him treated — and how could they get that? They ought to have a doctor, but where should they find one to whom they could entrust not only the Reformist's life, but the secrets of Maison-Close?

Monsieur de Vaudreuil's chest was laid bare, and examined. A deep wound made by a sabre stroke extended across its left side. The wound did not seem deep enough to have reached any vital organ, yet the sufferer was breathing so feebly, he had lost so much blood, that he might die of exhaustion.

After washing the wound with clean water, Bridget drew the two edges together and covered it with compresses. Would De Vaudreuil recover thanks to the careful treatment which she would give him, and the quiet he was sure of at Maison-Close, if only the soldiers left the village? Jean and his mother dared not entertain such a hope.

Two hours after his arrival, although he had not yet opened his eyes, the wounded man muttered a few words. Plainly all that bound him to life was the thought of his daughter. He was calling her — perhaps for her to help him, perhaps because he was thinking of the peril that now threatened her at St. Denis.

Bridget held his hand listening, while Jean, standing by her side, tried to keep the wound from being opened by some sudden movement. He also sought to make out the words, which were interspersed with sighs. Would De Vaudreuil say something that Bridget ought not to hear?

And then they caught a name, muttered amid some incoherent phrases.

It was that of Clary.

'The poor man has a daughter, then? ' Bridget looked at her son.

'Yes, Mother, he has.'

'And he's asking for her! He doesn't want to die till he's seen her. If his daughter were near him, his mind would be easy! Where is she now? Couldn't I find her and bring her here... in secret?'

'Here!' exclaimed Jean.

'Yes! Her place is near her father, who's calling her and who's dying.'

Then, in a fit of delirium, the wounded man tried to sit up in bed; he gasped, in tones of anguish: 'Clary... alone... there... at St. Denis!'

179

Bridget got up.

'St. Denis?' she said, ' it's there that he's left his daughter! Did you hear that, Jean?'

'The loyalists — at St. Denis!' the wounded man continued. ' She can't possibly escape them! The scoundrels will take their revenge on Clary de Vaudreuil.'

'Clary de Vaudreuil?' repeated Bridget.

Then, lowering her head, she added: 'Monsieur de Vaudreuil... here!'

'Yes! It's Monsieur de Vaudreuil,' said Jean. ' And as he's at Maison-Close, his daughter must come here!'

'Clary de Vaudreuil,' murmured Bridget.

Standing motionless at the side of the bed, she looked at him whose blood was flowing for the cause of independence, he who a dozen years before had nearly lost his life through the treachery of Simon Morgaz. If he knew what house was giving him shelter, what hands were fighting with death on his behalf, would he not be overwhelmed with horror, and if he had to drag himself away on his knees, would he not hasten to escape from this infamous contact with this family?

Like a long groan the name of Clary again rose to his lips.

'He may be dying,' said Jean, ' and he mustn't die till he's seen his daughter.'

'I'll go and fetch her,' replied Bridget.

'No! I'll go, mother.'

'You, whom they're hunting for all over the whole country! You to fall before you have accomplished your work! No, Jean, I will go and look for Clary de Vaudreuil!'

'Mother, she'll refuse to follow you!'

'She won't refuse when she knows that her father is dying, and that he's calling for her! Where is she — at St. Denis?'

'In the house of Judge Froment. But it's too far for you, mother! You won't be strong enough. There and back is twelve miles! If I start at once, I'll have time to get to St. Denis and bring her back before daylight. No one will see me go out; no one will see me come back.'

'No one?' said Bridget, ' and the soldiers who are watching the roads — how are you going to avoid them?

And if you fall into their hands, how are you to get away? Even assuming they don't recognise you, will they let you go? But I, an old woman, why should they stop me? Enough talk! Jean, Monsieur de Vaudreuil wants to see his daughter! He must see her, and I'm the only one who can bring her here! I shall go!'

Jean had to give in to his mother's arguments. Although the night was very dark, for him to venture into the roads guarded by the patrols would be to risk being unable to accomplish his task. Clary de Vaudreuil would have to cross the threshold of Maison-Close before sunrise. Who knew if her father would live till then? Could he — Jean-Sans-Nom, and known as such now that he fought in the open, could he get as far as St. Denis? Could he get back with Clary de Vaudreuil? Would that make it much more likely for her to fall into the loyalists' hands?

This last thought decided him, for he cared little for his own personal danger. He told Bridget how to find Judge Froment's house, and gave her a letter containing only the words, ' Trust yourself to my mother and follow her! ' — that ought to give the girl confidence. Then he opened the door and shut it behind his mother and went back to sit at the bedside.

It was a little after ten when Bridget started along the deserted road. The glacial cold of the long Canadian nights had frozen the ground, and the road facilitated quick walking. The moon, now in its first quarter, had just disappeared over the horizon, leaving a few stars gleaming between the clouds.

Bridget walked quickly through the dark solitude without fear or weakness. To carry out her task she had regained her one-time energy, of which she had already given proof. The road she knew quite well, having often been along it in her youth. Her only fear was that she would fall in with some of the detachments of the soldiers.

This happened three times within two miles of St. Charles. But why should they stop this old woman? She was greeted with a few words from men more or less drunk, but that was all. Colonel Weatherall had not got as far as St. Denis. Before attacking that unfortunate village he meant to reconnoitre carefully, and to avoid imperilling his victory by a premature attack.

For the rest of her journey Bridget met with no danger. The only people she came up with and passed were fugitives from St. Charles, who were scattering over the country, homeless now that their houses had been given to pillage and the flames.

But, as was only too certain, where Bridget could move freely Jean would have found it impossible to get through. On the approach of the soldiers he would have had to leave the main road and get across the country by devious routes, which would have made it impossible for him to return to Maison-Close before daylight. And if a cavalry picket were to capture him, they would have left him only when they had landed him in jail. They might even have recognised him, and then he knew what fate awaited him.

Half an hour before midnight Bridget reached the Richlieu.

The house of Judge Froment, she knew, was situated on the bank of the river, a little out of St. Denis, so there was no need for her to cross to the far side, which she could only have done in a boat. All she had to do was to go down beside the river for a quarter of a mile to reach the door of the house.

The place was completely deserted, and a deep silence reigned all over the valley.

In the distance a few lights were gleaming in the windows of the village, which was then plunged in a peace undisturbed by any rumour.

Had the news of the defeat at St. Charles not yet reached St. Denis?

That was what Bridget surmised. Then Clary de Vaudreuil would know nothing of the disaster, and she herself would be the bringer of evil tidings.

She went up the steps, and knocked at the door.

There was no reply.

She knocked again.

Footsteps could be heard in the hall, and a feeble light appeared. Then a voice asked: 'What do you want?'

'To see Judge Froment.'

'Judge Froment isn't at St. Denis, and in his absence I can't open the door.'

'I've got important news for him,' Bridget declared.

'You can give it to him when he gets back.'

The speaker seemed so determined not to open the door that Bridget did not hesitate to use Clary's name.

'If Judge Froment isn't at home,' she said, 'Mademoiselle de Vaudreuil ought to be, and I must have a word with her.'

'Mademoiselle de Vaudreuil has gone away,' said the voice, though not without a certain hesitation.

'When did she go?'

'Yesterday.'

'Do you know where she's gone?'

'No doubt to meet her father.'

'Her father?' said Bridget. ' But it's from Monsieur de Vaudreuil that I've come!'

'My father?' exclaimed Clary, who was at the back of the hall; ' open the door.'

'Clary de Vaudreuil,' Bridget lowered her voice, ' if I've come — it's to take you to your father, and it was Jean who has sent me...'

Already the door-bolts had been drawn back when Bridget added in low tones: 'No — don't open! Wait!'

And she moved quietly down the steps. It was important for her not to be seen, and especially so for her not to be seen entering the house; and a number of men, women and children had now come into sight, moving towards her along the river bank.

It was the first group of fugitives, who had reached St. Denis after crossing the country to avoid the road. Among them were some of the wounded, being helped along by all that remained of their family; and a few of the patriots who had escaped unscathed from the fight and the fire. Some of them might recognise Bridget, and she did not want it to be known that she had left Maison- Close. So, hidden in the shadow of the wall, she waited for the fugitives to pass.

But during these few moments what could Clary think as she heard those cries of despair! For many hours she had been waiting for the news from St. Charles. Perhaps it would be her father, perhaps Jean himself who would bring it, if they were not marching on Montreal after another victory? No. Through the door she dared not open she could hear the sound of groans.

At last the fugitives had gone by and were making their way along the river bank until they could find some way to cross.

The road had again become quiet, although more of the cries could be heard further down the stream.

Bridget went back to the door. At her knock it opened, to shut the instant she entered.

Clary de Vaudreuil and Bridget Morgaz were face to face. They were in one of the rooms on the ground floor, lit only by a lamp whose gleam could not be seen through the tightly-closed shutters.

They looked at each other while the servant stood a little aside.

Clary was pale; she had a foreboding of some great misfortune, and she dared not speak.

'The patriots at St. Charles?' she ventured.

'Defeated! ' Bridget replied.

'My father?'

'Wounded.'

'Dying?'

'I'm afraid so.'

Clary would have collapsed had not Bridget caught her in her arms.

184

'Courage, Clary de Vaudreuil!' she said, ' your father is asking for you! You must go, you must come to him, and follow me without losing a moment!'

'Where is my father? ' Clary had scarcely recovered from her faintness.

'At my home in St. Charles.'

'Who sent you?'

I told you — Jean! — I'm his mother! *

'You!' exclaimed Clary.

'Read this!'

Clary took the letter Bridget was holding out to her.

It was the writing of Jean-Sans-Nom, which she recognised at once.

'Trust yourself to my mother,' it said.

But how did De Vaudreuil come to be in that house? Was it Jean who had saved him, who had carried him from the battle-field at St. Charles, and taken him to Maison-Close?

'I'm ready, madame! ' Clary decided.

'Come on, then,' replied Bridget.

Nothing more was said.

The details of this disastrous affair Clary might learn later on. She knew only too much already, her father dying, the patriots dispersed, the victory of St. Denis annihilated by the defeat of St. Charles!

She hurriedly wrapped herself in a dark cloak. The door of the hall was thrown open, and the two went out into the road.

All that Bridget said as she pointed towards St. Charles, was: 'We've got six miles to go. For nobody to know we're at Maison-Close, we have to get there before it is daybreak.'

They quickly went along the river bank so as to reach the road which went northwards across country.

The girl would have liked to go more quickly, so anxious was she to reach her father's bedside. But she had to moderate her pace, for Bridget, although she was showing an energy beyond her years, could not keep up with her.

What was more, they met with hindrances. Occasionally they encountered groups of the fugitives. To mingle with them was to risk being dragged back towards St. Denis; so as the better to avoid them, Bridget and Clary hid in the thickets by the roadside. Here they could see and hear without being seen.

These poor people were in a wretched state. Many of them were leaving tracks of blood on the road. The women were carrying the young children in their arms. The stronger men were helping along the older people, who would have stayed behind only to lie down by the roadside to die. Then further cries were heard in the distance, and the groups disappeared into the darkness.

Were the soldiers and the volunteers in pursuit of these poor wretches, who now that their homes were destroyed were looking for shelter? Was Wetherall's column on the march to surprise the routed patriots at daybreak?

No. These were more of the fugitives. They passed in hundreds. And how many would have died during this terrible night if a few farms had not been open to receive them?

Clary, her heart wrung with anguish, watched the horrors of the flight. Yet she would not lose hope for the cause of independence, for which her father had just been mortally wounded.

When the road was clear she and Bridget continued their journey and for an hour and a half they went on. As they approached the village the delays were less frequent; the road was clearer. All who had been able to escape were already far away towards St. Denis or were scattered about the countryside. What they had to be wary of in the vicinity of St. Charles was contact with any of the soldiery.

At three in the morning they still had two miles to cover before reaching Maison-Close. And then Bridget fell, exhausted.

Clary stooped to help her up.

'Let me give you a hand,' she pleaded, ' lean on me, we can't be far off now.'

'Still another hour's walk,' said Bridget, ' and I can't...

'Rest for a minute or two. Then we'll start again. You must take my arm. Don't be afraid of tiring me. I'm quite strong.'

'Strong! Poor child, before long you'll have to give in, too!'

Bridget rose to her knees.

'Listen to me,' she said, ' I'll try to go a few more steps. But if I fall, you must leave me alone.'

'Leave you alone!' exclaimed Clary.

'Yes! You must get to your father tonight. The road is straight on. Maison-Close is the first house to the left as you enter the village. You will knock at the door, and give your name, and Jean will open to you.'

'I will never forsake you,' the girl replied. ' I won't go on without you.'

'You must, Clary de Vaudreuil. And then when you are safe, my son will return for me. He'll carry me just as he carried your father!'

'But try to walk, please try! I beg you!'

Bridget got up, though she could hardly drag herself along. Yet they succeeded in covering another mile.

Then the horizon began to brighten in the east towards St. Charles. Was it the first gleam of dawn, and would it not be impossible to reach Maison-Close before the day?

'Go on!' said Bridget. ' Go on, Clary de Vaudreuil! Leave me!'

'That can't be the dawn,' Clary assured her. ' It's scarcely four o'clock. That's the glow of a burning house...'

Clary did not finish the sentence. The same thought struck her as had struck Bridget, that it might be Maison- Close which was a prey to the flames, that De Vaudreuil's hiding-place had been discovered, that he and Jean had become the prisoners of Wetherall, or else had died in defending it.

The fear spurred Bridget on to a renewed burst of energy. She and Clary hastened on towards St. Charles. They came to a bend in the road, beyond which was Maison-Close.

They at least reached the bend in the road.

187

It was not Maison-Close that was burning, but a farm to the right of the village.

'There! It's there! ' Bridget pointed to her house with a trembling hand.

In a few minutes they would be in safety. But just then they saw a group of three men coming down the road — three volunteers staggering along, drunk with brandy, and stained with blood.

Clary and Bridget tried to avoid them by going to one side. They were too late. The volunteers had seen them, and now the fugitives had everything to fear. One of the men caught hold of Clary and tried to drag her away, while the other two held Bridget back.

The women called for help. But who could hear their screams unless it were some of the other soldiers — less intoxicated perhaps, and therefore more dangerous?

Suddenly a man leapt out of a thicket by the roadside; with a vigorous blow he felled the scoundrel who was holding the girl.

'Clary de Vaudreuil!' he exclaimed.

'Vincent Hodge!'

And Clary seized his arm. She had recognised him by the light of the flames.

When De Vaudreuil had fallen, Hodge had been unable to help him. Not realising that a few moments later Jean-Sans-Nom had dragged the victim out of danger, he had returned after the firing was over, and was waiting in the outskirts of the village at the risk of falling into the hands of the loyalists. When night fell he had tried to find his friend among the wounded and the dead. Having searched in vain until dawn was about to appear, he was going back along the road, when the cries for help had drawn him to the spot where Clary was struggling with a peril worse than death.

But Vincent Hodge had no time to be told that De Vaudreuil had been taken to the house a few hundred yards away. He now had to face the two scoundrels, who had released Bridget so as to attack him. Their shouts had been heard up the road, and five or six volunteers were hurrying to their help. There was only just time for Clary and Bridget to escape.

188

'Get away! Get away! ' Vincent Hodge urged them. ' I'll be able to get clear!'

Bridget and Clary ran up the road, while Hodge brought down his two half-drunken antagonists.

Then, before their comrades could rejoin them, he leapt into the thicket, followed by a shower of shots, none of which touched him.

A few moments later, Bridget knocked at the door of Maison-Close, which was at once opened. She first dragged Clary in, and then fell into her son's arms.

CHAPTER IV - THE NEXT WEEK

Maison-Close had thus for a time afforded shelter — precarious, no doubt — to De Vaudreuil and his daughter. They were under the roof of the ' family without a name,' under the same roof as the traitor's wife and son. That they knew nothing of the ties that bound to Simon Morgaz the old woman and young man who had risked their lives in sheltering them, Bridget and Jean realised only too well.

Towards the morning of 26th November, De Vaudreuil regained a little consciousness. His daughter's voice awoke him from his torpor and his eyes opened.

'Clary!' he murmured.

'Yes, father! I'm here! ' Clary assured him. ' I'm near you! I won't leave you.'

Jean was standing at the foot of the bed, in the shadow, as though he were anxious not to be seen. The wounded man's glance rested on him, and he murmured: 'Jean! Ah! I remember!'

Then seeing Bridget bending over his bed, he seemed to be asking who she was.

'It's my mother,' Jean explained. ' You're in my mother's house, Monsieur de Vaudreuil. You'll never lack for her care, nor for that of your daughter.'

'Their care! ' De Vaudreuil repeated feebly. ' Yes — I remember — wounded — beaten — my companions in flight — dead, perhaps! Ah! my poor country, my poor country — worse enslaved than ever!'

His head fell back, and his eyes closed.

'Father!' said Clary, kneeling beside him. As she took his hand she felt a light pressure answering to hers.

Jean reminded her: 'We'll have to get a doctor to come to Maison-Close. Where shall we find one? To whom shall we apply now that the whole region is occupied by the loyalists? Perhaps at Montreal! Yes! There alone will it be possible! Tell me some doctor in whom you've got confidence, and I'll go to Montreal.'

'To Montreal!' repeated Bridget.

'I'll have to, mother! For Monsieur de Vaudreuil's life it's worth risking my own.'

'It isn't for you I'm frightened, Jean. But if you go to Montreal you may be watched; and if anyone suspects Monsieur de Vaudreuil is hidden here, he's lost.'

'Lost!' murmured Clary.

'And won't he be even more surely lost if he doesn't get proper attention?' asked Jean.

'If the wound is mortal,' Bridget reminded him, ' nobody can cure it. If it isn't mortal, Heaven will give him recovery at the hands of his daughter and myself. The wound is a sabre-stroke which has only cut into the flesh. He's weak now from the loss of blood. It should be enough, I hope, to bathe the wound, and keep on with the cold water compresses so as to make it heal. Believe me, my son, Monsieur de Vaudreuil is comparatively safe here, and if we can help it, it's better for nobody to know where he is.'

Bridget spoke with an assurance whose first effect was to give Clary a little hope. It was above all things essential that no one should be allowed into Maison- Close. The life of Jean-Sans-Nom depended on it, as did that of De Vaudreuil. At the slightest alarm, indeed, Jean might get away across the country to the American frontier, but De Vaudreuil could not.

After the first day, the wounded man's condition justified the confidence Bridget had inspired. As soon as the loss of blood was checked. De Vaudreuil was, if still as weak, at least in possession of his senses. What he wanted above all things was freedom from anxiety, and that he would have now that his daughter was by his side at Maison-Close.

Wetherall's soldiers were soon to leave St. Charles and scour the country, so that the village would be relieved of their presence.

Bridget made arrangements for more comfortably installing her guests in her tiny home. De Vaudreuil occupied the room usually reserved for Joann or Jean. The other room, Bridget's, became Clary's, and the two women took it in turns to watch by the patient's bedside.

191

As to Jean, there was no need to worry about him, or about his brother, if ever the Abbé Joann did venture to visit his mother after what had happened. Any corner of the house would do for them.

Besides, Jean was not thinking of staying on at St. Charles. As soon as he was assured of De Vaudreuil's safety, as soon as he had consulted with him on the possibilities he foresaw, he would again get to work. The defeat at St. Charles could not have finally assured the ruin of the patriots' cause. Jean-Sans-Nom would know how to lead them on to their revenge.

The 26th November passed quietly enough. Bridget was able, without arousing suspicion, to leave Maison Close, as was her custom, to get some extra food, as well as suitable remedies, for as soon as the troops evacuated the village many of the houses were reopened.

But what a disaster, what ruin, especially in the upper part of the town, beside the camp; after a defence pushed to the extremes of heroism, this had been burned and devastated. A hundred of the patriots had shed their blood in this tragic fight, most of them killed or mortally wounded. Another forty had been taken prisoner. And then had come the excesses committed by the maddened soldiery, whom their leader had been unable to restrain.

De Vaudreuil slept for some hours quietly enough. There was no more delirium, no more of those incoherent words with which he had called for his daughter. He realised that Clary was near him, safe from the dangers to which she would have been subjected had the soldiery re-entered St. Denis.

While he was asleep, Jean explained to Clary the events of the previous day. She learnt all that had passed since her father had left with Judge Froment to join his comrades at St. Charles; how the reformists had fought to the last man; and how he had been carried from the scene of the battle into Maison-Close.

Clary listened with her heart oppressed, her eyes full of tears, but she steeled herself against despair. Misfortunes, it seemed, were being heaped up on Jean and herself; for both of them realised how much they were to each other.

Often Jean would rise in great distress, horrified at himself, and longing to escape from this friendship, which their position made even more dangerous. After the few days he had spent with Clary at the Villa Montcalm, he had calculated on the events he was preparing to take up all his attention. And now it was these very events which had brought her to his mother's home at the same time as they had forced him to seek its shelter.

Bridget soon realised the nature of her son's feelings. The terror which she felt was not less than that of Jean. The son of Simon Morgaz! The determined woman allowed no sign of her trouble to appear, but what suffering she foresaw for the future!

In the morning De Vaudreuil was told that the soldiers had gone. Feeling himself less enfeebled, he asked Jean what would be the consequences of the defeat at St. Charles, and what had become of his companions who had fought so bravely.

The others came and sat by his bed, and Jean replied by begging him not to tire himself with too much talking.

'I'll tell you what I know about your friends,' he began. ' They fought to the last, and were only overborne by numbers. One of my brave comrades at Chipogan, poor Remy Harcher, was killed at the very outset without my being able to help him. Then Michel and Jacques were also wounded, and they had to leave the battlefield, carried off by their father and their two other brothers. Where did they go when resistance became impossible? I don't know, but I hope they reached the American frontier. Gramont was made prisoner, and should now be in prison at Montreal, and we may guess the fate in store for him. Farran and Clerc have, I think, escaped from their pursuers. Were they unhurt? I cannot say. As for Vincent Hodge, I cannot say.

'Vincent Hodge has escaped,' Clary told him. ' That night he was roaming round St. Charles, looking for you, father. Madame Bridget and I met him on our way here. Thanks to him, we escaped from some drunken soldiers, who were molesting us. Probably he's now safe in some village in the United States.'

'He is a noble fellow, a brave patriot,' Jean agreed. ' What he did for Mademoiselle de Vaudreuil and my mother he's already done for me in the thick of the fight. He saved my life, and perhaps it would have been better for him to leave me to die! I ought not to have survived the defeat of the Sons of Freedom!

'Jean,' asked Clary, ' do you despair of the cause?'

'My son despair?' exclaimed Bridget. ' I shall never believe it.'

'No, mother! ' Jean assured her. ' After the victory at St. Denis, the insurrection will spread through the whole St. Lawrence valley. After the defeat at St. Charles, mastery has to be regained, and I mean to regain it. The reformists aren't beaten yet. Already they ought to be well enough reorganised to resist Sir John Colborne. I've been away from them too long, and I'll be off this very night.'

'Where shall you go?' asked De Vaudreuil.

'To St. Denis to begin with. There I hope to meet the leaders, under whom we repulsed the soldiers of Colonel Gore's troops.'

'Go on, then! Jean? ' Bridget gave her son a penetrating glance. ' Go. Your place isn't here. It's there — in the forefront.'

'Yes, Jean, you must go! ' Clary urged him. ' You must rejoin your comrades, and re-appear at their head! The loyalists must realise that Jean-Sans-Nom isn't dead!'

She could say no more.

De Vaudreuil raised himself in bed, and took Jean's hand.

'Go, Jean,' he said. ' Leave me to the care of your mother and my daughter! If you see my friends, tell them they'll find me with them as soon as I've strength enough to leave this house. But,' he added, in a voice which showed his extreme weakness, ' if you can keep us in touch with what's going on — if you can possibly return here — ah, Jean! I want so much to know what has become of all those who are so dear to me, and whom I may never see again.'

'You shall know it, Monsieur de Vaudreuil,' Jean assured' him. ' Take some rest now. Forget — until the time comes to fight.'

The wounded man was in such a state that all emotion ought to be avoided. He had fallen asleep, and the sleep lasted into the middle of the night. And he was still asleep when Jean left the house at eleven, after bidding farewell to Clary and embracing his mother, whose strength did not fail her even at the moment of separation from her son.

The conditions were not the same as they were when Bridget had dissuaded Jean from going to St. Denis. After Wetherall's departure the danger was negligible. St. Denis was now as quiet as St. Charles. After defeating the reformists on the 25th, the Government were temporising. It was astounding

194

that they were making no effort to complete their victory at St. Charles. Sir John Colborne was not the man to draw back before the reprisals which an offensive would provoke, and Colonel Gore was probably eager to avenge his defeat.

For some reason or other, at St. Charles, and consequently at Maison-Close, there was no news of such an aggression. Confidence had to some extent returned to the villagers. After their dispersal most of them had come back and set to work repairing the damage. In her occasional errands Bridget asked no questions, but she listened and reported to De Vaudreuil and his daughter. There was no serious news, no threats of an advance along the road from Montreal.

During the three days that followed, this calm was untroubled. Did the Government consider the rebellion finally crushed by the blow struck at St. Charles? It seemed so. Were they only in pursuit of the leaders of the opposition, those who had given the signal of revolt? Probably. But what no one would admit was that the reformists had given up the struggle, that they acknowledged themselves so completely defeated that they could do nothing but give in. No! And at Maison-Close, as in all Lower Canada, they were waiting for a new call to arms.

Thanks to Bridget and Clary, De Vaudreuil continued to improve. He was still very weak, but his wound began to heal. Unfortunately his recovery would be slow, and it would be long before he was able to leave his bed. At the end of the third day he was able to take a little food. The fever which had racked him had almost entirely disappeared. There was nothing serious to fear so long as no complication set in.

During these long hours Bridget and Clary sat beside his bed and told him all they knew about what was happening outside. Jean's name occurred frequently in their conversation. Had he been able to join his companions at St. Denis? Would he leave his friends at Maison-Close without any news?

And while Clary remained silent, her eyes cast down, and her thoughts far away, her father would praise the young patriot in whom was symbolised the national cause. Yes! Madame Bridget ought to be proud of such a son.

Bridget hung her head and did not often reply, if she did, it was simply to say that Jean was only doing his duty, no more.

195

There was nothing surprising in Clary's feeling a lively friendship, almost a daughter's love, for Bridget. It seemed natural for her to call her mother] But when she took her by the hand Bridget seemed to be trying to withdraw it, and when Clary kissed her she would suddenly turn her head away. Why this was, the girl could not understand. How gladly would she have known the history of this family, which had not even a name. But Bridget remained silent on the subject. On the one side was confidence and almost filial affection; on the other was extreme reserve; and an inexplicable distance separated the old woman and the young.

In the evening of 2nd December St. Charles was alarmed by disquieting news — by news so disquieting indeed that Bridget, who had heard it in the village, did not think it wise to report it to De Vaudreuil. Clary agreed, as it was useless to trouble the rest which her father needed so badly.

The report was that the loyalists had again fought the insurgents.

The Government had in fact not been satisfied with having put down the insurrection at St. Charles. They had now to avenge the check Colonel Gore had suffered at St. Denis. If they succeeded, they would have no more to fear from the reformists, who could be hunted down by the police, as they scattered about the countryside. Then all that would remain to be done was to inflict heavy penalties on their leaders, now imprisoned in Quebec and Montreal.

Two guns, five companies of infantry, and a squadron of cavalry had been put under the orders of Colonel Gore, who had arrived at St. Denis on 1st December.

The news of this expedition, somewhat vaguely at first, reached St. Charles that very evening, and a few people returning from the fields confirmed it.

It was this which Bridget heard and which, though she told Clary, she thought it wise to withhold from De Vaudreuil. The anxiety and anguish of the two women can well be imagined.

It was at St. Denis that Jean had gone to rejoin his companions, and to reorganise the insurrection. Would they be numerous enough, and well enough armed, to withstand the loyalists?

Unfortunately it was not likely that they would. And then would not the loyalists, once embarked on reprisals, pursue them to the bitter end? Would they not make requisitions on the villages chiefly concerned, and more especially on St. Charles? Would it not be subject to police surveillance, which was bound to have serious results? Would not the mystery of Maison-Close be revealed? What would become of De Vaudreuil, confined to his bed, whom it would be impossible to take across the frontier?

In what agonies Bridget and Clary heard these rumours! Already there was news from St. Denis, and it was heart-breaking. Colonel Gore had found the village abandoned by its defenders. Before so unequal a struggle they had decided to beat a retreat. The people had left their homes, and taken refuge in the woods, crossed the river, or sought shelter in the neighbouring villages. As to what had happened when the town was handed over to the soldiery — if they did not know it, this was only too easy to imagine.

The night had come. Bridget and Clary were at De Vaudreuil's bedside. Time and again they had to explain to him why the streets of St. Charles, which had been so quiet during the last few days, were now so full of noise. Clary racked her brain to find a reason which would not alarm her father. Then her thoughts flew further, and she wondered if the cause of independence had not received a last blow, from which it would never recover; whether Jean and his comrades had been forced to cross the frontier; whether some of them had fallen into the hands of the loyalists. And Jean, had be been able to get away? Or was he trying to return to Maison- Close?

Clary had a presentiment that this was so, and then it would be impossible to conceal the defeat of the reformists from De Vaudreuil.

Perhaps Bridget feared this also? And the two women, absorbed in the same thought, understand one another without exchanging a word.

About half-past eleven there were three knocks at the door.

'It's him!' exclaimed Clary.

Bridget had recognised the signal. It was indeed one of her sons who had knocked.

She thought it might be Joann, who had not been there for two months. But Clary was not mistaken. She repeated: 'It's him! Jean!'

And as soon as the door was opened, Jean appeared; he entered at once.

Jules Verne

CHAPTER V - THE INVESTIGATION

The door had hardly closed when Jean put his ear against it to listen. At the same time he gestured to his mother and Clary not to speak a word, not to make any movement.

And Bridget, who was just going to ask, ' Why have you come back, my son?' kept silent.

Outside they could hear people tramping up and down the road. There was a discussion going on between half a dozen men, who had just halted in front of Maison- Close.

'Which way has he gone?'

'He can't have stopped here.'

'He'll have gone into hiding in one of the houses higher up.'

'But he wasn't a hundred yards ahead of us.'

'To have let Jean-Sans-Nom give us the slip!'

'And those six thousand dollars on his head!'

As she heard the voice of the man who had last spoken, Bridget gave an involuntary start. She seemed to recognise the voice, without being able to remember whom it belonged to.

But Jean had recognised it, as he had the man who was on his track. It was Rip! And if he said nothing to his mother, it was because he dare not recall the horrible past which the name would bring back.

Soon, however, all was again silent. The police agents had gone up the road without suspecting that Jean had gone into hiding in Maison-Close.

Then Jean returned towards his mother and Clary, who were still standing motionless in the darkness of the passage.

Before Bridget could say anything, they heard the voice of De Vaudreuil. He had realised that Jean had come back, and was asking: 'Jean! Is that you?'

The three at once entered the invalid's room, and, deeply distressed, stood by the side of the bed.

'I've got strong enough now to bear anything,' he told them, ' and I want to know everything.'

'So you shall,' Jean replied; and he went on, while Clary and Bridget listened without interrupting him: 'The other night, two hours after I left you, I reached St. Denis. There I found several of the survivors of the disaster; Vincent Hodge, Farran and Clerc were among them. They were getting ready to defend the place, and all the people wanted was to help them. But yesterday we heard that Colborne had sent from Sorel a column of regulars and volunteers to pillage and burn the town.

'The column arrived in the evening, and it was in vain that we tried to resist it. Useless! It came right into St. Denis, and the villagers had to abandon their homes. More than fifty houses were destroyed by the flames. Then, so as not to have their throats cut by the ruffians, my comrades had to escape and make for the frontier, where Papineau and the others were waiting for them. And now the soldiers have invaded the district south of the St. Lawrence, burning and devastating, reducing the children and women to beggary, sparing them no ill-treatment or insult, and you can see their progress by the light of the fires they've raised. That's what has happened, Monsieur de Vaudreuil, and yet I don't despair. I will not despair of our cause!'

A distressed silence followed Jean's explanation, and De Vaudreuil let himself fall back on the bed.

Bridget was the first to speak. Addressing her son, and looking him straight in the face, she said: 'Then why are you here? Why aren't you with your comrades?'

'Because I've got reason to fear that the loyalists will return to St. Charles, that a house-to-house search will be made, that fire will destroy what's left of the village.'

'And can you stop it, Jean?'

'No, mother!'

'Then, I repeat, what are you doing here?'

'I'm here because I wished to see if it wouldn't be possible for Monsieur de Vaudreuil to leave Maison- Close, which will not be spared any more than the other houses.'

'It isn't possible,' said Bridget.

'Then I'll stay, mother, and I'll die defending you.'

'It's for your country you should die, Jean, and not for us,' De Vaudreuil pointed out. ' Your place is with the other patriotic leaders.'

'That's where your place is, too, Monsieur de Vaudreuil! Listen to me. You can't stay in this house, where you'd soon be discovered. This very night, half a mile from St. Charles, I was chased by a squad of police. There's no doubt they recognised me, for you heard them saying my name. They'll ransack the town, and even if I wasn't here, Maison-Close would not be overlooked. It's you that the police will find, Monsieur de Vaudreuil, it's you that they'll arrest, and you may expect no mercy.'

'What does that matter, Jean? ' De Vaudreuil replied. ' What does it matter so long as you're able to rally our friends on the frontier?'

'Listen, I'll tell you,' Jean insisted. ' All I can do for the cause I will do. But it is you who will have to be considered, Monsieur de Vaudreuil. Perhaps it may not be impossible for you to reach the United States. Once you are out of this district you'll be safe, and it'll only be a few miles before you're in American territory. That you aren't strong enough to drag yourself there, even if I'm with you to help you along, that's true. But in a cart, lying on a bed of straw just as you are now, couldn't you stand the journey? Well, my mother could get you this cart on some pretext or another — that of escaping like the others perhaps — or at least she can try! And when night comes, your daughter and yourself, and my mother and me, we'll leave this house, and we can be out of reach before the troops have come to do to St. Charles what they've done to St. Denis!'

Jean's scheme was worth consideration. A few miles further south, De Vaudreuil could find the safety which Maison-Close could no longer offer him, if the loyalists were to enter the village and make a house-to-house visitation. It was only too certain that Jean-Sans-Nom had been recognised by Rip's men. He had escaped them, but they would assume that he had taken refuge in one of the houses in St. Charles, and every effort would be made to capture him. The position was ominous. At all costs it was important that not only Jean, but De Vaudreuil and his daughter, should leave Maison-Close.

And flight was not impracticable if only Bridget could hire a cart, and De Vaudreuil could stand the jolting for a few hours. Even if he were too weak to reach the frontier, he could be sure of shelter at some farm in the south of the country. Anyhow, they would certainly have to leave St. Charles, for the police would search the house.

Jean had little difficulty in convincing De Vaudreuil and his daughter, and even Bridget agreed. Unfortunately, they could not start that night. Next day his mother could see about hiring the cart, and the following night they could put the plan into execution.

The day came. Bridget thought it was better to act openly. There would be nothing strange in her trying to get away from the scene of the insurrection. Many people had already done so, and her attempt would surprise nobody.

She had at first meant not to accompany De Vaudreuil with Clary and Jean. But her son easily made her understand that once her departure had been announced, if her neighbours were to see her still at St. Charles, they would suspect that the cart had been used by some other fugitive, and then the police would arrest her. In the interest of all, it was better for nothing of that sort to happen. Bridget had to give way. When the troubles were over she would return to St. Charles, and end her miserable life in the house which she had hoped never to leave.

Everything thus being decided, Bridget set about procuring the means of transport. If she could get a cart all would be well. She left the house next morning provided by De Vaudreuil with the money need to hire it — or rather to purchase it outright.

During her absence Jean and Clary did not leave the invalid's room. Already he had regained his strength and was bracing himself for the journey; a sort of reaction had set in. Despite his weakness, which was still very great, he was ready to get up; ready to travel in the cart when the moment came to leave. He could answer for himself at least for a few hours, but after that he would be in the hands of God. Nothing else mattered, so long as he again saw his comrades and could assure his daughter's safety, and so long as Jean-Sans-Nom was back among the French-Canadians ready for a final struggle.

Yes, their departure was essential. If De Vaudreuil did not survive his wounds, what would become of his daughter at Maison-Close, alone in the world, and with only an old woman to depend on? On the frontier he would meet his brothers-in-arms and his most devoted friends. And amongst them was one of whose feelings he approved. He knew that Vincent Hodge loved Clary, and he felt that Clary would not refuse to become the wife of him who had risked his life to save her. To what more generous, what more ardent patriot could she entrust her future? He was worthy of her, and she was worthy of him.

With God's help he himself would have the strength to reach his goal. He would not die until he had set foot on American soil, where the survivors of the Reformist party were waiting to take up their arms once more.

Such were the thoughts of De Vaudreuil, while Jean and Clary, seated at his bedside, exchanged only a few words.

Often Jean would rise and go across to one of the windows which opened on to the road, and whose shutters were always closed. Then he listened for any further noise that he could hear outside.

Bridget returned to Maison-Close after an absence of two hours. She had been to several people to ask about the horse and cart. She had mentioned her desire to leave St. Charles, and this had surprised nobody. The owner of a neighbouring farm had agreed to let her have a cart at a reasonable price, and it should be at the door of Maison-Close at nine that evening.

When he heard of her success De Vaudreuil felt a burden lifted from him.

'At nine o'clock we'll set out,' he said ' and I'll get up to take my place in the cart.'

'No, Monsieur de Vaudreuil,' Jean protested, ' you mustn't tire yourself needlessly. I'll carry you out to the cart; we'll spread a good thick layer of straw, and on that we'll put one of the mattresses from your bed. Then we'll go slowly, so as to avoid jolting, and I hope you'll be able to bear the journey. But as the temperature is low, you must see that you're well covered up. As to incidents on the road — have you heard anything fresh, mother?'

'No,' said Bridget,' but they're still expecting the troops.'

'And these police agents who've been after me?'

'I didn't see them, and they may have gone off on a false trail.'

'But they may return! ' Clary reminded her.

'We'll go as soon as the cart is at the door,' said De Vaudreuil.

'At nine o'clock,' added Bridget.

'You can trust the man who sold you the cart?' asked Jean.

'Yes! He's an honest farmer, and what he undertakes to do he'll do.'

In the meantime De Vaudreuil wished to take some nourishment, so Bridget, helped by Clary, quickly prepared a frugal lunch, which they all shared.

The hours went by without further incident. There was no noise outside. From time to time Bridget opened the door, and cast a rapid glance to right and left. The weather was fairly cold. The grey tint of the sky showed the complete calmness of the atmosphere. If the wind veered to the south-west, if the mist turned into snow, De Vaudreuil's journey would be very painful — at least, until he got far enough away to be safe.

However, everything seemed in favour of the journey — until three in the afternoon, when another alarm took place.

Distant sounds could be heard in the upper part of the town.

Jean opened the door and listened. He could not restrain a gesture of anger.

'Bugles!' he exclaimed. ' Troops advancing on St. Charles, probably!'

'What are we to do?' asked Clary.

'Wait,' replied Bridget. ' The soldiers may be only passing through the village.'

Jean shook his head.

But as it was impossible for De Vaudreuil to leave during the daytime, all that could be done, as Bridget had said, was to wait, unless Jean should decide to escape by himself.

Indeed, if he were, to leave Maison-Close at once, might he not be able to reach safety, before St. Charles was occupied by the loyalists? But that would mean leaving De Vaudreuil and Clary exposed to the greatest peril. Jean never even thought of it. Yet how, if their hiding-place were discovered, was he to defend them?

The sound of bugles came nearer. Then it ceased. The troops had reached the end of the village.

'All isn't lost yet,' said Bridget. ' The road is clear on the Laprairie side. The night will come, and we needn't change our plans. My house is not the sort to attract robbers; it stands by itself, and quite possibly it won't be visited.'

This was certainly to be hoped.

The preparations for departure were therefore continued. They would have to be ready for the cart as soon as it arrived. If the road were free for an hour, and the fugitives could get three miles away, De Vaudreuil could, if necessary, find shelter in one of the farmhouses.

The night arrived without any fresh alarm. A few detachments of volunteers, who had advanced along the main road, retraced their steps, but Maison-Close did not seem to have attracted their attention. The bulk of the column was encamped around St. Charles. Thence came a deafening uproar, which foreboded no good to the villagers.

At six Bridget asked Jean and Clary to have dinner, which she had just prepared, but De Vaudreuil hardly ate anything. Over-excited at the danger of the circumstances which he had to meet, he waited impatiently for the time to start.

A little before seven there came a gentle tap at the door. Was it the farmer who had brought the cart before the appointed time? It certainly could not be an enemy's hand that knocked so gently.

Jean and Clary went into De Vaudreuil's room, leaving the door half open. Bridget went along the passage and opened the front door, having recognised the voice of the farmer who had sold her the cart.

The honest man had come to say that it was impossible for him to keep to his bargain, and he had brought back the money that had been paid him. There were troops quartered on his farm, as on all the other farms nearby. The village was surrounded, and even if Bridget had the cart, she would not be able to use it. She must wait, whether she liked it or not, until St. Charles was evacuated.

Jean and Clary, from the patient's room, had heard what the farmer had said, as had De Vaudreuil.

The farmer added that there was nothing to be afraid of at Maison-Close, as the troops had only returned to St. Charles to help the police, who were making an investigation throughout the village. And why? Because of certain rumours that Jean-Sans-Nom was in hiding there, every means was being employed for his discovery.

When she heard the farmer mention her son's name, Bridget was careful not to make any movement that might betray her.

The farmer went away and, returning to the room, Bridget said: 'Jean! You must go, this instant!'

'You must! ' De Vaudreuil agreed.

'Go without you?'

'You have no right to sacrifice your life,' Clary told him. ' Before us, there's your country...'

'I won't go! ' Jean declared. ' I won't leave you exposed to these scoundrels' brutalities.'

'And what will you do, Jean?'

'I don't know, but I won't leave you.'

Jean's decision was so positive that De Vaudreuil did not attempt to argue with him.

Besides, it was obvious that flight would now be dangerous. According to the farmer, the village was surrounded, and the roads were being watched by the infantry and the country scoured by detachments of cavalry. Jean was too well known to escape. Would it not be better for him to stop at Maison-Close?

But it was not this he had thought of in coming to his resolution. He could not abandon his mother and Clary and De Vaudreuil.

His decision being final, did the three rooms of Maison-Close or the attic over them offer any hiding- place?

Jean had no time to find out.

Almost at once there was a violent knocking, which made the outer door rattle again.

The front yard was occupied by half a dozen of the police.

'Open!' came a voice from outside as the knocking redoubled. ' Open! or we'll break down the door!'

The door of De Vaudreuil's room was at once shut, while Jean and Clary tip-toed into Bridget's room, where they could hear better.

As Bridget went along the passage the door fell into fragments.

The passage was brightly lit by the torches which the police agents were carrying.

'What do you want?' asked Bridget.

'To search your house!' snapped one of the men. ' If Jean-Sans-Nom is here, we'll take him first, and then it will go badly with you.'

'Jean-sans-Nom is not here! ' Bridget told them calmly, ' and I don't know...'

The leader of the party suddenly stepped up to her.

It was Rip — Rip whose voice she had heard when her son had entered Maison-Close — Rip who had tempted Simon Morgaz into the most abominable of crimes.

Bridget, horror-stricken, recognised him at once.

'Eh!' exclaimed Rip, much surprised. ' Why, it's Madame Bridget! It's the wife of the brave Simon Morgaz!'

When he heard his father's name Jean recoiled to the end of the room.

Bridget, thunderstruck at this unexpected revelation, lacked the strength to reply.

' Eh? Yes? Madame Morgaz!' Rip continued. ' Really, I thought you were dead! Who would have expected to have found you in this place after twelve years?'

Bridget still kept silent.

' Come on, my friends! ' Rip turned to his men. ' There's nothing here! A brave woman, Bridget Morgaz! She's not the one to hide a rebel! Come, and let's look somewhere else. If Jean-Sans-Nom is in St. Charles, neither God nor the devil shall keep me from finding him.'

And, followed by his men, Rip had soon vanished up the road.

But the secret of Bridget and her son was now revealed! Even if De Vaudreuil had heard nothing, Clary had not lost a word.

So Jean-Sans-Nom was the son of Simon Morgaz! And with a movement of horror Clary fled from Bridget's room into her father's as though she were mad.

Jean and Bridget were left alone. Now Clary knew everything.

At the thought of appearing before her, before De Vaudreuil, before the friend of those patriots whom the treachery of Simon Morgaz had sent to the scaffold, Jean thought he would have gone insane.

'Mother!' he declared, ' I cannot stay here another instant. Monsieur and Mademoiselle de Vaudreuil no longer need me to defend them! They'll be safe enough — in the house of a Morgaz! Adieu!'

'My son — my son!' murmured Bridget. ' Do you think I haven't guessed it? You! the son of — you love Clary de Vaudreuil!'

' Yes, mother, but I'll die before I ever tell her! ' And he rushed from the house.

CHAPTER VI - WALHATTA

After the affair at Chipogan Farm, where the police and volunteers had been defeated, Thomas Harcher and his older sons had sought refuge beyond the Canadian frontier, whence they had returned to take part in the fight at St. Charles. After that tragic failure, which had cost Remy his life, Thomas and his four other sons had rejoined the reformists on the American frontier.

Mr. Nick had been careful not to return to Montreal. How could he explain his behaviour at Chipogan? Whatever might be the respect in which he was held, the police would not have hesitated to proceed against him for rebellion against the representatives of authority. The gates of the Montreal jail would certainly have closed on him, and in his company Lionel would have had plenty of leisure to cultivate the Muses intra muros.

Mr. Nick had acted for the best in the circumstances. He had followed the Mahogannis to Walhatta, and there he was waiting under his ancestral roof for the excitement to calm down. Then he would abandon the chieftainship of his tribe, and return modestly to business at his office.

Lionel was not of the same way of thinking. The young poet hoped that the lawyer would once and for all break his bonds with his office, and perpetuate among the Hurons the illustrious name of the Sagamores.

Two leagues from Chipogan Farm was the village of Walhatta, where Mr. Nick had been installed for some weeks. This was a new life for the placid notary. That Lionel was enthusiastic at the reception which all in the village gave his master need not be insisted on, but the notary failed to look at matters in the same light. The volleys of musketry that had welcomed him, the homage accorded to him, the palavers held in his honour, the flowery speeches addressed to him, the acknowledgements he had to make in the florid phraseology of the Far West, might be all very flattering to human vanity; but none the less the worthy man bitterly regretted the unfortunate affair which he had involuntarily engaged in. And if Lionel preferred the free air of the prairies to the stuffiness of the office and the parchments, and the eloquence of the Mahoganni warriors to the technical jargon of the law, Mr. Nick in no way shared his opinion. And between the master and the clerk there went on a vast amount of discussion which certainly did not increase their friendship.

Mr. Nick's fear was that matters could not remain as they were. He could foresee the Hurons having to take part in the struggle and throw in their lot with the patriots. And would he be able to stop them if they wanted to, if Jean-Sans-Nom called them to his side, if Thomas Harcher and his people came to Walhatta? Already he was dangerously compromised, but what would he be when he marched at the head of a savage tribe against the Anglo-Canadian authorities? How could he ever hope to take up his duties as a lawyer at Montreal?

But he comforted himself with the reflection that time is a great adjuster. Many weeks had elapsed since the outbreak at Chipogan, and if this were regarded merely as an isolated act of resistance to the police it might well be forgotten. Moreover the insurrectionist movement had not yet broken out, and nothing showed that a rising was imminent. If tranquillity continued to prevail in Canada, the authorities might show themselves tolerant and Mr. Nick might safely return to Montreal.

But this hope Lionel had no wish to see realized. To return to the office and practise engrossing for ten hours a day? Better become a backwoodsman or a bee-hunter! Let his master abandon the high position he held among the Mahogannis? Never! He was Mr. Nick no longer, he had become the legitimate descendant of the ancient race of the Sagamores! The Hurons would never permit him to exchange the tomahawk of the warrior for the quill of the lawyer.

Since he had reached Walhatta, Mr. Nick had resided in the wigwam whence his predecessor had departed to join his ancestors in the Happy-Hunting-grounds. Lionel would have given up every building in Montreal for this uncomfortable shelter where the young folks of the tribe did their best to serve his master. The Mahogannis regarded him as their chief's right hand man, and when Nicholas Sagamore had to make a speech at the council fire, Lionel could not keep from accompanying him with a wealth of impassioned gesture.

It follows that the young clerk would have been the happiest of mortals, had his master not obstinately refused to realize his dearest wish — for Mr. Nick to don the costume of the Mahogannis. Lionel desired nothing so much as to see him in full Huron attire, with moccasins on his feet, feathers on his head, and embroidered mantle on his shoulder. Many times he had broached the subject without success, but he did not despair.

'He'll come to it,' he said; ' I won't let him reign disguised as a lawyer. With his long coat, his velvet waistcoat and his white cravat, what does he look like, pray? He hasn't as yet put off the old Adam, and he must! Whenever he opens his mouth before the assembly of the notables of his tribe, I always expect him to say, ' In the presence of Mr. Nick and his colleagues.' That's not to be endured. I mean him to dress like the warriors, and when I get a chance to persuade him I shan't miss it.'

And a very simple idea occurred to him. In the conversations he had with the notables of Walhatta, he found that it was not without keen disappointment that they could see the descendant of the Sagamores clad in the European style; and at his suggestion the Mahogannis decided to proceed solemnly to the enthronisation of their new chief. Then was drawn up the programme of a ceremony to which were to be invited all the Indians in the neighbourhood. There would be shooting-matches, dances, feasts, at which Mr. Nick could not preside except in the national costume.

This resolution was definitely adopted during the last half of November, and preparations were at once begun, so that things could be done really well.

The duties Mr. Nick would have to perform when on the day fixed he received the homage of his people were kept a secret, to take him by surprise; but as he would have to dress and behave as a Huron chief the young clerk had to inform him of the fact. And this he did on 22nd November, much to Mr. Nick's displeasure.

When the lawyer heard that the tribe were preparing a festival in his honour, he promptly wished it to the devil, along with his young clerk.

'May Nicholas Sagamore deign to listen to the advice of the Paleface!' said Lionel. * Of what Paleface? ' Mr. Nick did not understand. ' Of your humble servant, great chief.'

' Well, take care I don't turn your pale face into a red one by a good slap!'

Lionel took no notice of the threat and continued cheerfully: 'May Nicholas Sagamore never forget that I am profoundly devoted to him! If he should ever become a prisoner of the Sioux, the Oneidas, or the Iroquois, if he is ever bound to the stake, it is I who will defend him from the insults and the claws of the old women; and when he is dead, it is I who will place on his grave his calumet and his tomahawk!'

Mr. Nick decided to let him talk, but to terminate the interview in a way that would leave its mark on his clerk's ears. He contented himself with saying: 'And so I must yield to the wishes of the Mahogannis?'

' To their prayers!'

'Well, if it comes to that I shall be present at the festival.'

'You cannot refuse, for the blood of the Sagamores runs in your veins!'

'The blood of the Sagamores mixed with a lawyer's! grumbled Mr. Nick. And then Lionel approached the delicate point. ' It is understood,' he said, ' that the great chief will preside at the ceremony. And he will present himself in the garb appropriate to his rank with a scalp-lock rising stiffly from the summit of his cranium.'

'And why?'

'Out of respect for tradition.'

'What! Tradition requires it?'

'Yes; and besides, should the chief of the Mahogannis ever fall on the war-path, is it not essential so that his enemy may brandish his head in sign of victory?'

'Indeed!' said Mr. Nick. ' My enemy must be able to brandish my head, must he? Holding it up by this scalp- lock, eh?'

'Such is the Indian custom, and no warrior would refuse to follow it. No other style of hairdressing would be in harmony with the costume which Nicholas Sagamore will assume on the day of the ceremony.'

'Ah! So I'm to assume...'

'At this very moment they are at work on the festive attire. It will be magnificent. The deer-skin jacket, the elk-skin moccasins, the mantle as worn by the predecessor of Nicholas Sagamore, the facial decoration as...'

'Facial decoration?'

'The most accomplished artists of the tribe are now preparing for the tattooing of the arms and chests...'

'Pray go on,' Mr. Nick clenched his teeth. ' This is most interesting. The facial decoration, indeed, the scalp-lock on my head, the moccasins of elk-skin, the tattooing of my chest. You have forgotten nothing.'

'Nothing,' the clerk assured him. ' And when the great chief shows himself to his warriors draped in the garb which will show him off at his best, I do not doubt but that the Indian ladies will fight for the honour of sharing his wigwam...'

'The Indian women will fight for the honour?'

'For the honour of assuring a long line of descendants to the elect of the Great Spirit!'

'And so it will be to the general satisfaction if I take a Huron squaw?'

'And who else could it be for the future of the Mahogannis? Already have they made choice of a squaw of high degree who will devote herself to the happiness of the great chief.'

'And may we inquire who is this red-skinned princess who is going to devote herself to me?'

'Certainly,' Lionel assured him; ' she is worthy of the lineage of the Sagamores.'

' And who may she be?'

' The widow of your predecessor.' It was lucky for the young clerk that he was able to dodge the blow that Mr. Nick levelled at him. But he had judged his distance, and his master had to content himself with saying: 'Listen to me, Lionel. If ever you return to the subject I'll pull your ears until they are as long as those of David La Gamme's donkey.'

At this comparison, which recalled one of the heroes of The Last of the Mohicans, Lionel very wisely retired. As to Mr. Nick, he was not more irritated against his clerk than against the notables of the tribe. To impose the Mahogannian costume upon him for this ceremony! To make him grow a scalp-lock, clothe himself, paint himself, tattoo himself, like his ancestors! But would he yield to the necessities of the case? Dare he present himself before his warriors in these civilian garments, the sombre attire of a lawyer, the most pacific of all the lawyers? Here was a problem that troubled him the more as the great day approached.

Fortunately — for the heir of the Sagamores — serious events created a diversion in the Mahoganni plans.

Important news reached Walhatta on the 23rd. The patriots of St. Denis had, it was reported, repulsed Colonel Gore's troops. The news provoked demonstrations of delight among the Hurons. At Chipogan Farm their sympathies had been won over for the cause of independence, and only an opportunity was needed for them to throw in their lot with the French-Canadians.

The victory — as Mr. Nick realised only too well — would not induce the warriors of his tribe to suspend the preparations for the festival in his honour. On the contrary, it would make them celebrate it with more enthusiasm, and their chief would escape none of the honours of his enthronisation. But three days later came bad news to follow the good. After the victory at St. Denis, the defeat at St. Charles.

On hearing of the bloody reprisals carried out by the loyalists, the atrocities, plunderings, burnings, murders, the destruction of both townships, the Mahogannis could hardly restrain their indignation. To rise as one man and rush to the help of the patriots was only a step, and Mr. Nick might well fear it would be taken. Was the lawyer, already somewhat compromised, to commit himself irretrievably? Would he have to put himself at the head of his warriors and make common cause with the insurrection? Anyhow, there could now be no question of ceremonies. But what was the reception he gave to Lionel when the clerk informed him that the time had come to dig up the tomahawk and to brandish it upon the war-path!

Thenceforward his one anxiety was to soothe his bellicose followers. When they came to him to be harangued, expecting him to declare himself against the oppressors, he exhausted his ingenuity in ways of saying neither yes nor no. They must be careful, he told them, not to act without careful thought, without seeing what would be the consequences of the defeat at St. Charles. Perhaps the whole region had already been invaded by the loyalists? Nothing was known of the plans of the reformists, who might be already dispersed. Where had they taken refuge? Where could they join them? Might they not have given up until a better opportunity presented itself? Were not the leaders in the power of the bureaucrats, and imprisoned at Montreal?

These were good reason enough for Mr. Nick to give his impatient Pretorian Guards, but they were not accepted without dispute. One of these days the warriors' rage might possess them and carry them away, and then their chief would naturally have to follow them. Perhaps he had some notion of giving his tribe the slip, but this would have been difficult, for they were watching him much more closely than he imagined. But where could he go? He did not care to leave Canada, where he had been born; and to hide himself in some village where the police were on the alert, would be to risk falling into their hands.

Besides, Mr. Nick did not know what had become of the leaders of the insurrection. Although some of the Mahogannis had gone up the banks of the Richelieu as far as the St. Lawrence, they had been unable to learn anything about this. Even at Chipogan Farm, Catherine Harcher knew nothing of what had happened to her husband or his sons, nothing of the De Vaudreuils, nothing of Jean-Sans-Nom, nothing of what had happened at Maison-Close after the affair at St. Charles.

All that could be done was to watch events, and this was not displeasing to Mr. Nick. To gain time, and with the time to see the excitement settle down, that was all he wanted.

But on this point there were further disputes with his clerk, who hated the loyalists. The latest news had overwhelmed Lionel. There was no longer anything here for him to make fun of. He no longer made jokes about the war-path, about digging up the tomahawk, about the blood of the Sagamores. All he could think of was the cause now so seriously compromised, what had become of the heroic Jean-Sans-Nom? Had he fallen at St. Charles? No! The news of his death would have spread abroad, and the authorities would have done their best to spread it, so that it would have been known at Chipogan as at Walhatta. But if he had survived, where was he? Lionel would have risked his life to know.

Several days elapsed, but there was no change in the situation. Were the patriots getting ready to take the offensive? Once or twice rumours of this reached the Mahogannis, but they were not confirmed. By Lord Gosford's orders the regions round Montreal and Laprairie were being searched. Large bodies of troops were occupying both banks of the Richelieu. Incessant house-to-house searches kept the people of the farms and villages on the alert. Sir John Colborne had his columns ready to march on the flag of rebellion

215

wherever it might be raised. If the fugitives tried to recross the American frontier, they would find themselves faced with considerable forces.

On 5th December, Lionel, who had gone out towards Chambly in search of information, learnt that martial law had been proclaimed in the district of Montreal. At the same time the Governor-General had offered a reward of four thousand dollars for the apprehension of the Deputy Papineau. Among the other rewards offered were those for De Vaudreuil and Vincent Hodge. Some of the reformists were said to be imprisoned at Montreal and Quebec, where they were to be tried by martial law, so that the political scaffold would soon be claiming further victims.

This was serious news. To the measures decreed against them would the Sons of Freedom respond by another call to arms? On the other hand, would they not be discouraged by this pitiless repression? That was Mr. Nick's opinion. He realised that if the reformists did not succeed at the outset, they had little chance of succeeding at all.

But this was not the opinion of his Mahoganni warriors, nor was it that of Lionel.

'No! 'he told the lawyer repeatedly, ' No! The cause is not lost, and so long as Jean-Sans-Nom is still alive we shall not despair of regaining our independence.'

On 7th December something occurred to thrust Mr. Nick back among the difficulties from which he fancied he had escaped, and to raise almost to madness the bellicose instincts of the Hurons.

For some days the presence of the Abbé Joann had been reported in the neighbourhood. He had traversed the Laprairie region, calling upon the French-Canadians to rise as one man. His fiery eloquence contended not without difficulty with the discouragement that had fallen upon the patriots after their defeat at St. Charles. But the Abbé Joann would never give in; he went straight ahead, he urged the people to take once again to arms as soon as their leaders reappeared in the district.

But his brother was not with him; the Abbé did not know what had become of him. Before setting out on his mission he had been to Maison-Close to embrace his mother, to have news of Jean.

Maison-Close had not been opened to him.

Joann had gone in search of his brother. He too could not think the man was dead, for the news of his death would have been reported far and wide. He told himself that Jean would reappear at the head of his comrades.

Meanwhile his efforts tended to raise the Indians, especially the Huron warriors, who were only waiting to be asked to intervene. It was in such circumstances that he arrived among the Mahogannis.

Mr. Nick could not but give him a cordial welcome; nor could he any longer resist the pressure brought to bear on him by his tribe.

' Well,' he said at last with a shake of his head, ' nobody can escape from his destiny. I don't know how the race of the Sagamores began, but I know only too well how it will end! It will end before a court-martial.'

The Hurons were in fact ready for the war-path, and Lionel had done not a little to rouse them.

As soon as the Abbé arrived at Walhatta, the young clerk had become one of his warmest supporters. Not only had he found in him all the ardour of his own patriotism, but he had been struck by the strange resemblance between the young priest and Jean-Sans- Nom, almost the same eyes, the same fiery look, almost the same voice and the same gestures. He thought his hero had returned disguised as a priest, he thought he could hear... Was it an illusion of his senses? He could not say.

For two days the Abbé Joann had now been among the Mahogannis, whose only demand was to join the patriots. These had concentrated their forces about fifty leagues to the south-west, at Navy Island, on the Niagara River.

Mr. Nick saw himself doomed to follow the warriors of his tribe. Their preparations were almost complete. As soon as they left the village the Mahogannis would traverse the neighbouring regions, raise the other Indians, reach the shore of Lake Ontario, and then, advancing to the Niagara, they would join the last supporters of the national cause.

On the evening of 9th December, one of the Hurons now returned from Montreal announced that Jean-Sans- Nom had been arrested by the police on the Ontario frontier, and that he was imprisoned in Fort Frontenac.

The effect of this news can be imagined. Jean-Sans- Nom in the power of the loyalists! The Mahogannis were aghast; and it is easy to imagine their

217

emotion when the Abbé Joann, as soon as he heard of the arrest, had exclaimed: ' My brother! ' Then he added: ' I'll save him from death!'

' Let me go with you!' pleaded Lionel. ' Come, my child!' the Abbé replied.

CHAPTER VII - FORT FRONTENAC

Jean was like a madman when he left Maison-Close. The incognito of his life so brutally torn apart; Rip's dreadful words, overheard by Clary, who now realised that it was in the home of the wife and the son of Simon Morgaz that her father had found refuge; De Vaudreuil having to be told all this if he had not already heard it in his room — it was enough to fill him with despair.

Stay in the house he could not — not even for a moment. Without asking what would become of the De Vaudreuils, without asking if his mother's infamous name could protect them further, without even remembering that Bridget would no longer be able to live in the place where she had been recognised, and from which she would undoubtedly be driven, he had fled into the forest, nor did he stop running throughout the night. He felt he could never get far enough from those to whom, for the future, he could be nothing but an object of horror and scorn.

And his work — not yet accomplished! His duty was to fight, simply because he was still alive! His duty was to get himself killed before his real name was revealed! When he was dead, when he had died for his country, if he could not gain the esteem of his fellow-countrymen, he might at least claim their pity.

At length he grew calmer, and with his self-control he regained that energy which no weakness could henceforth overcome.

As he fled he made for the frontier, to rejoin the patriots, and continue the struggle for independence.

At six in the morning Jean found he had got twelve miles from St. Charles, and near the right bank of the St. Lawrence, on the borders of Montreal County. The district was patrolled by detachments of cavalry, and it swarmed with the police agents; he would have to get away from it as soon as possible. But to strike direct for the United States seemed impracticable, and so he continued his flight obliquely through Laprairie County, which was watched as carefully as that of Montreal. The best thing he could do was to keep along the St. Lawrence to reach Lake Ontario, and then to cross the eastern territories to the nearest American village. And this is what he decided to do.

But he had to push on very carefully. The difficulties were great. To get through somehow, no matter how long it might take him, was his programme, which he could modify to suit contingencies. The loyalist volunteers were afoot. The police were making constant domiciliary visits in search of the insurgent leaders, and among them was Jean-Sans-Nom, the reward for whose apprehension he could see announced on the proclamations posted up on the walls.

It was only during the night that he could move; during the day he hid in abandoned huts, in the midst of impenetrable thickets where he found a thousand difficulties in getting food. And he would certainly have died of hunger had it not been for the charity of the local people, who gave him what he wanted without asking who he was or whence he came. But his progress was slow. It was not until he was out of Laprairie County, and in Ontario Province, that he could hope to make up for lost time.

From 4th to 8th December Jean hardly covered sixty miles. During these five days — it would be more exact to say these five nights — he had only just got away from the bank of the St. Lawrence, and reached the centre of Beauharnais county. The most difficult part of his task was over, for the western and southern parishes were much less patrolled at this distance from Montreal. Yet the dangers were thickening round him. A squad of police had come on his track on the county boundary. Once or twice his coolness managed to throw them off his trail.

During the night of 8th December, however, he realised that he was surrounded by a dozen men, with orders to take him dead or alive. After defending himself with truly terrific energy, and seriously wounding several of the police, he was captured. It was not Rip who had effected the capture, but Superintendent Comeau, so that six thousand dollars were absent from the right side on the books of the famous commercial house of Rip and Co.

The news of Jean-Sans-Nom's arrest soon spread far and wide, for the authorities had good reasons for making it known, and it reached the village of Walhatta the same day.

Fort Frontenac is situated on the north shore of Ontario, a few leagues from Kingson. It dominates the left bank of the St. Lawrence, the river which forms the frontier between Canada and the United States. The fort was then commanded by Major Sinclair, who had under his orders four officers and a hundred men of the 20th Regiment. It completed the defensive system which protected the outlying territories from Indian depredations.

It was to Fort Frontenac that Jean-Sans-Nom was taken. The Governor-General, informed of the important capture made by Comeau's detachment, did not think fit to send the prisoner to Montreal, or to any of the other important cities where his presence might provoke a popular rising. Hence the order from Quebec to take him to Fort Frontenac, and to hold the trial there. Normally Jean would have been executed within twenty- four hours, but there was a special reason for some delay in bringing him before the court-martial, convened under the presidency of Major Sinclair.

That the prisoner was the Jean-Sans-Nom, the determined agitator who had been the soul of the insurrections of 1832, 1835, and 1837 there was no doubt, but the Government wanted to know the real name of this man who concealed his identity under this pseudonym. Then they could inquire into his past life, and obtain information which might help them to unravel certain secret proceedings, and to identify his accomplices in the cause of independence. It was thus important to make out, if not the identity, at least the origin of this person, whose real name was still unknown, and which he might have some reason for keeping back. The court-martial therefore waited before proceeding to sentence, and Jean was closely interrogated. He refused point-blank to give any information, and declined even to answer any questions. So the attempt had to be given up, and on 10th December he was brought before his judges.

There was nothing to discuss. Jean declared that he had borne arms during the present as during the past revolts, and he proudly acclaimed the rights of Lower Canada, now withheld by England; he faced his accusers boldly; he spoke as if his words could cross the walls of the fort, and be heard throughout the country.

When Major Sinclair questioned him for the last time about his name, his birthplace and his family, he replied: ' I am Jean-Sans-Nom, a French-Canadian by birth, and that should be enough for you. It matters very little what the man is called when he is to be shot. Do you really want a name for a corpse?'

Jean was condemned to death, and Major Sinclair ordered him to be taken back to his cell. Then, in accordance with his instructions, he sent off a despatch- rider to Quebec, informing the Governor-General that he had been unable to ascertain his prisoner's real name, and asking whether, in the circumstances, he was to proceed with his execution?

For over a fortnight Lord Gosford had been very busy prosecuting those who had taken part in the insurrections at St. Denis and St. Charles. Forty-five of the leading patriots were in Montreal jail, eleven in that of Quebec. The Law Courts were in action with their three judges, the prosecutor general and the solicitor who represented the Crown, and there was also a Court Martial presided over by a major-general and composed of fifteen of the senior officers who had dealt with the insurrection.

While waiting for sentence, which would involve the most appalling penalties, the prisoners were subjected to treatment whose severity no political feeling could excuse. The jails contained hundreds of poor wretches, who were suffering intensely from the harshness of the Canadian winter. Tortured by hunger — for their rations were barely sufficient — they longed for the verdict and for their sentence, however pitiless it might be But before bringing them to trial, Lord Gosford wanted to wait until the police had completed their enquiries, so as to get into his hands as many of the patriots as he could.

When the news of Jean's capture reached Quebec, it was felt that the cause of independence had been struck to the heart.

It was nine in the evening when, on 12th December, Joann and Lionel came in sight of the fort. Like Jean, they had gone up the right bank of the St. Lawrence and crossed the river, at the risk of arrest at any moment. Though Lionel was in no special danger because of his behaviour at Chipogan. the Abbé was now "wanted by the police,' so that they had to take the needful precautions and this delayed them.

Moreover, the weather was frightful. For twenty-four hours there raged one of those snow-storms to which the meteorologists of the country give the name of blizzards. During such blizzards the temperature may sink thirty degrees, and the cold become so intense that its claims many victims.*

What did the Abbé hope for in coming to Fort Frontenac? What plan had he formed? Could he possibly get into touch with the prisoner? If he could make some prior arrangement, could he plot an escape? But it was certain that he felt it important to get into the cell that night.

Lionel, like the Abbé, was ready to lay down his life to save that of Jean-Sans-Nom. But what could they do? On coming within half a mile of the fort, they had skirted a copse which stretched down to the shore of the lake. There, through the trees, already stripped by the wintry breezes, swept the icy simoon which lifted the (*In some parts of Canada, in the St. John Valley, the thermometer has been seen to fall to 40° or 45° below zero. — J.V.) waters of Lake Ontario into tumultuous whirlpools.

'Lionel.' the Abbé told him, ' you stay here, but don't show yourself, and wait till I get back. The sentries at the gate mustn't see you. I'll try to get into the fort and get in touch with my brother. If I succeed, we can consider the chances of escape. If that's impossible, we'll discuss the possibility of an attack the reformists might make if the garrison of Frontenac isn't too strong.'

Such an attack would take some time to prepare, and the Abbé did not then know — for the tidings had not yet spread — that Jean had been sentenced to death, and that at any moment the order for execution might arrive. But he regarded the attack only as a last resource, and his real object was to enable Jean to escape.

'Monsieur l'Abbé,' asked Lionel, ' have you any hope of seeing your brother?'

'They cannot refuse admittance to a minister who comes to offer his services to a prisoner condemned to death.'

'That would be unworthy even of them! ' Lionel agreed. ' They can't refuse you. Go on, then, Monsieur l'Abbé, and I'll wait here for you.'

The Abbé gripped the clerk's hand, and disappeared along the edge of the wood.

In less than a quarter of an hour he had reached the gate of Fort Frontenac.

The fort was on the bank of the lake, and consisted of a central blockhouse, surrounded by high palisades. At the foot of the palisades, on the side facing the lake, was a bare, narrow beach, then hidden under a bed of snow which merged imperceptibly into the ice which covered the edge of the lake. On the other side was a village consisting of a few houses, inhabited chiefly by a population of fishermen.

Was an escape possible? Could Jean get away across the country? Could he slip out of his cell, clear the palisades, and outwit the guard? This was what must be looked into if Joann could get an interview with him. Once at liberty they could join Lionel, and make off, not towards the American frontier, but towards Niagara and Navy Island, where the patriots were rallying for a final effort.

The Abbé crossed the beach, reached the gate, and went up to the sentry, whom he asked to take him to the commanding officer.

A sergeant came out of the guard-room, accompanied by a soldier who carried a lantern, for the darkness was already deep.

'What do you want?' asked the sergeant.

'I want to see the commanding officer.'

'And who are you?'

'A priest, come to offer his services to the prisoner, Jean-Sans-Nom.'

* You want a word with the condemned man?'

'Sentence has been pronounced?'

'The day before yesterday. And he's been sentenced to death!'

Joann was sufficiently master of himself to show no sign of his emotion. He contented himself with replying: 'That is another reason why you should not refuse.'

'I will inform Major Sinclair, the commanding officer,' replied the sergeant.

And he went off towards the blockhouse, after letting the Abbé into the guard-room.

Joann sat down in a dark corner, thinking over what he had just heard. If sentence had been passed, was there time for his plans to succeed? But if the sentence — pronounced over twenty-four hours ago — had not yet been executed, was that because Major Sinclair had received orders to postpone it? The Abbé hoped so. But how long was it to be postponed, and would this be long enough for the prisoner to escape? Would the major let the Abbé enter the prison? But what would happen if he refused to call him until the very moment of execution? The agonies Joann suffered when he thought he might not be given time to act will be readily understood.

The sergeant returned and said: 'Major Sinclair will see you.'

Preceded by the sergeant, whose lantern lighted his way, Joann crossed the inner courtyard in whose centre rose the blockhouse. As well as the darkness allowed him he tried to make out the size of this courtyard, and the distance which separated the building from the gate, the only exit from the fort unless the palisades could be scaled. If Jean did not know the layout of the fort, Joann might describe it to him.

The door of the blockhouse was open. The sergeant entered, followed by the Abbé, and an orderly closed the door behind them. They climbed a narrow staircase to the floor above; and there the sergeant opened a door on the landing, and Joann found himself in the presence of Major Sinclair.

The major was a man of about fifty, typically English in his stiff manner and typically Saxon in his lack of sympathy for suffering. He might even have refused the condemned man the consolations of a priest had he not received orders too categorical to be infringed. He neither rose from his chair nor laid aside the pipe with which he was filling with tobacco smoke a room dimly lit by a small lamp.

' You say you're a priest?' he asked Joann.

' Yes, major.'

' You want to see the prisoner?'

' If you will permit me.'

' Where have you come from?'

' From Laprairie county.'

' You heard of his capture there, did you?'

' Yes.'

' And of his sentence?'

'I learnt that only when I arrived at Fort Frontenac, and I thought that Major Sinclair would not refuse me an interview with the prisoner.'

225

' Quite so, and I'll let you know when the time comes,' the major replied.

'It is never too soon,' the Abbé reminded him, ' when a man is condemned to death . ..'

'I tell you I'll let you know when the time comes. Wait in the village, where one of my men will come to fetch you.'

' Excuse my insistence, major,' the Abbé pleaded. ' I might be away just when the prisoner requires my services, so would you let me see him at once...'

' I've told you that I'll let you know,' the officer repeated. ' There is to be no communication with the prisoner until the time of execution. I'm expecting the order from Quebec, and when that order arrives the man will have two hours to prepare for death. Surely two hours is enough, devil take it, and you can use them in any way you think fit to save his soul. The sergeant will escort you back to the gate.'

With this answer Joann had to be content. But not to see his brother, not to be able to consult him, was to render impracticable any attempt at flight, and he was about to appeal further to the officer to alter his decision when the door opened and the sergeant appeared.

'Sergeant,' the major gave orders, ' show this priest out of the fort, and don't admit him again until I send for him.'

' Very good, sir,' the sergeant replied; ' but I came to tell you that an orderly has just arrived at the fort, sir.'

'From Quebec?'

'Yes, sir; and he has brought this letter.'

'Give it to me.'

And he snatched, rather than took, it from the sergeant.

The Abbé had become so pale, he felt so faint, that his weakness and pallor would have been noticed had the major looked up. But he did not, his attention being directed to the letter bearing Lord Gosford's seal, which he had torn out of the envelope.

He read it. Then he turned to the sergeant.

'Take this priest to the cell of Jean-Sans-Nom,' he told him. ' You'll leave him alone with the condemned man, and when he wants to leave, you'll escort him back to the gate.'

It was the order for the prisoner's execution.

Jean-Sans-Nom had but two hours to live.

CHAPTER VIII - JOANN AND JEAN

The Abbé left Major Sinclair's room much more fully in control of himself than when he had entered it. The thunder-clap of this news had only shaken him; God had inspired him with a plan, and the plan might succeed.

Jean knew nothing of the order which had just arrived from Montreal, and to Joann fell the sad task of telling him.

Well, he would not! He would not tell him! He would hide the terrible news that the sentence was to be carried out within two hours. If Joann's plan were to succeed, Jean must know nothing about it.

They could no longer count on a carefully prepared escape, nor on an attack on Fort Frontenac. Jean could escape death only by immediate flight. If two hours later he were still in the cell, he would leave it only to fall before a volley at the foot of the palisades.

Was the Abbé's plan feasible? Perhaps, if his brother would agree to it. It was certainly the only plan possible under the circumstances. But it was absolutely essential that Jean should not know that Major Sinclair had received the order for his execution.

Led by the sergeant, the Abbé descended the staircase. The prisoner's cell was in an angle of the ground- floor of the blockhouse, at the end of a long corridor. The sergeant lit the way with his lantern, and stopped at a low door secured on the outside with two bolts. As he was about to open it, the sergeant said quietly: 'You know that when you leave the prisoner my orders are to take you to the gate!'

'I know!' said the Abbé. ' Wait in this passage and I'll call you!'

The door of the cell was thrown open.

In the darkness, on a rough bed, Jean was asleep. He was not aroused by the noise the sergeant made.

The sergeant advanced to touch him on the shoulder, when Joann signed to him not to do so.

Instead he put the lantern on a table, went out, and gently shut the door.

The two brothers were alone, one asleep, the other on his knees.

Then Joann arose, and looked for a moment at this other self whom their father's crime had doomed to so miserable a life; he murmured: 'God, grant me Thy aid.'

Time was too short for him to lose even a few minutes. He touched his brother's shoulder.

Jean awoke, opened his eyes, sat up, and recognised him.

'Joann!'

'Quiet — Jean, speak quietly!' said Joann. ' They can hear us.'

And with his hand he made a sign that the door was guarded on the outside, where the sergeant's footsteps could be heard as he strode up and down the corridor.

Jean, half-dressed, under a coarse blanket that barely protected him against the chill of the cell, rose noiselessly and embraced his brother.

'How's mother?' he asked.

'She's not at Maison-Close.'

'Not there?'

'No.'

'And Monsieur de Vaudreuil and his daughter whom our house sheltered?'

'The house was empty when I last went to St. Charles.'

'When?'

'A week ago.'

'And since then you've had no news of mother or our friends?'

'None.'

What had happened? Had another search ended in the arrest of Bridget and the De Vaudreuils? Or, not wanting her father to remain another day under the roof of the Morgaz family, had Clary taken her father away in spite of the danger which threatened him? And Bridget, had she fled from St. Charles when the shame of her identity had been made public?

All this passed like lightning through Jean's mind. And he was about to tell his brother what had happened during his last visit to Maison-Close, when Joann leaned towards him and whispered in his ear.

'Listen, Jean. It isn't a brother who's here, but a priest come to fulfil his duty to a condemned man. It's in that capacity that the commander of the fort has allowed me to enter your cell. We haven't a moment to lose. You must escape this instant.'

'This instant? And how?

'Take my clothes and get away disguised as a priest. We resemble each other enough for nobody to see through the trick. Besides, it's still night, and there will hardly be any light from the lantern as you go down the passage, and across the courtyard. Your face will never be recognised under this hat. When we've changed clothes, I will get to the back of the cell there, and call out. As agreed, the sergeant will open the door. He has orders to escort me back to the gate. It's you he will be escorting . .

'Brother,' Jean grasped Joann's hand, ' you thought I'd ever consent to this sacrifice?'

'You must, Jean. Your presence among the reformists is more necessary than ever.'

'Haven't they despaired of the cause after their defeat?'

'No! They're concentrating at Niagara, on Navy Island, ready to continue the struggle.'

'They can do that without me, Joann. The success of our cause doesn't depend upon any one man. I won't let you risk your life to save mine.'

'And isn't it my duty, Jean? You know what our aim is? Have we attained it? No, we haven't even known how to die to atone for the evil...'

Joann's words moved his brother deeply, but he would not give in.

Joann continued: 'Listen once more. You're afraid for me, Jean; but what have I to fear? Tomorrow, when they find me in the cell, what can happen to me? Nothing. Here there's only a poor priest instead of a condemned man, and what can they do but let him go...'

'No! ' Jean was struggling with himself and against his brother's arguments.

'Enough talk! ' Joann told him. ' You must go, and you shall go. Do your duty as I am doing mine. You alone are popular enough to arouse a general revolt...'

'And if they make you responsible for my escape?'

'They won't condemn me without a trial, without an order from Quebec, and that will take several days.'

'Several days!'

'During which you will have time to join your comrades on Navy Island and bring them to Fort Frontenac to rescue me.'

'It's sixty miles from Frontenac to Navy Island, Joann. I shan't have time.'

'You refuse? Well, up to now I've implored you, now I command you. It is no longer a brother who is speaking to you, but a priest. If you do not die fighting for our cause, you will have done nothing to accomplish the task that has been assigned to you. If you refuse, I will make my identity known, and the Abbé Joann will fall before the firing-squad side by side with Jean-Sans-Nom!'

'Brother!'

'Go, Jean! Go! I will have it so! Our mother will have it so! Your country will have it so!'

Overcome by Joann's urgency, Jean could do nothing but obey. Moreover the chance of returning to Fort Frontenac in a few days with some hundreds of his followers overcame his last resistance.

'I'm ready!' he said.

The change of clothes did not take long. Under the Abbé's cloak it would have been difficult to recognise that the brother had taken his place.

And then for a few moments the brothers talked of what was going on among the Reformists and their foes. Then Joann said: 'Now I'll call the sergeant. When he opens the door, you go out and follow him along the passage. Once out of the blockhouse, you've only to cross the courtyard, about fifty yards wide, and then you'll reach the guardroom on the right hand of the palisading. Turn your head away as you pass it. The gate will be in front of you. When you get through it, keep along the shore until you reach the edge of a wood about half a mile from the fort. There you'll find Lionel.'

' Lionel? The lawyer's clerk?'

' Yes! He came with me and he'll take you to Navy Island. Now, goodbye!'

'Brother! ' Jean threw himself into his brother's arms.

The moment had come. Joann called loudly and went across to the back of the cell.

The sergeant opened the door and, turning to Jean, said: ' You're ready? ' Jean answered by a gesture. ' Come this way.'

The sergeant took the lantern, followed Jean oat of the cell, and shut the door.

In what agony did Joann pass the next few minutes! What would happen if Major Sinclair were in the corridor or the courtyard when Jean went by? If he stopped him; if he asked him about the prisoner? If the trick were discovered, the prisoner would at once be shot! And he knew that the preparations for execution had begun, that the garrison had received their orders, that the sergeant, thinking he was dealing with a priest, might mention this to Jean on the way out! And then Jean, learning that the execution was going to be carried out, would return; for he would never allow his brother to die in his place. With his ear at the door, the Abbé listened. His heart beat so violently that he could scarcely hear the sounds outside. At last a distant noise reached him. He fell on his knees and gave thanks to God.

The gate had just been shut.

'Free!' murmured Joann.

And indeed Jean had not been recognised. The sergeant, walking before him lantern in hand, had led him to the gate without saying a word. Officers and men alike were still unaware that the execution was to take place in an hour. As he passed through the gate Jean had turned aside his head, as his brother had told him.

'Will you come back to the prisoner?' asked the sergeant.

Jean nodded.

And a moment later he was free.

Yet he moved but slowly from the fort, as if some bond held him to the prison — a bond he dare not break. He reproached himself with having given in to his brother, in allowing him to take his place. All the perils of the substitution appeared before him with an alarming clearness. A few hours later, he thought, they'll go into the cell, at daybreak; the escape will be discovered, and Joann will be treated very harshly as he waits for the death with which they might punish his heroic sacrifice.

And then Jean felt himself seized with an irresistible desire to go back. But no! He must hurry on to join the patriots at Navy Island, to begin anew the insurrectional campaign, and to hurl himself against Fort Frontenac, to set his brother free. And for that there would not be a moment to lose.

He crossed the beach obliquely, turned along the edge of the lake, and made for the wood where Lionel ought to be waiting for him.

The blizzard was then raging in all its violence. The ice on the shore of the lake was piled up like the floes of the Arctic Ocean, and a blinding snow-storm swept along over them in furious squalls.

Jean, lost for a time in the storm and hardly knowing whether he were on the land or the lake, strove to find his way to the clump of trees he could just see in the darkness. At last he reached it, after taking nearly half an hour to cover the half-mile.

Lionel could not possibly have seen him, or he would certainly have come to meet him.

Jean went on under the trees, uneasy at not finding the young clerk at the appointed place, and not liking to shout to him for fear of running into danger if he were overheard by some belated fisherman.

Then the last two lines of the young poet's ballad recurred to his memory, and as he went into the wood he softly repeated: 'To be born with you, my frolicsome flame, To die with you, my will-o'-the-wisp.'

A moment afterwards Lionel emerged from a thicket and exclaimed: 'You, Monsieur Jean, you?'

'Yes, Lionel.'

'And the Abbé Joann?'

'He's in my cell! But now for Navy Island! In forty- eight hours we must be back with our comrades at Fort Frontenac.'

Jean and Lionel left the wood, and went southwards, so as to follow the shores of the Ontario to Niagara. It was the shortest way as well as the least dangerous.

Fifteen miles off they would cross the American frontier; then, safe from any pursuit, they could hurry on to Navy Island.

But to take this direction they had to pass the fort. In this terrible night, amid the thick whirlwinds of snow, they were not likely to be seen by the sentinels, even as they went along the beach.

If the lake had been navigable, instead of being choked with the masses of ice, it would have been better for them to have appealed to some fisherman, who could soon have taken them to the mouth of the Niagara river. But that was impossible now.

Jean and Lionel went along as fast as the storm would let them. They were scarcely a hundred yards from the palisades of the fort, when the sharp crackle of musketry rent the air.

There could be no mistake. A platoon had fired a volley somewhere inside the palisade.

'Joann!' exclaimed Jean.

And he fell, as if he had been hit when the soldiers opened fire.

Joann had died for his brother, for his country.

Half an hour after Jean had gone, Major Sinclair had given orders to proceed with the execution in conformity with the orders he had received from Quebec.

Joann had been taken out of the cell and out into the courtyard where he was to be shot.

The major read the order aloud.

Joann did not reply. At that moment he need only have said, ' I am not Jean-Sans-Nom! I am the priest who took his place to save him!'

And the major would have had to suspend the execution, and to get fresh instructions from the Governor-General.

But Jean was too near Fort Frontenac. The soldiers would have started out after him. He would inevitably be retaken. He would have been shot. And Jean-Sans-Nom must not die anywhere except on the battlefield.

Joann held his peace, and died with the thoughts in his mind of his mother, his brother, his country.

The soldiers had not recognised him when he was alive, nor did they recognise him when he was dead. They at once buried him in a grave dug just outside the palisades.

In him the Government believed they had struck down the hero of Canadian independence.

He was the first victim offered in expiation of the crime of Simon Morgaz.

CHAPTER IX - NAVY ISLAND

Navy Island is situated about three miles above Niagara Falls, and it was there that the Reformists had raised the last rampart of insurrection, at a camp midway between Canada and the United States on the Niagara River, the natural boundary between the two countries.

The leaders who, after St. Denis and St. Charles, had escaped from pursuit by the loyalists, had left Canadian territory and crossed the frontier in order to concentrate on Navy Island. If the fortune of war should betray them, if the royalists were to cross the left arm of the river and drive them from the island, they would still be able to escape to the other bank, where there were sympathisers in plenty. But doubtless those who sought shelter among the Americans would be few in number, for this last game they would play out to the end.

The Reformists, and more particularly the so-called Bonnets-bleus, occupied Navy Island, although the river no longer sufficed to protect it. For although the cold was very severe, thanks to the speed of its current the Niagara was still navigable, and communication was still possible by means of boats between Navy Island and both of the banks. The Canadians and Americans kept coming and going between the camp and the village of Schlosser, on the right bank of the Niagara; and many of these boats were carrying ammunition and arms and stores in readiness for the approaching attack by the royalists.

A citizen of the United States, named Wills, the owner of the small steamer Caroline, allowed his boat to be used for these purposes in return for a small fee.

On the opposite bank of the Niagara, and consequently facing Schlosser, the British were stationed in the village of Chippewa, under the orders of Colonel MacNab. There were quite enough of them to overwhelm the reformists on Navy Island whenever they decided to attack. A number of large boats had been collected at Chippewa with a view to this attack, which would take place as soon as Colonel MacNab had completed his preparations. The end of the struggle was thus imminent on the Canadian frontier and within view of the Americans.

It is not surprising that those who have played the chief parts in this narrative were assembled at Navy Island. Farran, recently cured of his wound, as well as William Clerc, had hastened to the camp, where Vincent Hodge soon joined them. Sebastien Gramont, then in prison at Montreal, was the only one who did not take his place among his comrades.

After making certain that thanks to his intervention Bridget and Clary de Vaudreuil had been able to reach Maison-Close, Vincent Hodge had got away from the drunken soldiers who had surrounded him and threatened to cut off his retreat. He had then taken to the woods, and by daybreak was out of danger of falling into the hands of the royalists. Forty-eight hours later he had reached St. Albans, beyond the frontier. When the camp was formed at Navy Island he had gone there, accompanied by a few Americans, who were devoted to the cause of independence.

There too were Thomas Harcher, and four of his sons, Pierre, Tony, Jacques and Michel. To return to Chipogan after the disaster of St. Charles would have been to endanger not only themselves but Catherine Harcher. They had therefore taken refuge at St. Albans, where Catherine had been able to send them news of herself and her children. During the first week of December they had come to Navy Island, ready for another struggle, and determined to avenge the death of Remy, who had fallen under the bullets of the loyalists.

As to Mr. Nick, if the most far-seeing medicine man of the Far West had ever prophesied, ' The day will come when you, a respectable lawyer, peaceful by character and prudent by profession, will be fighting at the head of a Huron tribe against the constituted authorities of your country!' he would have been thought worthy of being shut up in the local lunatic asylum. But, nevertheless, there Mr. Nick was at the head of his warriors.

At a solemn palaver, the Mahogannis had decided to join the reformists, and a great chief, in whose veins flowed the blood of the Sagamores, could not remain behind. He might object, but his objections were not even listened to. And the day after Lionel and the Abbé Joann had left Walhatta, as soon as the council fire had been extinguished, Mr. Nick followed — no, preceded — by fifty warriors had set out for Lake Ontario.

It may well be imagined what a reception he met with. Thomas Harcher had gripped his hand so vigorously that for twenty-four hours afterwards Mr. Nick would have found it impossible to wield bow or tomahawk. And he was as warmly welcomed by all those who had been his friends or clients at Montreal.

'Yes... yes...' he stammered. ' I thought it my duty, or rather these brave fellows...'

'The warriors of your tribe?' they asked.

'Yes — of my tribe!' he repeated.

In short, although the excellent man looked so pitiful that Lionel was ashamed of him, it was an important development that the Hurons had lent their aid to the reformist cause. If the other Indian tribes followed their example, if their warriors, animated by the same sentiments, allied themselves with the Reformists, the authorities would no longer find it easy to cope with the insurrection. Events had, however, compelled the reformists to pass from the offensive to the defensive, and if Navy Island were to fall into the hands of Colonel MacNab, the cause of independence would be definitely lost.

The leaders of the Bonnets-bleus were busy organising resistance in every way possible. A number of entrenchments had been dug in various parts of the island, obstacles were devised against attempts at landing, and arms, ammunition, and stores were brought in from Schlosser — and all this was done hastily but with enthusiasm. It was unfortunate for the Reformists that they had to wait for an attack which they could not provoke, for they were not in a position to cross the Niagara. With their scanty equipment, how could they launch an assault on Chippewa, on a camp so strongly placed on the river bank?

And the longer this state of affairs lasted the worse it would be for them. The forces of Colonel MacNab were daily increasing, while preparations for crossing the Niagara were being actively pushed forward. Driven to the frontier, the last defenders of the insurrection had vainly endeavoured to get into touch with the people of the regions about Ontario and Quebec. Under these circumstances how could the people unite in an armed rising, and what leader would put himself at the head of the rebellion now that the royal columns had overrun the regions bordering the St. Lawrence?

Only one man could do this. Only one had influence enough to raise the people, and that was Jean-Sans-Nom. But since the disaster at St. Denis he had disappeared. It seemed probable that he had perished obscurely, for he had not appeared anywhere on the American frontier. To suppose that he had fallen into the hands of the police was impossible; such a capture would never have been kept secret by the authorities at Quebec or Montreal.

It was the same with De Vaudreuil. Neither Hodge, Farran, nor Clerc knew what had become of him. That he had been wounded at St. Charles they knew. But nobody had seen Jean carry him off the field of battle, and no news had come that he had been taken prisoner. And as for Clary de Vaudreuil, Hodge had been unable to trace her since he had saved her from the violence of those drunkards.

Imagine then their delight when, on 10th December, they saw De Vaudreuil land on Navy Island, accompanied by his daughter and by an old woman who was unknown to them.

It was Bridget.

After Jean had left them their best plan would doubtless have been to remain at Maison-Close, where De Vaudreuil was in no danger of being found. Where could his daughter find a safer hiding-place? The Villa Montcalm had been burnt by the volunteers and was now in ruins. But De Vaudreuil did not know why Rip had kept Maison-Close from being searched by the police. Clary had kept the shameful secret that had protected them, and he did not know he was the guest of — Bridget Morgaz.

Fearing the consequences of another visitation by the police, and more on account of his daughter than of himself, he had made no change in his plans. And on the following evening, as soon as he learnt that the royalists had left St. Charles, he had taken his place with Clary and Bridget in that friendly farmer's cart, and the three had gone into the south of St. Hyacinthe. Then, as soon as they heard that the patriots were concentrating on Navy Island, they had hastened across the American frontier, and after a dangerous eight days' journey they were now among their friends.

And had Bridget consented to follow Clary de Vaudreuil, who knew of her past life?

Yes! The unhappy woman had been unable to resist Clary's entreaties.

After Jean's flight, and seeing, as he did, that she could inspire nothing but horror in her guests, Bridget had retired to her room. And terrible was the night she had spent! Would Clary conceal from her father what she had just heard? No! And in the morning he would more than hasten — he would fly — from Maison-Close! Yes! Fly — at the risk of falling into the hands of the royalists, he would fly, rather than remain an hour longer beneath the roof of a Morgaz!

Moreover, Bridget could no longer stay at St. Charles. She would not wait to be driven away by public scorn.

She would go far away, and ask only that God would free her from her odious existence.

But next morning, at dawn, Bridget saw Clary enter her room. She would have hastened away to avoid meeting her had not Clary spoken to her in a voice of sorrowful affection: 'Madame Bridget, I have kept your secret from my father. He does not know, he shall not know anything of your past, and I want to forget it myself. I will only remember that you are the most unfortunate and the most honourable of women! ' Bridget did not raise her head. ' Listen to me,' Clary pleaded. ' I respect as you deserve to be respected. For your misfortune you've all the pity and sympathy they deserve. No, you are not responsible for the crime you have so cruelly expiated. That abominable treachery has been atoned for, and more than atoned for, by your son. Justice will be done you some day; and meanwhile let me love you as if you were my own mother. Give me your hand, Madame Bridget, your hand!'

At this touching manifestation of feelings to which she was quite unaccustomed, the unhappy woman broke down completely; and she clasped the proffered hand, while her eyes flowed with tears.

'Now,' said Clary, ' as there's an end of all that, let's talk about the present. My father is afraid your house will not escape further investigation. He wants us to go away together — this very night if the roads are clear. You cannot stay at St. Charles; and I want you to promise to go with us. We will go to our friends, we will find your son, and I will tell him what I have told you, that I feel a truth far above all human prejudice, the truth of my own heart. Have I your promise, Madame Bridget?'

'I will go, Clary de Vaudreuil.'

'With my father and me?'

'Yes, though it might be better for you to leave me to die far away in shame and misery.'

Clary stooped to raise Bridget, who knelt sobbing at her feet. And next evening all three left Maison-Close.

It was at Navy Island, twenty-four hours after their arrival, that they learnt the news so disastrous for the reformist cause, that Jean-Sans-Nom had been arrested by Commeau and taken to Fort Frontenac.

This last blow overwhelmed Bridget. What had become of Jean, she knew not. What had become of Jean she knew she was going to die.

'But at least, may no one ever know that they are the sons of Simon Morgaz!' she murmured.

Mademoiselle de Vaudreuil alone knew her secret. But what could she say to console Bridget? Moreover, in the grief she felt when she heard of the arrest, she knew that her love for Jean was still unchanged. All she could see in him was the ardent patriot devoted to death!

The capture of Jean-Sans-Nom spread deep discouragement throughout Navy Island; this was the result the authorities had counted on when they spread the news. As soon as it reached Chippewa Colonel MacNab had given orders that it should be proclaimed far and wide.

But how had the news crossed the frontier? No one knew. It seemed inexplicable that it could have been known at Navy Island before it was even heard of at Schlosser. But this was of little importance.

Unfortunately, it was only too true; and Jean-Sans- Nom would be missing at the very time when the fate of Canada would be in the balance on the last field of battle.

As soon as his arrest was reported on 11th December a conference took place between such leaders as Hodge, Farran and Clerc, while De Vaudreuil, who commanded the camp at Navy Island, acted as president.

Vincent Hodge opened the discussion by suggesting that some attempt should be made to rescue Jeans-Sans- Nom.

'It's at Frontenac that he's in prison,' he pointed out. ' The garrison is a small one, and a hundred determined men would compel its surrender. It would not be impossible for us to get there in twenty-four hours.'

'Twenty-four hours!' exclaimed M. de Vaudreuil. ' Are you forgetting that he was condemned before he was taken? It's within twelve hours, it's this very night that we should have to be at Frontenac.'

'We'll be there,' Hodge assured him. ' All along the shore of Ontario there's no obstacle to stop us until we reach the frontier at the St. Lawrence, and as the royalists haven't had any notice of our plan they can't offer us any resistance.'

'Go, then,' M. de Vaudreuil decided, ' but in the greatest secrecy. The spies from Chippewa Camp must know nothing of your movements.'

The expedition having been decided on, it was not difficult to collect the hundred men who were to take part in it. To save Jean-Sans-Nom from death, there was no lack of volunteers. The detachment, commanded by Vincent Hodge, went off along the right bank of the Niagara; and after crossing the United States territory obliquely, arrived at about three in the morning on the right bank of the St. Lawrence, which could easily be crossed on the ice. Fort Frontenac was not more than five leagues to the northward, and before daylight Vincent Hodge would have surprised the garrison and rescued the condemned man.

But he had been anticipated by a despatch-rider sent from Chippewa. The troops who were guarding the frontier had occupied the left bank of the river.

The attempt to cross the river had to be abandoned. The reformists would have been annihilated. The cavalry would have cut off their retreat, and not one of them would have returned to Navy Island. Vincent Hodge and his companions had to take the road back to Schlosser.

And so warning of the attempted surprise attack on Fort Frontenac had been given to the camp at Chippewa?

That the preparations necessitated by the mustering of a hundred men could not be kept quite secret, that was probable enough. But how could Colonel MacNab have heard of them? Were there spies among the Reformists, spies in touch with the camp at Chippewa? Already suspicions had been aroused that the English knew everything that took place on the island. This time there could be no doubt of it, for the troops stationed on the Canadian frontier had been warned in sufficient time to stop Vincent Hodge.

But in any case the attempt to reach Fort Frontenac would not have saved the prisoner. Vincent Hodge would have arrived too late.

The very next day, on the morning of the 12th, the news spread abroad that on the previous evening Jean- Sans-Nom had been shot.

And the loyalists were congratulating themselves at having no more to fear from the popular hero who had been the soul of the insurrection.

CHAPTER X - BRIDGET MORGAZ

Meanwhile two more blows, not one whit less terrible, fell upon the reformist party, and discouraged the last defenders of Navy Island. And, indeed, there was every chance of their being seized with despair at the series of disasters with which ill-fortune now assailed them.

In the first place, the proclamation of martial law in the district of Montreal rendered a common understanding among the parishes of the St. Lawrence almost impossible. On the one hand the French clergy, though they did not abandon their hopes for the future, advised the insurgents to submit. On the other, it was not easy to succeed without the aid of the United States; but, notwithstanding what was being done by the Americans on the frontier, it did not seem that any help was to be obtained from that quarter. The Federal Government carefully abstained from openly assisting the French. Good wishes, yes! but deeds, no! And then there were a number of Canadians who, though still protesting against manifest abuses and claiming their rights, were doing their utmost to bring about peace.

From this state of things it resulted that the insurgents in arms in this last month of 1837 did not amount to a thousand, scattered through the whole country. In place of a revolution, history would only have to chronicle a revolt.

A few isolated attempts were made at Swanton. On the advice of Papineau, a small party of eighty men entered Canadian territory, reached Moore's Corner, and came across a detachment of four hundred volunteers who had been sent to bar their way. The Reformists fought with admirable courage, but they were driven back in confusion across the frontier. And the Government, having nothing further to fear in that district, concentrated its forces in the north.

On 14th December there was a fight at St. Eustache in Deux Montagnes county. There, among his brave companions, Doctor Chenier, for whose head a reward had been offered, especially distinguished himself. Two thousand infantry sent by Sir John Colborne, nine guns, a hundred and twenty cavalry, and a company of eighty volunteers, attacked St. Eustache. The resistance of Chenier and his people was heroic: exposed to cannon-balls and bullets, they fortified themselves in the presbytery, the convent, and the church. Many of them had no fire-arms.

'Take those of the men who are killed,' Chenier advised them coldly.

But the circle of assailants crept closer round the village, and fire came to the aid of the royalists. Chenier realised that he had to abandon the church. A bullet struck him to the ground. He rose and fired again. A second bullet struck him in the chest. He fell. He was dead.

Seventy of his companions perished with him.

The damage done to the church is still visible, and the French still visit the spot where the brave doctor fell. In the country the saying still persists: ' As brave as Chenier.

After the rout of the insurgents at St. Eustache, Sir John Colborne ordered his troops to St. Benoit, where they arrived next day. It was a beautiful and wealthy village, situated a few miles to the northward in Deux Montagnes county.

This was the scene of a massacre of unarmed men who were prepared to surrender. How could they possibly defend themselves against the troops from St. Eustache and the volunteers from St. Andrew, more than six thousand in all, with the general himself at their head?

Devastation, destruction, plunder, arson, all the excesses of an infuriated soldiery, who respected neither age nor sex, profanation of the churches, the sacred vessels given to the most odious use, priestly vestments draped round the necks of the horses, such were the acts of vandalism and inhumanity of which this parish became the scene. And, it must be admitted, though these crimes were mostly committed by the volunteers, the regular forces were restrained little, or not at all, by their leaders. More than once, these gave the orders to deliver the houses of the local gentry to the flames.

When, on 16th December, these tidings reached Navy Island, they aroused great excitement. The Bonnets-bleus demanded to be led across the Niagara to the attack on MacNab's camp, and it was with difficulty that De Vaudreuil could keep them back. But the wave of anger was soon over, and deep discouragement set in. And at last desertions began and a hundred of the insurgents fled across the American frontier.

The leaders saw their influence lessening, and they were divided amongst themselves. Vincent Hodge.

Farran, Clerc, were in frequent disagreement with the other patriots, and De Vaudreuil alone seemed to be able to moderate the rivalries produced by this desperate state of affairs. And unfortunately, although he had lost none of his old energy and strength of character, he felt that his bodily strength was diminishing from day to day, and he was only too well aware that he could never survive another defeat.

And amid his apprehensions for the future of the cause was his growing anxiety regarding the fate in store for his daughter.

Farran, Clerc, and Hodge did not cease to struggle against their companions' discouragement. If the attempt had failed this time, they repeated, they could wait till the time came to try again. After leaving behind them the leaven of a future rising, they could retire to the United States and prepare for a new struggle against the oppressors. No, there was no need to despair of the future; so even Mr. Nick thought, as he explained to De Vaudreuil: 'Though the rebellion hasn't yet succeeded, the reforms we demand will be granted through the force of circumstances. Sooner or later Canada will regain her rights; she will get her autonomy; she will be only nominally dependent on England. You will live to see it, Monsieur de Vaudreuil. We shall find ourselves together once again at the Villa Montcalm, and I shall get rid of this mantle of the Sagamores, which is so uncomfortable on my legal shoulders, and I shall return to my office in Montreal.'

When De Vaudreuil mentioned his anxiety on his daughter's account to Thomas Harcher, the farmer replied: 'If you have any fear about Mademoiselle Clary, why don't you send her to my wife Catherine? At Chipogan she'd be in perfect safety, and you could come to her there as soon as circumstances allow you.'

But M. de Vaudreuil had no illusions about himself; he knew his life was nearing its end, and he was anxious to arrange Clary's future in the way he had always desired. Knowing Hodge's love for his daughter, he had reason to believe that his love was reciprocated. He had no suspicion that Clary could be thinking of anyone else. If she were to consider the position in which the death of her father would leave her, she would feel the need of support. And where could she feel herself safer than with Vincent Hodge, to whom she was bound not only by love but by patriotism? De Vaudreuil resolved to bring about at once the realisation of his fondest hopes. He had no doubt of Hodge's feelings; he could not doubt those of Clary! He would bring them together; he would speak to them; he would join their hands; and when he died, he would only have one regret — that he had not been able to gain independence for his country.

So Vincent Hodge was invited to come on the evening of 16th December.

It was a small house on the eastern shore of the island and facing the village that De Vaudreuil occupied with his daughter. Bridget lived there too, but she never went out in the daytime. Generally the poor woman went out only at nightfall, absorbed in the memory of her two sons, of Jean, who was dead for the cause, and Joann, of whom she had heard nothing, and who was probably awaiting his death-hour in the prisons of Quebec or Montreal. Nobody ever saw her in the house where De Vaudreuil and his daughter returned the hospitality she had given them at Maison-Close. Who would have suspected that she was the wife of Simon Morgaz?

Vincent Hodge arrived at the time appointed, eight in the evening.

Bridget had already gone out, and was wandering about the island.

Hodge shook hands with De Vaudreuil, and turned towards Clary, whose hand was extended towards him.

'I have something serious to talk to you about, my dear Hodge,' said De Vaudreuil.

'I'll leave you, father,' Clary turned towards the door.

'No, my child, stay here. What I have to say concerns both of you.'

He motioned to Vincent Hodge to be seated in front of his arm-chair, and Clary sat down by his side.

'My friend,' he began, ' I haven't long to live. I feel I'm growing weaker from day to day. Listen to me, then, as if you were at the death-bed of a dying man, listening to his last words.'

'My dear Vaudreuil,' Vincent Hodge protested, ' you're exaggerating!'

'And you are making us very unhappy, father,' Clary added.

'It will make me even more so,' replied De Vaudreuil, ' if you refuse to believe me.'

He looked at them fixedly for a moment. Then, turning towards Hodge, he said: 'My friend, up to the present we have only spoken of the cause to which you and I have devoted our lives. On my part, nothing could be more natural, for I am of French blood, and it is for the triumph of French Canada that I have fought. You, who are not bound to our country by ties of birth, have not hesitated to put yourself in the front rank of the Reformists...'

'And aren't the Americans and the Canadians brothers?' asked Vincent Hodge. 'And who knows but that some day Canada will form part of the American Confederation?'

' Would that that day were come!' sighed De Vaudreuil.

'Yes, father,' said Clary, ' it will come, and you will see it...'

' No, my child, I shall never see it.'

' Do you think our cause is lost for ever because we've been defeated?' asked Hodge.

' A cause which is based on justice and right,' De Vaudreuil assured him, ' will always conquer in the end. The time which will fail me will not fail you. Yes, Hodge, you will see the success of the cause, and at the same time you will have avenged your father who died on the scaffold through the treachery of a Morgaz.'

At this name, so unexpectedly mentioned, Clary felt struck to the heart. Did she fear that the blush which rose to her face would be visible? Apparently she did, for she rose and went to the window.

' What's the matter, Clary? ' Vincent Hodge rose and went across to her.

' You're not well?' asked De Vaudreuil, making an effort to rise from his chair.

' No, father, it's nothing! A little air will soon put me right!'

Hodge opened one of the windows and went back to De Vaudreuil.

They waited a few moments, till Clary returned to them. Then her father took one of her hands, and at the same time he said to Hodge: 'My friend, although patriotism has filled your whole life, it has nevertheless left room in your heart for other feelings. Yes, Hodge, I know that. You love my daughter, and I also know how highly she thinks of you. I shall die more at ease if you have the right and the duty to look after her, left alone in the world after I am gone! If she consents, will you take her for your wife?'

Clary had withdrawn her hand from her father's grasp. Looking at Vincent Hodge, she awaited his reply.

'My dear Vaudreuil.' he said ' you are offering me the realisation of the greatest happiness I could dream of. Yes, Clary, I love you, and I have loved you for a long time and with my whole heart. Before I spoke of my love, I wanted to see the triumph of our cause. But the position has become serious, and recent events have made a great difference to the Reformists. A few years may well elapse before we can continue the struggle. Will you spend these years in this America, which is almost your native land? Will you give me the right to take your father's place, and give me the happiness of calling myself his son? Tell me, Clary, will you do this? ' The girl was silent.

His head lowered in response to her silence, Vincent Hodge dared not repeat his question.

'Well, my child,' said De Vaudreuil, ' you have heard me. You have heard what Hodge has said. It depends on you whether I am to be his father, and, after all the sorrows of my life, whether I shall have the supreme consolation of seeing you united to a patriot who is worthy you, and who loves you.'

Then Clary in a voice broken with emotion, gave the reply which left them no hope.

'My father,' she said, ' I have the greatest respect for you! Hodge, I have more than a high esteem for you. I feel for you as if I were your sister. But I can never be your wife.'

'You cannot... Clary? ' De Vaudreuil grasped her arm.

'No, father.'

'And why not?'

'Because my life belongs to another.'

'Another! ' Vincent Hodge could not restrain a spasm of jealousy.

'You must not be jealous, Hodge! ' Clary assured him. ' He whom I love, and to whom I have never spoken of my love, but who loved me and never has spoken to me of his love, is no more! Perhaps, even if he had lived, I should never have been his wife! But he is dead, dead for his country, and I shall remain faithful to his memory.'

'It is Jean, then?' asked De Vaudreuil.

'Yes father, it is Jean...'

Clary was unable to complete her sentence.

'Morgaz! Morgaz!' such was the name which could be heard shouted in a distant tumult that was rapidly getting nearer. The uproar came from the north of the island, from the bank of the Niagara on which stood De Vaudreuil's house.

At the sound of the name thus loudly shouted, Clary turned alarmingly pale.

'What's that noise?' asked De Vaudreuil.

'And why that name? ' Vincent Hodge got up and went across to the open window.

The bank was ablaze with light. A hundred and more of the reformists, carrying blazing torches, were coming towards the house.

These were men and women and children, all yelling the accursed name of Morgaz, and thronging round an old woman who could not escape from their insults, for she was hardly able to drag herself along.

It was Bridget!

Clary rushed to the window, and, seeing the victim of the demonstration, whose cause she knew only too well, she screamed: 'Bridget!'

She ran to the door; she opened it; she rushed out, without even replying to her father, who was following her with Vincent Hodge.

The crowd was not fifty yards from the house. The uproar was increasing. Mud was being thrown at Bridget's face; angry fists were being shaken at her; stones were being picked up to be hurled at her.

In an instant Clary de Vaudreuil was at Bridget's side, and had covered her with her arms, while the yells resounded with greater fury: 'It's Bridget Morgaz! She's the wife of Simon Morgaz! Death to her! Death to her!'

De Vaudreuil and Vincent Hodge, who were about to intervene between her and the mob, suddenly checked themselves.

Bridget, the wife of Simon Morgaz! Bridget, who bore that name — that odious name!

Clary supported the wretched woman, who otherwise would have fallen on her knees.

'Kill me! Kill me!' she murmured.

'Wretches! ' Clary turned on those who were threatening her. ' Respect this woman!'

'The wife of Morgaz, the traitor!' repeated a hundred furious voices.

'Yes, the wife of the traitor!' said Clary, ' but the mother of him...'

She would have uttered the name of Jean — the only one, perhaps, that could give Bridget protection.

But, recovering all her strength, Bridget stood erect and whispered: ' No, Clary! No. Out of pity for my son — out of pity for his memory!

Then the shouts broke out with renewed violence, and with them came the threats. The crowd had increased, a prey to one of those irresistible paroxysms that lead to the most dastardly deeds.

De Vaudreuil and Hodge tried to rescue the victim, while some of their friends, attracted by the tumult, came to their help. But in vain they strove to drag away Bridget — and Clary who was clinging to her.

'Death! Death to the wife of Simon Morgaz!' yelled the frantic mob.

Then, tearing his way through the crowd, and hurling them aside, there suddenly came a man.

Freeing Bridget from the hands raised to deal her the death-blow, he cried: 'Mother!'

It was Jean-Sans-Nom; it was Jean Morgaz!

251

CHAPTER XI - EXPIATION

These were the circumstances in which the name of Morgaz had been revealed to the defenders of Navy Island.

On several occasions the preparations made for resistance, the points which had been fortified to repulse a royalist attack, and the attempts which had been made to force the crossing of the Niagara, had all been known in the British camp. It was clear that there was a spy among the Reformists who kept the enemy informed of everything that happened on the island. In vain was a search made for this spy, so that he might be brought to summary justice. He had escaped every attempt to find him in the villages on the American side of the river.

The spy was none other than Rip.

Infuriated at his lack of success, which meant a heavy loss to his business, the head of the house of Rip and Co. was endeavouring to recover himself by a bold stroke that would fully atone for his recent failures. He had failed at Chipogan Farm, where his men had had to beat a retreat. At St. Charles he had inadvertently given Jean-Sans-Nom, then hiding in Maison-Close, his only chance of escape. And then it had not been his own men, but those of Comeau, who had captured the fugitive.

Rip, eager for revenge, gave no further thought to Jean-Sans-Nom who, he had every reason to suppose, had been executed at Fort Frontenac. He had come in disguise to Navy Island; and there, by means of a prearranged code of signals, he kept Colonel MacNab informed of the defensive works and the places at which a descent on the island was practicable.

To venture among the reformists was obviously to risk his life. If they recognised him, he could hope for no mercy: they would kill him like a dog. But a considerable sum of money would fall to him if he helped in capturing the island, inasmuch as the insurrection would end with the disappearance of its leaders. And so Rip landed on the American bank of the Niagara, and at Schlosser he took passage on the Caroline, like any ordinary visitor, and so he had crossed to Navy Island.

Thanks to his disguise, to his beard which he now sported, to the changes he had made in his gait and in the tone of his voice, the audacious detective was unrecognisable. And although he was amongst people who should have known him — such as De Vaudreuil and his daughter, Thomas Harcher and his sons, whom he had met at Chipogan, and also Mr. Nick, whom he had never expected to meet on the island — fortunately for him his disguise was so perfect that no one had any suspicion regarding him. So he could without difficulty pursue his occupation as a spy, and when necessary he could communicate with Chippewa. He it was who had warned Colonel MacNab of Hodge's attack against Fort Frontenac.

A chance encounter might have been his ruin. During the eight days he had been on the island he had often met Thomas Harcher, Mr. Nick, and the others, but he had never met Bridget. And how could he have suspected that she was there? The wife of Simon Morgaz among the Reformists was the most unlikely thing in the world. Had he not left her at Maison-Close, after sparing her the reprisals taken against the inhabitants of St. Charles? And then for twelve years, since he had known her at Chambly, they had met only once, during the house-to- house search. So Bridget would not have recognised him any more than Mr. Nick or Thomas Harcher.

And indeed Bridget had not recognised him. He it was who betrayed himself under circumstances which he could not possibly have foreseen.

That evening — 16th December — Bridget had left the house where Vincent Hodge had been asked to meet De Vaudreuil. The darkness of night covered the whole of the Niagara valley. There was no sound, neither in the village occupied by the British troops, nor in the reformist camp. A few sentries were pacing up and down the bank and guarding the left arm of the river.

Without taking any notice of them, Bridget had reached the farthest point of the island up-stream. There, after a rest of a few seconds, she was preparing to return, when her eye was caught by a light which was moving about at the water's edge.

Surprised and uneasy, she went down to the rocks, which here rose above the Niagara.

Here there was a man swinging a lantern, whose light could easily be seen on the Chippewa shore; and, what was more, a light from the camp at once flashed out in reply.

Bridget could not help crying aloud at seeing this exchange of suspicious signals.

On hearing her cry, the man scrambled up the rocks.

Standing before her, he held the lantern up to her face.

'Bridget Morgaz!' he exclaimed.

Bridget stepped back astounded that the man should know her name. But he had not taken the precaution of changing his voice, and the voice betrayed the spy.

'Rip!' stammered Bridget. ' Rip! — here!'

' Yes, Rip himself.'

' Rip... at this trade...'

'Well, Bridget,' Rip spoke very quietly. ' What I'm doing is what you're here to do, isn't it? Why is the wife of Simon Morgaz in this camp, if it isn't to communicate...'

'You scoundrel!'

'Silence! ' Rip seized her roughly by the arm. ' Be quiet, or...'

And with one push he could have hurled her into the current of the Niagara.

' Kill me? ' Bridget took a step backwards. ' Not before I've given the alarm — not before I've denounced you.' And she began shouting for help.

At once there came a sound that showed the sentries were on the alert and were running towards her.

Rip saw he would have no time to get rid of Bridget before they came up.

'Take care, Bridget,' he warned her. ' If you say who I am, I'll say who you are.'

'Say it, then! ' Not even this threat made her hesitate.

Then, even more loudly, she shouted, ' Help! Help!'

A dozen men had already surrounded them, and others were running up from all sides.

'This man,' Bridget told them,' he's the detective Rip, and he's a spy in the service of the royalists.'

'And this woman,' Rip snarled, ' is the wife of the traitor Simon Morgaz.'

The effect of the detested name was immediate; it wiped out all thoughts of Rip. Shouts of ' Bridget Morgaz! Bridget Morgaz!' rose above the din, and it was towards this woman that all the threats and insults were turned. Rip took advantage of this. Cool as ever, seeing that attention had been diverted from him, he disappeared. And no doubt he crossed the Niagara and took refuge in Chippewa Camp long before any search could be made for him.

And this was how Bridget, pursued by the infuriated mob, had come to De Vaudreuil's house.

And it was just as she was about to fall under their blows that Jean had appeared, and with the one word ' Mother!' had revealed the secret of his birth.

Jean-Sans-Nom was the son of Simon Morgaz.

After the sound of the firing from within Fort Frontenac, he had fainted in Lionel's arms. He had at once realised what had happened: Joann had just died in his place. His young companion brought him to, and then having crossed the St. Lawrence on the ice, they had followed the shore of the Ontario, and at daybreak they were far from the fort. To reach Navy Island, to rally the insurgents against the royal troops, and to die if he failed in this last effort, that was what Jean had resolved to do. As he traversed the shore of the lake, where the news of his execution had been made known, he could see for himself that the Anglo-Canadians believed they were finished with him. Very well! He would reappear at the head of the reformists, he would fall like a thunderbolt on Colborne's soldiers. Perhaps his reappearance, which might almost be thought miraculous, would spread terror in their ranks, while at the same time it would arouse irresistible enthusiasm among the Sons of Freedom.

But however anxious Jean and Lionel might be to reach the Niagara, they had to go a long way round, and this took time. The risks they ran were so great, until they reached American territory, that they could travel only by night. Hence it was not until the evening of 16th December that they reached first the village of Schlosser, and then the camp on Navy Island.

And now Jean was face to face with the howling mob, which had closed up around him. But such was the horror inspired by the name of Simon Morgaz that the shouts did not cease. They had recognised him. Yes, it was Jean-Sans-Nom, the popular hero, whom they had thought fallen under the English bullets! Yet his legend had lost its power. To the threats hurled at Bridget were added those hurled at her son.

Jean was unmoved. Supporting his mother on one arm, he kept off this enraged multitude with the other. In vain De Vaudreuil, Farran, Clerc, and Lionel tried to restrain them.

Vincent Hodge, finding himself in the presence of the son of the man who had betrayed his father, of the man he knew Clary loved, was seized with an impulse of anger and hatred, Then, overcoming his instincts of vengeance, he thought only of defending the girl against the hostile demonstrations brought upon her by her devotion to Bridget Morgaz.

And, indeed, that such feeling should be showed against the unhappy woman, that she should be held responsible for the treachery of Simon Morgaz, was a revolting injustice. But this was something the crowd had not realised: from the outset they had not stopped to think.

But that the presence of Jean-Sans-Nom should not have calmed their frenzy after what they knew of him, that went beyond all bounds.

Jean's indignation at this abominable conduct was so great that, no longer red with shame but pale with anger, he shouted in a voice that was heard even above the uproar: 'Yes! I am Jean Morgaz, and this is Bridget Morgaz! Strike us down, then! We care no more for your pity than for your scorn. But, mother, look up, and forgive those who would hurt you — you, the most worthy of women!'

Before his attitude the threatening arms were lowered. Then once again the shouting began: 'Get out of this, family of the traitor! Get out of this, Morgaz!'

And the crowd pressed closer round to the victims of this hateful outburst to drive them from the island.

Clary threw herself before them.

256

'You wretches!' she cried. ' Before you drive out his mother and himself you must listen.'

Taken aback by the girl's energetic protest, the crowd recoiled.

And then Jean continued, in a voice in which scorn was mingled with indignation: 'There's no need to dwell on what my mother has suffered on account of the infamy of the name she bears. But what she has done to atone for that infamy you ought to know. Her two sons she has brought up to become accustomed to the idea of sacrificing and renouncing every earthly happiness. Their father had betrayed the Canadian fatherland; they were to live only to restore its independence. Renouncing a name which horrified them, while one went from county to county and parish to parish, rousing support for the national cause, the other threw himself into the very front rank in every insurrection. He stands before you. The elder of the two brothers was that patriot, the Abbé Joann, who took my place in the prison of Frontenac, where he fell shot by the executioners...'

'Joann! Joann dead!' exclaimed Bridget.

'Yes, mother, dead as you made us swear we should die — dead for his country!'

Bridget knelt beside Clary de Vaudreuil, who threw her arms around her, and the two mingled their tears.

From the crowd, who were touched by this moving scene, there came only a low murmur, in which, however, there could still be detected the insurmountable horror inspired by the name of Morgaz.

Jean continued in more excited tones: 'You see what we have done; not in the hope of rehabilitating a name which is for ever disgraced, a name which you learnt by sheer accident, and which we had hoped to bury in oblivion with our accursed family! But God has willed it otherwise. And now that you know everything, will you reply by cries of hatred or words of scorn!'

Yes! Such was the horror provoked by the traitor's memory that one of the most frantic in the crowd dared to reply: 'Never will we suffer the wife and son of Simon Morgaz to soil with their presence our patriotic camp!

'No! No!' shouted his hearers, transported with fury.

'Wretches!' exclaimed Clary.

Bridget had risen to her feet.

'My son!' she said, * forgive them; all we have is the right to forgive them...'

'Forgive them!' exclaimed Jean, his whole being roused against this injustice. ' Forgive those who hold us responsible for a crime which is not ours, and in spite of all we have done to atone for it! Forgive those who would visit treachery on the wife, and on the children, of whom one had shed his blood for them, while the other asks only to do the same! No! Never! We will never remain with the patriots, who would think themselves defiled by our touch! Come, my mother, come!'

'My son,' Bridget replied, 'we have to suffer! It is our lot here below. It is our expiation!'

'Jean!' murmured Clary.

A few more shouts were heard; then there was silence. The ranks opened before Bridget and her son, who made their way towards the shore. Bridget had hardly the strength to move. The horrible scene had exhausted her. Clary, helped by Lionel, supported but could not console her, while Vincent Hodge, Clerc, and Farran stayed among the crowd to calm them. De Vaudreuil had followed his daughter. Like her, he felt his heart revolt against this flood of injustice; against the abominable prejudices of this mob, who carried, beyond all bounds, this doctrine of human responsibility. With him, as with her, the past of the father was effaced by that of the sons. And when Bridget and Jean had reached one of the boats that was going to take them across the stream, he said: 'Your hand, Madame Bridget! Your hand, Jean! Think no more of these wretches who have insulted you; they will soon see that you are above their insults. Some day they will come and ask you to forgive them...'

'Never!' said Jean, as he entered the boat.

* Where are you going?' asked Clary.

'Where we shall be safe from these men's insults!'

'Madame Bridget,' the girl spoke in a voice that was heard by all; ' I respect you as if you were my own mother! Only a few minutes ago, believing that your son was dead, I swore to be faithful to the memory of him to whom I would willingly have devoted my life. Jean, I love you! Shall I come with you?'

Jean, pale with emotion, almost fell at the feet of this noble girl.

'Clary,' he replied, ' you have given me the only happiness I have ever had in my wretched existence! But as you see that nothing can lessen the horror that our name inspires, this horror I could never ask you to share.'

'No,' exclaimed Bridget, ' Clary de Vaudreuil must never become the wife of a Morgaz!'

' Come away, mother,' Jean implored her. ' Come.' And he helped Bridget into the boat, which left the shore while the traitor's name still resounded amid the clamours of the mob.

***

On the morrow, in a lonely hut outside the village of Schlosser, to which he had taken his mother, Jean knelt by her side, to receive her last words.

No one knew that the hut was sheltering the wife and son of Simon Morgaz. But it would not shelter them long. Bridget was dying. In a few hours she would end this existence in which there had been heaped upon her all the suffering and misery by which a human creature could be overwhelmed.

When his mother was no more, when he should have closed her eyes, when he should have seen the earth close over her poor body, Jean had made up his mind to leave the country which had thus driven him out. He would disappear; no more would be heard of him, not even after death had come to deliver him also.

But the last words of his mother led him to give up his idea of abandoning the task which had been set him, of making reparation for his father's crime.

'My son, your brother is dead, and after my long sufferings I am dying at last. I do not complain. God is just! This was our expiation! To make it complete, Jean, you must forget those insults. You must return to your work! You have no right to desert it. Your duty, Jean, is to sacrifice yourself for your country until you fall . .

And Bridget died with these words on her lips.

Jean kissed the dead woman and closed the eyes which had shed so many tears.

CHAPTER XII - THE LAST DAYS

The position of the reformists on Navy Island had become extremely critical, and could not possibly last. It might be only a question of days, perhaps only of hours.

Although Colonel MacNab still hesitated to attempt the crossing of the Niagara River, he began to render the camp of the besieged untenable. A battery installed on the Chippewa side had just been brought into action, and the Bonnets-bleus were unable to reply to it, as they did not possess even a solitary gun. A few hundred muskets — the only weapons they could use at a distance to hinder a landing — were helpless against the royal artillery.

Though the Americans were interested in the success of the Franco-Canadian insurrection it was deplorable that the United States Government had kept the strictest neutrality since the outbreak of the struggle. They alone could have furnished the guns which the reformists lacked; but such an action would have provoked recriminations from England at a time when the slightest incident might have brought about a rupture — as indeed happened a few months later. The means of defence of Navy Island were very limited. Even ammunition and provisions were running out. although, as far as the resources of the country permitted, food was obtainable from Schlosser, Buffalo, and Niagara Falls. There was a

continual coming and going of boats large and small, across the right arm of the river, although Colonel MacNab, so as to command this means of access obliquely, had stationed his guns both up and down stream. The little steamer Caroline still ensured speedy communication between the camp and the Schlosser bank, and she was especially patronised by the sightseers who came to visit the defenders of Navy Island.

In such circumstances it demanded an extraordinary display of energy from the leaders of this handful of men not to abandon the struggle. Unfortunately the number of the combatants was diminishing every day, large groups, now completely discouraged, went over to Schlosser never to return.

Since the lamentable scene which had resulted in Jean's departure, De Vaudreuil had not been out of his house. He could scarcely keep alive, and his daughter did not leave him for an instant. They both felt as though they had been soiled by the filth of the insults hurled at Bridget and her son. Nobody had suffered more than they from the taunts with which their comrades had overwhelmed this unhappy family, already crushed beneath a name they had renounced. Yet when they thought of the crime of Simon Morgaz, of the heroic victims that the traitor's work had sent to the scaffold, they bowed their heads beneath the weight of a destiny against which no justice could prevail.

In the house where De Vaudreuil's friends met every day, no allusion was ever made to what had passed. Vincent Hodge, with a discretion worthy of his character, maintained extreme reserve, not wishing to let it be suspected that he blamed Clary in any way for expressing her sentiments. And indeed had not the brave girl been right to protest against this odious prejudice, which would extend to the innocent the responsibility of the guilty, and would transmit a heritage of shame from father to son. as if it were some physical or moral resemblance?

And when he thought of this terrible state of affairs, Jean, now quite alone in the world, felt his whole being revolt. Joann dead for his country, Bridget dead from the insults she had received, was not that enough to compensate for the past? No! And when he exclaimed, ' It is unjust!' he seemed to hear the voice of conscience replying: ' Perhaps it is only justice!'

Then Jean remembered Clary, braving the insults of the crowd that was pursuing him. Yes! She had had the courage to defend a Morgaz! She had almost offered to link her existence with his! But he had refused her: he would always refuse her! And yet how sincerely did he love her! And he would wander along the banks of the Niagara, like Natty Bumppo of the Mohicans, who had preferred to engulf himself in its cataracts, rather than to leave Mabel Denham.

During the whole of the 18th, Jean stayed beside his mother's body, envying the rest which she now enjoyed. His only wish was to rejoin her. But he remembered her last words: he had no right to die except at the head of the Reformists. That was his duty — he would fulfil it.

When the night came, a sombre night, hardly lighted by the * Blink ' of the snow — a sort of whitish reflection, which fills the sky in the polar regions — Jean left the hut where Bridget lay, and a few yards away, beneath the trees heavy with rime, he began to dig a grave with his large Canadian knife — alone. Alone, on the outskirts of the forest; lost in the darkness where no one could see him — nor did he wish to be seen. No one should ever know where

Bridget Morgaz lay buried. No cross would indicate her tomb. If Joann lay in some unknown corner, at the base of Fort Frontenac, his mother at least was buried on American soil, the soil of her native country. Jean would get killed in the coming attack, and his body would disappear, borne away with many others in the rapids of the Niagara. And then there would remain nothing, not even a memory, of what had once been the Morgaz family.

When the trench was deep enough for the corpse to be safe from the talons of the wild beasts, Jean returned to the hut; he lifted his mother's body in his arms, he carried it under the trees, he pressed a last kiss on its forehead and laid it in the grave, wrapped the cloak about it, and covered it with the soil. And then he knelt and prayed, and his last words were: 'My poor mother, rest in peace.'

And when, in spite of everything, MacNab's forces tried to land on Navy Island, Jean would be in the first line of the defenders, where he might seek his death.

He had not long to wait.

In the early hours of the morning of 19th December, it was obvious that Colonel MacNab was preparing a direct attack. Large flat-boats were drawn up along the shore below Chippewa Camp. Having no artillery, the Bonnets-bleus were without means either of destroying these boats before they moved off or of stopping them when they tried to cross. Their one resource was to withstand the attacking forces as they landed, and to concentrate at the threatened points. But what resistance could a few hundred men offer to the assailants if they attacked several points at the same time? As soon as the royalists had gained a footing, the camp would be carried and the defenders, too numerous to escape in the boats to Schlosser, would be massacred before they could take refuge on American soil.

It was these possibilities which made De Vaudreuil and his friends anxious. They fully realised the danger of the position. To escape, it is true, all they had to do was to get to Schlosser, while it was still possible to cross the Niagara. But nobody was willing to retreat without defending the camp to the last.

Perhaps after all they imagined themselves strong enough to offer serious resistance, and over-estimated the difficulties of making a landing.

But one of them was under no illusions. That was Mr. Nick. But his position at the head of the Mahoganni Indians did not allow him to say anything.

As for Lionel, his patriotism allowed of no hesitation whatever. The young clerk no longer concerned himself about the revelations which had followed the unexpected reappearance of his hero. What! Jean-Sans-Nom, the son of Simon Morgaz! The Abbé Joann the son of a traitor!

'No matter,' he said to himself. ' Are they any the less good patriots for all that? And was not Mademoiselle Clary right to stand up for Jean and his mother? Ah! the brave girl! That was splendid! That was noble! That was worthy of a Vaudreuil!'

Thus reasoned Lionel, who never spared his enthusiasm, and could not believe that Jean had left Navy Island never to return. Yes! Jean-Sans-Nom would reappear, were it only to die in defending the national cause!

And then the young clerk was led to this reflection, certainly judicious enough: 'Why shouldn't the children of Simon Morgaz be the most loyal of men when the last descendant of a warlike race has none of the qualities of his ancestors, when the race of the Sagamores ends in a lawyer?'

As Lionel thought of Jean-Sans-Nom, so likewise did Thomas Harcher and his sons. Had they not seen him at work for many a year? In risking his life a hundred times, had he not atoned for the crime of Simon Morgaz? Truly, if they had been present at the hateful scene they would have been unable to restrain themselves, they would have thrown themselves upon the crowd, and made them pay for so abominable an outrage. And if they knew where Jean had gone they would go and bring him back to the Bonnets-bleus and put him at their head.

And it must be added, for the honour of humanity, that since Jean and Bridget had been driven off, a change had come over the mood of the crowd. The feelings of Lionel and the Harchers were now shared by most of the patriots.

About eleven in the morning the preliminaries of the attack began. The first shots from the batteries of Chippewa came ploughing through the camp, and the shells brought destruction and fire upon the island. No shelter was possible from the projectiles on what was almost a flat plain dotted with clumps of trees, divided by narrow hedges, and having only a few earthworks along the riverside.

Colonel MacNab was striving to breach the banks before attempting to cross, but this operation was not without its difficulties in spite of the restricted number of the defenders.

These were mustered around De Vaudreuil's house, less exposed to the artillery because of its position on the right bank opposite Schlosser.

As soon as the firing began De Vaudreuil ordered all non-combatants to cross to the American territory. The wives and the children, whose presence had so far been tolerated, now had to embark, after bidding farewell to their husbands, their fathers, and their brothers. This was not without danger, for the guns above and below Chippewa menaced them with their cross-fire. A few shots even reached the United States frontier, provoking justifiable protests from the Federal Government.

De Vaudreuil urged his daughter to take refuge in Schlosser, and there to await the outcome of the attack. Clary refused to leave him.

'Father,' she said, ' I ought to stay with you, and I shall stay with you. It is my duty.'

'And if I fall into the hands of the royalists?'

'Well; they won't refuse to let me share your prison.'

'And if I should be killed, Clary?'

The girl made no reply; but De Vaudreuil could not overcome her opposition. And so she was by his side when he went to take his place among the leaders who were assembled in front of his house.

The sound of the guns was getting louder. The position of the camp was becoming untenable. But the attempt at landing had not yet been made. Otherwise the Bonnets- bleus posted behind the entrenchments would have given the alarm.

In front of the house were Vincent Hodge, Clerc and Farran, Thomas, Pierre, Michel, and Jacques Harcher.

And there too were Mr. Nick and Lionel and the Mahoganni warriors, as coldly impassive as usual.

De Vaudreuil addressed them: 'Comrades,' he began, ' we have to defend the last rampart of our independence. If MacNab gains this fight the insurrection is at an end and who knows when new leaders and new men will again begin the struggle? If we repulse the assailants, if we manage even to hold our own, help will come to us from other parts of Canada. Our partisans will again take hope, and we shall convert this island into an impregnable fortress, where the national cause will always find a stronghold. Are you determined to defend it?'

'To the death!' replied Vincent Hodge.

'To the death!' repeated his companions.

At this moment several bullets struck the ground a few yards away, and ricochetted into the distance, throwing up a cloud of snow.

Not one of the Bonnets-bleus had moved. They were awaiting their chief's orders.

'It is time to get to the river-bank,' M. de Vaudreuil continued. ' The Chippewa artillery will soon stop firing, for the royalists are going to force a landing. Scatter along the bank, take cover behind the rocks, and wait until the boats are within range — MacNab's men must not land.'

'They shall not land,' Clerc assured him, ' and if they do we'll hurl them back into the Niagara.'

'To your posts, my friends!' exclaimed Vincent Hodge.

'I shall go with you,' De Vaudreuil told them, ' although my strength is failing me...'

'Stay here, Vaudreuil,' replied Farran; ' we shall keep in touch with you...'

'No, my friends,' said De Vaudreuil, ' I shall be where I ought to be! Forward!'

'Yes! Forward! The boats have already begun to leave the Canadian shore!'

The words were spoken in a ringing voice. The men turned towards the speaker.

It was Jean. During the previous night a boat had landed him on the island. No one had recognised him. Hidden on the shore opposite Chippewa, he had watched MacNab's preparations, heedless of the shot that battered the ground nearby. Then seeing that the assailants were getting ready to force a landing, he had come — openly — to take his place among his former comrades.

'I knew he would!' exclaimed Lionel.

Clary de Vaudreuil stepped towards the young patriot just as Thomas Harcher and his sons ranged themselves around him. De Vaudreuil held out his hand but Jean did not take it.

'Defenders of Navy Island,' he addressed them, ' my mother is dead, dead under the insults to which you subjected her. Now I alone am left of this family devoted to horror and scorn. Submit to the shame of seeing a / Morgaz fight on your side, and die for the Franco- Canadian cause.'

These words evoked thunders of applause. Every hand was raised towards Jean. And again he refused to touch them.

'Adieu, Clary de Vaudreuil!' he said.

'Adieu, Jean!' the girl replied.

Then, ahead of De Vaudreuil and his companions, and all who like him were marching to their death, he led the way to the island's left bank.

CHAPTER XIII - THE NIGHT OF THE 28th OF DECEMBER

Three o'clock was striking from the little church at Schlosser. A grey, glacial mist filled the humid valley of the Niagara. The air was very cold. The sky was covered with motionless clouds, which the least rise in the temperature would condense into snow, under the influence of the easterly wind.

The roar of the Chippewa guns was rending the air. In the intervals between the salvoes there could be distinctly heard the distant roaring of the cataract.

A quarter of an hour after they had left De Vaudreuil's house, the Reformists, advancing among the clumps of trees and defiling along the hedges and the walls, had reached the left bank of the river.

Many had already fallen. Some, hit by shell fragments, had had to return to the rear; others were lying stretched on the snow never to rise again. Altogether twenty had been lost from the two hundred who had remained.

The guns of Chippewa had done great damage. The earthworks that were to serve as cover for the Bonnets- bleus had been almost entirely destroyed. The defenders had therefore to take up their position at the foot of the bank among the rocks around which swirled the impetuous current. It was there that Jean and his men would strive to prevent the landing until their supply of ammunition gave out.

But their movements had been seen from Chippewa. Colonel MacNab, already advised by the signals Rip had sent, and now by word of mouth — for the spy was then in his camp — redoubled the fire, concentrating it on the fortified positions. Around Jean thirty of his comrades were struck by the fragments of rock wrenched away by the projectiles.

In spite of the shot which fell at his feet or rent the air above his head, Jean was moving about the beach observing the manoeuvres of the foe. A number of large flat-boats were being rowed out from the Canadian shore, and as a last effort to clear the ground three or four volleys were fired over them, falling upon the island to ricochet into the distance.

Jean did not move.

'Patriots!' he shouted, ' get ready!'

They waited till the boats came within range.

The attackers, lying down in the boats so as to offer the smallest possible targets, numbered from four to five hundred, half of them volunteers and half regular soldiers.

A few minutes later, and the boats had reached midstream, and were near enough to the island for the artillery to have to cease fire.

The first shots were at once fired from the shelter of the rocks. The men in the boats replied, and as they were now badly exposed to the fire from the island they plied their oars more vigorously than ever.

A few minutes were enough to bring them to the beach, and both sides prepared for a hand-to-hand conflict.

Jean took command amid a hail of bullets, which whistled around him like machine-gun fire.

'Get into cover! ' Vincent Hodge told him.

'Me? ' Jean replied.

Then, in a voice of thunder he shouted to the men who were about to leap from the boats: 'I am Jean-Sans-Nom!'

The name was received with bewilderment, for the royalists believed that Jean-Sans-Nom had been shot at Fort Frontenac.

And then, hurling himself at those in the first boat, he shouted: 'Forward, Bonnets-bleus! On to the red-coats!'

The struggle was very fierce. The first of the men who strove to land were repulsed, some falling into the water and being swept towards the cataract. The reformists, leaving the shelter of the rocks, spread along the bank, and fought with such fury that the advantage at first lay with them. There was even a moment when the boats had to recoil. But more of the boats were coming to reinforce them. Hundreds of men landed on the island, and numbers gained the advantage over valour.

Before so numerous an enemy, the defenders had to retire from the bank. Though they did not yield until they had inflicted severe losses on the assailants, they too had suffered cruelly.

Among them Thomas Harcher, Pierre and Michel had been shot, and were despatched by the volunteers, who gave no quarter. William Clerc and Andrew Farran had been wounded and were taken prisoners, and had it not been for the intervention of an officer, they would have shared the fate of the farmer and his sons. But Colonel MacNab had given orders that the leaders should be spared wherever possible, so that the Government might try them by court martial at Quebec or Montreal. It was for this reason alone that the two had escaped the general slaughter.

The Bonnets-bleus fought desperately. The Mahogannis, after defending themselves with that cool courage and contempt of death which distinguishes the Indian race, had to take cover among the trees, and were pursued from wall to wall, attacked from their flanks, and charged from the rear. It was a miracle that Lionel was not killed a score of times, and that Mr. Nick likewise escaped the carnage. How many of the Hurons would never again see their wigwams at Walhatta!

When Mr. Nick reached De Vaudreuil's house, he tried to persuade Clary to enter one of the boats and escape to Schlosser.

'So long as my father is on the island,' she declared, ' I shall never forsake him.'

Yes! Her father, and perhaps also Jean, although she knew he had come back only to die.

At five, De Vaudreuil saw that resistance was no longer possible against the hundreds of assailants who had now mastered much of the island. If the survivors were to save their lives, they could do so only by escaping to the right bank of the river.

But he himself had scarcely strength enough to stand upright or to regain the house where his daughter was waiting for him.

Vincent Hodge tried to help him away, but at that very moment De Vaudreuil fell shot through the chest. He died murmuring: 'My daughter! Hodge! My daughter!'

Jean-Sans-Nom had heard him.

'Save Clary!' he shouted to Vincent Hodge.

Then a dozen volunteers threw themselves upon him. They had recognised him. To capture the celebrated Jean-Sans-Nom, to drag him alive to the camp at Chippewa, that indeed would be a stroke of luck!

With a last effort Jean struck down two of the volunteers who were trying to seize him, and disappeared in the midst of a volley that left him unharmed.

Vincent Hodge, dangerously wounded, was taken prisoner.

Where had Jean gone? Did he then think of surviving now that the finest of his comrades had been killed or were in the hands of the royalists?

No! Had not De Vaudreuil's last word been his daughter's name?

Very well! As Vincent Hodge could not save her, he, Jean would save her, he would take her across to the American shore; then he would return to his comrades, who would still be fighting on.

Clary de Vaudreuil, standing alone before the house, heard the sounds of the battle, the shouts of fury, the cries of pain, the crackle of the musketry, and watched all this tumult approach her amid the flashing of the firearms. Already fifty or more of the Reformists, most of them wounded, had taken to the boats, and were on the way to Schlosser. Only the little steamboat Caroline remained, crowded with fugitives, to make the journey across the river.

Suddenly Jean appeared, covered with blood — the blood of the royalists — safe and sound, after vainly seeking that death which twenty times he had given to others.

Clary rushed towards him.

'My father?' she asked.

'Dead!'

Jean answered unhesitatingly, for it was essential that Clary should be willing to leave the island.

She fainted, and he caught her in his arms just as the volunteers came running round the house to cut off his retreat. Carrying his burden, he ran to the Caroline and laid the girl on her deck; then he rose: 'Adieu, Clary!' he said.

As he stepped on the steamer's rail to jump ashore, there came the crackle of musketry, and Jean, shot in two places, fell backwards, just as the Caroline put off under full steam.

But, by the light of the gun-flashes, he had been recognised by the volunteers who had pursued him across the island, and there arose a shout of: 'Jean-Sans-Nom is dead!'

At the sound Clary recovered consciousness.

'Dead!' she murmured, as she dragged herself towards him.

A few minutes later the Caroline was moored alongside the quay at Schlosser. There the fugitives might deem themselves to be in safety under the protection of the American authorities.

Some landed at once, but as the only inn in the village was full and the hotels at Niagara Falls were three miles away, many of them preferred to stay on board.

It was then eight in the evening.

Jean lay on the deck; he was still breathing. Kneeling by his side, Clary raised his head and spoke to him. He did not reply. Perhaps he could not hear her.

She looked around. Where could she seek for help in this confusion, in a village crowded with fugitives, encumbered with so many wounded but without surgeons or medical supplies?

Then Clary saw all her past life return to her memory. Her father dead for the cause! The man she loved dying in her arms after fighting to the very last! Now she was alone in the world, friendless, in despair...

She covered Jean with a boat-cloth to shelter him from the cold, and tried to ascertain whether his heart was still beating, whether a sigh did not escape from his lips.

On the other side of the river the firing was nearly over, but the flashes could still be seen among the trees on Navy Island.

At last all was silent, and the whole Niagara valley seemed asleep.

The girl unconsciously murmured her father's name, and that of Jean, saying to herself — a supreme anguish! — that the young patriot had died with the thought that the curses of mankind would pursue him even beyond the tomb! And she prayed for both of them.

Suddenly, Jean moved, his heart began to beat a little more strongly. Clary spoke to him. He did not answer.

Two hours went by. Now all was quiet aboard the Caroline. No sound either in the cabins or on the deck. Watching alone, Clary de Vaudreuil knelt, like a sister of charity, at the bedside of the dying.

The night was very dark. The clouds began to swirl down on the river — great wreaths of mist swathed the skeletons of the trees, whose branches, heavy with hoarfrost, were drooping over the river.

Nobody noticed that four boats were coming round the upstream end of the island and that they were noiselessly making for Schlosser bank.

They were manned by fifty volunteers, commanded by Lieutenant Drew of the militia. By the orders of Colonel MacNab, this officer was about to perform an act of revolting cruelty, in defiance of the law of nations. Among his men was a certain MacLeod, whose cruelties were to bring about serious international complications a few months later.

The four boats came silently across the river and ran alongside the Caroline. The men at once climbed on deck, went down into the cabin, and began a frightful slaughter. Wounded or asleep, their victims were unable to defend themselves. Their cries were heart-rending, but it was all in vain. Nothing could stop the scoundrels, among whom MacLeod, pistol in one hand and axe in the other, was howling like a cannibal Jean had not regained consciousness; so Clary, in her terror, dragged the sail-cloth over her so that it covered them both.

At last some of the victims managed to escape, either by jumping on to the quay, or by throwing themselves overboard to reach some point on the shore, where MacLeod and his cut-throats could not follow them; and the alarm had been given in the village, where the people were rushing out of their homes to the rescue.

The massacre had not lasted long, and many of the victims would have escaped, had not MacLeod been leading the assassins. He had brought a supply of inflammable materials with him, and he now piled them up on the deck and set them on fire. In a few minutes hull and rigging were ablaze. Meanwhile he had cut through the hawsers, and the steamer, thrust forcibly from the quay, had drifted out into the current.

Her position was terrible.

Three miles down stream the Niagara was engulfed in the abyss of its cataract.

It was then that five or six of the poor wretches, mad with fear, jumped into the river, but only a few of them reached the shore after struggling against the ice that floated on the water. Nor was it ever known how many victims had been suffocated or had drowned in trying to escape the flames.

The Caroline drifted away down between the river banks like a blazing fireship.

The fire spread aft and Clary, desperate with terror, stood up and shouted for help.

Jean at last heard her. He opened his eyes, he raised himself a little, he looked around.

In the light of the flames the banks of the river swept rapidly by.

Jean realised that the girl was close beside him.

'Clary!' he murmured.

If he had had the strength, he would have taken her in his arms; with her he would have thrown himself into the stream; he would have tried to save her. But, unable to support himself, he collapsed on the deck. The roar of the cataract could be heard less than half a mile away. It was death for her and for him, as for the other victims which the Caroline was carrying down the Niagara.

'Jean,' Clary told him, ' we are going to die — to die together! Jean, I love you. I should have been proud to bear your name! God would not have it so.'

Jean had just strength enough to clasp her hand. Then his lips repeated the last words his mother had spoken: 'Expiation! Expiation!'

The boat sped along with frightful rapidity as she swept round Goat Island, which separates the American from the Canadian fall. And there, in the middle of the horseshoe, where the current has cleft its gorge, the Caroline leaned over the abyss and disappeared into the gulf of the cataract.

CHAPTER XIV - THE LAST PHASES OF THE INSURRECTION

This act perpetrated by the English, in violation of international law and the rights of humanity, had endless repercussions in the Old and the New Worlds alike. An enquiry was ordered by the authorities at Niagara Falls. MacLeod had been recognised by several of those who had escaped the massacre and the flames. Moreover, the wretch was not slow in boasting quite openly of having ' got the better of those dam' Yankees.'

The question now arose of demanding an indemnity from England when in November 1840 MacLeod was arrested in New York.

The British representative demanded his release; the Federal Government refused to give him up. So, by Lords and Commons alike, the Minister was instructed to get him set free, as he had acted under orders from the Throne. Congress replied to this claim by publishing a claim setting out the rights of New York State. The report might have been considered as a real casus belli, and the United Kingdom took measures accordingly.

On their side, after having ordered the assassin to be brought to trial on a charge of murder, the Federal Government voted subsidies. And no doubt war would have been declared had not McLeod, under the pretext of an alibi which was barely justified but which allowed English and Americans alike to hush up the affair, put an end to the action.

It was thus that the victims of the horrible attack on the Caroline were to be avenged!

After the defeat of the insurgents at Navy Island, Lord Gosford received information that the Reformists would no longer resist the constituted authorities. Their principal leaders had been dispersed or imprisoned, and Jean-Sans-Nom was no more.

In 1838, however, a few risings took place at several points in the Canadian provinces. The first attempt occurred during March under Robert Nelson, the brother of him who had taken command at St. Denis, and it failed at the very outset. At Napierville, in a second attempt, two thousand insurgents were attacked by Sir John Colborne at the head of six hundred regulars, with five hundred Indians and four hundred volunteers, and put to flight in one day at

Odeltown. In November there was a third attempt at insurrection, the reformists rising in two groups each of one hundred men. One attacked a seignorial manor, the other seized upon a steamboat at Beauharnais quay. At Chateauguay the insurgents forced the Indians to surrender their arms, and began a campaign which ended in disaster. Then came the last of these movements, which marked the end of the insurrectional period of 1837 and 1838.

Then came the reprisals, and the government acted with an energy so pitiless that it amounted to cruelty. On 4th November, Sir John Colborne, having been invested with superior authority, proclaimed martial law, and suspended the Habeas Corpus Act throughout the province. The Court Martial was set up, and over a dozen men, whose names were never to be forgotten in Franco Canadian martyrology, were sent to the scaffold. To their names must be added those which have appeared in this record, the lawyer Sebastien Gramont and Vincent Hodge, who died as his father had died, with the same courage and for the same cause.

William Clerc had succumbed to his wounds in American territory, and Andrew Farran, who also had fled to the United States, was the sole survivor of this group of comrades.

The list of exiles included fifty-eight of the foremost patriots, and many years were to elapse before they were allowed to return to their country.

The Deputy Papineau, the statesman whose personality had dominated all this period of national demands, had managed to escape. A long life enabled him to see Canada in possession, if not of her complete independence, at least of her autonomy, and he died in an honoured old age.

There remains to be told what became of Catherine Harcher. Of her five sons who had accompanied their father to St. Charles and Navy Island, only two returned to Chipogan Farm, after several years of exile, and they did not leave it again.

As to the Mahogannis, who had taken part in the climax of the insurrection, the Government wanted to forget them just as it wanted to forget that excellent man who, in spite of himself, had been forced to meddle in matters for which he cared but little. So Mr. Nick returned to Montreal and there, disgusted with the honours he had never sought, he resumed his former life. And if Lionel returned to his desk in the office on Bon Secours marketplace in the employment of a Sagamore, it was with a heart which would always remember those for whom he would gladly have sacrificed his life. Never would he forget the family of the Vaudreuils, nor that of Jean-Sans- Nom, rehabilitated by death, and now one of the legendary heroes of Canada.

The insurrection had failed, but it had sowed its seed in good ground. In course of time the seed bore fruit. It was not in vain that patriots had shed their blood in seeking to recover their rights. The governors sent to the colony gradually gave up many of the claims of the Crown. And then the Constitution of 1867 established the Canadian Confederation on a sound basis. It was at this time that the question of removing the capital to Quebec was finally settled in favour of Ottawa.

Today all control by the mother-country has virtually ceased.

Canada is now, practically speaking, a free power under the name of the Dominion of Canada, and all its inhabitants, French-Canadian and Anglo-Saxon alike, now enjoy equal rights. And of a population of five millions, about a quarter still belong to the French race.

Every year an affecting ceremony unites the patriots of Montreal at the foot of a column erected to the memory of the political victims of 1837 and 1838. There, on the day of its inauguration, an address was given by M. Euclide Roy, President of the Institute, and his closing words well sum up the moral of this narrative: 'To glorify self-sacrifice, is to make heroes.'

The End

Printed in Great Britain
by Amazon.co.uk, Ltd.,
Marston Gate.